Julia Franck

THE BLINDNESS OF THE HEART

TRANSLATED
FROM THE GERMAN
BY

Anthea Bell

Grove Press
New York

Originally published in German with the title *Die Mittagsfrau* in 2007
By S. Fischer Verlag GmbH, Frankfurt am Main

First published in English in Great Britain in 2009 by Harvill Secker,
an imprint of Random House, London

Printed in the United States of America

ISBN-13: 978-0-8021-1967-4

Grove Press
an imprint of Grove/Atlantic, Inc.
841 Broadway
New York, NY 10003
Distributed by Publishers Group West
www.groveatlantic.com

10 11 12 13 14   10 9 8 7 6 5 4 3 2 1

The author would like to thank the German Literary Fund
for support in her work on this book.

There is nothing bad to fear; once you have crossed the threshold, all is well. Another world, and you do not have to speak.

Franz Kafka, *Diaries*, Volume 12, 1922

PROLOGUE

A seagull stood on the windowsill, uttering its cry, as if the Baltic itself were in its throat, high as the foaming crests of the waves, keen, sky-coloured, its call died away over Königsplatz where all was quiet, where the theatre now lay in ruins. Peter blinked, he hoped the gull would take fright at the mere flutter of his eyelids and fly away. Ever since the end of the war Peter had enjoyed these quiet mornings. A few days ago his mother had made up a bed for him on the kitchen floor. He was a big boy now, she said, he couldn't sleep in her bed any more. A ray of sunlight fell on him; he pulled the sheet over his face and listened to Frau Kozinska's soft voice. It came up from the apartment below through the cracks between the stone flags on the floor. Their neighbour was singing: *My dearest love, if you could swim, you'd swim the wide water to me.* Peter loved that melody, the melancholy of her voice, the yearning and the sadness. These emotions were so much larger than he was, and he wanted to grow, there was nothing he wanted more. The sun warmed the sheet over Peter's face until he heard his mother's footsteps, approaching as if from a great distance. Suddenly the sheet was pulled back. Come on, come on, time to get up, his mother told him sternly. The teacher's waiting, she claimed. But it was a long time since Herr Fuchs the teacher had minded whether individual children were present or absent. Few of them could still attend school regularly. For days now his mother and he had

3

been going to the station every afternoon with their little suit-case, trying to get a place on a train bound for Berlin. If one did come in, it was crammed so full that they couldn't climb aboard. Now Peter got up and washed. Sighing, his mother took off her shoes. Out of the corner of his eye, Peter saw her untie her apron and put it to soak. Every day, her white apron was stained with soot and blood and sweat; it had to be soaked for hours before she could take the washboard and rub the fabric on it until her hands were red and the veins on her arms swollen. Peter's mother raised both hands to her head, took off her nurse's cap, pulled the hairpins out of her hair and let it tumble softly over her shoulders. She didn't like him to watch her doing that. Glancing at him out of the corner of her eye, she told him: And that too. It seemed to him that she meant his little willy and with some repugnance was telling him to wash it. Then she turned her back to him and passed a brush through her thick hair. It shone golden in the sun and Peter thought he had the most beautiful mother in the world.

Even after the Russians had taken Stettin in the spring – some of the soldiers had been sleeping in Frau Kozinska's apartment ever since – their neighbour could be heard singing early in the morning. Once last week his mother had sat down at the table to mend one of her aprons while Peter read aloud, because Herr Fuchs the teacher had told him to practise that. Peter hated reading aloud and he had sometimes noticed how little attention his mother paid when he did. Presumably she didn't like to have the silence broken. She was usually so deep in thought that she didn't seem to notice at all if, in mid-sentence, Peter suddenly read on to himself instead of aloud. He'd been listening to Frau Kozinska at the same time as he was reading to himself. I wish someone would wring her neck, he heard his mother say abruptly. Startled, Peter looked at her, but she just smiled and put her needle through the linen.

4

The fires last August had completely destroyed the school and since then the children had met Herr Fuchs the teacher in his sister's dairy, where there was hardly ever anything for sale now. Fräulein Fuchs stood behind the empty counter with her arms crossed, waiting. Although she had gone deaf, she often put her hands over her ears. The big shop window had been broken out of its frame, the children sat on the windowsill, and Herr Fuchs the teacher showed them numbers on the board: three times ten, five times three. The children asked him to show them the places where Germany had lost battles, but he didn't want to. We're not going to belong to Germany any more, he said, adding that he was glad of it. Where, then, asked the children, where will we belong? Herr Fuchs the teacher shrugged his shoulders. Today Peter planned to ask him why he was glad of it.

Peter stood at the washbasin and dried himself with the towel: his shoulders, his stomach, his willy, his feet. If he did it in a different order, and he hadn't done that for a long time, his mother lost patience. She had put out a clean pair of trousers and his best shirt for him. Peter went to the window, tapped the pane and the seagull flew up. Now that the row of houses opposite was gone, along with the backs of the buildings and the next row of houses too, he had a clear view of Königsplatz, where the ruins of the theatre stood.

Don't be too late home, said his mother, as he was about to leave the apartment. Last night, she said, a nurse at the hospital had told her there were going to be special trains laid on today and tomorrow. We're leaving. Peter nodded, he had been looking forward for weeks to travelling by train at last. He had only ever been on a train once, two years ago, when he was starting school and his father had visited them. His father and he had gone by train to visit a colleague of his father's in Velten. Now the war had been over for eight weeks and his father still didn't come

5

home. Peter wished he could have asked his mother why she wasn't waiting for his father any longer, he'd have liked her to confide in him.

Last summer, on the night between the sixteenth and seventeenth of August, Peter had been alone in the apartment. His mother often worked two shifts back to back during those months, and she had stayed on at the hospital after the late shift to work the night shift as well. When she wasn't there Peter felt afraid of the hand that would come out from under the bed in the dark, reaching up through the gap between the wall and the sheet. He felt the metal of his clasp knife against his leg, he kept thinking how fast he would have to whip it out when the hand appeared. That night Peter had lain face down on his mother's bed and listened, as he did every night. It was better to lie in the very middle of the bed; that way there was plenty of room on both sides for him to see the hand appear in good time. He'd have to thrust the knife in fast and firmly. Peter sweated when he imagined the hand coming up; he saw himself so paralysed by fear that he wouldn't be able to raise the clasp knife to strike it.

He remembered exactly how he had taken the velvet of the heavy bedspread in both hands, one of those hands also clutching the knife, and rubbed his cheek against it. Faintly, almost gently, the first siren sounded, then it howled, rising high to a long, penetrating screech. Peter shut his eyes. The sound stung his ears. Peter didn't like the cellar. He kept thinking up new ways of avoiding going down to the shelter there. The siren sounded again. His heart was beating fast, his throat felt tight. Everything about him was stiff, rigid. He had to breathe deeply. Goose down – Peter pressed his nose into his mother's pillow and drew in the smell of her as if it could satisfy his hunger. Then all was still. Terribly still. Peter raised his head and heard his teeth chattering; he tried to keep his jaws together, he clenched his teeth with all his might, lowered his head again and pressed his face into the goose down. As he rubbed his face against the pillow, which meant that he had to move his head back and forth, something underneath it crackled. Carefully, he put his hand under the pillow and his fingertips touched paper. At the same moment a sinister roaring sound filled his ears, the sound of the first bombs dropping. Peter's breath came faster, there was crashing and splintering, glass couldn't withstand the pressure and the windowpanes broke, the bed where he was lying shook and Peter suddenly felt that everything around him was more alive than he was. Silence followed. In defiance of the events outside, he drew out a letter with his free hand. Peter recognized the writing. He laughed wildly, he couldn't help it, oh, his father had entirely slipped his mind although he would always protect him. That was his writing, look, his M for My, A for Alice. The letters stood firmly side by side, nothing could touch them, no siren, no bomb, no fire. Peter smiled lovingly at them. His eyes stung and the writing threatened to blur. His father was sorry about something. Peter had to read the letter from his protector, he had to read what it said, as long as he was reading nothing would harm him. Fate was putting all Germany severely to the test. The sheet of paper trembled in Peter's hands; that must be the shaking of the bed. As for Germany, Peter's father was doing his best. She asks if he couldn't work in one of the shipyards. Shipyards, of course, sirens were howling but not ships' sirens, the other kind. Peter's eyes streamed. Civil engineers like him, said the letter, were urgently needed. There was a hissing very close, as if it were right outside the window, a crash, a second and even louder crash. They were finishing work on the Reich Autobahn, there wasn't much to do in the east. Not much to do? Once again Peter heard the roaring, the smell of burning tickled his nose at first, then it became acrid and sharp, but Peter was still smiling, he felt as if nothing bad could happen to him with his father's letter in his hands. Alice. Peter's mother. She reproached him, said the letter, for writing so seldom. There was smoke in the air but it didn't smell of smoke; was that a fire crackling? It had nothing to do with her origins. *It*, what was *it*? And what origins, what was his father writing about? A remittance? Did that say remittance? Things were happening, wrote his father, that changed matters between them.

It had been such hard work, deciphering that letter. If only he'd been able to read better, as well as he could now almost a year later, at the age of nearly eight, perhaps he could have believed in the power of the letter to protect him, but the letter had failed, Peter hadn't been able to finish reading it.

When he set off for the dairy and Herr Fuchs the teacher that morning, everything was all right and he didn't need a letter from any father to help him through the night now, not ever. The war was over and today they were leaving, Peter and his mother. Peter saw a tin can in the gutter and kicked it. It made a wonderful clattering sound as it scudded along. The horror would be over, it would be left behind, not a single dream would ever remind them of it. Peter remembered the first air raids in winter, and once again he felt his friend Robert's hand as they scrambled over the low, white-painted fence at the roadside. They were about to cross the street near the Berlin Gate and jump down into the ditch by the newspaper stand. Their shoes had slipped on the ice, they had skidded. Something must have hit his friend, severing his hand from his body. But Peter had run on alone over the distance they had yet to go, as if he had been speeded up when his friend was torn away from him. He had felt the firm, warm hand, and it was a long time before he let go of it. When he realized, later, that he was still holding Robert's hand he couldn't just drop it in the ditch, he had taken it home with him. His mother had opened the door to him. She had made him sit on a chair and encouraged him to unclench his fingers. Then she crouched down on the floor in front of him, holding one of the white fabric napkins with her initials on it, and waited; she had stroked and kneaded his hands until he let go.

To this day Peter wondered what she had done with it. He gave the tin can a hefty kick, sending it rolling over to the other side of the street, almost all the way to the dairy. It still felt as if he were holding Robert's hand – then, next moment, as if the hand were holding him, and as if his father referred solely to that incident in the letter. Yet he hadn't seen his father for two years; he had never had a chance to tell him about the hand.

Last summer, that August night when the bombs dropped, when Peter had read his father's letter, he'd been able to decipher only every third or fourth sentence. The letter had been no help. His hands had been shaking. His father wanted to do what was right by the mother of his son, he wrote, he would be frank, he had met another woman. There were steps to be heard on the staircase and another little sound so close that, for the fraction of a second, it stopped your ears; then came a crash and screaming. Hastily, Peter skimmed the remaining lines. They were to be brave, he was sure the war would soon be won. He, Peter's father, would probably not be able to come and see them any more, a man's life called for decisive action, but he would soon send more money. Peter had heard a noise at the door of the apartment, hard to say if it was a shell howling, or a siren, or a human being. He had folded up the letter and put it back under the pillow. He was trembling. The smoke stung his eyes, making them stream, and waves of heat from the burning city were coming closer.

Someone took hold of him and carried him downstairs to the cellar on his shoulders. When he and the others crawled out into the open air, hours later, it was light outside. The stairs up to their apartment were still there, only the banisters had come away and were lying on the steps. There was smoke in the air. Peter climbed the stairs on all fours, had to clamber over something black, then he pushed open the door of the apartment and sat down at the kitchen table. The sun was shining right on the table, shining so brightly that he had to close his eyes. He was thirsty. For some time he felt too weak to stand up and go over to the sink. When he did turn on the tap he heard only a gurgling and no water came out. It could be hours before his mother was home. Peter waited. He fell asleep with his head on the table. His mother woke him. She took his head in both hands and pressed it against her, and only when he put his arms round her did she let go. The door of the apartment was open. Peter saw the black thing in the stairwell. He thought of the screaming last night. His mother opened a cupboard, threw sheets and towels over her shoulder, took candles out of a drawer and said she had to go straight out again. She told Peter to help her carry things; they needed bandages and alcohol for use as a disinfectant. They climbed over the charred body outside the door of their apartment. It was the shoes more than anything that told Peter this had been a human being, the body was so shrivelled, and he saw a large gold pocket watch. Something that was almost a feeling of happiness flooded through him that morning, for the watch couldn't possibly have belonged to Frau Kozinska.

The photograph of the handsome man in the fine suit, leaning on the shiny black bodywork of the car with one arm elegantly crooked and glancing up at the sky, clear-eyed, as if he were looking at the future or at least at birds in the air, still stood in its frame on the glass-fronted kitchen cabinet. Peter's mother said that now the war was over his father would come and take them to Frankfurt, where he was building a big bridge over the river Main. Then Peter would be able to go to a proper school, said his mother, and it made him uncomfortable to hear her telling these lies. Why doesn't he write, asked Peter in a moment of rebellion. The post isn't working any more, replied his mother, not since the Russians came. Peter looked down, feeling ashamed of himself for his question. From now on he waited, with his mother, day after day. After all, it was possible that his father might change his mind.

One evening, when Peter's mother was at work in the hospital, he had looked under her pillow. He wanted to make sure. The letter had disappeared. Peter had opened his mother's desk with a sharp knife, but he found only paper and envelopes and a few Reichsmarks that she kept in a small box. He had searched his mother's wardrobe, he had lifted her ironed, neatly folded aprons and her underwear. There were two letters from her sister Elsa there, sent from Bautzen. Elsa's handwriting was such a scrawl that Peter could read only the opening words: Dear little Alice. He hadn't found any more of his father's letters, not a single one.

This morning, when Peter entered the dairy, Herr Fuchs the teacher and his sister were not there. The children waited for them in vain and looked at the other people who came into the shop, first diffidently, then boldly, and opened all the cupboards, crates, tubs and cans. The people cursed and swore, there wasn't a drop of sour cream left, not a bit of butter. An elderly lady kicked a cupboard and the door fell off.

As soon as the last of the grown-ups had left the shop the oldest boy knelt down on the floor, expertly lifted one of the tiles, and underneath it there was a cool storage space. One of the boys whistled and the girls nodded appreciatively. But the space was empty. Whatever had been inside it, butter or money, wasn't there any more. When the boy looked up and his dis-approving glance happened to fall on Peter, he asked why he was all dressed up like that. Peter looked down at himself in his best shirt and only now did he remember that he had to be home in good time. That was the last thing his mother had told him.

Even in the stairwell, he could hear the pots and pans clattering. His mother had been on night shift for the last week and spent her days cleaning up the apartment, as if it had ever been dirty; she polished the floors, dusted the chairs and cupboards, cleaned the windows. The door of the apartment wasn't locked and Peter opened it. He saw three men round the kitchen table, and his mother half sitting, half lying on it. The bare behind of one of the men was moving back and forth level with Peter's eyes, and his fleshy buttocks wobbled so much that Peter wanted to laugh. But the soldiers were holding his mother firmly. Her skirt was torn, her eyes were wide open, Peter didn't know if she could see him or was looking straight through him. Her mouth was wide open too, but no sound came out. One of the soldiers noticed Peter, held the waistband of his trousers closed and tried to push him out of the door. Peter called for his mother. Mother, he cried, Mother. The soldier kicked his legs, hard, so that Peter collapsed outside the door. One foot kicked his backside and then the door was closed.

Peter sat on the stairs and waited. He heard Frau Kozinska singing: *A bird on a green bough sat singing its song, on a cold wintry night, yet it sang loud and long.* But this was summer and Peter was thirsty, and the trains would soon be going. He wanted to leave with his mother. Peter pressed his lips firmly together. He looked at the door and the gap where the lock had once been. There were still splinters of wood on the floor. Peter's teeth nibbled scraps of thin skin off his lips. Soldiers had visited his mother once before, only a few days ago; they'd had to kick the door down, knocking the lock out. They had stayed all day, drinking and bawling. Peter had kept on hammering at the door. Someone must have pushed something up against it on the inside, perhaps there was a chair wedged under the handle. Peter had peered through the hole left by the missing lock, but there was such thick smoke inside that he couldn't make out anything. So Peter had sat on the stairs, waiting, as he was sitting now. You couldn't sharpen your teeth. Peter carefully chewed a scrap of skin that he had nibbled off. As he bit his lips he rubbed both forefingers over his gums. Although his mother kept his nails as short as possible, he always managed to loosen the skin over his gums with his forefinger, using the place where the nail lay embedded.

When the door finally opened last time the soldiers had stumbled out into the stairwell one by one. They went downstairs and knocked at Frau Kozinska's door. The last of them had turned and called something up to Peter in German: I have a lad like you at home, keep an eye on your mother. And the soldier, smiling, had wagged one forefinger. When Peter went into the smoke-filled kitchen he had seen his mother bending over in a corner of the kitchen, smoothing out a sheet. You're a big boy now, she had said without looking at Peter, you can't sleep in my bed any more.

She hadn't looked at him, unlike today. He had never seen such an expression in his mother's eyes before. They were icy.

It was hard for Peter to wait outside the door. He stood there, he sat down on the stairs and stood up again. Peter tried to see something through the gap left by the lock when it was broken out. He stood on tiptoe on the last step and leaned forward. That way he could easily lose his balance. Peter felt impatient, his stomach was grumbling. Whenever his mother was on night shift she came home in the morning, woke him to get ready for school and had a meal waiting when he came home at midday.

13

She made soup with water, salt and fish-heads. Later she took the fish-heads out and put some sorrel in the soup. She said it was healthy and nourishing. Very occasionally, when she had got hold of a little flour, she made it into small dumplings and simmered them in the soup. There'd been no potatoes since last winter. There was no meat, no lentils, no cabbage. Even in the hospital they had nothing but fish to feed to the children. Peter's eyes were fixed, as they had been before, on the closed door and the hole left by the lock. He sat down on the top step. He remembered that after last time his mother had asked him to go and find a new lock. There were locks everywhere, in every building, in every godforsaken apartment. But Peter had forgotten.

Now Peter was chewing at the ragged skin round his thumbnail, where you could pull it off in long, thin strips. If he hadn't forgotten about the lock, his mother could have locked the door. Peter's eyes wandered over the charred door frame in the abandoned apartment next door. You could see the marks left by the fire everywhere; the walls, ceilings and floors were black. He and his mother had been lucky, only the apartment above them and their old neighbour's apartment next door had burned out.

Suddenly the door opened and two soldiers came out. They were clapping each other on the back, in high good humour. Peter wondered if he could go into the apartment. He had counted three men before, so one of them must still be inside. Peter quietly got to his feet, went to the apartment door and opened it a crack. He heard sobbing. The kitchen seemed to be empty. This time none of the soldiers had been smoking; it all looked as clean and comfortable as it had in the morning. His mother's cleaning rag lay on the kitchen dresser. Turning, Peter saw the naked soldier behind the door. Legs drawn up, head in his hands, the man sat on the floor sobbing. Peter thought it a strange sight, because the soldier was wearing a helmet, although

14

otherwise he was entirely naked, and the war had been over for weeks.

Peter left the soldier sitting behind the door and went into the next room, where his mother was just closing the wardrobe. She was wearing her outdoor coat, she took the small case off the bed. Peter wanted to say he was sorry he'd forgotten the lock, sorry he hadn't been able to help her, but he got out only a single word and that was: Mother. He reached for her hand. She shook his off and went ahead of him.

They passed the sobbing soldier sitting on the kitchen floor behind the front door of the apartment, they went downstairs, they walked straight along the street to the fish quay. Peter's mother, with her long legs, walked so fast that he had trouble keeping up with her. He hopped and skipped along, and as he scurried after her, almost running, a great feeling of happiness came over him. He was filled by the certainty that they would be catching the train today, they would be setting out on their great journey, the journey west. Peter guessed that they wouldn't be going to Frankfurt, perhaps they'd go to Bautzen and his mother's sister, but first they would travel in the direction of Berlin. Once upon a time his mother used to tell him, as he dropped off to sleep, about the river, the beautiful market place in Bautzen, the wonderful smell in her parents' printing works. Peter clapped his hands and began to whistle, until his mother suddenly stood still and told him to stop it. Once again Peter tried to take her hand, but his mother asked if he couldn't see that she had the case and her handbag to carry.

I can carry the case, Peter offered, but his mother wouldn't let him.

Peter had often been to the fish market with his mother. One of the few fishwives still working there knew her well. She was a very young woman, her face still burned from last August, so that you could hardly see her youth. While the burns appeared a blemish at first, that blemish might have protected the young woman these last few weeks. She was the only one who still put up a big red sun umbrella early every morning, just like back in the old days, people said. In the old days – and by that they meant not so very long ago – the whole fish market had been full of big red sun umbrellas. They had disappeared over the last few years and months. It was from this fishwife that Peter's mother often fetched the fish for the children, eels, zander, bream, tench, pike, sometimes a fish from the sea that had found its way in from the lagoon, they were glad of any kind of fish at the hospital, and in spring Peter's mother had brought home a shad. By the time they reached the quay the fishwife had long ago set up her crate on her little wooden cart, with the sun umbrella right above it. There was a smell of tar and fish in the heat of the summer day. Cats lived among the ruins of the fish quay. Peter watched a thin tomcat run along the bank, rolling slightly from side to side, and jump down on to the little wooden landing stage. There wasn't a single boat left now where the broad, solid, flat-bottomed boats used to rock side by side with the fishing smacks. The cat dipped one paw into the water, its head jerking back again and again as if something had alarmed it. Was there a fish there or not? Peter's mother opened her handbag and took out some banknotes. This was what she owed the fishwife, she said. The fishwife wiped down her hands on her apron, where thousands of scales glittered, making it look like a robe, a mermaid's robe, as she took the notes and said thank you. Her eye fell on the case, and when his mother shook hands with her she said: Have a good journey. The fishwife's lips had almost escaped injury; they looked plump, full and young. Her voice rippled as if she were about to start chuckling. She had no eyebrows left and her eyelashes hadn't grown back very far yet.

16

Peter liked it when she turned aside and cast her eyes down, sounding embarrassed as she said something like: Well, good luck, then. He felt that she was looking at him and it was him she meant. He stood very close to his mother and laid his head against her arm, rubbed his nose over her elbow as if by chance, until she moved aside and changed her case to the other hand.

They walked briskly to the station. But even as they were going down the steps, a uniformed nurse with a big belly came towards them, obviously a colleague of his mother's, saying that the special trains weren't coming into Stettin, they'd have to walk to the next station in Scheune. The trains were leaving from there.

They went along between the tracks. The nurse was soon breathless. She kept close to Peter's mother and he walked behind them, trying to understand what they were talking about. The nurse said she hadn't been able to sleep a wink for thinking about the corpses they'd found by night in the hospital yard. Peter's mother did not reply. She said nothing about the soldiers and their visit. Her colleague was sobbing; she said she really admired Peter's mother for taking action, although everyone knew that there was something, well, not quite right about her background. The nurse laid a hand on her big belly, puffing and panting, but she wouldn't dwell on that now, she said. Who'd have the courage, after all? She herself could never have taken one of those stakes to thrust it into a woman's body and pull it out again, impaled like animals they'd been, with their female parts shredded. The nurse stopped, leaning heavily on Peter's mother's shoulder for support, she breathed deeply, the survivor kept on calling for her daughter, she said, but the daughter had bled to death long before, lying there beside her. Peter's mother stopped and told the nurse brusquely to keep quiet. For God's sake shut up.

The narrow platform at Scheune was crammed with people

waiting. They sat on the ground in groups, suspiciously watching the new arrivals.

Nurse Alice! The cry came from a group sitting on the ground, two women were waving their arms in the air. Peter's mother followed the voice of the woman who had obviously recognized her. She crouched down among the seated group. Peter sat down beside his mother, and the pregnant nurse followed them but stood there looking undecided, shifting from foot to foot. The women whispered together, and two women and a man went off with the pregnant nurse. When a woman needed to pee, she took several other people with her for company, if possible. Ivan was said to lurk behind the bushes waiting to attack women.

Several more hours were to pass before a train came in. The people crowded round it even before it stopped, trying to grab handles and rails. It almost looked as if the crowd itself were stopping the train, bringing it to a halt. The train didn't seem to have enough doors. Arms flailed, feet kicked, people struck out and brought sharp elbows into play. There was swearing and whistling. Those who were too weak were pushed aside, left behind. Peter felt his mother's hand on his back as she propelled him through the crowd, he had fabric against his face, coats, a case struck him in the ribs, and finally his mother picked him up from behind and raised him above the shoulders of the crowd. The conductor blew his whistle. At the last moment, Peter's mother fought her way the crucial final metre forward, pushing Peter, shoving him, forcing him into the train with all her might. Peter turned, holding her hand tightly, clutching it, the train jolted and began to move, the wheels were going round, Peter held on to the door, held on to his mother too, he'd show her how strong he was. Jump! he cried. At that moment their hands lost touch. The people left on the platform were running along beside the train. Someone must have pulled the emergency brake, or perhaps the engine was labouring, because the wheels squealed on the rails. A fat lady in a hat at the back of the crowd called out: Sausages, there's sausages over there! Sure enough, many people turned to look at her, stopped, stood on tiptoe, craned their heads to see who had uttered that cry and where the sausages were. The fat lady took her chance to fight her way several metres forward. The crowd pressed Peter's mother and the case into the train. Peter put both arms round his mother. He was never going to let go of her again.

Once on board, they stood in the corridor, people were pushing and shoving, children had to stand on suitcases. Peter was happy to stand on theirs; it made him almost as tall as his mother. When she turned, as she kept doing, her hair tickled him. It was pinned up but a lock had fallen loose. She smelled of lilac. Beside her, the door to the compartment with seats in it was open, and two young girls stood there on their cases in short-sleeved dresses, holding on to the overloaded baggage rack. The first sparse little hairs were growing in their armpits and Peter craned over his mother's shoulder to get a better look at their dresses, which curved out here and there. Peter felt the pleasant friction of his mother's coat rubbing under his chin. She must be sweating, but she hadn't wanted to leave her coat behind. The train jerked and slowly began to move. Outside the window, those who hadn't managed to board it moved by. One of the two girls was waving and crying, and Peter saw that little hairs were sprouting under her other arm too.

Hold tight, his mother told him, nodding her head towards the door frame of the compartment. Her little nurse's cap was still perched on her blonde, pinned-up hair, although they weren't in the hospital. Are you dreaming? Hold on tight, she snapped. But Peter put his hands on his mother's shoulders, thinking of the soldier who had been sitting sobbing behind the door. He was glad they were getting out of that place at last, and he wanted to fling his arms round his mother. Then someone's elbow struck him in the back, pushing him against his mother so hard that she almost overbalanced, the case under Peter's feet gave way, tipped over, and Peter fell on top of his mother. She staggered back into the compartment. She would never have cried out, she just uttered a sound of annoyance. Peter put his hand on her hip so as not to lose touch with her. He tried to help her up. Her eyes were sparkling angrily, Peter said he was sorry, but his mother didn't seem to be listening; her mouth stayed closed, her lips were narrowed, she pushed his hand away. Peter wanted her attention at any price.

Mother, he said, but she didn't hear him. Mother, he repeated, taking her hand again. It was cold and strong, and he loved it. Next moment the train jerked, people tumbled against each other, and his mother held tight with one hand to the baggage rack and with the other to the door frame for the rest of the journey, while Peter clung to her coat without her noticing or being able to prevent him.

Just before Pasewalk the train stopped on an open stretch of line. The doors were opened, and the passengers pushed and shoved each other out of the train. Peter and his mother let the mass of humanity sweep them along until they reached the platform. A woman was shouting that her baggage had been stolen. Only now did Peter notice that they had lost sight of the pregnant nurse. Perhaps she hadn't gone back to Scheune at all after answering the call of nature? Peter's mother was walking fast now, people came towards them and stood in their way, Peter was jostled repeatedly and held his mother's coat all the more tightly.

You wait here, his mother said when they came to a bench. An old man had just that moment got up from it. Trains leave for Anklam and Angermünde from here, perhaps there'll be tickets. I'll be right back. She took Peter by the shoulders and pressed him down on the bench.

I'm hungry, said Peter. Laughing, he clung to her arms.

I'll be right back, she repeated, you wait here.

I'm coming with you, he said.

She said: Let go of me, Peter. But he was already getting to his feet to follow her. At that she thrust the little case his way and pressed him and the case back on the bench. Now that Peter had to hold it on his lap he couldn't reach for her any more.

You wait. She said that sternly. A smile flitted over her face, she patted his cheek and Peter was glad. He thought of the sausages back in Scheune, that lady had been shouting about them, maybe there'd be some sausages here, he'd help his mother look for them, he wanted to help her anyway. He opened his mouth, but she was determined to have her own way, she turned and plunged into the crowd. Peter watched her go and spotted her by the door to the station concourse.

He badly needed to pee and looked around for a toilet, but he wanted to wait until she was back. After all, people could easily lose each other on a station like this. The sun slowly set. Peter's hands were cold, he held the case firmly and jiggled his knees. Small particles of colour from the case stuck to his hands, deep red. He kept looking towards the door where he had last seen his mother. People streamed by. At some point the family sitting on the bench beside him stood up and others sat down. Peter kept thinking of his father, building a bridge over the river Main somewhere in Frankfurt. He knew his name, Wilhelm, but not where he lived. His father was a hero. What about his mother? He knew her name too, Alice. There was something suspect in her background. Once again Peter looked at the door to the station concourse. His neck was stiff from sitting like that

21

for hours, staring the same way. A train came in, people picked up baggage, reached for their nearest and dearest, you had to hold on to everything. Anklam – the train wasn't going to Angermünde, it was for Anklam. The crowd was happy so long as it was going somewhere, anywhere. It was after midnight now and Peter didn't need to pee any more, he was just waiting. The platform had emptied, so presumably those who were still waiting had gone into the station concourse. If there was a ticket office wouldn't it have closed long ago? Perhaps there wasn't a concourse beyond that door at all, perhaps this station had been destroyed like the one in Stettin. A blonde woman appeared at the far end of the concourse; Peter stood up, jamming the case between his legs, he strained to see, but it wasn't his mother. Peter stayed on his feet for a while. When he was sitting down again, gnawing at his lips, he heard his mother complaining of the way he persisted in peeling off bits of his body and eating them, he could see her expression of revulsion in his mind's eye. Someone or other, Peter told himself, someone or other is bound to turn up. His eyes closed, he opened them, he mustn't go to sleep or he wouldn't notice if someone came looking for him; he fought against sleep, thought of his mother's hand and drew his legs up on the bench. He laid his head on his knees and never took his eyes off the station door. When daybreak came he woke up thirsty, and the wet fabric of the seat of his trousers was sticking to his skin. Now at last he stood up to go in search of a toilet and some water.

THE WORLD IS
ALL BEFORE US

T wo girls lay on a white-enamelled metal bedstead, taking turns to put their bare feet against the warm copper of the hot-water bottle. The little one kept trying to get the bottle over to her side of the bed, pushing with her toes and shoving with her heels. However, at the last moment her sister's long leg would stop her. Helene admired the length of Martha's legs and her slender, graceful feet. But the apparently effortless determination with which Martha claimed the hot-water bottle for herself, against Helene's wishes, drove her to despair. She braced her hands against her sister's back and tried to find a way for her cold toes to get past Martha's legs and feet under the heavy covers. The candlelight flickered; every breath of air caused by the scuffling under the blanket as it suddenly rose and fell made the flame gutter. Helene wanted to laugh and cry at once in her impatience, she compressed her lips and reached out for her sister, whose nightdress had ridden up, so that Helene's hand came down on Martha's bare belly, Martha's hips, Martha's thighs. Helene wanted to tickle her, but Martha twisted and turned, Helene's hands kept slipping away, and soon Helene had to close her fingers and pinch to get hold of any part of Martha at all. There was a tacit agreement between the two sisters: neither of them must utter a sound.

Martha didn't cry out, she just held Helene's hands tight. Her eyes were shining. She squeezed Helene's hands between hers so hard that her finger joints cracked, Helene squealed, she whimpered, Martha squeezed harder until Helene gave up and the little girl kept whispering: Let go, please, let go.

Martha smiled. She wanted to read a page or so of her book now. Her little sister's blonde eyelashes fluttered, the curve of her eyes showed under them. How fine the network of veins was round the eye. Of course Martha would forgive Helene sooner or later. All this just because of a copper hot-water bottle at their feet. Helene's pleading was a familiar sound, it soothed Martha. She let the little girl's hands go, turned her back to her sister and pulled the quilt away with her.

Helene was freezing. She sat up. And although her hands still hurt she reached out with them, touched Martha's shoulder and took hold of her thick braid, which had little curls escaping from it everywhere. Martha's hair was both soft and unruly, almost as dark as their mother's black hair. Helene liked to watch when Martha was allowed to comb Mother's hair. Then Mother would sit with her eyes closed, humming a tune that sounded like a cat purring. She purred contentedly in several different musical registers while Martha brushed and combed her thick, long hair, grooming it like an animal's coat. Once Helene had been at the sink washing a sheet, and when all the soap was rinsed away she wrung it out over the big bucket, taking care not to splash any water on the kitchen floor. It was only a matter of time before Mother cried out. Her cry was not a high, clear sound, but low and throaty, uttered with the fervour of some large animal. Mother reared. The chair she had just been sitting on crashed to the floor. She pushed Martha away, the brush fell to the floor. She flailed out with her arms, violent, aimless movements, her hairslides and combs flying off the table, she hooked her foot round the chair, picked it up and flung it in Helene's direction. Her loud cries re-echoed as if the earth itself had opened up and was growling.

26

The crochet work lying on the table shot right across the room. Something had pulled a strand of Mother's hair, tweaking it.

But while Mother shouted at her daughters, cursing them, complaining that she'd given birth to a couple of useless brats, Helene kept on and on repeating the same thing like a prayer: May I comb your hair? Her voice quivered: May I comb your hair? As a pair of scissors flew through the air she raised her arms to protect her head: May I comb your hair? She huddled under the table: May I comb your hair?

Her mother didn't seem to hear. Not until Helene fell silent did Mother turn to her. She bent over to see Helene under the table more clearly. Her green eyes were flashing. Stop that, snorted Mother. Straightening up, she brought the flat of her hand down on the table so hard that it must have hurt her. Helene had better come out from under that wretched table this minute. She was even clumsier than her big sister. Martha looked at the girl with the bright golden curls crawling out and carefully standing up as if she were a stranger.

You want to comb my hair, do you? Mother laughed nastily. Huh, you can't even wring out the laundry properly! Mother snatched the sheet out of the bucket and flung it on the floor. Maybe your hands are too fine for such work? Mother gave the bucket a vigorous kick, and then another, until it fell over with a clatter.

Helene instinctively jumped and flinched away. The girls knew their mother's fits of rage well; it was only when they came on so suddenly, without the slightest warning, that they were taken by surprise. There were tiny bubbles on their mother's lips, new ones formed, shining. There was no mistaking it, Mother was actually foaming at the mouth, seething, boiling over. Slavering, she raised her arm. Helene stepped sideways and grasped Martha's hand. Something brushed Helene's shoulder in passing and, as

27

Mother screeched, clattered to the floor and broke in half. Glass shattered. Thousands of tiny splinters of glass, thousands upon thousands. Helene whispered the unimaginable, incredible number, thousands upon thousands. Thousands upon thousands of them glittering. Mother must have snatched her Bohemian glass vase off the dresser. Helene wanted to run away, but her legs felt too heavy.

Mother doubled up, sobbed and sank to her knees. The broken glass must be coming through the fabric of her dress, but that didn't bother her. Her hands ploughed through the green splinters and the first blood sprang between her fingers; she cried like a child in a thin little voice, asked if no damn God would help her; she whimpered, and finally she kept on stammering the name Ernst Josef, Ernst Josef.

Helene wanted to bend down, kneel beside her mother, comfort her, but Martha firmly held her back.

This is us, Mother. Martha spoke sternly and calmly. We're here. Ernst Josef is dead, like your other sons, he was born dead, do you hear me, Mother? Dead, ten years ago. But we are here.

Helene could hear the anger and indignation in Martha's voice. It wasn't the first time she had faced up to their mother.

Ah! Mother cried out as if Martha had thrust a dagger into her breast.

Martha went out of the room, taking Helene with her.

Nauseating, whispered Martha, we really don't have to listen to such things, little angel. Come on, let's go.

Martha put her arm round Helene. They went into the garden and hung out the washing.

Again and again, Helene felt impelled to look up at the house, where Mother's wailing and screaming could be heard through the open window, but dying down now and becoming intermittent, finally stopping altogether, so that Helene was afraid their mother had bled to death or done herself some really serious injury.

And in addition Helene thought, as she sat up in bed beside Martha, that perhaps their mother assumed her screaming might work only in front of the children. On her own, it must seem pointless. What use was screaming if there was no one to hear you? Helene shook herself, she felt so cold, and touched her sister's braid, the braid that put out tiny curls, soft, fine little curls, the braid that was part of her kind sister who always protected her in any difficulty.

I'm freezing, said Helene. Please let me come in with you.

And she was glad when the mountain of bedclothes in front of her opened and Martha reached out a hand, holding the quilt up with her arm so that Helene could get underneath it and snuggle down. Helene nuzzled her nose into her sister's armpit, and when Martha went back to her book Helene pressed her face into her back, taking deep breaths of the warm, familiar scent. Helene wondered whether she ought to say her bedtime prayers. She could always fold her hands. She felt good. A surge of gratitude passed through her, but she was grateful to Martha, not God.

Helene played with Martha's braid in the shadow cast by the candlelight. Its muted glow made her hair look even darker than it was; those tiny curls were almost black. Helene stroked her forehead with the end of Martha's braid; the hairs tickled her cheeks and ears. Martha turned a page of her book and Helene began counting the freckles on her sister's back. Helene counted Martha's freckles every evening. Once she was sure of the number on her left shoulder as far as the birthmark at the top of her spine, she moved the braid aside and counted the freckles on Martha's right shoulder. Martha didn't object; she turned another page and chuckled softly.

What are you reading?

It's not your sort of book.

Helene loved counting. It was exciting and soothing. When Helene went to the baker's, she counted the birds she saw on the way to the shop and the people she met on the way back. If she left the house with her father she counted the number of times his big sandy dog Baldo lifted his leg, and how often people greeted them, and she liked to score high numbers. Once she played them off against each other: each greeting cancelled out one lift of the dog's leg. Now and then acquaintances addressed Helene's father as 'Professor', which was more an expression of flattery than a misunderstanding. Everyone knew that although Ernst Ludwig Würsich had been publishing philosophical and literary books for some years now, setting them in his printing works, that didn't make him a professor. Mayor Koban stopped and patted Baldo's head. The two men discussed the number of copies of the commemorative Town Council volume to be printed, and Koban asked Helene's father what kind of dog his was. But Father always declined to speculate on the mixture of breeds in Baldo and just replied: A good dog.

Helene was surprised to see how many of their acquaintances hurried past in silence as soon as she came out into the street with her mother. Mother herself didn't seem to notice. Helene counted quietly, in secret, and often she scored no more than a single greeting. Frau Hantusch the baker's wife, who almost hugged Father when they met, didn't even look at mother and daughter. Instead she lowered her umbrella slightly, holding it in front of her like a shield to make sure that no glances were exchanged. Helene supposed it must have been Martha who once told her that Mother wasn't really known as Frau Würsich at all. The people who lived in Tuchmacherstrasse spoke of her as 'the foreign woman'. It was true that she had married that highly regarded citizen of Bautzen Herr Würsich the master printer, but she was still a foreigner, even behind the counter of his printing works or out in the street with their daughters. Although it was very usual in Lusatia for couples to marry in the bride's home town, even ten years after the marriage there was still gossip about the origins of this particular bride. It was said that husband and wife had been married at a registry office in Breslau. A registry office – there was a dubious sound about that. Everyone knew that the foreign woman didn't go to St Peter's with her husband on Sundays. Rumour said she was ungodly.

Her daughters had been baptized in the cathedral, but that made no difference. The inhabitants of Bautzen obviously felt that a wedding not celebrated in church tainted their own respectable reputation. No one would deign to pass the time of day with the foreign woman. Every glance was accompanied by whispering and a disapproving shake of the head, even if Selma Würsich couldn't meet that glance because, with wise foresight, she paid more attention to the rare finds she might spot on the paving stones than to the citizens of the town. Whether proudly or awkwardly, the people in the street ignored Helene and her mother, looking over the head of the woman crouching on the ground or right through her. If Helene met her father's friend Mayor Koban while she was holding her mother's hand, the mayor crossed the road without a word. Judge Fiebinger's sons laughed and turned to stare, because they thought the flimsy fabrics Mother wore in summer were improper and her voluminous skirts in winter odd. But Mother seemed to notice none of this. She bent down, radiant, and showed Helene a little glass bead she had found. Look, isn't that lovely? Helene nodded. The world was full of treasures.

Whenever Mother left the house she collected things she found on the ground – buttons and coins, an old shoe that looked as if it had another few months' wear in it, perhaps it would be good for something, at least the shoelace was new, unlike the sole, and the hooks on the upper part seemed to Mother very rare and particularly valuable. Even a coloured piece of broken china down by the river would elicit a cry of delight from her if its edges were washed smooth by the water. Once, right outside their door, she found a goose's wing that could be used as a feather duster and wept tears of emotion.

On that occasion Martha had said it was more than likely that someone had left the feather duster there on purpose, just to see the foreign woman bend down and pick it up. The feathers were already worn short with use, and several of the quills stuck out like broken teeth, shiny and bare.

Mother collected such feather dusters, although she seldom used them. She hung up the birds' wings on the wall over her bed. A flock of birds to escort souls, that was how she described her collection. Only wings that she had found herself earned a place there above her bedhead. There were nine now, this one included, and she was hoping for a tenth. Once there were ten, she could complete the twenty-two letters of the alphabet and cast light on the roads ahead, as she put it. Neither of her two daughters asked where which souls were coming from and where they were to be escorted. The significance of a wandering soul, founded on or borrowed from the idea of parallel worlds, seemed to them eerie. It implied that side by side with their own world, where an inanimate object was an inanimate object and a living being a living being, there was another in which a reciprocal relationship between lives and objects existed. Helene covered her ears. Wasn't it difficult enough even to imagine what a soul was made of? And what might happen to a soul if it went wandering? Did it stay the same soul, individual, identifiable? Were we really destined to meet again in another world at a given time? That was what Mother threatened them with. When I'm dead we'll meet again, we'll be united. There's no escaping it. Helene was so scared that she didn't want to know any more about souls. Mother knew of an alleged purpose for every object, inventing one if necessary. Over the years of her marriage the house had filled up with things, not just in the closets and glass-fronted cupboards; a landscape with a will of its own was always threatening to grow in the attic among the pieces of furniture there. Mother laid out hills and mounds of objects, collections of items for purposes both certain and uncertain. Only Marja the housekeeper, who was called Mariechen by her employers and was no more than a few years older than Mother herself, managed, by dint of great patience and perseverance, to create any visible kind of order in some of the rooms. Mariechen ruled the kitchen, the dining room and the narrow stairs to the two upper storeys. In Mother's bedroom, however, and the room next to it you could hardly find any path to tread, and there was seldom a chair clear enough for anyone to sit on it. Mother collected branches and pieces of string, feathers and pieces of fabric, and no broken china could be thrown away; no box, however battered; no stool eaten away by woodworm, even if it wobbled because one of the rotten legs was now too short. If Mariechen turned anything out of the kitchen Mother took it to the upstairs rooms, where she would deposit the pan with the hole in it or the broken glass, confident that one of these days she would find a place and a use for the item. No system was discernible in her collection, only Mother herself had any idea which pile to search for a certain newspaper cutting and under which heap of clothes she had put the valuable Sorbian lace. Wasn't the filigree pattern of that lace wonderful, where had such delicate lilies ever been seen as those growing vigorously in it?

In search of a woollen winter dress now to be Helene's, a dress that Martha hadn't worn for nearly ten years, Mother had been rummaging inside the highest mountain of clothes, which rose almost to the ceiling. She had soon disappeared entirely under it and finally crawled out with a different dress, one that was already too small for her younger daughter. In the course of her search the pile of clothes had been scattered far and wide, and now covered the bookshelves, two chairs and the beaten track through the room itself. It seemed to Helene as if the house must soon burst apart from the sheer volume of stuffing inside it. Mother bent down, picked up something here and something there, put those items aside to left and right of her, and thus worked her way to the corner of the room. There she came upon a round hatbox near the floor. She clasped the hatbox to her breast as if it were a prodigal son.

She had once brought back the hat she wore at her engagement party to her married home in this box, an unusually wide-brimmed hat with a veil and magpie feathers shimmering in shades of dark blue, almost black. Tenderly, she stroked the fine grey paper of the lid and caressed its almost pristine sides. But then she eyed the hatbox suspiciously, she turned it this way and that, she shook it and there was a clinking inside as if the engagement hat had turned into nails or coins. For a while, Mother tried undoing the violet satin ribbon wound several times round the box with shaking fingers, until she lost patience and her face twisted with anger. She flung the box at Martha's feet with a cry of: You do it!

Martha picked up the hatbox, which now had a large dent in it. She looked around; she couldn't see a place clear for her to put down this treasure. So she took the box to the kitchen and placed it on the table there. Helene and Mother followed her. Martha's quick hands skilfully undid the knots.

Mother wanted to lift the lid herself. She sighed when she

looked into the box. A sea of buttons and other sewing things came into view, flowers worked in lace, small scraps of fabric presumably kept for covering buttons still bare or in need of renovation.

Mother had to sit down on a chair and breathe deeply. As she did so her ribcage rose and fell as if she were fighting off rising excitement with all her might. She sobbed, tears ran down her cheeks and Helene wondered where, in her slender mother, such an apparently inexhaustible supply of tears could be stored.

Mother had gone to lie down late in the afternoon, and now the girls were sitting by her bed, Helene on the stool, Martha in the rocking chair. Helene was bending over the round box, busy fishing out hooks and eyes both large and small, gold and black, white and silver. She found a clump of moth cocoons in the tangle of tapes and braid. The empty shells of the larvae still stuck to the fabric. Helene looked round. Mother was propped against a tall pillow. She had laid one hand on the little chest with two drawers that held picture postcards and letters, as well as dried flowers and loose playing cards – you never knew, you might assemble a full pack some day, or a particular card might be needed for a pack that was incomplete without it. The lower drawer of the little chest contained mainly postage stamps and coupons from packs of coffee. Mother had closed her eyes after telling her daughters to keep quiet and do their work. She had been suffering from a violent headache for hours, and lines of pain were traced on her forehead between her eyes. Obviously Martha thought this was a good opportunity. The task she had been given must seem to her laborious and pointless: she was supposed to be disentangling the threads of cotton reels thrown carelessly into the needlework box and winding them up tidily again. Then she was to sort the reels by colour and type of thread.

As soon as Mother's arm slipped heavily off the little chest in her sleep and her breath came regularly, Martha took out a slim, mustard-coloured book from under her apron and began reading it. She chuckled to herself, while her feet jiggled up and down as if she were about to start dancing or at least jump up any minute now. Helene looked longingly at Martha; she would have loved to know what made her so cheerful. Helene examined the tangled tapes in her hands. She spotted a white maggot on the dark-blue velvet of her dress, laboriously crawling in the direction of her knees, and felt nausea. And now another tiny maggot dropped out of what she had thought were the empty cocoons in her fingers, to land on her lap not far from the first. The maggot writhed, unsure which way to go. Hoping that Martha could rescue her, Helene whispered: Can I throw this away?

Leaf-green light shone through the drawn net curtains. From time to time a breath of wind made them billow out and tiny motes of dust danced in the narrow shaft of sunlight that shone briefly through the window. Martha rocked forward, stopped the rocking chair there for a few seconds, then rocked back. She turned a page and did not deign to give the tangled tapes in Helene's hand so much as a glance. When she shook her head sternly, but still smiling, Helene wasn't sure whether Martha had even heard her; perhaps she was lost entirely in her own world and her thoughts were with her book, or perhaps she was simply glad not to be holding this tangle of moth-eaten tapes and larvae herself. Helene retched. She cautiously put the tangle down on Mother's bed. Assorted suspender belts, stockings and items of clothing that Mother had worn over the last few days were draped over the end of it.

Martha leaned back in the rocking chair and stretched her legs. With a delicate movement, she put the curl that had slipped out of her thick braid back behind her ear. Now and then she clicked her tongue, crossed one leg over the other and narrowed her eyes, licking her lips as if she particularly liked the flavour of whatever she had been reading. Only when Father came into the room with his dog did she start in surprise. Baldo had his tail between his legs and immediately lay down in front of the stove.

But Father did not notice his elder daughter's red cheeks or the book that she hastily hid under her apron. He had eyes only for his wife. He didn't know how he was going to say goodbye, and sighed as he walked up and down in his hussar's uniform. Every time he turned, he looked at his wife as if asking her for help, turning to her for advice. It looked to Helene as if Father were about to say something, but he just breathed heavily, swallowed and finally sent the girls out of the room.

Later Helene knocked at the closed door; she wanted to say goodnight, and hoped for a glimpse of her father's new sword and the sash of his uniform. As Helene saw it, the fear that Martha and her mother felt at the thought of Father going to join the army was entirely unfounded. With his imperial moustache, which he wore a little shorter than the Kaiser himself, more out of admiration and respect than because of any initial insidious doubts, with his rock-hard confidence and his love for the girls' strange mother, Father seemed to her absolutely invulnerable. That impression was reinforced by the gleam and sparkle of the new curved sword. Even as Helene knocked, the door opened just a crack. Father was kneeling on the dark oak of the wooden floor that had been polished only a few days ago. It smelled of resin and onions. He was resting his forehead on Mother's hand.

Goodnight, Helene whispered, and glanced at the sword that Father had put down casually on the rocking chair. When he did not reply, Helene supposed he was asleep. She tiptoed over to the rocking chair, ran her finger over the blade and was surprised to find how blunt it was, how cool. A faint click of the tongue startled her; she saw Father waving one hand, indicating that she was to go away so that he could be alone with Mother. He didn't mind Helene's feeling the blade of his sword, but he didn't want her there. He had to say goodbye to his wife. Selma Würsich lay stretched out on the bed with her eyes closed; perhaps it was her high collar keeping her neck straight and the smell of onions luring tears from her closed eyes. Mother heard nothing, saw nothing, said nothing.

Helene retreated quietly to the door, walking backwards, and waited, hoping that Father would ask her some question, but he had laid his forehead on the back of Mother's hand again and was repeating the words: my love, my little pigeon. Helene admired her father for his love. The war could never hurt anyone who loved her mother.

Next evening neither of the girls said goodnight to their father. They heard him pacing up and down in the room next door, and knew he was getting no advice or help. Sometimes he said something, it sounded like: Joy! and then again like: God! Only occasionally, between those words, did they hear his dog whining.

The girls lay snuggling close together. Helene pushed her nose between her big sister's shoulder blades; from time to time she stuck out her chin and took a breath of air, while Martha turned the pages of her book regularly and laughed quietly to herself. But then, loud and clear, the girls heard their mother's voice, deep and slightly husky from all her smoking: If you go I shall die.

Helene caressed the faint brown birthmark. Martha's back was thin and delicate, and she stroked its freckles too, running her finger up and down along the fine lace edging of her sister's nightdress.

Please, just one word – please.

No begging.

Please. Just one word.

Go on doing that first. Up there, yes, further up.

Helene followed her sister's instructions and ran her hand over the skin, up the nightdress and Martha's shoulders, circling there, then down her arm, over its bare skin, once again over her back under the linen nightdress, then down along Martha's backbone, vertebra by vertebra, she could clearly feel every one of them under the fabric. Then she stopped.

One word.

Star.

Helene moved her hand very slightly, tracking the points of a star, stopped and demanded: More.

Though the star of my fate hath declined.

Helene rewarded Martha. She tickled the back of her neck. Line by line, stanza by stanza, Helene's hands lured Byron's words out of her sister's mouth.

A horse and cart passed by under their window, and as the cart jolted over the cobblestones something jingled and clinked as if it were loaded with glasses. It must be carrying a delivery from the Three Ravens inn, which had moved into its new premises in Tuchmacherstrasse in the spring. The opening had enlivened their street a good deal. The drayman had cluttered up the pavement with his barrels, ladies of the middle class went to the Three Ravens in the middle of the day to drink coffee, while their cooks and housekeepers went shopping up in the Kornmarkt, and in the evening there were hussars bawling at the top of their voices in the street itself, which suddenly seemed too narrow and too small.

At weekends, the town south of the Kornmarkt was now all activity on a Saturday night. Men and women sang and stamped until the small hours to familiar tunes played on a piano. If the piano-player tired and his keyboard fell silent, someone else would bring out an accordion. People came from the little mountain villages at weekends, from Singwitz and Obergurig, even from Cunewalde and Löbau. They went to market in the morning, sold their ladders and ropes, their baskets and jugs, their onions and cabbages, and bought what wasn't to be had at home, oranges and coffee, fine pipes and coarse tobacco. Then they danced the night away at the Three Ravens, before harnessing the horses to their carts early in the morning and climbing in, or some of them simply pushed handcarts back to their villages in the mountains. But Bautzen was a quiet place during the week.

Helene stroked her sister's back, she ran the ball of her thumb down Martha's backbone.

Harder, said Martha, with your nails.

Helene crooked her fingers so that her nails, which were short, could at least touch her sister's skin. Perhaps she'd let her fingernails grow long for Martha's sake, file them to points, the way she'd seen a girlfriend file hers.

Like that? Helene traced a star map on Martha's shoulder blade, drawing lines from freckle to freckle, joining them up to make the constellations she knew. The first was Orion the hunter, wearing Martha's birthmark on his breast like a shield; the central star of the three on his belt was slightly raised. Helene knew the moments when Martha would stretch, and when she would arch, luxuriating, go rigid and then double up. Cassiopeia merged directly with the Serpent in the star map, a snake with a large head. Ophiuchus the Serpent-Bearer rose in the middle of it. Helene knew that one from a book she had found on Father's shelves. There were many days when Martha writhed under the touch of Helene's hands, and if Helene listened carefully she thought Martha's breathing sounded like a hiss. Helene imagined what it would be like to lift Martha up in the air, carry her, wondered how heavy she would be. Martha's sighs were unpredictable, Helene teased them out; she thought she knew every nerve and fibre under her sister's skin, stroked her as if she were playing an instrument that would make music only if the strings were touched in a particular way. In Helene's eyes, Martha was already a grown woman. She seemed to her perfect. She had breasts with curving little buds, clear and tender and soft, and on some days of the month she secretly washed her little cloths. Only when she wanted to punish Helene for stealing raisins or saying something she didn't like would Martha give her those little cloths to wash instead. Helene was afraid of Martha's brusque instructions. She washed Martha's blood out of the linen, took the little brown bottle of oil of turpentine, unscrewed the top and counted out thirty drops into the water for the final rinse. In winter she hung the little cloths up to dry in the attic, in front of the south-facing window. The turpentine evaporated, and the sun helped to make the cloths bright and white again. It would be years yet before Helene had to wring out any little cloths of her own; she was nine years younger than Martha and had started school only last summer.

Further down, said Martha, and Helene did as she was told, she stroked her sister's sides further down, all the way to the place where her hips curved gently, then on back and round to the base of her spine.

Martha sighed deeply and there was a faint smacking noise as if she were opening her mouth to say something.

Over your kidneys, here, said Helene.

Yes, and up to my ribs, up to my lungs, dear heart.

Helene hadn't heard Martha turn a page for several minutes now. Martha was lying on her side, her back turned to Helene, still and expectant. Helene's hands came and went, she heightened Martha's craving, she wanted to hear another sigh, just one, her hands flew softly over the skin now, no longer touching everything, only a few places, very few, desire made them breathe faster, first Helene, then Martha, and finally both of them; it sounded like the gasping noise you made wringing out laundry when you stood at the sink by yourself, hearing nothing but your own breathing and the gurgling of the laundry in the enamel basin of water, the effervescence of the washing powder, the foaming soda; here it was the gasping of two girls, no gurgling yet, only fast breathing, an effervescent bubbling, until Martha suddenly turned round.

My little angel. Martha took Helene's hands, the hands that had just been stroking her, she spoke softly and clearly: I come off duty at four tomorrow and you must meet me outside the hospital. We'll go down to the river. Martha's eyes were shining, as they often did these days when she announced that they were going for a walk beside the Spree.

Helene tried to free her hands. It was hardly a question, more of a statement when she said: With Arthur.

Martha laid her forefinger on her sister's lips. Don't mind.

Helene shook her head, although she did mind. She opened her eyes very wide, she wasn't going to cry. Even if she had wanted to cry, it wouldn't be any use. Martha stroked Helene's hair. Little angel, we're going to meet him in the old vineyard on the other side of the railway line. When Martha was happy and excited, her laughter gurgled in her throat. He's going to study botany in Heidelberg. He can live with his uncle there.

What about you?

I'm going to be his wife.

No.

The *No* came out of Helene's mouth faster than she could

think it, came bursting out. She added, quietly: No, that's impossible.

Impossible? Anything's possible, my angel, the world is all before us. Martha was radiant, joyful, but Helene squeezed her eyes shut and obstinately shook her head.

Father won't let you.

Father won't let any man come near me. Martha released Helene's hands and, in spite of her remark, she had to laugh. He loves me.

Father or Arthur?

Arthur, of course. Father just owns me. He can't give me up. Even if he wanted to, he simply can't do it. He won't let anyone have me.

Well, not Arthur, that's for sure.

Martha turned on her back and clasped her hands as if about to pray. God, what can he do about it? I have two legs, I can walk away. And a hand to give Arthur. Why are you so stern, Helene, why are you so anxious? I know what you're thinking.

What am I thinking?

You think it's because of Arthur's family, you think Father has reservations of a certain kind. But that's not true. Why would he mind? They don't even go to synagogue. Sometimes Father says bad things about those people, but haven't you noticed his smile? He's making fun of them in a friendly way, like when I call you a grubby sparrow, little angel. He'd never have married Mother if he thought the same way as he talks.

He loves Mother.

Has he told you how they met? Helene shook her head and Martha went on. How he travelled to Breslau and met Fräulein Steinitz with her striking hats in the printing works there? She was stylish, he says, a stylish young lady in a sea-green coat, the colour the printers call cyan. She still has it. And she wore a different hat every day.

Stylish, murmured Helene to herself. The word sounded like a chocolate; it was meant to describe something high-class, but chocolates just tasted bitter.

Her uncle was a hat maker and she was his favourite model. She won't throw out any of those felt confections that look so odd today. I once heard Father telling her angrily she'd been in love with her uncle, that was why she couldn't part with those old hats. Mother only laughed, she laughed so much that I thought Father's suspicions must be right. Do you think he minded her being Jewish?

Helene looked at Martha incredulously and narrowed her eyes. But she isn't. Helene shook her head to reinforce what she said. I mean, not really.

You just don't notice because she doesn't wear a wig. And what synagogue would she go to? She doesn't keep separate sets of dishes, she leaves the cooking to Mariechen. But of course she's Jewish. You think they call her the foreign woman here in Bautzen because she speaks with a Breslau accent. Do you? Do you really believe it's a Breslau accent? I don't, it's the way her whole family talk. She uses all those words that seem to you familiar, and you have no idea that they show what she is.

Martha, what are you talking about? Helene kept shaking her head slowly and firmly, as if that would silence Martha.

It's true. She doesn't have to pretend to us. Why do you think she never goes to church? She gives the cathedral a very wide berth.

It's because of the meat market, that's why. She says the butchers' stalls smell horrible. Helene wished Martha would keep quiet.

But there was no stopping Martha now. When we go to Mass

44

at Christmas with Father and Grandmother, she says someone has to stay at home and cook the meal. What a fib! Why does she have to cook the meal at Christmas, of all times? Because she wants to give Mariechen time off, because she has such a kind heart? No, it's because she has no business in church with our God at Christmas, that's all, little angel. Did you never notice before?

Helene leaned her head on her hand the way she saw Martha do it. Have you talked to her about that?

Of course. She says it's none of my business. I tell her if I want to get married she won't be found in any church register, and I don't have her family records so half of my own are missing. Guess what she said? She told me not to be impertinent, she said if I went on like that no one would ever want to marry me.

Helene looked at Martha and knew that Mother was lying. Martha was at least as beautiful as Mother, with the same attractive, narrow nose, the same freckled white skin, the same curving hips. Who'd bother about some kind of old family records?

Martha said it was no good Mariechen teaching them the stitches to embroider their initials on linen for a trousseau. Never mind their initials, their origin tainted them.

Mariechen was considered a wonderful needlewoman and lacemaker, even among her own Sorbian relations. But although women often knocked at the door in Tuchmacherstrasse wanting to order lace handkerchiefs and caps and tablecloths from her, she turned them all down. She was in a steady job, she replied with the smile of a faithful servant. Only very occasionally did she give something as a present to a sister, cousin or niece. Most of the lace and little mats that Mariechen crocheted and embroidered in her spare time stayed in the house. Her absolute loyalty created a strange bond between Sorbian Marja and her mistress, Frau Selma Würsich. Perhaps they simply shared a love of fine fabrics?

Helene looked at Martha. She could see no flaw. Martha appeared to her perfect. Arthur's glances were by no means the only ones that lingered on her fine features. When Helene crossed the Kornmarkt with Martha, it wasn't just the young men who looked at her, whistling cheerfully, and wished them good day. Old men too made sounds like grunts and groans. Martha's steps were light, her strides were long, she stood proud and erect, so that people showed respect when they met her, or that was how Helene saw it. The men clicked their tongues and smacked their lips as if tasting sweet syrup on their tongues. Even the market women addressed Martha as *pretty young lady* and *my beauty*. More and more men who would have liked to marry her were to be found every day near the little printing works in Tuchmacherstrasse. If Martha stood behind the counter in the small shop area helping to serve customers, several young men would gather there during the afternoon, getting her to show them different kinds of paper and different typefaces, seldom able to make up their minds. They weighed up the pros and cons, got talking to each other, they boasted of their own businesses or studies with unconcealed glances in Martha's direction and courted her as best they could. Only when one of them ventured to ask her out for coffee, and she declined with a smile, saying she never went out for coffee with customers, did the point where he decided to order a small print run come closer. But the young men came back another day, they kept watch on each other; every single one of them wanted to make sure that no one else was higher than he was in Martha's favour. Helene could understand how those men felt, for she herself would have loved to sleep beside beautiful Martha and wake up at her side all her life. Marriage to a man seemed to Helene totally point-less and unnecessary. Marriage was the last thing anyone needed.

So why do you think Father wouldn't let you marry someone like Arthur Cohen?

Why? Martha put her head back on the pillow, looking annoyed rather than thoughtful, and when she brought out a handkerchief from under the pillow and blew her nose very thoroughly, as Mother did after a long fit of tears, Helene was sorry she'd asked. But then, unexpectedly, Martha's smile spread over her face, a smile that she could hardly keep back these days, a smile that easily turned to a chuckle and – only if neither Mother nor Father was around – occasionally to wholehearted, exuberant laughter.

Little angel, who'd there be for him to rely on then? Mother? If Mother goes to a fair she isn't seen for days. Very likely she stays at inns in Zwickau and Pirna dancing with strange men until morning!

Never. Helene couldn't help smiling, because she didn't know whether Martha expressed such a supposition just to anger her or whether there was a grain of truth in it.

And who would look after you? Father can't get on his horse and go off to the war without knowing we're provided for. He's afraid, that's all it is. And he wants me to look after you. I will, too. You wait and see.

Helene didn't reply. She guessed that every word she said would only make Martha think harder and in more detail than ever about possible escape routes. She was sure that for weeks Martha had thought of nothing but how to begin a new life with Arthur Cohen.

Who's that book you're reading by?

It's not your sort of book.

But I want to know.

You want to know everything. Martha wrinkled her nose; she

liked Helene's curiosity and she liked still being so far ahead of her sister. A year ago, when Helene was finally old enough to start at the Municipal School for Girls on Lauengraben, she could already read and write. She had learned to play the old piano from Martha, who watched with admiration and a little envy to see how smoothly her hands slipped over the keys without practising, how fast her runs were even in the lower octaves, how surely she remembered the melodies that Martha often had to learn laboriously, note by note. And numbers raced around in Helene's head even faster and more confidently than her fingers moved over the piano keyboard; no matter what numbers Martha threw out for her, Helene had no trouble in making other numbers out of them, taking them apart, dividing them, fitting them together into something new. After only a few weeks the teacher moved Helene up to do lessons with the older girls, giving her exercises for ten-year-olds. Helene was seven at the time. It began to look as if the teacher would have passed on all she knew to the little girl within a few months, before she was supposed to be the right age for it. Helene was ashamed of herself for not growing up fast enough. She was frightened, too. At fourteen, sixteen at the latest, girls left school and went home to their parents, to take over the running of the household and be introduced to men who were believed to be well off and to enjoy a good reputation, one to which a young wife would add. Only a few girls were allowed to go on to the High School, and the other girls in the town knew very well who they were and envied them. If one of Martha's friends said she would like to be a nursery schoolteacher, her parents asked in disparaging tones whether that kind of thing was really necessary. The family had enough money, they said, the girl was well enough educated, she could already choose between two suitors and have a good, well-to-do husband. Martha's tales of her girlfriends sounded to

Helene like a horror story. She would pause for effect as she described how one particular friend, for instance, wanted to marry for love and had told her parents so. The parents just laughed. In a tone of wise superiority, the girl's father pointed out that the right man had to present himself first, and love could follow. Meanwhile Judge Fiebinger, whose sons were not to begin their studies until they had done military service in the local regiment, was sending his daughters straight to Dresden, one to the conservatory, the other to the women's teacher-training college. Martha often told Helene about the judge's daughters. It was a good thing to be a teacher. A few years ago, Martha used to sit beside that budding teacher the judge's daughter in school and help her with her sums. Perhaps the girl would never have made it to the High School without her help? Martha whispered in Helene's ear that if she herself went on like this, Father would send her to study too, to Dresden and Heidelberg, she was sure he would. Her whispering lips touched Helene's ear, they tickled pleasantly and Helene couldn't get enough of it. Their father had allowed Martha to train as a nurse, so surely in view of Helene's clever mind he would consider his younger daughter his pride and joy, he'd send her to Heidelberg where she could be one of the few women to study medicine. When Martha painted such a picture of her future, Helene held her breath, hoping Martha wouldn't stop telling that story, would go on and on, and picture Helene studying human anatomy some day in a huge lecture room at Dresden University, enumerating the funny names of parts of the body, like spinal cord and verte-bral canal. Helene drank in such words when Martha came home with them and repeated them to her sister once or twice, only to forget them soon herself. Helene wanted to know more about the rhomboid fossa and the arteries at the base of the skull, but Martha stumbled over her words, as if she had been caught out.

At a loss, she looked at Helene and confessed that the names were all she knew, not where those things were and what they were for. She stroked her little angel's head and comforted Helene, not very long now and she'd be studying the subject herself, only a few more years, she'd soon see. As soon as Martha's narrative flow stalled – perhaps she had dropped happily off to sleep beside her sister – less attractive ideas occurred to Helene. She remembered that although Father had recently got her to help with the bookkeeping for the printing works, he just muttered quietly, talking crossly to himself, if she found a mistake in the accounts somewhere. He didn't want to acknowledge that his younger daughter was clever. All the time Helene sat in her father's office in the evening doing arithmetic, he never once showed any surprise or pleasure. She drew up whole columns of figures just to get him to stop and marvel at them for a change, to notice that she was soon dealing with his accounts more easily than he did himself. But Father ignored Helene's efforts. When the teacher asked her parents to visit the school building on Lauengraben and talked to her father, telling him that in the course of the school year Helene had studied all the material supposed to occupy the first four years in many subjects, he smiled in a kindly way, shrugged almost impercep-tibly, as was his habit, and looked lovingly at his wife, who was ceremoniously taking a needle she had brought out of the lapel of her coat, who then produced the darning thread she had put in her pocket at home and, in mid-conversation and despite the teacher's presence, set about darning a hole in her dress with the red yarn. While Helene's parents were relieved to find that their daughter had not stolen anything and had not been naughty in any other way, they did not understand why the teacher had asked them to come to the school to tell them that she would soon be unable to teach their daughter anything else. She was simply plan-ning to let her read rhymes and fairy tales, if her parents had no objection, she said. Helene's mother bit through the thread with her teeth; the hole was mended. The dog impatiently slapped his master's leg with his long tail. The teacher's enquiring look made Helene's father uneasy. It was not for him, after all, to tell the teacher what she was to do with his daughter.

When they came home they didn't say a word to Helene about their visit to the teacher. It was as if their younger daughter were an embarrassment.

Helene wanted to stay on at school, but she entertained doubts, both niggling and more serious, of the dream that Martha had spun for her. Neither of her parents had ever said a word about Heidelberg or studying. Helene did not want to be sent home ahead of time to keep house for her mother and be set to work clearing cupboards of the debris left by moths.

Martha sometimes asked Helene: What do you want to be when you grow up?

But she knew the answer; it was always the same. I want to be a nurse like you. Helene pressed her nose against Martha's shoulder and breathed in her sister's scent. Martha smelled like a warm roll and only very slightly of the vinegar that she rubbed into her hands when she came off duty. Helene observed Martha's smile. Was she glad of Helene's ever-reliable answer? Did it flatter her to think that the little girl wanted to be just like her? Next moment, however, Helene realized that Martha's smile had nothing to do with her answer. Martha was stroking the gold-embossed lettering on the cover of her book.

What a lovely present.

Let me see.

Close your eyes, yes, that's right. You can read it blind.

Helene felt Martha taking her hand, but did not guide it to the book. Instead, she found that she was feeling Martha's stomach and her navel. Martha's navel was set in a little hollow, unlike Helene's, which stood out like a button. Helene squeezed both eyes tight shut and felt Martha taking her finger and pushing it into the pit of the navel.

There, what can you decipher?

Martha felt the slight curve of Martha's belly. How soft her sister's skin was. Unlike their mother's belly, which spread out, particularly below the navel, Martha had a beautiful stomach with only the gentlest swelling. Helene felt Martha's ribs and thought of the gold letters on the mustard-coloured book. She had deciphered them in secret long ago. Byron, said the letters. So she said: Byron.

Byron. Martha corrected Helene's pronunciation. Keep your eyes closed and go on reading.

Helene could tell from her sister's voice that Martha was pleased with her ability to read blind. Go on reading, Martha told her for the second time. And Helene felt Martha taking her hand and guiding it over her belly, circling, running Helene's hand over her hips, stroking them. Read.

A Selection of Lyrical Poetry.

Helene had noticed the gold letters and had been wondering for some time what exactly lyrical poetry was. But then Martha took her hand again and placed it on her bottom rib.

Can you see under my skin too, little angel? Do you know what's underneath the ribs here? The liver lies here.

Sisterly knowledge. Remember that, you'll have to learn it all later. And this is where the gall bladder is, right beside it, yes, there. The word spleen was on Helene's lips, but she didn't want to say it, she just wanted to open her eyes, but Martha noticed and told her: Keep your eyes closed.

Helene felt Martha take her hand and guide it up to the next rib, and finally still higher, up to her breast.

Although she kept her eyes tightly closed and couldn't see, Helene noticed her own feelings and how hot her face was all of a sudden. Martha was still guiding her hand, and Helene clearly felt her nipple and the firm, soft, perfect curve of the breast. Then down into the valley below, where she felt a bone.

A little rib.

Martha didn't answer, and now her hand was climbing the other hill. Helene peered through her lashes, but Martha's eyes weren't on her any more, they were wandering aimlessly, blissfully, under her own half-closed lids, and Helene saw Martha's lips opening slightly and moving.

Come here.

Martha's voice was husky; with her other hand she drew Helene's head towards her and pressed her own mouth on Helene's. Helene was startled; she felt Martha's tongue on her lips, demanding, she could never have imagined how rough and smooth at the same time Martha's tongue on her lips would feel. It tickled, it almost made Helene laugh, but Martha's tongue grew firm and pressed on Helene's lips as if searching for something. That tongue opened Helene's lips and pushed against her teeth. Helene had to breathe, she wanted air, she opened her lips, and now Martha's tongue was filling her whole mouth. Helene felt her sister's tongue moving about in it, back and forth, pushing at the insides of her cheeks, pressing against her own tongue. Helene thought of their last walk beside the Spree, and how Martha had told her to stay a few steps behind her and Arthur. Suddenly she noticed that her hand was lying on Martha's breast all by itself, while for some time Martha's hands had been moving in her hair and on her back.

They had walked to the causeway lying concealed beyond the vineyard; you could reach it only by passing the willows that grew there. The ground was black and slippery. Come on, called

Martha, several metres away, and she ran ahead with Arthur. They jumped from tree stump to tree stump, the soft ground yielded, their bare feet sank into it. Little puddles of gurgling water stood everywhere. Swarms of tiny midges were swirling in the air. Here, at this bend of the river, the Spree had made itself a small bay where the ground underfoot was not firm, land on which few people out for a stroll would ever tread. Marsh marigolds were flowering wherever you looked. The daisy chain that Martha had made Helene on the meadow by the river bank threatened to slip off her head; she held it on with one hand, using the other to carry her shoes and hold up her dress to keep it from getting muddy. It was difficult to see where the ground was at all firm, it kept giving way and, fast as they ran, putting their toes down first, their feet were soon black up to the ankle. The sword-shaped leaves of water lilies had a silvery sheen in the sunlight.

Arthur had put on his bathing costume behind a willow tree and was first into the water; he had flung himself into the current and was flailing about frantically with his arms to keep from being carried downstream. He looked as if he were treading water. The wind blew through the reeds, they swayed and bent down to the surface. Next moment the wind blew everything the other way, the yellowish-green twigs, the curving blades of grass as they bowed down. The rushing sound broke against Helene's ears. Although Arthur kept calling to them, Martha couldn't make up her mind to follow him. She didn't have a bathing costume, she had grown so fast last year that her old one didn't fit any more.

Let's leave our petticoats on and just paddle in the water.

Martha and Helene took off their dresses and hung them over the branch of a low-growing willow. The water was icy cold, the chill went right through their calves. When Arthur came close to the bank and made as if to splash them with water, the girls fled. Martha squealed and laughed, and kept calling Helene's name. Arthur wanted to lie on the grass with Martha at the foot of the slope further downstream, but Martha took Helene's hand and said she couldn't go anywhere without her little sister. And there might be grass stains if they lay down in their petticoats. Arthur said she could sit on his jacket, but Martha declined. She pointed to her mouth and showed Arthur how her teeth were chattering.

I'll warm you up. Arthur put his hands on Martha's arms, he wanted to stroke them and rub them, but now Martha made her teeth chatter as loudly as she could.

Arthur brought Martha her dress, told her to put it on again and Martha thanked him.

Later the two sisters sat snuggling together on the slope, side by side. A little way further up, Arthur had found some small wild strawberries, and now he was crawling around the meadow on all fours. From time to time he came back to the girls, knelt down in front of Martha and offered her a handful of berries on a vine leaf.

No sooner had he left again than Martha took the berries and put them alternately in Helene's mouth and her own. They fell on the grass and looked up at the clouds. The wind had died down around them and now carried only a faint scent of wood from the sawmill. Helene breathed in the aroma, mingled with the sweet perfume of some kind of flowers. Martha saw the shape of a hussar in the sky; his horse had only forelegs and even those disappeared if you watched for any length of time. While there seemed to be almost no wind down here, the clouds up above were driving eastwards faster and faster. Helene said she could see a dragon, but Martha said dragons have wings.

No wonder everyone's talking about mobilization, Arthur

called down to them. Seeing you two lying there like that, I don't feel as if picking berries were difficult!

The sisters exchanged meaningful glances. Arthur's main interest was in being close to them, they were sure, not in mobilization. Neither of them had any idea, in fact, what he meant by that word. They suspected that his notion of the term was as vague as their own. They heard the wind whistling fitfully up above, whistling a cheerful march. Who was going to war, and what for? Was there a more beautiful place anywhere than the banks of the Spree? And for months the warmth of the sun had inspired such confidence! The holidays would never end; no one would follow the call to mobilization.

That's all there are, said Arthur when he came back some time later with two handfuls of wild strawberries and sat down in front of the sisters. Would you like them? He reached out his hands to Martha; the berries were rolling about and threatened to fall into the grass.

No, I don't want any more.

Would you like some?

Helene shook her head. For a moment Arthur looked at his hands, undecided.

Darling, he begged Martha, laughing. They're for you.

Never mind that, let's feed the little angel.

Martha held up her hands and took the strawberries from Arthur. Some of them fell on the grass.

Grab her. Martha indicated Helene with a nod of her head. Arthur did as she said, flung himself on Helene, forced her down under him and knelt on her small body, his strong hands pressing her arms to the ground. While Arthur and Martha laughed, Helene struggled, clenched her fists, shouted to Arthur to let her go. She tried arching her spine to throw him off, but he was heavy, he laughed, he was so heavy that her back gave way under the strain. Now Martha forced berry after berry between Helene's lips as she pressed them together as firmly as possible. Juice was running out of the corners of her mouth and down her chin and throat. Jaws clenched, Helene tried begging them to leave her alone. Now Martha stuffed the little berries up Helene's nose so that she could hardly breathe and the juice stung the inside of her nostrils. Martha squashed the berries on Helene's mouth, on her teeth, squeezed them so that the skin around Helene's mouth was itching from the sweet juice of the berries, until she opened her mouth and not only did she lick the strawberries off her teeth, she licked Martha's fingers too when her sister pushed them into her mouth.

That tickles. Martha laughed. It feels like, like . . . feel for yourself.

Helene could already feel Arthur's fingers in her mouth. She didn't stop to think, she simply bit. Arthur screeched and jumped up.

He had run some way off.

Are you crazy? Martha had looked at Helene in horror. It was only a bit of fun.

And now, feeling Martha's tongue in her mouth, Helene wondered whether to bite that too. But she couldn't, there was something she liked about Martha's tongue, although at the same time she felt ashamed.

Martha shook her awake. It was still dark and Martha was holding a candle. Apparently the girls were to follow their father into the next room. Mother lay there on the bed, rigid. Her eyes were dull, with no light in them. Helene tried to see a gleam of some kind there, she propped her hands on the bed and bent over her mother, but Mother's eyes never moved.

I'm dying, said Mother quietly.

Father said nothing; he looked grave. He was nervously fingering the pommel of his curved sword. He didn't want to waste any more time talking about the point of the war and his part in it. He had been expected at the barracks on the outskirts of town since last week and the regiment wouldn't put up with further delay. His departure could not be postponed or evaded. It was no surprise to Ernst Ludwig Würsich to hear that his wife would rather die than say goodbye. She had frequently toyed with the idea before, had said so, in tones both loud and soft, to herself and to others. Every child she had lost after the birth of Martha had seemed to her a demand for her life to end. The pendulum of the clock on the wall shattered time into small, countable units.

Carefully, Helene approached Mother's hand. She was going to kiss it. The hand moved and was withdrawn. Helene leaned over her mother's face. But Mother moved her head aside without giving her daughter one of her usual strange looks. Her four dead children would have been boys. One by one they had died, two still in the uterus, the other two just after birth. They had all had black hair when they were born, thick, long black hair, and dark skin that was almost blue. The fourth son had been breathing noisily on the morning of his birth, breathing with difficulty, he seemed to take a deep breath and then all was still. As if the breath couldn't leave his little body any more. Yet he was smiling, and newborn babies don't usually smile. His mother had called the dead child Ernst Josef; she had taken the baby's body in her arms and wouldn't let him go for days. He lay in her arms, in bed with her, and when she had to visit the smallest room in the house she took him with her. Later, Mariechen had told Martha and Helene how their father had asked her to make sure that everything was all right, and how she had gone into the bedroom where Mother sat on the edge of the bed with her hair down, cradling her dead baby. Only after days was she heard praying; it was a relief. Mother had recited a long *Kaddish* for Ernst Josef, although there was no one to say amen, no one to join her in mourning. Father and Mariechen were worried about her, and neither of them wept for the dead child. Whenever anyone spoke to Mother over the next few days, said something to her or asked a question, her voice rose, murmuring words as if she were constantly talking to herself, and the murmuring died down quietly to inaudibility only in the hours when no one spoke to her. Even now she was heard praying every day. The strange sounds coming out of Mother's mouth sounded like an invented language. Helene couldn't imagine that Mother knew what she was saying. There was something both all-inclusive and exclusive about them; to Helene's ear they had no meaning at all, yet they screened the house from the world, rested on it like a silence full of sound.

When Mariechen opened the curtains in the morning Mother closed them again. After that there were only one or two months in the year when Mother woke from her darkness, and then she remembered that she had a living child, a little girl called Martha, and she was ready to play with her in silly ways as if she were a child herself. It was Easter, so Mother thought she would roll eggs down the Protschenberg. She seemed to be in high spirits, she was wearing one of her feather-trimmed hats. She threw it up in the air like a discus and let herself drop in the grass, she rolled over the meadow and downhill, and lay there at the bottom of the slope. Martha ran after her. Ladies and gentlemen with sunshades watched from a safe distance; no longer surprised by the foreign woman's behaviour, they shook their heads disapprovingly and turned away. Their eggs must seem to them more important than the woman who had just rolled down the hill. Martha's father had followed his wife and daughter; he bent over his wife and offered her a hand to help her up. Martha, then eight years old, held her mother's other hand. Mother uttered a throaty laugh, she said she liked his God better than hers, but both of them were just the same, merely the shared imaginary creation of a few deluded people, human worms who for hundreds and thousands of years had spent a large part of their lives brooding over some plausible reason for their existence. A strange, a ridiculous characteristic of living beings.

Ernst Ludwig Würsich took his wife home to calm her down.

Martha was entrusted to the maidservant's care, and the husband sat beside his wife's bed. He never expected her to show him respect, he said gently, he would ask her to keep quiet only to show respect for God. He stroked his wife's brow. Sweat was running down her temples. Was she hot, her husband asked, and he helped his wife to take off her dress. He carefully stroked her shoulders and arms. He kissed the rivulet at her temple. God was just and merciful, he told her. Next moment he knew he had said the wrong thing, for his wife shook her head and whispered: Ernst Josef . . . Only when he closed her mouth with a kiss a few seconds later, and tried to soothe her, did she complete her sentence in a whisper: . . . was one of four. How can you call a God who has taken four sons from me just and merciful?

Tears flowed. Her husband kissed her face, he kissed her tears, he drank her unhappiness and lay down in bed beside her.

In the evening she told her husband: That was the last time, I don't want to lose any more sons. She didn't have to ask if he understood her, for whether he liked it or not, he surely did.

Almost ten months later a baby was born. Big and heavy, fair-skinned with a rosy glow, a bald head with huge eyes which within a few weeks were a radiant blue that alarmed its mother. The baby was a girl, her mother could not recognize her as her own. And when her father wanted to take his daughter to the pastor, it was Mariechen who chose the child's name: Helene.

Helene's mother paid her no attention, she wouldn't pick up the baby and could not hold her close. The baby cried as time went on, she grew thin, couldn't digest the goat's milk she was given and spat out more of it than she drank. Mariechen put the baby to her own breast to soothe her, but her breast was old and had never smelled of milk, it could give no nourishment, so the baby screamed. A wet-nurse was found to breastfeed Helene. The baby sucked the milk, she grew plump and heavy again. Her eyes seemed brighter every day and her first hair came in, a pale gold down. Her mother lay motionless in bed, turning away her face when anyone brought her the baby. When she spoke of the child she did not say her name, she could not even say *my daughter*. She called her just *the child*.

Helene knew about these early years of hers. She had heard Mariechen talking to Martha about them. Her mother would not hear of any god. She had made one room in the house hers, a room for herself alone, and she slept there in a narrow bed under the feather dusters and spoke of them escorting souls. When Helene lay in Martha's bed in the evening, counting freckles and pressing her nose to Martha's back, she increasingly found herself adopting, without meaning to, the viewpoint that she supposed was really reserved for a god. She imagined all the little two-legged creatures scrabbling over the globe of earth, devising images of him, thinking up names for him, telling creation stories. The thought of them as ridiculous earthworms, as Mother called them, seemed to her reasonable in one way; in another she felt sorry for them, creatures who, in their own fashion, were doing only as the ants and the lemmings and the penguins did. They set up hierarchies and structures suitable to their species with its thoughts and doubts, both of those part of the system, since a human being free of doubts was unimaginable. She knew how touchily Father reacted to these ideas. And he was especially silent and serious when Mother said, laughing, that she had spent a night with all souls, or he might call it god, and now that she was carrying a son below her heart she felt blessed, so she would soon be going away with the souls, her flesh would be going with them for ever. Helene heard Father's friend Mayor Koban trying to persuade him to put Mother in an asylum. But Father wouldn't hear of it. He loved his wife. The idea of an asylum hurt him more than her withdrawal from the world. It did not disturb him that she spent many months a year in the darkened rooms of the house, never setting foot out in Tuchmacherstrasse.

Even when the footpaths through the house grew narrow because his wife kept dragging things indoors during her few wakeful months, collecting them, adding them to various piles over which she spread lengths of cloth in different colours, Father preferred this kind of life with his wife to the prospect of living without her.

While he had once protested against the collecting and gathering, occasionally telling her that she ought to throw some object out, whereupon she would explain to him at great length the possible use of that object – perhaps a particularly battered crown cork which she expected to metamorphose in some way if she kept her eye on it – over the last few years he asked his wife what use something could possibly be only when he felt like listening to a declaration of love. Her declarations of love for what generally seemed to be worthless, superfluous objects were the most exciting stories that Ernst Ludwig Würsich had ever heard.

One day Helene was sitting in the kitchen, helping Mariechen to bottle gooseberries.

Where's that orange peel I hung up in the storeroom to dry?

I'm sorry, madam, the housekeeper made haste to say. It's still up there in a cigar box. We needed the space for the elderflowers.

Elderflower tea! Mother scornfully distended her nostrils. It smells of cat pee, Mariechen, how often have I told you so? Pick mint by all means, dry yarrow, but never mind about the elderflowers.

My little pigeon, Father interrupted, what were you going to do with the orange peel? It's dried already.

Yes, like leather, don't you think? Mother's voice was velvety, she waxed lyrical. Orange peel cut from the fruit in a spiral strip and hung up to dry. Isn't the smell of it in the storeroom lovely? And you should see the spirals twist and turn when you hang them over the stove by a thread – oh, so beautiful. Wait, I'll show you. And Mother was already racing up to the storeroom like a young girl, looking for the cigar box, carefully taking out the strips of orange peel. Like skin, don't you agree? She took his hand so that he could feel it, she wanted him to stroke it the way she did, to feel what she was feeling, so that he'd know what she was talking about. The skin of a young tortoise.

Helene noticed how lovingly her father looked at his wife, his eyes followed the way her fingers stroked the dried strips of orange peel, raised them to her nose, lowered her eyelids to distend her nostrils and smell the peel, and obviously he wasn't going to tell her that this wasn't the time of year to heat the stove. She would keep the orange peel strips in the cigar box until next winter, and the winter after next, for ever, no one must throw anything away, and Helene's father knew why. Helene loved her father for his questions and his silences at just the right moment; she loved him when he looked at her mother as he was looking at her now. In silence he was surely thanking God for such a wife.

Just under two years after the war had ended, Ernst Ludwig Würsich finally managed to set off for home, accompanied by a male nurse from Dresden who was also on his way back. It was a difficult journey. He spent most of it sitting in a cart pulled along by the male nurse, who swore at him for various reasons depending on the time of day: in the morning because he kept apologizing for giving the man such discomfort, at noon because he wanted to go much too far in a day and in the evening because in spite of his missing leg he still weighed several kilos too much.

To his disappointment, and because he had not reported to the barracks until some weeks after the beginning of the war, he had not been accepted into the 3rd Saxon Hussars, a regiment set up four years earlier. How could he tell anyone that his wife said she was dying, and without her in his life he might well not feel any inclination to be a hero? But even worse, certainly – and perhaps it was why he couldn't talk to anyone about his wife's threat of her imminent death – this was by no means the first time she had felt impelled to make it. Although he had lived with her words ringing in his ears for several years, and although she gave a different reason every time, he could not accustom himself to that most extreme threat. He was also aware how little such a reason could affect a garrison, how little it could ever be a valid reason for defying orders from a state requiring unconditional obedience. The threat of his Selma's death appeared plain ridiculous and insignificant in the face of a German Reich for which he was in duty bound to risk his life.

On his arrival at the Old Barracks on the outskirts of town, he was immediately stripped of the hussar's uniform and curved sword he had acquired only a few months earlier, and was told that another man had ridden his horse to France, where he had already died a hero's death. The artillery had also left, so he was to report to the new infantry barracks. On all these journeys he was accompanied by his dog, old Baldo. He had told him to go away, but Baldo was having none of that; he simply would not leave his master. God with us! Ernst Ludwig Würsich had shouted at Baldo, gesturing to him with outstretched arm to go away. Perhaps it wasn't so hard to understand that a dog called after Chancellor Theobald von Bethmann-Hollweg could not part with his master on hearing him utter the Chancellor's own slogan. Baldo lowered his head and wagged his tail hard. The dog followed him so persistently from barracks gate to barracks gate that tears came to Ernst Ludwig Würsich's eyes and he had to threaten to strike Baldo with his bare hand to make him go home, where no one expected him. At the infantry barracks they handed Citizen Würsich, until recently a hussar, a private soldier's uniform that had obviously seen action already, then they pondered for some weeks which way to send him. In mid-January he set off for Masuria. He could hardly move for the driving snow. While the men in front of him, behind him and beside him spoke of revenge and striking back, he longed to be at home under the warm goose feather quilt in his own bed in Tuchmacherstrasse in Bautzen. Not long afterwards the army he had been sent to join did indeed fight a battle among frosty fields and frozen lakes, but before Ernst Ludwig Würsich could even use his gun in a copse of oak trees – the saplings were still young and not very tall – he lost his left leg to his immediate neighbour's hand grenade, which went off at the wrong time as the troop attacked. Two comrades carried him over the ice of Lake Löwentin and in February took him to a field hospital at Lötzen, where he was to lie forgotten and thus unable to return home for the rest of the war.

As soon as the pain brought him back to consciousness on his sickbed, he asked someone to look for his talisman: the stone that his wife had pressed into his hand on one of the days of their long-drawn-out farewell. At first she probably hoped that the talisman would change his mind and get him to stay, but later, when he was polishing his sword, she had told him to think of it as something to keep him safe. It was sewn into the inside pocket of his uniform and was shaped like a heart. His wife, claiming to have recognized it as a linden leaf, ascribed curative powers to it and told him to lay it on any wound to heal it. The wound below his torso seemed to him too large for that, and for the first few weeks after his injury he shrank from looking down at it at all, let alone touching the sore flesh in any way, so he placed the stone on his eye socket. It felt heavy and pleasantly cooling there.

While the stone lay on his eye socket, Ernst Ludwig Würsich murmured words of comfort to himself, words reminding him of what his wife had said, good words – oh, my dear, she had called him – encouraging words saying that it would be all right again. Later he took the stone in his hand and held it tight, and he felt as if not only his pain, that keen and now familiar companion which kept appearing, white and shining, to deprive him of sight and hearing, but also the last of his strength were being pressed out into the stone, breathing life into it. At least just a little, so little and yet so much that the stone soon felt to him hotter than his hand. Only when it had been lying on the sheet beside him for some time could he use it to cool his eye socket again. So he spent days occupied with this simplest of actions. Those days appeared to him at first anything but dull, for the pain kept him awake, kept his wound alive, nagged until he would have liked to run away from it on both legs, and he knew just where he would go. Never before had he thought so passionately of his wife, never before had his love seemed so clear and pure to him, manifest as it was without any kind of distraction, without the faintest doubt, as in these days when all he did was to pick up her stone and put it down again.

But the pain went on and on, exhausting his nerves, and fine cracks appeared in his clarity of mind of those first few days; his insight into his pure love crumbled and collapsed. One night the pain woke him and he could turn neither to left nor to right, the pain was not white and shining any more but fluid, black, lightless lava, and he heard the whimpering and whining under the other sheets on the beds close to him. He felt as if all his love, all his understanding of his existence, had been merely a courageous but vain rebellion against the pain. Nothing seemed pure and clear any more; there was only pain. He didn't want to groan, but there was no time or space for what he wanted now. The auxiliary nurse was tending another wounded man who wouldn't last much longer, he was sure of that, the man's wailing at the far end of the hut must stop soon, before his own. He longed for peace. He cried out, he wanted to blame someone, he had no memory of God or faith in him. He begged. The auxiliary nurse came, gave him an injection, and the injection had no effect whatsoever. Only after dawn did he manage to sleep. At midday he asked for a sheet of paper and a pencil. His arm felt heavy, there seemed to be no strength in his hand, he could hardly hold the pencil. He wrote to Selma. He wrote to keep the bond between them from breaking, so faint now did the memory of his love seem, so arbitrary the object of his desire. He devoted the next few days to his stone out of mere loyalty. A chivalrous feeling ran through him when he touched it. He wanted to cry. Cautiously, his thoughts circled around ideas like honour and conscience. Ernst Ludwig Würsich felt ashamed of his own existence. What use was a one-legged, wounded man, after all? He hadn't so much as set eyes on a Russian, he hadn't looked an enemy in the face. Still less had he risked his life in some honourable action in this war. The loss of his leg was a pitiful accident and could not be considered any kind of tribute to the enemy. He knew he would go on picking up the stone and putting it down again until the next infection of his wound or his guts struck, setting his body on fire, burning it out, and he sank into fever and the twilight of pain.

Although the winter battle had been won, that success was to remain as remote from Ernst Ludwig Würsich as the question of there being any point in the war. When the field hospital closed down one day just after the end of hostilities, he and the other wounded men were to be taken home. But transport turned out difficult and tedious. Halfway through the journey some of them deteriorated; typhoid spread among them, many died and the survivors were temporarily accommodated in a small colony of huts near Warsaw. From there they went on to Greifswald in a larger convoy of the injured. Week after week now he was told that they were only waiting for his health to improve before sending him back to Bautzen. But however much it improved, there were still stumbling blocks: he needed the financial means to get back and someone to help him physically, and those he did not have. He wrote two or three letters home a month, addressing them to his wife, although he had no way of knowing whether she was even still alive. No answer came. He wrote telling Selma that the stump of his leg refused to heal, although the injuries to his face near the socket of his right eye had healed nicely and the skin around the scars was smoothing out more every day. Or at least, so his sense of touch told him; he couldn't know for certain because he had no mirror. He hoped she'd recognize him. Of all his features, his nose was almost the same, he said. Yes, his face had healed up extremely well, he assured her, very likely it was only on close inspection, and by drawing conclusions from the rest of his physiognomy, that anyone could see where the right eye had once been. In future, when they went to the theatre, he'd be glad to borrow the gilded opera-glasses he had given her for their first wedding anniversary, and then at last he'd offer her his monocle in exchange. He knew she'd always thought the monocle suited her better than him, he added.

That, he thought, might at least make his wife smile her enchanting smile if she were still alive, if she read his letter, if she learned about his injuries from it. Merely imagining the sparkle of her eyes, their colour changing between green and brown and yellow, sent a shiver of desire and a sense of well-being down his spine. Even the pain, so far unidentified, that sprang from a sore place on his coccyx, throbbing and spreading up his back as if the upper layers of skin were being sliced into very thin strips, even that he could ignore for minutes at a time.

How was he to guess that his wife Selma handed the letters to her housekeeper Mariechen for safe keeping, unread and still sealed?

With abhorrence, Selma Würsich told Mariechen that she felt more and more disgusted to be receiving wartime letters from That Man – as she now referred to him – a man who, allegedly for love of her but against her express wish, had wanted to go off and be a hero. She thought that in these signs of life from him she detected a kind of mockery, something of which she had suspected her husband for no real reason ever since they

69

had known each other. Inwardly, she was waiting for the day of his return and her chance to say, with a shrug of her shoulders expressing utter indifference, the following words of welcome: Oh, so you're still with us, are you?

After the first weeks when he went missing, and the following weeks and months of fury that he had ever gone away at all, such a display of indifference promised to be her ultimate triumph. The Wendish housekeeper, that old maid, as Ernst Ludwig had once described Mariechen in their daughters' hearing, was now the only person to whom she ever spoke, not that she spoke much at all.

Selma Würsich lay in wait season by season. She had no time to spare; an inner restlessness chased her out of doors in spring. Suddenly, there stood one of her daughters in front of her asking something, the word Ascension came into it, and Selma was turning away, for such words, she thought, were none of her business, but still they rang in her ears; a pair of eyes belonging to one of her daughters was fixed on her, but it couldn't possibly be anything to do with her. She simply said she didn't want to be disturbed, and demanded peace and quiet.

She left decorating the Easter eggs to Mariechen, who was better at it anyway. Indeed, Selma found being with other people more and more of a burden, she simply lacked the patience to tolerate her daughters' chattering and questions. How gratefully, in secret, she thanked heaven for Mariechen, who kept their cheerful company at a distance from her.

In summer Selma picked the last few cherries from the large unpruned tree that had been plundered for weeks by the street urchins and her own daughters. To go cherry-picking she wore one of her broad-brimmed hats, a hat with a veil beneath which she could watch the Kornmarkt less conspicuously, and as she stood on the ladder she kept looking the way she thought she would see her husband approaching. Sitting on the steps in front of the house with her basket full of cherries, she nibbled the meagre, maggoty fruit off the stones. It tasted sour and slightly bitter. She laid out the stones to dry in the sun, where they bleached like bones. Every few days she took a handful of cherry stones and shook them in the hollow of her hands. The sound warmed her. Happiness might sound like that, thought Selma.

In autumn she once thought she saw her husband trudging through the fallen leaves on the opposite side of the street, and turned back quickly so that she would be at home when he arrived. She tried hard to feel nothing but indifference. But her efforts were wasted; the doorbell was silent and he did not appear. The man trudging through the leaves must have been someone else, probably a man who, welcomed home with a passionate embrace, was now sitting laughing with his wife over their supper of hot cabbage soup.

Early in winter Selma Würsich removed any green walnut husks and those already black and dried from the inner shells with a knife, and as she worked she looked out of the window into slowly drifting snow. Flakes tumbled up and down as if ignorant of the force of gravity. She often saw him coming down Tuchmacherstrasse. He would have aged in these last few years, he would smell of strange places. If he came back – well, he'd soon see!

But her long wait for next spring and summer, for the delightful revenge she longed for, was followed by a time of exhaustion. Business was slow; hardly anyone wanted anything printed. Paper was getting expensive. While Selma sat at the window, empty-eyed, Helene worked out new prices for letterheads and death announcements every quarter. Sales of picture postcards were so poor that she hadn't been able to get any more printed for months, and there were hardly any orders for menus, since most landlords and café owners wrote up the names of their few dishes on blackboards. The savings of the pre-war period, when the printing works were still flourishing and Helene's father had begun printing marriage advice manuals, collections of crossword puzzles and finally poems, suddenly lost their old value. The number of copies of the calendar they sold annually had recently dropped to less than a hundred. Designing the calendar pages for 1920 looked like costing more than prospective sales would bring in.

Acting on an idea that came to her one night, Helene's mother had begun paying the wages of the typesetter who had worked for the firm for many years several months in advance. She obviously thought that this was a way to counter the price rises and help her to get around them, so to speak. But fewer and fewer orders came in, and the typesetter sat around without any work to do, solving crossword puzzles. Booklets of the puzzles piled up in the stockroom because no one was buying them any more. The army hadn't accepted the typesetter as a wartime recruit because he was too small and his legs were too short. His wife and eight children went hungry with him, many of the children begged for bread and lard in the Kornmarkt, and they were always being caught stealing apples and nuts.

One evening Selma found a handful of sugar cubes in the typesetter's overall pocket, after he had hung it up beside the door before going home from work. Because of the shape and colour of the sugar cubes, she found it easy to believe they had been stolen from her kitchen. Next morning she felt sorry for the man when she saw him sitting there with no work to do. Selma felt a great reluctance to speak to him about the sugar and how much he was costing her. She expected excuses and thought she would rather find a way to stop employing him. She would get him to teach her younger daughter how to set type, and handle the characters and the press. After all, she wouldn't have to pay Helene for the few jobs and orders that still came in.

The girl was bored to death in her last year of school; it was time she made herself useful. Helene's mother would not give in to her ardent wish to go on to a High School for Girls. If she had found school so tedious until now, it seemed to Selma far too expensive an indulgence to pay for her to do nothing in comfort for another two years.

Selma Würsich stood at the window and looked up Tuchmacherstrasse, holding her dressing gown closed. It was days since she had been able to find its belt. The bells were ringing; her daughters would soon come out of church. Selma was not at all happy with the idea that her younger daughter might become a teacher and had once, in her artless, childlike way, even expressed a wish to study medicine. That child is unruly and rebellious, she whispered to herself.

Martha was arm in arm with Helene as they strolled down the street from the Kornmarkt. Selma saw a violet satin gift-wrap ribbon lying on the glass display case. Mariechen must have rolled it up tidily and put it down there. Selma put it round her dressing gown instead of the missing belt. With great care, she tied a bow and smiled at her idea. Now she heard the shrill sound of the doorbell ringing.

Come up here, I want to speak to you two! Their mother was standing on the landing, beckoning to Helene and Martha to join her. She didn't wait until the girls were sitting down.

You've been doing the accounts for years, Helene, it wouldn't hurt you to learn the practical side of the business too. Their mother cast a cautious glance at her elder daughter, whose criticism she feared. But Martha's mind seemed to be somewhere else. Even now I couldn't manage the deliveries without your bookkeeping, and you see to buying paper and the maintenance of the press. The typesetter will eat us out of house and home one of these days. It would be a good idea to get him to show you what you need to know, and then we could fire him.

Helene's eyes were shining. Wonderful, she whispered. She flung her arms round Martha's neck, kissed her and cried: First of all I'll print us some money and then I'll print a book of family records for you.

Martha shook Helene off. She went red and said nothing. Their mother took Helene by the arm and forced her down on her knees.

What nonsense! I don't like to hear you sound so delighted, child. The work won't be easy, you know. Then she let go and Helene was able to stand up again.

Untroubled, Helene looked at her mother. She wasn't surprised to find that Selma thought the work difficult; after all, her mother very seldom entered the rooms housing the printing works – she had probably never seen type being set, and from a distance the business must seem to her mysterious. Helene thought of the clicking and quiet chuffing of the press, the crunch of the rollers. How differently people could see something! What appeared all right to the typesetter made Helene uneasy. She had a clear picture of herself spacing the letters and words properly at long last, with the gaps between them ensuring harmony and clarity. The idea of operating the big press on her own was exciting. She had often wanted to improve on the typesetter's work.

Selma was watching Helene. Those shining eyes seemed uncanny to her. The child's joy made her seem even taller and more radiant than usual.

What you lack, said her mother sternly, is a certain sense of proportion. Her voice was cutting, every word finely judged. You don't understand the natural order of things. That is why you find it hard to recognize order among us all. Subordination, my child, is important and you'll be able to learn it from our type-setter. Subordination and humility.

Helene felt the blood rise to her face. She lowered her eyes. Darkness and light broke apart, colours blurred. She had no idea yet what to say in reply. The kaleidoscope went round and round, several times a rusty nail moved near some walnut shells, you never knew when that nail or those shells might come in useful. It was some seconds before she had a clear picture inside her again. Her mother, who as Helene now saw was wearing the violet satin ribbon, looked all done up like a present. The violet bow shook as Mother spoke. It wants to be undone, Helene thought, it really does. Helene scrutinized the maternal land-scape, consisting as it did of remnants of clothes, feather dusters encrusted with black blood at the ends of the quills, pillowcases with cherry stones coming out of the holes in their corners and mountains of old newspapers. She could not make out the summit from which her mother was trying to tell her something about understanding the established order of things. Helene could not raise her eyes to meet her mother's. She looked for help to Martha, but this time Martha did not come to her aid.

Within a few weeks Helene lost her veneration for the *pièce de résistance* in her father's printing works. The platen press, which bore the brand name Monopol, no longer inspired awe in her but demanded physical effort. While the typesetter, who was too small for his legs to reach the pedal from her father's stool, skil-fully raised one of those short legs and kept the pedal in motion by kicking it vigorously, at Helene's first attempts she couldn't move it a millimetre. Although she could work the sewing machine and had no difficulty in keeping it going by stepping on the treadle, the Monopol press obviously called for a man's strength. Helene put both feet on the pedal and pushed down. The wheel simply jerked forward once. The typesetter laughed. Perhaps he'd like to show her how to clean the rollers, said Helene sharply, looking pointedly at the thick layer of dust lying on them.

She wasn't going to accept that she wasn't physically strong enough to learn to use the press. As soon as the typesetter had left in the evening, she went over to the Monopol and practised with her right leg. She leaned on the paper holder and trod down and down again, until the big wheel was turning faster and faster and the friction of the rollers made a wonderfully deep sound. She was sweating, but she couldn't stop.

By day the typesetter showed her how to use the stitching machine, the pressing machine and the stapling machine. He taught her assiduously, as he had been told to do, but he kept saying, with a twinkle in his eye, that the Monopol would obey only its master. And since her father had gone away, he obviously felt that he was its master now. The certainty that, as he thought, he was indispensable cheered the typesetter.

No one knew that over the past few years a friendly working relationship had developed between the typesetter and Helene. He was the first adult to take her seriously. Ever since she began helping with her father's accounts at the age of seven, and now, because he was away in the war, had taken over the purchase of supplies as well as the bookkeeping, the typesetter had treated her with great respect. He called her Fräulein Würsich. Helene liked that. And he accepted all her calculations without demur.

Even when Helene could not comply fully with his request for higher wages after the war, nothing about his friendly attitude changed. He discussed the work on hand with her. And if one of the machines needed servicing, he referred back to Helene, particularly now that her mother was disappearing into the upper part of the house for months on end, closing the net curtains and turning her back on the windows. Helene liked the typesetter. It was she who would go up to the kitchen, search the pantry, look round several times to make quite sure no one could see her and fold newspaper to make a paper bag, fill it with pearl barley, put semolina into another bag and finally place a cucumber, a kohlrabi and a handful of nuts in a third. When she found the huge cardboard box of sugar cubes on the top shelf of the pantry one day, she unhesitatingly tore a page off the Bautzen Household Calendar, wrapped a heap of cubes in it and gave that to the typesetter too.

As soon as he had left in the evening Helene went back to practising on the Monopol press in secret. After a few days she practised with her left leg as well as her right. She practised until she couldn't go on. And when she couldn't practise any more she practised overcoming not being able to practise any more, and got on with it. In the evening she could feel how strong her legs were growing, and next morning she felt an unaccustomed tugging in them. She knew what it was, but before now she had only ever heard boys say they had cramp in their legs.

One evening she sat high up on her father's stool, which was fixed to the floor. To her surprise she didn't even have to stretch her legs; the stool could have been made specially for her. She put both feet on the pedal and trod away. She had to pull in her stomach firmly, which caused a pleasant, tickling sensation; she felt a fluttering inside, as if she were on a swing. She was reminded of Martha's hands and Martha's soft breasts.

Only when Selma Würsich asked, a few weeks later, whether her daughter had learned all about the printing press now, did the typesetter demonstrate the cutting machine to her. So far he had avoided even taking her anywhere near it. A dark presentiment now took shape in his mind. He looked at her fair hair,

77

which she wore plaited into a thick braid, and found that he could bring out the words only reluctantly. His comments were brief. First open it. Then adjust it. The typesetter placed the rulers one above the other like battens. Place the paper here.

Without a word of apology, the typesetter pushed Helene slightly aside and showed her, in silence, how she must first knock the stack of paper together and then straighten it to fit it into the machine. As he saw it, the cutting machine was dangerous, not because Helene was a tender young girl of only just thirteen, but because now she could operate all the machinery, everything but the Monopol press.

Mother told Mariechen to roast a joint of beef with a thyme-flavoured crust for Martha's twenty-second birthday. As always when there was meat, she ate none of it herself. No one discussed her reasons, but her daughters agreed in thinking they were to do with certain dietary regulations. There was no kosher butcher in Bautzen. It was said that the Kristallerer family asked the butcher to slaughter meat specially for their needs, and there was a rumour that they even took him their own knives for the purpose. But Mother obviously didn't feel comfortable about getting such things done if everyone in town would know about it. And perhaps she meant it when she said she simply didn't like meat.

Martha had been allowed to ask her friend Leontine to her birthday party. Mother wore a long dress of coffee-coloured velvet. She had lengthened the hem herself with lace that looked to Helene unsuitable and a little ridiculous. Helene had put Martha's hair in curlers the evening before and let it dry overnight. Now she spent the afternoon pinning up her sister's hair and weaving silk mallow flowers into the little braids, so that in the end Martha looked like a princess, and a little like a bride too. Then Helene helped Mariechen to lay the table. The valuable Chinese porcelain came out of the sideboard, napkins were placed in silver rose-petal rings that had come with Mother's trousseau and were otherwise used only at Christmas.

When the bell rang, Martha and Helene hurried to the door at the same time. Leontine was standing outside, her face hidden behind a big bunch of flowers and grasses that she had obviously picked in the meadows: cornflowers, rue, barley. She laughed merrily and turned once in a circle. She had cut her hair short. Where there used to be a chignon severely pinned back behind her head, you could now see her ear and her white neck as her short hair swirled in the air. Helene couldn't take her eyes off the sight.

Later, at dinner, Helene's eyes were fixed on Leontine. She tried to look away, but she couldn't. She admired Leontine's long neck. Leontine was both slender and strong. Helene could see every vein and sinew in her forearms. She worked with Martha at the Municipal Hospital, not as a ward sister yet, she was much too young for that, but at the age of twenty-three she had been head nurse in the operating theatre for several months. Leontine was the surgeon's favourite nurse. She could lift any patient by herself, and during operations her hands were so steady and sure that the surgeon, who had only recently been appointed professor, was always asking her to stitch up difficult wounds.

When Leontine laughed, her laughter was long and deep.

Helene spent her time with Martha and Leontine whenever she had a chance. The way Leontine laughed went far down inside you. When she sat down, you could clearly see her bony knees parted under her skirt. She sat there with her legs spread, not at all embarrassed, as if that position were perfectly natural. Now and then she put her hand on her knee and bent her arm slightly, so that the elbow stood out at an angle. These were short, sharp movements that told a tale of unhappiness, but then her deep laugh would follow. Leontine usually laughed on her own. Martha and Helene listened open-mouthed to her laughter; perhaps that would help it to seep down inside them too and reach the pit of the stomach. It took Martha and Helene some time even to guess what Leontine had been laughing at. They must look silly, sitting there. They didn't shake their heads out of any idea that Leontine's laughter was misplaced, but because it amazed them. Helene specially liked Leontine's voice, which was firm and clear.

As they sat around the table on Martha's birthday, with the roast beef in front of them, Leontine said: My father's going to let me study.

Study? Mother was surprised.

Yes, he thinks it would be a good idea. I could earn more money then.

Mother shook her head. But studying *costs* money. She handed Leontine the dish of potato dumplings.

I don't want to study, though. Leontine pushed the dark hair back from her forehead. It now fell sideways, like a man's.

Mother nodded in agreement. Very understandable. Who wants to learn useless things? Nurses are in constant demand. A nurse can always find a job anywhere, at any time.

What sort of useless things? Helene looked enquiringly at Leontine, who was just putting a large piece of roast beef in her mouth.

Well, perhaps not so very useless, replied Leontine, but I don't want to go away. Away from what, Helene wondered. As if Leontine could hear her thoughts, she said: Away from Bautzen. Helene accepted that, although she doubted it.

Mother nodded again. Helene wondered whether she really understood what Leontine was saying; after all, she had never taken root in Bautzen herself in all these years, far from it.

Mother was always restless in Bautzen. As Helene saw it, there couldn't be many reasons why Leontine would want to stay here. Her father was a well-respected lawyer; he was also a widower and a drinker, both in moderation, as he saw it. He preferred his younger daughters to Leontine and if he went away on work he always took one of the younger girls with him, bringing her back in a new dress or carrying a fashionable parasol. Leontine's father was a prosperous man; you couldn't call his eldest daughter a Cinderella forced to do menial work, nor was she ill-used, but she seemed to be in her father's way. It troubled him that Leontine didn't get married. From time to time he made suggestions to her, and then they quarrelled. Since the death of his wife over ten years earlier, he had lived alone with his three daughters and his mother-in-law, whose mind had been confused for years. On Sundays he went to St Peter's Cathedral, walking past the Town Hall arm in arm with his younger daughters, one to right and one to left of him. His mother-in-law followed a few steps behind with the cook, and it looked as if Leontine had no established place in this family. It was left to Leontine herself to choose her company. She usually helped her grandmother along, but as soon as they reached the church and she saw Martha among the cluster of people in the porch, she seized her chance to go to a pew hand in hand with her friend. Here she sat between Martha and Helene, in the place that, in their thoughts, they left free for their father. Even though the war was over, he wasn't home yet. She liked it when, during the service, Martha placed her hand with its long and beautiful fingers beside her own and they linked fingers. Then she sometimes felt a warm weight on her other side: it was Helene leaning her face against Leontine's arm as if she had found a mother in her.

Hardly a day passed when Martha didn't bring Leontine home from the hospital with her to Tuchmacherstrasse. They did the housework together and, depending on their shifts at work, they helped out on the big bleaching ground in the meadows by the Spree. They were inseparable.

Wild horses wouldn't drag me away from here, Leontine assured them as she took a rather small potato dumpling, and it did not escape Helene's notice that Martha's elbow was touching Leontine's, although the two of them avoided exchanging any glance that might give them away.

Eat up your meat, girls. Helene, how are you getting on in the printing works? Mother smiled with a certain derision. You usually learn so fast. Can you do it all? Is there anything you don't yet know?

How am I to know what I don't yet know? Helene helped herself to a slice of beef.

Mother rolled her eyes. She sighed. Perhaps, miss, you would be kind enough just to answer my question.

How am I supposed to answer the question when I don't know the answer?

Then I'll answer it for you, dear.

Mother had never before called her dear. It sounded like a foreign word, sharply spoken as if Mother wanted to show Martha's friend how kind she was to her children, although it didn't come easily to her. It's been ten weeks now, she said, plenty of time for you to have learned all that matters. What you don't know yet, you'll have to learn as you go along. I'm dismissing the typesetter tomorrow. Without notice.

What? Martha dropped her fork. Mother, he has eight children.

So? I have two children myself, don't I? We have no man around the house. We can't pay the typesetter any longer. We aren't making any profit these days. You know that better than anyone, Helene. What did last year look like in the accounts?

Helene put down her knife and fork. She picked up her napkin and dabbed her mouth with it. Better than this year.

And worse than any year before, am I right?

Helene did not nod. She hated the idea of presenting Mother with the words and gestures she expected.

There we are, then. The typesetter is dismissed.

Helene found the next few weeks a difficult time. She wasn't used to being alone all day. The typesetter hadn't been seen since the day he was dismissed. He was said to have left the town with his family. Helene sat in the printing works day after day, waiting for customers who never came. She was supposed to be studying from Martha's book for the admission examination she must take for nursing, but she just leafed through it and found hardly anything she didn't already know. The exact sequence of compresses and bandaging to be used for various illnesses was part of the final nursing exam rather than this one. Most of the book was concerned with what you would have to learn during your training, and after she had leafed through it the few details she hadn't known before were fixed in her memory. So Helene began reading other books, the books that she found on her father's shelves. His daughters were forbidden to take any volumes out of that mighty bookcase, but even in the old days when Father was still here, his daughters had felt that it was a particularly exciting adventure and a test of their courage to borrow those precious books. They would push Stifter's *The Condor* further to the left so as not to leave a gap where Kleist's *The Marquise of O.* had been standing. The books stood in no particular order on their father's shelves, which upset Helene a little, but she wasn't sure whether her mother kept an eye on this disorder, or what might happen if she took it upon herself to rearrange the books in alphabetical order. As she read, Helene kept her ears pricked, and as soon as she heard a sound she hid the book under her apron. She often looked out of the door when she thought she heard Leontine's deep voice. Once, quite unexpectedly, the door opened and Martha and Leontine came in, laughing, with a big basket.

Goodness, how red your cheeks are! said Leontine, passing her hand briefly over Helene's hair. I hope you aren't running a temperature?

Helene shook her head. She had a treasure tucked under her apron. She had found it on the very top shelf of the bookcase, wrapped in newspaper and lying behind the other books as if hidden away. It was more than a hundred years old. The cardboard binding was covered with coloured paper and there was an embossed title: *Penthesilea. A Tragedy.* Helene apologized briefly to Martha and Leontine, bent down behind the big wooden counter and hid her treasure in the lowest drawer there. She put some of the old Bautzen Household Almanacs over the book to conceal it.

A farmer from the Lusatian Hills had given Leontine the basket of peas as a thank-you present. Months ago, she had splinted a difficult break of his wrist. Now Leontine put the big basket on the counter in front of Helene. It was full of plump green pea pods. Helene immediately plunged both hands into the basket and ploughed them through the pods. They had a young, grassy smell. Helene loved popping pods open with her thumb and the sensation of pushing out the smooth, gleaming, green peas from top to bottom in order of size, to roll down her thumb and into the bowl. She would put the tiny peas that weren't fully mature yet straight into her mouth. Martha and Leontine were talking about something that Helene wasn't supposed to understand, giggling and gurgling. They spoke only in mysterious half-sentences.

He was asking all the nurses and the patients about you. Oh, and to see his face when he finally found you! Martha was amused.

Dear child. Leontine rolled her eyes as she spoke, obviously imitating the farmer.

Oh, I come over all peculiar when I see you, nurse! Martha put in. She was spluttering with laughter. Nurse, I'm yours heart and soul!

He didn't say that? Leontine was laughing too.

He did. You should have seen the way his hand kept going to his trousers. I thought he was going to fall on you there and then.

But our dear professor didn't think it was funny at all: oh, take your peas and go away, you seem to have finished work at noon today. Leontine sighed. And usually I can never stay too long for him.

Are you surprised? Didn't you hear what he said to the ward sister about you the other day: she may look like a flapper, but she's something of a bluestocking!

He thinks highly of you, but his fears are growing.

Fears? Leontine waved the idea away. Our professor doesn't know the meaning of fear. Why, anyway? I'm a nurse, that's all.

The girls were shelling the peas now.

A long silence followed. But suppose you do go away after all? Martha was bracing herself for anything.

Helene didn't want to see her sister's grave face now. She tried to imagine she was invisible.

Leontine did not react.

Go away to Dresden, I mean. To study. That's what everyone is saying you'll do.

Never. Leontine hesitated. Not unless you come with me.

That's stupid, Leontine, just plain stupid. Martha sounded both sad and stern. You know I can't.

There you are, then, said Leontine. In that case nor can I.

Martha put her hand on the nape of her friend's neck, drew her face close and kissed her on the lips.

Helene's breath faltered; she quickly turned away. There must be something she ought to do, look for something on the top shelf of the bookcase, or maybe take a stack of paper out of its pigeonhole and put it on the desk. The picture seemed to be burned on her retina: Martha drawing Leontine towards her, Leontine pursing her lips ready for the kiss. Perhaps Helene had mistaken what she saw? She risked a cautious glance over her shoulder. Leontine and Martha were bending over the basket full of pea pods, and it was as if there had never been a kiss at all.

But suppose you took her with you? She could train as a nurse in Dresden. Leontine was speaking quietly, now, and her glance went to Helene. Helene acted as if she had heard nothing and hadn't realized that they were talking about her. Out of the corner of her eye, she saw Martha shaking her head. There was another long silence. Helene felt that her presence was inhibiting their conversation. At first she thought of leaving the two of them alone and going out, but next moment she felt rooted to the spot. She couldn't move her feet; she severed the umbilical cords of the peas and felt a sense of shame. She didn't want Leontine to leave them, she didn't want Martha and Leontine to stop talking because of her, and she didn't want Martha and Leontine to kiss each other either.

That evening in bed, Helene turned her back to Martha. Martha could scratch her own back, she thought. Helene didn't want to cry. She breathed deeply and her eyes swelled, her nose felt smaller and stuffed up. Breathing was difficult.

Helene didn't want to count freckles either, or feel for Martha's stomach under the blanket. She thought of the kiss. And while

86

she imagined kissing Leontine, knowing that only Martha would kiss her, tears escaped from her eyes.

Mother expected Helene to run the printing works so that no red figures had to be written in the accounts books. She found that easier every day. A profit recently entered could easily compensate for the losses of the early part of the year, which appeared numerically slight by comparison. What that meant wasn't clear to Mother. She was just surprised to see how seldom Helene ran any of the machines.

Not wishing to waste stocks of paper, Helene designed simple calculation tables. She suspected that people could make good use of her ready reckoners in these times of rising prices.

The mere sight of one of her ready reckoners cheered Helene up. How nice and straight her figures were! It had been worth giving the figure 8 more space than the others, and the margin was so neat.

When news of the typesetter's dismissal got around town, it wasn't long before Frau Hantusch the baker's wife put an unusually small and over-baked loaf down on her counter when Helene went to buy bread.

Helene asked if she could please have one of the two larger, lighter-coloured loaves still on the shelf instead. But the baker's wife, who used to press little pieces of butter-cake into her hand only a few years ago, shook her head as well as anyone with almost no neck could. The deep line marking the short distance between her breasts and her head didn't move at all as she shook it. Helene ought to be glad she could still buy a loaf at all, she said. Helene took it.

You poor thing. The baker's wife was short of breath, her heavy lids covered her eyes, her words expressed sympathy but her tone was both indignant and injured. Operating heavy machinery these days. A girl, working machinery! The baker's wife shook her head again in her laborious way.

Helene stopped in the doorway. It's not hard to learn, she said, and felt as if she were lying. I've printed some very nice ready reckoners. I can bring you one on Monday if you like, we could do a deal – you get a ready reckoner, I get four loaves of bread.

Nothing doing, said the baker's wife.

Three?

To think of girls at a man's work these days, we can't have that kind of thing. Your mother's well off. Why didn't she let the typesetter keep his job?

Don't worry, I'll be starting to train as a nurse in September. We don't have anything left. Most of what we did have was money, and money's worth nothing now.

The baker's wife raised her eyebrows sceptically. These days everyone suspected their neighbours of owning more than they did. Helene remembered how, early this year when she had wanted to do something to please her mother, she had gone into her room and stripped the sheets off the bed to do a big wash. Only when she lifted the mattress to put a clean sheet on it did she see the banknotes. Huge quantities of them tucked into its stuffing. Notes of many different currencies, bundles of them tucked among the feathers and held together with paperclips. The numbers printed on the notes were of small denominations, ridiculously small. As Helene, alarmed by her unintentional discovery, hastily threw the old sheet over the mattress again, she heard her mother's voice behind her.

You little devil. How much have you stolen from me already? Come on, how much?

Helene turned and saw her mother leaning on the door frame, so angry that she could hardly stay upright leaning against it.

She was drawing on her thin cigar as if extracting information from it.

I've been asking myself for years: Selma, I've been asking myself, who in this house is stealing from you? Her voice sounded low and threatening. And all these years I've been telling myself, well, it won't have been your daughter, Selma, never, not your own child.

I was only going to change the sheets, Mother.

What an excuse, what a mean, shabby excuse. And with these words her mother went for Helene, clutching her throat so tightly that she could breathe only by raising her hand against her mother to push her away with all her might. She pinched her mother's arms, but they would not loosen their grip. Helene tried to scream and couldn't. Not until footsteps came up the stairs, and Mariechen audibly cleared her throat, did her mother let go.

Helene had not set foot in her mother's room since then. She remembered how scared she had been at the sight of those banknotes and wondered how, with her own faultless bookkeeping, her mother could have contrived to put them all aside. Money that, as Helene was sure, was worth hardly anything now. Money that, if it had been spent at the right time, would have kept the whole household going and might have allowed her to study.

Helene looked at Frau Hantusch the baker's wife. She couldn't help thinking that the woman's doubts arose from discontent with her own situation.

Last week we had some particularly good stout paper in. Paper with a high proportion of wax in it. Helene smiled as nicely as she could. It stands up to moisture well, it would be just the thing in your shop.

Thanks, Lenchen, thank you very much, but I can tell my customers the daily price of bread myself. The baker's wife pointed to her mouth with one fat forefinger. It's all in here, that's what counts. Having it on paper would just be a waste of money.

When Ernst Ludwig Würsich, arriving unannounced one evening in late November, asked the male nurse who had brought him the last few kilometres to Bautzen in a cart to knock on the front door of his house, and Mariechen, alarmed to be roused so late, opened it, hardly recognized him, but finally let him and the male nurse into the parlour as a few words of explanation were exchanged – when he came home his wife's mind was clouded. Her chamber pot was left outside her door every few hours; that was all anyone saw of her. It was usually Mariechen who emptied it, and three times a day she left a small tray with a meal there. The girls' mother lay in bed, and for several weeks she had managed to prevent either of her daughters or Mariechen from entering the room.

Their father was taken into the parlour and settled in his armchair. He looked around and asked: My wife, doesn't my wife live here?

Of course. Mariechen laughed in relief. The mistress is just tidying herself. Would you like a cup of tea, sir?

No, I'd rather wait for her, said Ernst Ludwig Würsich, and with every word he spoke more slowly.

How are you feeling, sir? Mariechen's voice was higher than usual, clear as a bell, she was anxious to while away the time for him as he waited for the lady of the house to come down, even make him forget it was taking so long.

How am I feeling? The girls' father looked into space with his one remaining eye. Well, usually I feel as if I'm the man whom my wife sees in me. He suppressed a groan. It looked as if he were smiling.

Although Mariechen said she had let the girls' mother know as soon as he arrived, her mistress still did not appear. Helene warmed up the soup left over from midday and Martha found something for the male nurse to eat. The man left soon afterwards. Ernst Ludwig Würsich found speaking as difficult as standing up. He spent the first few hours after his return huddled in his big armchair. His daughters sat with him, taking a great deal of trouble not to show that they noticed his missing leg. But looking into his face was difficult; it was as if their own eyes kept moving from his one remaining open eye to the socket now closed by skin that had grown over it, again and again their glances kept slipping that way until they couldn't stop. The girls tried to find some kind of lifeline; it was more than they could manage to keep looking at just that one eye. They asked about these last few years. Their questions were general; to avoid anything personal, the sisters asked about victory and defeat. Ernst Ludwig Würsich could not answer any of their questions. When his mouth twisted it looked as if he were in great pain, but he was trying to smile. The smile was intended to keep these young ladies, as his daughters now appeared to him, from asking questions. His tongue stuck to the roof of his mouth. He was filled with pain.

Helene knocked on her mother's door and pushed it open, in spite of the books and clothes and lengths of fabric stacked up just inside.

Our father has come home, Helene whispered into the darkness.

Who?

Our father. Your husband.

It's night-time. I'm sleeping.

Helene kept still. Perhaps her mother hadn't understood what she said? She stood in the doorway, unwilling to go yet.

Oh, go away. I'll come down as soon as I feel better.

Helene hesitated. She couldn't believe that her mother was going to stay in bed. But then she heard her turning over and pulling up the blankets.

Quietly, Helene retreated and closed the door.

Obviously her mother didn't feel well enough to come down over the next few days either. So the injured master of the house was carried past her bedroom door and up to the top floor, where they laid him down on the right-hand side of the marital bed. Within a few days the dusty bedroom that he and his wife once shared had been turned into a hospital ward. On Martha's instructions, Helene helped Mariechen to carry up a washstand. During his arduous journey home Ernst Ludwig Würsich's stump had become inflamed again, and in addition he now had a slightly raised temperature. Pain numbed all his other senses. Not for the first time, it was in the missing leg that he felt it.

For her father's own sake, Martha arranged to keep him in a carefully calculated state of intoxication. It was meant to last until she had managed to abstract morphine and cocaine in sufficient quantities to be effective from the Municipal Hospital. Martha had been working with Leontine in the operating theatre for some time, and she knew the right moment when such substances could be purloined. The ward sister was of course the only one who had the key to the poison cupboard, but there were some situations in which she had to entrust it to Leontine. Who, later on, was going to measure exactly how many milligrams this or that patient had been given?

* * *

Next morning Mariechen made Father a new nightshirt. The window was open; you could hear the crows perching in the young elms outside. Mariechen had hung the girls' quilts over the windowsill to air. In the evening they smelled of wood and coal. Helene had gone down to the printing works, and had spent some time sitting over the big book with the monthly accounts when the bell rang.

A well-dressed gentleman was waiting outside the door. He stooped slightly and his left arm was missing. With his right arm he was leaning on a walking stick. Helene knew him by sight; he had sometimes come to the printing works in the old days.

Grumbach, he introduced himself. He cleared his throat. He had heard, he said, that his old friend, the master printer who had published his own first poems, was home again. More throat-clearing. It was six years since they had met, he said, and he really felt he must pay his friend a visit. The moist sound as he cleared his throat was obviously not shyness but a frequent necessity. No, Grumbach wouldn't sit down.

It's a long time since we last met, Helene heard him telling her father. She couldn't take her eyes off Herr Grumbach; she was afraid that he was coming too close to her father with all that throat-clearing. Her father looked at him. His lips moved.

Perhaps he might feel better tomorrow? The visitor seemed to be asking himself this question rather than anyone else; he looked neither at Helene nor the maid. Clearing his throat once more, he left.

Contrary to expectations, the visitor did ring the bell again next day. His eyes lit up when he saw Martha, who was not on duty at the hospital that day. He left his umbrella at the door, but politely declined the cup of tea that Helene offered him.

Next day he did accept a cup of tea, and after that he came to visit daily, without waiting to be expressly invited. He drank a great deal of tea, emptying cup after cup, and noisily munching the sugar lump in it. The sugar bowl had to be refilled at every visit. With his remaining thumb, the one-armed guest indicated his back, which still had a shell splinter from the war left in it, so that he walked with a stoop and needed a stick. He avoided mentioning the word hump, but said he was feeling fine. He cleared his throat. Helene couldn't help wondering whether the splinter in his back might have injured his lungs and that was the reason for the constant throat-clearing. Over the past few months, said the guest happily, he had written so many poems that he now had enough to put together in a seven-volume edition of his complete works. He deliberately ignored the fact that his old friend couldn't answer him, for after the latest injection given to the invalid by his tall and beautiful daughter, his mouth seemed too dry to speak.

Although Martha told Helene to go downstairs and help Mariechen to stone, gently heat and bottle plums, she stayed where she was. The winy aroma of the plums rose to the top storey of the house, getting into every nook and cranny, and clinging to Helene's hair. She leaned back. She had no intention of leaving the visitor alone with her father and her sister Martha.

How nice that we have time for a good chat at last, said Grumbach, probably appreciating his friend's customary silence.

Helene looked at the walking stick. Its finely carved ivory handle was in curious contrast to the three little plaques he had screwed to the stick itself. One of them was in several colours, one gold and one silver. At a distance, Helene could not make out what was embossed on them. The further carving at the lower end of the stick showed that it must once have been short-ened above the metal tip. Very likely Grumbach had owned that stick for years and years, and after the war its original length had had to be adjusted.

The visitor never took his eyes off Martha as she reached up to open the top of the window. You remember me, don't you? Old Uncle Gustav? Uncle Gusti? said the visitor, looking Martha's way, and he must have been glad of her kind smile, which might mean anything, either that yes, she did remember him or that she was pleased to see him again.

Grumbach had settled into the wing chair near his friend's bed, but he could sit there only if he stooped over. He was sucking his sugar lump to the accompaniment of the familiar throat-clearing and a slight smacking of his lips. Such a big lump of sugar called for good strong teeth, but since his third back molar had recently broken he preferred to suck it.

Uncle Gustav, whispered Helene to Martha at the next opportunity, she couldn't help giggling. The attempt at familiarity and the term Uncle that he used to convey it struck Helene as so outlandish that, in spite of Uncle Gustav's obvious frailty, she was on the verge of laughter. The silence was punctuated by his slurping tea with his mouth half open. Helene couldn't take her eyes off him. She saw his gaze wandering over Martha as if their hospitality gave him licence to stare openly at her. At her shining hair pinned up on top of her head, her long white neck, her slender waist, and most of all at what lay below the waist. To all appearances, the sight made Uncle Gustav feel proud and happy. Until a few days ago he had been permitted only to watch Martha from afar; now he felt really close to her at last. Like most of the men who lived near the printing works, he had watched her growing up with a strangely mingled sense of amazement and desire, the latter suppressed only with difficulty. Grumbach made sure that her other admirers remained at a suitable distance, keeping as beady an eye on them as they did on him. Seeing his old friend at home again gladdened his heart no less than the chance it gave him of gaining access to the house and the company of his friend's daughters. As the guest now watched Martha carefully cleaning the hypodermic needle, turning her back to him, busying herself at the washstand with cloths and essences to help the wound to heal, it was easy to let his walking stick and the hand resting on it move a few centimetres sideways, so that next time Martha turned he could feel the rough fabric of her apron on the back of his hand. That slender waist and what lay just below it. Obviously Martha didn't even notice the touch; the folds of her dress and apron were too thick; she kept moving this way and that near the washstand. With sly glee the guest relished the way her movements stroked the back of his hand.

Helene watched Uncle Gustav widen his nostrils and sniff. She felt sure that nothing escaped him, that he noticed the aroma of coffee in the air, and while Martha's involuntary stroking excited him, he might be wondering whether to ask Helene to bring him a cup. He enjoyed sending his friend's two daughters around the house in search of this and that. Although Martha had warned him not to smoke when he was with her father, he had asked her to bring first an ashtray for his pipe, then a glass of wine, and later he had not turned down the porridge that Helene had made for her father, although Father could eat hardly any of it.

What smelled so good, Grumbach wanted to know every day as he arrived at the house around noon, as if by chance. Rhubarb pudding, a casserole of beans baked with caraway, mashed potatoes with nutmeg. Grumbach said he hadn't had a watch since the war, adding that without a wife or children you could easily lose track of the time of day. So it was all the more surprising that he came to visit just in time for the midday meal.

When Martha and Helene had helped him to some of everything, hoping he would feel well fed and go away again,

96

Grumbach just stayed put in his chair, cheerfully rocking back and forth, and making himself at home. As if it were the most natural thing in the world, he would unstrap his wooden arm and hand it to Helene to be put in the corner.

How wonderful to see everything growing and flourishing, said the visitor, as his eyes caressed Martha's back. When she made her father's bed, bending far over it, her apron parted slightly at the back to show the dress underneath. It seemed to the man that she was bending over just for him.

All gone to rack and ruin, said Helene's father, blinking.

What, Father? What's gone to rack and ruin? Martha was at the washstand again, and the guest in the wing chair was getting the back of his hand stroked by her apron.

The house, just look at the paint peeling, flakes of coloured paint everywhere, big ones.

It was true that little had been done to maintain the house in the years of his absence. No one had bothered about the paint, which was fading up here under the roof and peeling off the wall like dead skin.

Grumbach was not to be distracted from his silent lust by his friend, the girls' father, deploring the state of the house. The touch of Martha's dress seemed to him too sweet for that. Only when Helene stood up did Martha turn to face them. Her slightly flushed cheeks were shining, her little dimples looked enchanting. The innocence that the guest could read in her wide eyes might make him feel some shame. Helene hoped so.

Can I help you? Helene asked Martha, with a sharp glance at the guest who liked to be called Uncle Gustav.

Martha shook her head. Helene squeezed past Martha and the visitor, and knelt at the head of the bed.

Are you awake? Helene whispered to her father. Since his return she had felt she must speak to him formally. He lacked the ability to overcome the reserve between them in words or by showing her any attention.

Father, it's me. Your little girl. Your golden girl.

Helene took her father's hand in hers and kissed it. I'm sure you wonder what we were doing all the time you were away. Her tone was imploring. She wasn't sure whether her father heard what she was saying. We went to school. Martha taught me to play piano studies: Desolation and then the Well-Tempered Klavier, Father. I'm afraid I don't have the patience to play the piano. And three years or more ago we went to the railway station with Arthur Cohen and his baggage to see him off. Did Martha tell you about that? But just think, Arthur couldn't join up to fight in the war. They didn't want him.

A Jew, said Grumbach, interrupting Helene's whispering. He leaned back in the wing chair and added, with a derisive click of his tongue, who'd want the likes of him?

Helene half turned to him, just far enough for him to have to see her gaze fixed on the back of his hand as it touched Martha's dress, and narrowed her eyes. The guest breathed heavily, but he left his hand where it was, on Martha's apron. Helene supposed he saw that as his due reward for saying no more. She turned back to her father, kissed the palm of his hand, his forefinger, each finger separately, and went on.

When Arthur reported for military service, they said they couldn't call him up without proof of his residence in Bautzen and they wouldn't send him to any regiment. Arthur objected, until they finally gave him a medical and told him he had rickets, he'd be no use in the war. He'd better go to Heidelberg and study there, they said, if he had the money and recommendations he'd need. In case of doubt, a young doctor would be more use than a soldier with rickets.

Helene's father cleared his throat. She went on.

You remember him, don't you? Arthur Cohen, the wigmaker's nephew. He went to school here in Bautzen; his uncle paid the fees. He was a good student.

Her father began coughing harder, and Martha glanced up from what she was doing at the washstand to look sternly at Helene. Her expression showed that she was afraid her relationship with Arthur Cohen might come to light. She didn't want either her father or his guest to know about those walks by the Spree; she didn't want anyone to know.

So now he's studying in Heidelberg. Helene paused, took a deep breath; it wasn't easy for her to utter the word Heidelberg and the explanation: Botany, that's what he's studying. And he sent us a letter, he wrote saying that there are women studying medicine in Heidelberg.

Now her father coughed so noisily that Helene's words were lost, although she had taken great trouble to raise her voice. What else could she say to her father about Heidelberg and studying there? What would fire him with enthusiasm? She hesitated, but next moment he vomited as he coughed. Helene flinched back, taking the visitor's walking stick with her. If she hadn't clutched Martha's dress, and then pushed herself off from the guest's knees as he sat behind her, she would probably have stumbled and fallen straight on top of him. Since he stooped in the chair, she could easily have fallen on his head and shoulder.

As it was, Helene landed on the floor. Her eyes fell on the badges adorning Grumbach's walking stick. The civic emblems of Weimar, Cassel, Bad Wildungen. Helene rose to her feet and handed back the stick.

Their guest shook his head. He got up too, took his wooden arm off the bed and placed himself beside Martha. He whispered, loud enough for Helene to hear him: I'm going to ask for your hand in marriage.

No, you are not. There was more contempt than fear in Martha's voice.

Yes, I am, said their guest. Then he hurried downstairs and out of the door.

Martha and Helene washed their father. Martha showed Helene how to change the compresses on the stump of the leg and what proportion of morphine to add to the injection. She must go carefully, because the last dose wasn't long ago. Under Martha's watchful eye, Helene gave her father an injection, the first she had ever given anyone. She was pleased to see the relaxed smile that appeared on his face a little later, a smile that must be meant for her.

Next day, around noon, Grumbach knocked on his friend's door again. Mariechen opened it. It had been snowing over the Lusatian Hills all night, and when she opened the door the light coming in from the street was so dazzling that Mariechen blinked. Snowflakes lay on the visitor's hair. He was obviously wearing his best suit. He held not just his stick in his one hand, but also a little basket of walnuts, and they too wore little caps of snow.

Ah, whenever I come visiting there's such a wonderful aroma in this house, said the uninvited guest. He stamped his feet to get the snow off his shoes. Mariechen stood in the doorway as if she wasn't sure how far in the visitor could be allowed. Grumbach looked through the open door and spotted the dining table in the parlour. Three full plates stood on it. The guest made his way past Mariechen and into the house. There was a smell of beetroot in the air. Soup spoons lay in the steaming plates as if the company had had to jump up in a hurry and leave the table. The vacated chairs stood a little way apart. While the visitor ceremoniously removed his boots, he ventured a second inquisitive glance at the dining room. Mariechen lowered her eyes, for bumping and clattering sounds were coming from the floor above. Suddenly Selma Würsich's voice rang out loud and clear.

Your father needs looking after? This was followed by a malicious cackle of laughter. Do you know what looking after someone means? Acting so sweet, and you don't even fetch a glass of water for your mother! Another bumping sound. Your mother, do you hear? Just you wait, you'll have to look after me one of these days. Aha. Me, do you hear? Until I die. You'll have to take my excrement in your hands.

The cackle of laughter died away, changed and turned to sobbing.

Let's see what's going on, said the guest, climbing the stairs with determination ahead of Mariechen.

As he reached the top step, a boot flew just past his face and hit the wall. Helene had ducked, so her mother took the second boot and threw that at her too, with all her might.

You brat, you little tick, you'll be the death of me yet!

Helene put her arms over her head for protection. Her answer came soft but clear: I wouldn't do you the favour.

No one had noticed the advent of the visitor. He could hardly believe his eyes. If Mariechen had not followed him upstairs, close on his heels, and if she hadn't been standing behind him now and barring his way down, he would have turned to beat a retreat unseen. There stood Frau Selma in her nightdress, which was cut so low that it showed more of her breasts than surely she could like. Embroidered marguerite daisies ran along the lace edge. But her loose hair swirled in the air and fell in ringlets to her bare shoulders as if it were alive. The silver threads in it gleamed, winding over her breasts like worm trails. Obviously she hadn't been expecting a visitor, and she still didn't see him as he stood hesitantly on the top step but one, looking for a way out.

You shameless, spoilt brat!

So who brought me up, Mother?

And to think I've been feeding such a child in my house. Her mother snorted. Aren't you ashamed of yourself?

Martha feeds us, Mother, haven't you noticed? Helene's voice was level but challenging. Maybe I write the red and black figures in the printing works accounts books for you, but it's Martha who feeds us. Whose money do you think we use to pay for goods at the market on Saturday? Yours? Do you have any money?

Oh, you little devil, get away from here, clear out! Mother snatched a book from the shelf and flung it in Helene's direction.

Heavens above. Helene kept her voice low. Why did you give birth to me, Mother? Why did you do it? Why not abort me and send me off to join the angels?

Before the guest could dodge, another book ricocheted off his shoulder.

Don't say you didn't know how!

Only now did Selma Würsich notice their visitor. Tears flowed from her eyes, she sank to her knees and said to the guest, in a pleading tone: Did you hear that, sir? Help me! And she calls herself my daughter! She was sobbing uncontrollably.

Excuse me, please. The guest was stammering. He stood hesitantly on the stairs, leaning on his stick with his one hand: Weimar, Cassel, Bad Wildungen, where are you now? He was trembling as he leaned against the banisters for support.

Oh yes, she calls herself my daughter! Mother was shouting now; she wanted the whole town, the entire human race, to hear about her misfortune. It was her soul wanted to come to me, she was the one who chose me.

Helene did not deign to glance at the guest. She murmured quietly: Wanting never came into it.

She straightened up, tidied her hair, and went purposefully upstairs to her father, who was lying there on the right-hand side of the marital bed and did indeed need her care and help. Even before the guest could follow her up, probably assuming that he would find Martha, his old friend's wife was barring his way. She seized hold of his leg, clasped it in both her hands, she groaned, she whimpered. The visitor turned, looking for Mariechen, but Mariechen had disappeared. He was alone with the foreign woman.

Upstairs, Helene tried to open the door, but it wouldn't budge. So she sat on the top step in the dark and, unseen, looked down at her mother through the banisters. She was clutching Grumbach's leg and crawling over the floor at the same time. Grumbach was trying to free himself, but in vain.

Did you see that? Her nails were clawing at Grumbach's ankles.

Excuse me, repeated the visitor, er, please excuse me. Can I help you up?

At least there's one person in this house who has a heart. Helene's mother gave the visitor her hand, hauled herself up heavily, and was finally supporting herself on him and his stick with her bare arms, making him totter. His glance fell on her bosom, moved on to the delicate daisy embroidery, then returned to the locks of dark and silver ringlets falling over her breasts. Finally he tore his eyes away and, with an effort, fixed them on the floor.

As soon as she was upright again she looked down at the stooping man in front of her.

Who are you? she asked in surprise. She pushed back her hair from her face, still ignoring her deep décolleté. Suspiciously, she looked at the man. Do I know you? What are you doing in my house?

Grumbach is my name, Gustav Grumbach. Your husband

printed my poems *To the Fair One*. Grumbach cleared his throat, trying to summon up a trusting smile out of the confusion of the moment.

To the Fair One? The girls' mother broke into a peal of laughter.

The change from heart-rending tears to loud laughter was so sudden that it sent a shiver running down the visitor's spine. Perhaps his heart was thudding; at least, he dared not look the woman in the eye. In fact, he didn't know where to look at all, since he could hardly consider it proper for his eyes to rest on the tiny breasts showing above her nightdress either. For over twenty years he had known Selma Würsich only at a distance. In the past she used to stand behind the wooden counter in the printing works now and then; he must have spoken to her a few times, he just couldn't remember it at the moment. She had retreated from the life of Bautzen over the years and had been forgotten, had to be forgotten.

Since his return from Verdun, Grumbach had seen her only once, again from a distance. If it had been her. The people of the town said there was something wrong with her. Gustav Grumbach should have felt all the more relieved that the foreign woman had never crossed his path since he began visiting the Würsich household.

To the Fair One? Selma Würsich had assumed a serious expression. She made it a question, and kept hold of the visitor's shoulder. And who is this Fair One? Who is she supposed to be? While she was still asking, she seemed to be searching for something; she felt in her dressing gown pocket and looked uneasily over the guest's shoulders. Cigarette? she asked, putting out her hand for a packet standing within reach on the narrow bookshelf.

No, thank you.

Selma Würsich lit one of the slender cigarettes and inhaled deeply. So do you know who this Fair One is? I assume you have someone special in mind, am I right? You know Daumer's poem, I take it? *Waft, ye zephyrs, soft and sweetly.* Selma's voice was hoarse. *Waft!* she said in a deep and menacing tone. *Waft!* She laughed, and the cackle hurt Helene, who put both hands over her ears.

Tentatively, Selma Würsich inhaled the smoke of her cigarette and let it out through her nostrils in tiny, cloudy puffs.

Grumbach managed to get out the words: Yes, of course.

This was more of an assertion than anything else, or so at least Helene interpreted the pressure she detected behind the sounds he uttered and his restless eyes.

If thou thine heart wouldst give me . . . Her mother began the line in a voice laden with meaning.

. . . then secret let it be./ That others may not guess it when they see you with me. Oh yes, of course, that too, said the guest, making haste to complete the couplet. But he seemed unable to summon up much real pleasure in their complicity.

But have you thought what craftiness lies behind that vow of love? No? Yes? What a polemic! I'll tell you: he wants her to keep her mouth shut so that he's the only one with any say about their being a couple. And she's not happy about it. Did you understand that? I mean, it's monstrous. The reader can but weep to see her words so obviously dismissed, to see him reject her. At least, a woman reader must, she whispered barely audibly, adding out loud: But I don't see you shedding any tears. You want to triumph over her. *To the Fair One!* I ask you!

Once again Helene heard her mother's malicious laughter. A guest like this would have difficulty understanding the depths below it.

As for Heine, the likes of you ought not even to read him. Do you hear me? You betray him rather than understanding him. Oh, you still read him, do you? Are you in your right mind?

One ought not to read him?

Not you. You and your misunderstandings, what a gang! *To the Fair One*. You know, it won't do. It's not simply bad, it is wicked, wicked.

Please be gracious enough to forgive me, madam. The guest was stammering now.

But Helene's mother seemed to find forgiving difficult.

Gracious? There's no grace among mankind. Grace is not our business.

Forgive me, dear lady. Perhaps you are right and I've just been talking hot air. Forget it, dear Frau Würsich. It's not worth discussing.

Talking hot air? Listen, Grumbach, talk as much hot air as you like, but spare your fellow men yourself and your nonsense! You must seek true grace and forgiveness only from your God, sir. Helene's mother had been regaining control of herself, and spoke those last few words with stern clarity.

I really would like to ask you, Grumbach began.

To the Fair One! And again Helene heard her mother's laughter, the laughter with depths that a guest like this could never guess at, could never plumb, which was just as well.

Helene's mother offered the guest the remains of her cigarette.

So now, sir, take this outside with you. You'd like to ask me? No beggars here, no hawkers, no itinerant musicians . . . you'll forgive me.

From her safe retreat in the darkness above, Helene saw the guest nod. He took the glowing cigarette, which must be burning close to his fingers. As her mother withdrew into her bedroom, coughing, and closed the door, the guest nodded. Carefully, stick and glowing cigarette in his hand, he climbed down the steep stairs. He was still nodding as he reached the front door and went out into Tuchmacherstrasse. The door latched behind him.

Helene stood up and tried to open her father's door again. She shook it.

Let me in, it's me.

At first all was still behind the door, but then Helene heard Martha's light footsteps inside.

Why didn't you open the door?

I didn't want him to hear her.

Why not?

He's forgotten her. Have you noticed that he hasn't asked about her these last few weeks? I couldn't tell him she's living on the floor just below and simply doesn't want to see him.

Martha took Helene's hand and drew her over to their father's bed.

How relaxed he looks, Helene remarked.

Martha said nothing.

Don't you think he looks relaxed?

Martha still did not answer and Helene thought he must be glad to have a daughter like her, a nurse who not only dressed the inflamed stump of his left leg daily, but injected him with painkillers and was careful, day after day, to talk herself and him out of the fear that he might have typhoid. Their father could not keep down any fluids now, but there were several possible reasons for that, which Martha hastily listed, while Helene read medical manuals, allegedly to prepare herself for training as a nurse, in fact so as not to lose sight entirely of her wish to study medicine.

Helene sat down on the chair and, when Martha set about washing their father's yellow foot, she took the top book off the pile lying beside her. She glanced up only now and then, to suggest that her father's steadily rising temperature might be a symptom of typhoid after all, developing after some delay.

Martha said nothing to that. It had not escaped her that their father's condition had deteriorated considerably. But she said: You don't understand anything about it yet.

Over the last few weeks, Martha had shown Helene how to do everything she did. They handled their father's body in turn as he lay there, looking so defenceless, Helene thought. There was nothing he could do but suffer his daughters' hands on his body. They were not caressing him lovingly but exploring his body as if to find out something and as if, when they did, it would do them some good. Martha told Helene where every organ was, although Helene had known all that for a long time. Martha couldn't help noticing how his spleen was swelling by the day; she must know what that meant.

For some time now, Martha had been unable to go to the hospital in the morning. She stayed at home, watching over her father's life, easing it for him. Helene noticed that Martha was scraping and scrubbing herself more frequently every day. After each visit to her father's bedside Martha scraped at her hands thoroughly, right up to the elbows; she called in the aid of the hairbrush and openly scrubbed her back with it.

At first she asked Helene to empty the bedpan with some hesitation, but then they came to take it for granted that Helene would carry the bedpans of fluids out of the room, rinse them with boiling water and clean the thermometer. Helene washed her hands and her arms up to the elbows, she scrubbed her fingers and the palms and backs of her hands with the nailbrush. It was not supposed to itch, it mustn't itch. Cold water on her wrists, soap, plenty of soap, which had to foam into a lather. It didn't itch, she just had to wash herself. Helene conscientiously entered the temperature from the thermometer on the curve of the chart recording it. Martha watched her.

You know what it means when the spleen swells, said Helene. Martha didn't look at her. Helene wanted to help Martha, she wanted at least to take her father's pulse, but Martha pushed her away from the bed and the sick man in it.

One evening the sweetish smell met Helene on her way upstairs. The stench of rotting almost took her breath away. She opened the window; the smell of damp leaves rose to her nostrils. A cool October day was drawing to its close. The wind blew through the elms. Her father wouldn't open his one eye any more. He was breathing through his mouth, which was wide open.

Not without her. Martha was standing beside Helene. She reached for her hand, squeezed her little sister's hand so hard that it hurt them both, and repeated what she had said. Not without her here.

Martha left the room, determined to break down the door to her mother's bedroom by force if necessary.

This was the first time for days that Helene had been alone with her father. She carefully kept her breathing shallow and went over to his bed. His hand was heavy, the skin roughened. When Helene picked up that yellow skin in two fingers it did not drop back into place again. Helene was not surprised when, in the light of the lamp, she saw the red rash on his chest where his nightshirt opened. Her father's hand was pleasantly warm, his temperature had risen daily by tenths of a degree until it reached forty.

From below, she heard clattering and furious shouts. No one was supposed to disturb Mother. Helene changed the sheet that they were using instead of a blanket, now that their father was so hot inside. Her glance went instinctively to the festering stump. Its sweet smell had enticed maggots out. She didn't want to look; it was as if his wound were alive, as if death were licking its way towards it. Helene swallowed as she uncovered his genitals – they looked to her small and dried-up, as if they had withered away and just happened to be lying where they were by chance. The instrument of her conception. Helene laid her hand on her father's forehead; she bent over him.

She didn't even whisper the words: I love you. Her lips formed them, that was all, as she kissed his forehead.

Hoar frost, only a small one. My little pigeon. We're not freezing any more, her father stammered. He hadn't spoken for weeks. She hardly recognized his voice, but it must be his. Helene stayed with him, she touched his forehead with her lips and stayed there. Her head suddenly felt so heavy that she wanted to lay her face on her father's. She knew that her father had always called her mother his little pigeon.

The body is only a disguise, her father whispered. That's all, and invisible. It's warm inside the house, come in to me, little pigeon, no one can find us, no one can scare us. Father put his hands to his ears and held them there. Stay with me, my words, don't run out. My pigeon is coming, my little pigeon is coming.

For a moment Helene was ashamed; she had heard the words spoken to her mother, or at least meant for her mother, and would be keeping them to herself.

Only when the shivering began did Helene stand up. She caressed her father's head. Countless numbers of his hairs, grown long now, stuck to her hand. So many hairs sticking to Helene's hand. Full of surprise, she wondered how he could still have any left on his head. What had begun as shivering became more violent; her father's body was shaking, spittle flowed from the corner of his mouth. Helene expected him to turn blue as she had seen him do a few days ago. She said: It's me, Helene.

But through his shivering, his words sounded unnaturally clear. Such a sweet smile, you have. We two together. Only the shells explode and give us away, they're so loud and we are so soft. Too soft. It's spurting, take care!

Helene took a step back to avoid her father's fist as it lashed out.

Father, would you like something to drink?

A legbone, a legbone, a legbone dancing on its own. Her father laughed and with his laughter the shivering died down. Ripples moving away from their point of origin. Helene was not sure whether he was talking about his lost leg.

Something to drink?

Suddenly her father's hand shot out, unexpectedly strong, to seize Helene and hold her firmly by the wrist.

Helene was alarmed. She turned, but there was no sign of Martha coming back. Indistinct sounds from the floor below showed that she and Mariechen had managed to get into the room, that was all. Helene twisted out of her father's grasp, and next moment he seemed to fall asleep. She took the carafe of water from the bedside table and poured some of it into the little bottle that Martha had been using for the last few days to get liquid into her father's mouth.

As soon as she put the little bottle to his lips he said, still in the position of a sleeping man: Drunken women in my mouth.

He couldn't drink, couldn't take any more water. Helene moistened her father's lips with her fingers. She resorted to the syringe for aid, taking out the needle and dripping water into his mouth from it.

Then she replaced the needle and filled the syringe with morphine to the lowest mark, held it up and expelled the air. Her father's arm was covered with puncture marks, so she looked for somewhere on his neck. An abscess had formed there, but next to it she found a good place for the injection. She pressed down slowly.

Later, she must have fallen asleep at his bedside from exhaustion. Twilight was falling as she raised her head and heard her mother cursing as she approached. Obviously she was being forcibly brought upstairs. Martha's voice was heard, loud and determined: You must see him, Mother.

The door was opened, their mother was resisting, she didn't want to enter the room.

I won't, Mother kept saying again and again, I won't. She hit out. But Martha and Mariechen were having none of that; they propelled her to the door and then, now that she was clinging firmly to them both, hauled her over to Father's bed with all their strength.

There was a moment's silence. Mother stood up straight. She saw her husband, the man she hadn't seen for six years. She closed her eyes.

Just what did he do to you? Martha asked her, breaking the silence and unable to hide her indignation. For the first time in her life, Helene heard Mariechen speaking her own Sorbian language, a soft sing-song. She was familiar with its rhythm from the women in the market place. Mariechen folded her hands, clearly in prayer.

Ignoring that, Mother groped her way towards the bed like a blind puppy, a creature that doesn't yet know its way but is instinctively getting the hang of it. She took hold of Father's sheet and bent over the sick man. When he opened his sound eye, she whispered, with a tenderness that frightened Helene: Just say you're still alive.

Her head sank on Father's chest and Helene was sure that now she would shed tears. But she stayed where she was, motionless and still.

My little pigeon, said Father, laboriously searching for words. I didn't give you a room in my house just for you to shut yourself up in it.

Mother withdrew from him.

Yes, you did, she said quietly. All the things in my room, all the hills and valleys they make, that's where I'm at home. Nowhere else. They are me. Who knows what care I put into laying out my paths? Clearings. Your daughters wanted to throw away the *Bautzen News*, tidying up they call it. They tore away the chiffon as if it wasn't hiding anything, they took last December's editions apart, I worked for days stacking them up again. By subject. According to subject, theme, material, putting them together, stacking them, putting them in order that way, not by the date. I'm a nocturnal creature. It's dark in me, but never dark enough.

Helene glanced at Martha, looking across the bed and over her parents' heads. They were so preoccupied with each other that Helene felt as if she were at the theatre. Perhaps Martha was thinking the same. Mother's heart has gone blind, Martha had once said when Helene asked what was wrong with her. She can only see things, not people any more, that's why she collects those old pots and pans, scarves with holes in them and common-or-garden fruit stones. You never knew when this or that might come in useful. Only the other day she'd been sewing a peach stone to her woollen cape. Mother could see a horse in a piece of bent tree root and would tie a tail of hair recently cut from one of her daughters' heads to the back of it. She had drawn a strand of wool through the hole in an enamel dish which said SOAP on it in large letters, and tied assorted buttons and pebbles collected over the years to the strand. This soap dish now hung over her bedroom door to act as a bell, so that she would have warning, even in a drowsy state, if anyone came in. Helene remembered a walk many years ago, perhaps their last outing together before Father left for the war. Mother had gone on this walk with her family only with reluctance and after repeated requests from her husband. She had suddenly bent down, picked up a curved piece of iron from the rim of a cartwheel and cried happily:

Eureka! She recognized the earth in the iron and the fire in the shape of it, picked it up, held it in the air and took it home, where she found it a new function as a shoehorn, discerning a soul in the thing. She talked a soul into it, gave it a soul, so to speak. Mother in the role of God. Everything was to have its being through her alone. Eureka: Helene often wondered about the meaning of the word. But her mother could no longer recognize her younger daughter, her heart had gone blind, as Martha said, so that she couldn't see people any more. She could tolerate only those whom she had met before the death of her four sons.

Helene looked at her mother, who described herself as a nocturnal creature, pointing out the attention she paid to the existence of her paths and clearings, making all these confessions like a brilliant actress. Malice had become second nature to her: it was the effect that counted. But Helene could be wrong. The appearance of malice was Mother's only possible armour, malicious words her weapons, in her triumph over what had once bound the couple together as man and wife. Something about this woman appeared to Helene so immeasurably false, concentrating as she did so mercilessly on herself, without the faintest trace of love or even a glance for her father, that she could not help hating her mother.

Father moved his mouth, struggling with a jaw that wouldn't obey him. Then he said distinctly: I wanted to see you, my little pigeon. I'm back because of you.

You never should have gone.

There was no grief left in Mother's voice; all the grief had frozen into certainty. Your daughters wanted to get rid of my books, but I saved a quotation for you, one of my favourites, to console me for your absence.

I'm glad you had consolation. Father's voice was faint and free of any mockery.

It's from Machiavelli, I expect you remember him? *The first law for every creature is: Preserve yourself! Live! You sow hemlock and act as if you saw ears of corn ripening!*

I've lost my leg, look, I'll be staying here now. Father tried to force a smile, a kind one. An understanding, gentle smile. The kind with which he could once smooth over any disagreement between them.

It would never have been lost here, not here with me.

Father did not reply. Helene felt a strong wish to defend him; she wanted to say something to justify his leaving six years ago, but nothing occurred to her. So she said: Mother, he went to the war for all of us, he lost his leg for all our sakes.

No, said Mother, shaking her head. Not for me.

She rose to her feet.

She walked out of the door, turning back once, without a glance for Helene as she told her: And you keep out of this, child. What do you know about me and him?

Martha followed their mother to the stairs, undaunted and unimpressed.

Then her mother, whose heart had gone blind, of whom Helene knew nothing much but the orders she gave and the thoughts that cut her off from the world, went back to her dying husband, knowing that her daughters were there behind her, yet still she said: This isn't the first time I've been dying.

Helene took Martha's hand; she almost laughed. She had so often heard her mother say that! Usually it led to demands for them to do more housework, show greater respect, or run an errand; sometimes it was a mere explanation, although its intention was not easy to decipher and its purpose could keep the girls guessing for hours on end. But here at her husband's deathbed, obviously nothing meant anything to their mother but her own emotion, the darker side of feelings that were sufficient only for herself.

Martha removed her hand from Helene's. She took her mother by the shoulder. Can't you see he's the one who's dying? Father is dying. Not you. Can't you finally understand that this is not about your death?

It's not? Mother looked at Martha in surprise.

No. Martha shook her head as if she had to convince her mother.

Mother's baffled gaze suddenly fell on Helene. A smile came to her lips, as if she were setting eyes on someone she hadn't seen for a long time. Come here, my daughter, she said to Helene.

Helene dared not move. She didn't want to get an inch closer to her mother, not the smallest step. She would have liked to leave the room. She was avoiding not so much the threat of her mother's imminent rejection as her touch, as if that touch might carry some kind of infection. Helene felt her old fear that some day her heart might go as blind as her mother's. Mother's smile, still confident a moment ago, froze. Helene had a recurrent nightmare that had tormented her for years, about two gods who looked like Apollo in the engraving hanging over the shelf for paper in the sales room of the printing works. The two gods who resembled Apollo were arguing, each claiming his sole right at the top of his voice: Me, me! I am the Lord thy God, they both cried at the same time. And everything went dark around Helene. So dark that she couldn't see anything any more. In this dream she groped her way forward, she felt something slippery as slugs, felt heat, fire and finally she fell into a void. Before she could hit the bottom of the abyss, she always woke up with her heart racing, pressed her nose to Martha's back as her sister lay breathing regularly, and while her nightdress stuck to her back, cold and clammy, she prayed to God to free her from the nightmare. But God was obviously angry. The nightmare came back again. Perhaps his feelings were hurt, and Helene knew why: he guessed that she was thinking of him in a certain shape, as the figure of a stately Apollo, and not only that, she saw him double, she saw his brother, and while she prayed to one she turned her back on the other – and in the end her prayer itself left no god any choice but anger.

Next moment, as she stood there frozen rigid, when it had become clear that she would not and could not do as her mother asked, she remembered how her mother had talked, years ago on the Protschenberg, about her God and Father's God, as if their faiths were rivals. When Mother described human beings as earthworms, Helene took it as an expression of the hatred that Mother had always tried imparting to her, and it bore fruit when Helene dreamed of slugs and fell into a void that appeared to her like her mother's womb.

Helene wanted to wash, wash her hands up to the elbows, her neck, her hair. She must wash everything. Her thoughts were going round and round. She turned away and stumbled down the stairs. She heard Mariechen calling after her, she heard Martha calling her name, but she couldn't think, couldn't stop, she had to run. She opened the front door of the house and ran up Tuchmacherstrasse and over the Lauengraben to the bridge, to Kronprinzenbrücke. Then she made her way further, on tiptoe in the dark, below the Bürgergarten and down the slope of the bank to the River Spree. Sometimes she could cling to the stout foundations of the bridge with her hands, sometimes she held on to trees and bushes. She went along the lower road to the Lattenzaun, past the Hop Flower restaurant, where there was still lively company and loud dance music. People wanted to be done with the war and silence and defeat at last. Only when she came to the weir, and heard nothing in the darkness but the gurgling and rushing of the river, was she able to stop. Crouching down, she held her hands in the icy water. Mist hung low over the river, and Helene listened to her breath as it calmed down.

It was late when the music from the restaurant had stopped, and her clothes were damp and cold from the night air and the river, and she went home. On tiptoe, she went up to her dark bedroom, felt around for Martha and slipped into bed with her under the blanket. Martha put an arm over her and a leg, her long, heavy leg, and under it Helene felt safe.

Helene stood at the window, scratching away the leaves of the frost flowers with her fingernail. A fine layer of ice, still smooth, the frosty white shavings. Small heaps, tiny crystals. Father is dead. Martha had told her this morning. Helene tried out the words singly, for their meaning. You shouldn't contradict yourself, but how did dead and the verbs to be or to have go together? He had no life any more – so the person who could call something his own was still somehow there. How did such a life want to be, to possess itself? She wondered why Martha hadn't woken her in the night so that she too could have held her father's hand. Martha had been alone with him.

What was it like?

What?

How did he die?

You saw him, didn't you, little angel?

But the last breath. What came after that?

Nothing. Martha looked at Helene, eyes wide open. Unblinking eyes trying to say they couldn't tell a lie. Helene knew that Martha wouldn't tell her any more about it, even if there was anything else to know. She'd keep it to herself. So nothing came after that. Helene breathed on the frost flowers, touched the jagged blooms with her lips. Her lips stuck to the ice and burned. Skin came off, the delicate skin of her lips. Martha will have folded his hands, drawn the sheet over his face and turned the bed to the window so that his soul could look out at God. Her lips felt sore.

Helene would have liked it if Martha had woken her. Perhaps he wouldn't have died if she had been holding his hand. At least not like that, so simply, not without her.

Candles were burning in every room in the house; day refused to begin. The clouds lay low and heavy over the rooftops, they hung between the walls, night was still swaying back and forth in the clouds above.

We'll wait for the pastor, said Martha, sitting down on the stairs.

You wait. I'm going upstairs to read my book, replied Helene. She went up, but not to the room they shared, where her familiar friends were waiting, Young Werther and the Marquise of O, whose fainting fit Helene still thought extraordinary and incredible. She went up yet another floor. Overnight it had turned cold in here. No one had lit the small stove this morning. She went over to the bed and saw his nose poking up under the sheet. She wondered what he looked like now, but no picture would form before her eyes. Even the memory of how he had looked when he was still alive failed her; yesterday she had tried to get a little water down him and he wouldn't open his mouth, not even a crack, she could find no trace of memory in herself of the way he'd looked yesterday. There had been hairs left all over the pillow, his long, ashen and finally yellowish hairs. She had plucked his hair off the pillow and held it in her hand for a long time, not knowing where to put it. Could she throw away her dying father's hair? She could. She had taken his hair into the little closet in the yard and was going to drop it down the frozen hole in the ground there. The hair wouldn't just drop in. It hadn't wanted to leave her hand. Even in the closet she'd had to pluck it off her hands, hair by hair. And it had not fallen, it floated in the air so slowly that she felt revulsion and didn't want to watch. Helene remembered that, remembered his hair yesterday, but not how he himself had looked. The sheet was white, that was all. Helene lifted it, first tentatively, then all the way off, and looked at her father. The skin over his eye socket shone, spotlessly smooth. He had a bandage round his head, to keep his jaw closed before rigor mortis set in. Helene was surprised to see his skin still shining, his face still gleaming. She touched his cheek with the back of her hand. The nothingness there was only slightly cool.

She put the sheet over him again and left the room on tiptoe. She didn't want her mother in the room below to hear her footsteps, she mustn't hear and know that Helene had been with him. Helene climbed downstairs again and stood by the window. She took a deep breath and puffed a hole in the frost flowers. Helene could see through the hole as the pastor, walking by, came down from the Kornmarkt, keeping close to the sooty walls of the houses, crossed to the other side of the street and came over to their house. He stopped. He looked for something in the skirts of his long coat, found a handkerchief and blew his nose. Then he rang the bell.

Martha offered the pastor tea. They spoke softly, and Helene could hardly hear them. The bell rang once and Mariechen opened the door to six black-clad gentlemen. Helene recognized one of them as Mayor Koban, who hadn't once visited his friend's sickbed, and another as Grumbach, but he was too shy to raise his eyes and meet hers. A carriage and pair stood waiting outside the door. The horses wore blankets to keep out the cold. They were snorting, and their breath looked like the vapour from a small steam engine. The six gentlemen carried the coffin upstairs, and a little later they carried it down again.

We must go, the people are waiting at the graveyard, they'll be freezing, the chapel lost its stove as well as its bell in the war, said the pastor, adding: Is your esteemed mother ready to set out?

Only now did Helene prick up her ears.

No, said Martha. She won't be coming.

She won't be . . . ? The pastor looked blankly from Martha to Helene and finally back to Martha, who cast down her eyes.

No, said Helene, she doesn't want to.

She says she's tired, Martha explained, her voice sounding curiously weak.

Tired! The pastor's mouth dropped open. Helene liked his Rhineland accent; he had been in this parish only two years. And she liked his sermons; she thought that in his language she heard something of the wide world, something that rose far above the world of the God of which he spoke.

Martha firmly took her coat. The pastor stayed sitting where he was. But on the last journey to the grave, he objected and fell silent. Where were his words about disobedience now?

We should go and let her do as she wants, Martha told the pastor sternly.

No, faltered the pastor. We can't go without her, without his wife, without your esteemed mother. I will speak to her. May I? The pastor rose, hoping that Martha would take him to the lady of the house. But Martha barred his way.

Believe me, it's no use. Martha was already smoothing her hair down, ready to set out.

Please. The pastor was not giving way. He showed clearly that he was not abandoning the attempt.

As you like. But you said yourself that people are waiting at the graveyard.

Martha nodded to Mariechen, indicating that she could show the pastor the way up to their mother's room.

Is Leontine coming? Helene put on her coat and saw Martha blushing.

The girls heard the clink of the pebbles and buttons in the bell their mother had made for her room coming from up above. Then there was unaccustomed silence, no shouting, no banging. Martha's blush left red marks on her face and down to her throat. She looked unhappy.

What's the matter? Have you two quarrelled?

What gives you that idea? Martha was indignant. She quietly added: Leontine's been prevented from coming.

The pastor and Mariechen came down the stairs. Mariechen put on her coat and opened the door.

Mother didn't want to come, am I right? Helene looked searchingly at the pastor.

We won't force her. Everyone must find his own way to God.

Not her. Don't you know she's Jewish?

The Jews too will stand before God some day. The pastor spoke devoutly and with stern but inescapable kindness. He seemed to feel so certain of his faith that Helene had to respect him.

Martha had booked a table in the Town Hall cellar for the funeral meal. None of the black-clad gentlemen said a word. They kept quiet and drank. Mariechen was crying quietly. And as the pastor kept quoting from the Book of Job, Helene wanted to close her ears in spite of his pleasant voice. She put her foot out to Martha under the table, gently touching Martha's calf, but Martha did not respond by giving any sign, however small.

And so you see, Fräulein Martha, God takes to him those whom he loves best. And he gives joy and love to all who still have their path to tread through this life. We have only to look around in our own community. Fräulein Leontine is a good friend

123

of yours, is she not? You see, her engagement to be married is the beginning of a new path, the path of her children and her happiness.

The familiar chord of A major rang out from St Peter's Cathedral. The pealing bells seemed to be agreeing with the pastor.

Engagement to be married? Helene was astonished. Had her question been drowned out by the sound of the bells?

Martha was crying now, sobbing uncontrollably.

Fräulein Leontine is getting married in Berlin. Mariechen smiled at the gentlemen present with a certain pride, or perhaps just pleasure, dried her tears and patted Helene's arm. No doubt she was relieved to think that a young lady who presented such difficulties as Leontine was to have a husband after all. Obviously Helene was the only person at the table who hadn't known about Leontine's engagement.

Did you know? Helene leaned forward, hoping Martha would look at her. But Martha wasn't looking at anyone, she just nodded almost imperceptibly.

Even if you do not care to think of such things at this moment, Fräulein Martha, God the Father will provide for you too. You will marry and bear sons. Life, my dear child, has so much waiting for you.

So much? Martha blew her nose. Do you understand God, do you understand why he allows us to suffer?

The pastor smiled indulgently, as if he had expected Martha to ask this question. Your father's death is sent as a trial. God means well by you, Martha, you know that. It is not a case of understanding, my dear child, facing the trial is what counts. When the pastor put his hand out over the table to place it consolingly on Martha's, she jumped up.

Please excuse me. I ought to go and see to Mother.

Martha ran up the stairs from the Town Hall cellar and left. There was nothing Helene could do but remain seated at the table, although she guessed that Martha had simply been looking for a good excuse to run away.

She loved her father very much, said Grumbach, raising his voice in this company for the first time. The other men nodded and amidst the general assent he added grimly: She loved him too much.

God's love is great. A daughter cannot love her father too much. She can learn to love and give only from God. Martha will withstand this trial, we do not for a moment doubt that. The pastor believed what he said and knew the effect his words would have. The gentlemen nodded.

Both his children loved him, both of them. Mariechen was still patting Helene's arm.

When the funeral meal was over, Helene sent Mariechen to see her women friends ostensibly to buy yarn for new lace, but really so that she could return to Tuchmacherstrasse alone. All was still in the house. Helene knocked at her mother's door once, twice, and when there was no answer she opened it.

Has Martha been here?

Her mother was lying in bed, her eyes wide open, and stared at Helene. You two are always looking for each other. Don't you have anything better to do?

We've just buried Father.

Her mother said nothing, so Helene repeated it: We've just buried Father.

Oh.

Helene waited, hoping Mother would think of a few more words to say, even a whole sentence.

What is it? Why are you hovering in the doorway like that? Martha isn't here, surely you can see that.

Helene went downstairs and out of the back door. Frost still lay on the black trees and foliage. It looked as if day could not break fully, as if it would be morning for ever, now, a November morning although it was early in the afternoon. Helene went into the garden and trudged over to the outside closet, with the dead leaves crumbling underfoot. The door was bolted.

Are you in there? Helene knocked hesitantly at the door. She heard rustling inside and finally Martha opened it.

It's all right. Martha pushed her hair back from her face, suddenly radiant.

Is it? Helene saw Martha's glazed eyes. She didn't want to hear any lies.

Yes, everything's all right! Martha took a deep breath and spread her arms. Helene clasped Martha round the waist. Oh, not so stormy, little one! Martha laughed out loud. Don't forget, we're out of doors, everyone can see us!

Oh, Martha, you're dreadful. Helene smiled, she was ashamed of herself, for all she had been thinking of was comfort. She wanted to comfort Martha, she wanted to know everything about Leontine and Martha, yet she had firmly resolved to ask no questions.

Shall we go upstairs? Martha gave Helene a lustful glance.

Helene couldn't say no, but she did say: I only wanted to comfort you.

Yes, you do that, comfort me! Martha was breathing audibly and deeply again, in and out. Under her thick coat she wore her new black dress with its high collar. Mariechen had made it specially for the funeral. Its black was a pretty contrast with Martha's white skin. Her cheeks and her large, delicate nose were reddened by the cold. Her glazed eyes looked brighter than usual. Comfort me!

Helene tried to take Martha's hand, but Martha snatched it

away. She was holding something in that hand, something that now disappeared into her coat pocket.

The sisters went upstairs and closed the door of their room. They dropped on to the bed that they shared and undressed. Helene returned Martha's kisses, receiving every one of them as if it were meant for her, as if they were not both thinking of Leontine.

My breasts aren't getting any bigger, Helene whispered later in the blue twilight.

Never mind, said Martha, they're getting prettier. Isn't that something?

Helene bit her tongue. Martha could have said that Helene had only to wait another two or three years, after all, and time allowed her to hope, but her kindly answer showed Helene how difficult it was for Martha to pay attention to her sister today. Yet Helene too was thinking mainly of Leontine and her engagement to a man in Berlin. Perhaps Leontine had written Martha a letter, and Martha had been reading it in secret in the closet and put it in her coat pocket before she could take Helene's hand. A goodbye letter to explain where this fiancé of hers had come from all of a sudden, and why she was going away after all, in spite of her previous promises. Helene wondered what would become of Martha now. But Martha obviously didn't want to talk about Leontine.

I'm thirsty, said Martha.

Helene got up. She took the water jug off the washstand, poured some water into a mug and handed it to Martha.

Lie down on me, little angel, come on.

Helene shook her head. She sat on the edge of the bed and stroked Martha's arm.

Please.

Helene shook her head again.

Then I'll go downstairs. I think I heard Mariechen just now. I'll help her with supper. Martha stood up, fastened her woollen stockings and put on the black dress.

As soon as Martha had gone out of the door and her footsteps had died away on the stairs, Helene reached out to pick up the coat lying on the floor. She did not find a letter in the pocket, but a handkerchief wrapped round a syringe. A memento of their father? Helene's thoughts were all in disorder. Why would Martha hide their father's syringe? Helene found tiny drops of blood on the handkerchief. She quickly rewrapped the syringe in the handkerchief, and the handkerchief fell open once more. Helene rolled it all up together and put the little bundle back where she had found it – why was it in her sister's coat pocket; why did she go into the closet with that syringe and not with a letter from Leontine?

NO FINER MOMENT

In the winter after the death of the girls' father the Spree froze over from its banks, until in January the ice floes were so close together that the boys of Bautzen tested their daring by crossing the river on them. To Helene, the spectacle was evidence of biblical truth. Couldn't water freeze even in the desert, and wasn't Jesus walking on water historical evidence of that fact? Smoke rose from chimneys early in the morning, clouds of it enveloping the town where it stood on its granite rock. Only the tip of the Lauenturm, the Cathedral of St Peter and the leaning Reichenturm, visible from afar, emerged from the mists of Bautzen in the morning hours. Even the high walls of the Ortenburg and the Alte Wasserkunst, the Old Water Tower, were lost in the vapours. Most households ran out of firewood at the end of January, and where money was short and coal deliveries slow people chopped up small items of furniture, stools and benches, garden furniture that seemed useless to them in midwinter. Martha and Helene saw their cash running out. If they managed to sell a calendar or a picture postcard, the money was spent right away. Bread had never been as expensive as it would be tomorrow. They tried to find someone to lease the printing works, but nothing came of all their advertising and enquiries. The factories down by the river were laying off workers, and anyone who could leave went to Breslau, Dresden or Leipzig. Any big city offered better chances of finding food and heated accommodation.

Helene cleared the stockrooms and the office shelves. Thick dust lay on the upper shelves, along with a number of small composition patterns for type that no one would be needing now. Helene had kept paper in the lower compartments in past years, but much of it had found its way into the stove these last few weeks. The brief warmth as it burned was better than no warmth at all. The long planks forming the top shelves would be sure to give a good heat and there'd be no need to take all the shelving apart. Helene planned to use only the wood from those two planks at the top, which were firmly anchored in their supports. The shelving covered the whole long wall of the room from floor to ceiling, then ran from the far corner to the door and beyond. There would still be plenty of space without the top shelves. Helene climbed the ladder with a hammer in her hand. A piece of cardboard had slipped behind one shelf and was stuck there between the plank, the wall and the support. Helene leaned forward, held on to a shelf with one hand and tried to pull the cardboard out. Then she intended to knock the top shelf right out of its anchoring. The cardboard was still stuck. Helene groped her way along the wall and was trying to free one corner of it from the supporting post when she was aware of something metallic moving. She felt behind the outer support for the object, pulled it out and found that she was holding a key. It was a little rusty, but Helene knew at once what it was. She was familiar with its shape and the unusual ornamentation of its head, even with its weight, yet she had never held it in her hand before. It looked a little smaller, as if it had shrunk. Helene well remembered how, before the war, her father used to clear the till at the end of the day, take the key and go into the back room with the money in his hands. Then he opened the large cupboard. Although Helene might already be turning to the door when he opened the till, he winked at her every evening with the eye that

132

would be missing later and said: You stand guard at the doorway, will you? And if anyone comes, just whistle. Sometimes Helene said: Girls aren't supposed to whistle. Then he would smile and reply: Oh, are you a girl, then? And once, half hidden by the open cupboard door, he chanted the lines he had written in her album: *Sweet as the violet be, /virtuous, modest and pure, /not like the rose whom we see/flaunting her full-blown allure.* Then he changed his tone of voice, adjuring her almost menacingly: But all girls must know how to whistle, just you remember that.

Helene knew that the door to the safe was in the back wall of that cupboard. In all the years of her father's absence the key had not turned up, and after his return there had been no opportunity to ask him about it. Helene loved her father and, in the old days, when he stroked her hair and drew her head towards him as if it were the head of his big dog, she wouldn't for anything have endangered that sense of security; she would keep still until he sent her out to the kitchen or into the street with a kindly little tap on the behind. All the same, Helene didn't care for those lines about the violet. She liked the sweet scent of violets and their delicate appearance, but she admired the upright growth of roses at least as much, the thorns they grew to protect themselves and their bright colours, pink unfolding like dawn, yellow like late October sunlight. In particular she loved the old song about the Virgin Mary walking through a wood of thorns, which all burst into flower and bear roses. Leontine had taught it to them before she went to Berlin. Weren't those thorns showing Mary how much they respected and even worshipped her by flowering? Everything about the rose seemed to Helene admirable, even enviable. Out of respect for her father she made an attempt to like the allegory of girls seen as flowers, but it was only an attempt and went no further. Since last year Helene had been growing roses, not violets, in the garden outside the house. They were not really garden flowers but wild roses that she had found and dug up on the slopes of the Schafberg.

Now, when Helene and Martha opened the safe for the first time, they found old banknotes arranged in several wads, amounting in all to a good two thousand marks, which made them laugh. To think what they could have bought with that years ago! Now it might buy a whole loaf, or anyway half a loaf. At least half a pound of bread. Two thousand loaves back then, claimed Martha. They discovered a leather address book with the cut edges of the pages gilded, and a folder containing lithographs of various sizes and, judging by the typography, of different origins, arranged in no particular order. The lithographs were pictures of women with nothing or very little on. Curvaceous women, very unlike the sisters themselves and their mother. Women in just their stockings, women with veils and tight-fitting basques, as well as women wearing nothing whatsoever.

The sisters set to work to write the names and addresses from the leather book on envelopes. They put a death announcement for their father in each envelope. Under 'S' they found the name of an aunt or maybe cousin they had never heard of before. It said: Fanny Steinitz. Under the name their father had written, in the fine script of a meticulous bookkeeper, a note in brackets: (Selma's cousin, the daughter of Hugo Steinitz's late brother). The address for Fanny Steinitz was number 21 Achenbachstrasse, W 50, Wilmersdorf, Berlin.

Even before Helene managed to catch her mother at a moment of mental clarity during the next week and took the opportunity of asking about her cousin who lived in Berlin, she wrote a short letter on her own initiative. Dear Aunt, she began, unfortunately we are sending you sad news today. Our father, your cousin Selma Würsich's husband, died on 11 November last year from the consequences of his war wounds. You will find our death announcement enclosed. Helene wondered whether, and in what words, to mention and explain her mother's condition. After all, the cousin would be surprised to get a letter from her nieces, not her cousin in person. She added: I am sure our mother would send you her best wishes, but sad to say she has been in very poor heath for the last few years. With our very best wishes, your nieces Martha and Helene Würsich.

Helene could not be sure whether their aunt still lived at the same address. Wouldn't she have married some time over the past years, in which case her surname would not be the same today? Their aunt might well be surprised to find them getting in touch after such a long time – moreover, there must be some reason for the absence of any mention of this maternal cousin of theirs in the family stories they had been told. But Helene wanted to write this letter. Her curiosity and her hope of receiving an answer from Berlin outweighed her doubts, and she quickly dismissed them all.

It was Easter before the postman brought a strangely narrow, folded envelope addressed to Fräulein Helene Würsich. Their aunt wrote in a bold hand, the letters leaning far to the right, the upper loops of the 'H' in Helene's name just touching the finely traced letter 'e'. This, wrote Aunt Fanny, was a wonderful surprise! After that exclamatory opening she left two lines blank. It was a long time since she'd heard anything of that crazy cousin of hers. She was delighted to hear that two children had obviously arrived over the years, for they had not been in touch since the birth of the first child, Martha. She had always wondered whether her cousin had broken off contact with her because of their old quarrels, or might even have died in childbirth. In a postscript Aunt Fanny asked her nieces whether their mother was seriously ill.

A correspondence began. There was little to say about their

mother, Helene replied, she hadn't been well for years and it was unlikely that any doctor could help her. She consulted Martha about the best way to describe their mother's condition. To say she was in poor health did not mean much, particularly as there was nothing organically wrong with her. They remembered Lady Midday, the Noonday Witch whom Mariechen mentioned now and then, saying with a curious smile that her lady, as she called the girls' mother, just wouldn't speak to the spirit who appears in the harvest fields at noon and can confuse your mind or even kill you, unless you hold her attention for an hour by talking about flax. There was nothing to be done about it, said Mariechen, shrugging her shoulders, although all her lady had to do was talk to the Noonday Witch for an hour about the working of flax, that was all. Mariechen's eyes twinkled. Just passing on a little wisdom, she told the girls. Martha and Helene had known the tale of the Noonday Witch as long as they could remember; there was something comforting about it, because it suggested that their mother's confused state of mind was merely a curse that could easily be lifted. Nothing to be done about it, however, Mariechen repeated, shrugging again, and her smile showed she was sure of the spirit's powers and felt only a tiny scrap of sympathy for her disbelieving mistress. On the other hand, as things were Mariechen had her lady to herself, along with her beliefs. Her lady couldn't run away. But Martha and Helene did not write to their aunt in Berlin about the Noonday Witch; they did not want Fanny Steinitz thinking of them in connection with rustic superstition and supposing that they must be simple-minded. So they merely gave a factual account of some malady that no one could explain: it was hard to pin down any cause for their mother's mental anguish and it seemed impossible to treat it.

Ah, well, that wouldn't surprise her, Aunt Fanny wrote back.

Such disorders ran in the family; and in that case, she asked, who was looking after the girls now?

They looked after themselves, Martha said proudly and she asked Helene to put that in her next letter. Both of them did. And she told Helene to tell their aunt that after just two years of training, and although she was the youngest of the student nurses, she, Helene, was going to take her examination in September. She should say that she was already helping in the hospital laundry and earning a little money there, so the two of them had enough to live on in a modest way. So far what remained of the family fortune had just been able to provide for their mother, the household and their faithful maid Mariechen.

Helene hesitated. Wouldn't it be better to say what little remained of the family fortune?

Why? A fortune can't be little, my angel.

But it's all gone now.

Does she have to know that? We're not beggars.

Helene didn't want to contradict Martha. She liked the invincibility of her sister's pride. She went on writing: So far we haven't found anyone to lease the printing works, but we can probably sell some of the machinery. We'll have to sell the Monopol press too, since our money is running out as the currency loses value and we have had no news of our legacy from Breslau. Did Aunt Fanny know anything about her late uncle the hat maker Herbert Steinitz, and the big salon he was said to have opened on the Ring in Breslau?

Ah, yes, the hat maker, Aunt Fanny wrote back. Her well-heeled uncle had liked only one person in the world, and that was her strange cousin Selma. She was sure he had left everything to Cousin Selma. Herself, she had never really cultivated the acquaintance of her Uncle Herbert. Perhaps she ought to make up for that now, after the event? The fact was that her uncle's reputation depended solely on his fortune. She could ask her brothers about him; one of them still lived in Gleiwitz, the other in Breslau.

It was to be autumn before Martha and Helene received the legacy left to their mother. It consisted of the regular income from the rents of an apartment block with business premises on the ground floor that Fanny's uncle had had built in Breslau, some securities that were worth hardly anything now and finally a large, brand-new wardrobe trunk that came by cart on one of the first cool days of late September.

The carrier said the trunk weighed so little that he'd be willing to carry it upstairs by himself.

It was lucky that Mother was in her bedroom and didn't see the trunk. Martha and Helene waited until Mariechen had gone to her own little room that evening, then broke open the lead seals with a knife and a hammer. A scent of thyme and southern softwoods rose to their nostrils. The trunk contained a large number of unusual hats packed in tissue paper, lavishly trimmed with feathers and coloured stones, and inside them square wooden hat blocks that gave off a resinous aroma. The blocks were planed smooth but were sticky at the sides. Each hat had a flat little bag of yellow hemp on it, filled with dried herbs, probably to keep moths away. Among the hats were two curious small round ones that looked like pots and fitted closely on Martha's and Helene's heads. At the bottom of the trunk, wrapped in heavy moss-green velvet, lay a menorah and a peculiar fish. The fish was made of horn in two different colours, adorned with carving, and the two sections fitted ingeniously together. Its eye sockets, pale horn set in horn of a darker hue, might once have held jewels, or at least so Martha thought. Inside the hollow horn body Helene found a rolled-up paper. The will. I bequeath all my property to my dear niece Selma Steinitz, married name

Würsich, now resident in Bautzen. Uncle Herbert had signed his will. Further inside the belly of the fish was a thin gold necklace with tiny deep-red translucent stones. Rubies, Martha surmised. Helene wondered how Martha came to know anything about precious stones. Instinctively she let the stones slip through her hand and counted them. Twenty-two.

We'll keep the fish here in the glass-topped display cabinet, said Martha, taking the fish from Helene's hands and opening the cabinet. She put the fish in one of the lower compartments where it couldn't be seen from outside. It was tacitly agreed that Helene and Martha would not ask their mother what to do with the fish. If she said they should keep it, that might mean for as long as she lived. They told her nothing about the fish and they hid the two modern cloche-shaped hats in their wardrobes.

When Martha finally, with Helene's assistance, pushed the wardrobe trunk containing the other hats, the will and the menorah into their mother's darkened bedroom one morning, then carried it, stepping cautiously, from clearing to clearing, because there was no space for the big trunk on the floor, she looked up in alarm. Like a frightened animal, she watched her daughters' movements. They lifted the trunk over a pile of fabrics and clothes, over two little tables full of vases and twigs, caskets and stones, and countless other items unidentifiable at first glance, raised it in the air and finally put it down at the foot of Mother's bed. Martha opened the trunk.

From your uncle the hat maker in Breslau, she said, holding up two large hats heavily trimmed with paste gems, stones and beads.

Uncle Herbert in Breslau, Helene confirmed.

Their mother nodded so eagerly, then glanced at the door, the window and back to Helene again with such a hunted look, that the girls didn't know if she had understood them.

Don't open the curtains, Mother snapped at Helene. She snorted with derision as Helene put the menorah on the windowsill beside her smaller candleholder. Candles had last burned in Mother's menorah on the day of her husband's death. She had lit only six of them, and when Helene asked why her mother had left out the middle candle she had whispered in a toneless voice that there was no Here any more, hadn't her child noticed that? Helene opened the window as she suddenly heard a chuckle behind her. Her mother was struggling to catch her breath; something evidently seemed to her incredibly funny.

Mother? Helene tried just speaking to her at first; after all, there were days when a question could be asked to no purpose whatsoever. Her mother chuckled again. Mother?

Suddenly her mother fell silent. Well, who else? she asked, and broke out laughing once more.

Martha, on her way downstairs, called out to Helene. But when Helene reached the doorway her mother spoke again.

Do you think I don't know why you were opening the window? Whenever you come into my room you open it, unasked.

I just wanted to . . .

You don't think, child. I suppose your idea is that my room stinks? Is that what you want to show me? I stink, do I? Shall I tell you something, stupid girl? Old age comes, it will come to you too and it rots you away. Mother raised herself in her bed, rocking on her knees, looking as if she might tip forward and off the bedhead first. And she was laughing, the laughter was burbling out of her throat, physically hurting Helene. I'll tell you a secret. If you don't come into the room it doesn't stink. Simple, eh? Mother's laughter was not malicious now, just carefree, relieved. Helene stood there undecided. She was trying to make sense of the words. What's the matter? Off you go, or do you want to leave me stinking, you pitiless girl?

Helene went away.

And close the door behind you! she heard her mother calling after her.

Helene closed the door. She put her hand on the banisters as she went downstairs. How familiar they seemed to her; she felt almost happy to think of these banisters leading her so safely down to the ground floor.

Downstairs, Helene found Martha sitting in their father's armchair. She was helping Mariechen to mend sheets.

Helene and Martha thanked Aunt Fanny for her help over the legacy in a long letter full of detailed accounts of the weather and descriptions of their everyday life in the town of Bautzen. They told her that they had made a second sowing of winter salad greens in the garden behind the house and next day it would be time to sow overwintering cabbage varieties. No one would expect a flower garden to be kept going in times like these, but they did it for love. Although the water rates were rising in an alarming way, they had managed to keep the flower bed in front of the house from drying up all summer. Late summer meant a lot of outdoor work. Now Helene had cut off all the rose leaves and burned them. They had made a copper brew to spray the roses against rust, and a lime and sulphur brew to ward off mildew. The Michaelmas daisies were in full flower. They just weren't sure when to put in flowering bulbs: Mariechen said now was the time to plant scilla and daffodils, tulips and hyacinths, but last year they had planted those bulbs early and they had frozen during the winter. They liked spinach and lamb's lettuce very much, and had sown plenty for the winter, for no one could say when the general situation would improve. Last year, after all, they had printed small calendars for the coming year on a little press that had been standing idle in the workshop, fully operational but covered up, and now they were colouring them in by hand in the evenings. They hoped very much that the calendars would sell at the autumn fairs, or at the latest at the Christmas fair in winter. Thank goodness, they wrote, the Christmas market was reserved for local traders, or the hill farmers would force down prices. People had to look out for themselves these days. Only yesterday they had designed a little calendar with texts quoting rustic lore and maxims giving good advice. The provincials here liked to be exhorted to be virtuous in the sight of God, and it increasingly seemed to Helene, she added, that agreement on such matters was what created a sense of community here in Lusatia, bringing consolation and giving courage. And what could be more important these days than confidence and hope? What, for instance, did her aunt think of such precepts as: moderation and hard work are the best doctors; work sharpens the appetite and moderation prevents its wrongful satisfaction? People so often confuse education and good conduct with etiquette and will forgive a boy's prank more easily than anything offending against the usual forms of social intercourse. The surest way to spoil a young man is to lead him to value those who think as he does more highly than those who think otherwise. A resolution cannot be more certainly thwarted than by being frequently uttered.

These reflections appeared to Helene and Martha like the yearning of their own graceful souls for the heaven of Berlin, and they hoped for nothing more fervently than to touch their aunt's heart by writing in such terms. True education enables you to set the right tone with anyone, striking a note that chimes harmoniously with your own, don't you agree, dear Aunt Fanny? And you are a sacred example to us there.

Helene and Martha went to great pains to show their aunt, line by line, how cheerfully independent they were and at the same time how grateful to her. Their very existence was a real joy! Helene thought this assertion too fine not to be written down. Martha, however, felt that such an expression was a demeaning lie in view of the sheer exhaustion that came over her when she thought of her life in Bautzen. Adopting a tone that trod the narrow line between pride and modesty appeared to them the real challenge of the letter they were writing. Time and again sentences were crossed out and rephrased.

Sacred example, said Martha doubtfully, she might take that the wrong way.

How do you mean, the wrong way?

She might think we're making fun of her. Maybe she sees herself as anything but sacred, so she wouldn't want to be a sacred example.

You think not? Helene looked enquiringly at Martha. Well, in that case at least she'll have a good laugh. We really must put that in or we'll never meet her at all.

Martha shook her head thoughtfully.

It was hours before they could get down to the fair copy, which had to be written out by Helene, because Martha's handwriting often looked unsteady and crooked these days. Something wrong with her eyes, Martha claimed, but Helene didn't believe her. She put in the bit about the sacred example and finally, in the last sentence of all, she politely asked their aunt if she would like to visit them in Bautzen some day.

When days passed, then a week, then two weeks and no answer came Helene began to worry.

There was nothing at all the matter with Martha's eyes. If they went for a walk and Helene pointed out a dog a long way off, a sandy-coloured dog like their father's old Baldo, who had disappeared on the day when he went away to the war, or if she showed her a tiny flower by the roadside, Martha had no difficulty in making out in detail both dog and flower. Helene suspected that her untidy handwriting, like her sudden dreamy moods, was to do with the syringe she had sometimes seen these last few months lying beside the washbasin, where Martha had obviously left it. Often as Helene handled syringes herself at the hospital now, the sight of one on their washstand at home made her throat tighten. Everything in Helene protested against the sight of that syringe when she didn't want to see it. The first few times she was so shocked and ashamed on Martha's behalf that she wanted to hide it before Mariechen found it, or Martha herself noticed her carelessness. But if she hid it that was sure to be noticed and would make it impossible for them to go on saying nothing about it.

As time went on, Helene became used to the idea that Martha had formed the habit of using the syringe every day. She did not speak directly to her about it. Nor could she honestly have asked questions, since she knew perfectly well that since their father's death and Leontine's departure Martha had been injecting small quantities of drugs now and then, presumably morphine, perhaps cocaine.

In the time just after her father's death it was Aunt Fanny's letters more than anything else that kept Helene hoping for a life beyond the town of Bautzen, a life she did not yet know. Even the pictures of Berlin that she had seen made her wax enthusiastic about the many different aspects of the city. Wasn't Berlin, with its elegantly dressed women and never-ending nights, the Paris of the east, the London of Continental Europe?

But no reply came from Aunt Fanny all through October in response to that letter from Martha and Helene, the best, most detailed letter they had ever written her. Early in November Helene couldn't bear the waiting any longer and wrote again. She hoped, she said, that nothing was wrong with her aunt?

Here in Bautzen, anyway, they were more than grateful to her for getting in touch with Uncle Herbert's relations in Breslau. Had their last letter arrived? Life went on in the usual way in Bautzen. After passing her examinations successfully (Helene had first put brilliantly, but struck it out again), she had begun work in the surgical department of the hospital in September. It meant that she was earning more, but she specially liked the work for its own sake anyway. Martha took the pen from Helene's hand and added, in her scrawl, that Helene had filled the position left vacant by Nurse Leontine, a friend of theirs, when she moved to Berlin two years ago. The professor wanted to have Helene beside him more and more often these days, when he needed someone with great powers of concentration and sure hands to help with difficult operations, because she was very talented in that way. Helene wanted to strike out what Martha had said; it seemed to her boastful and ill-judged. But Martha said Helene's worst mistake could be to hide her talents under a bushel, it would mean she ended up a helpless little thing in some man's arms, begging for his favours. She held out the pen to Helene.

You don't really believe that, do you? Helene wished Martha wouldn't keep challenging her in that way of hers. She took the pen and went on writing.

Thanks to their uncle's legacy, she said, their mother was now provided for. Aunt Fanny was warmly invited to visit them and would be a welcome guest at any time. With best wishes and hoping to hear from her soon.

Helene wondered whether she ought to apologize for the extensive account of their household arrangements in her last letter. Such matters, after all, might well bore and repel her aunt. Helene refused to entertain the idea that she might have thought the bit about being a sacred example insulting. But perhaps it seemed presumptuous of her two Protestant nieces from a small town in Lusatia to have chosen her as their example?

More weeks passed and the much desired letter did not arrive until just before Christmas. It was longer and seemed to have been written in more haste than Fanny's earlier missives; it was hard to decipher the closely written characters. She had so much to do, she said, preparing for the coming festivities; her cousin's children were looking forward to Chanukah and she was going to buy them little presents, even her lover was counting on Christmas, taking some notice of it. He'd see what came of that, she said. She was expecting the cousins from Vienna and Antwerp to visit at Chanukah, oh, the whole clan of them. She had her hands really full today, she had to discuss the menus for the festive season with her new cook, who was still wet behind the ears, an inexperienced young girl, so she, Fanny, had to keep helping in the kitchen. She liked that – after all, she was fond of cooking herself and she hadn't cared for the way her old cook, before she finally retired, used to add so much flour to every sauce that it came out stodgy. The older the cook grew, the thicker were her sauces, with more and more floury lumps in them; perhaps her clouded eyes hadn't been able to see them any more, or perhaps she had let the sauces go lumpy on purpose. Was it overwork? Or maybe she'd been cross with her husband who was making her stay at work until the day he died, using his empty sleeve as the excuse for exploiting her industry. She had suspected the old cook of using the wrong pans for milk or cream, although she'd been forbidden to do any such thing several times. Not that she, Fanny, was going to come over all hypocritical and claim to live strictly by the old dietary rules. No, she couldn't be doing with all that milky messing about. But in the end it was the woman's constant complaints about her lazy husband at home that bothered her more than the lumpy sauces. And that was saying quite something, for the sauces hardly deserved to be called sauces at all! In the end her fricassees were pieces of meat wedged solid in a floury paste, not a trace left of the flavours of bay leaf and lemon. Just a meat pudding, simply disgusting!

Helene and Martha couldn't help laughing when the letter they had been waiting for so long was in their hands. A whole world unfolded before their eyes. Every sentence had to be read several times.

The girls wondered whether these cousins from Vienna and Antwerp were their own relations too. The description, and the fact that Aunt Fanny hadn't mentioned a husband in any of her letters, made it seem likely. Imperceptibly, Martha and Helene sat up rather straighter. They were sitting on the bench by the stove, warming their backs. It seemed to them as if the letter cast a net all around the world, and Aunt Fanny was close friends with that world, an expert on it, if not its very essence. In a postscript she wrote that while her travels certainly didn't look like taking her to Lusatia in the near future, she thought maybe the girls might like to visit her in Berlin some time? She'd be happy if they could come for a long stay. The girls would find two first-class railway tickets from Dresden to Berlin enclosed. She thought Dresden must be their nearest real railway station, wasn't it? Her apartment was large enough, for she had no children herself, and she was sure the two girls could find work in Berlin. She would be only too happy to help them make their way and succeed.

Helene and Martha looked at each other. They shook their heads, laughing. Two years ago, when their father died, they had thought that from now on their lives would consist of working at the hospital and growing old here in Bautzen, at the side of their increasingly confused mother – but here was this letter, the prelude to their future, and only now could they really dream of it. Helene took Martha's hand and wiped a tear from her eye.

She looked at her big sister, her older sister, whom she had always admired for her modest conduct, whose wide-eyed gaze derived its attraction from her perfect appearance of purity, yet also owed something to those kisses that Helene had seen Martha and Leontine exchange. Helene understood the appearance of female virtue very well, the look of a modest, well-behaved, pure girl – it was exactly what a girl should be, it was the making of her. But this letter struck another note, and it aroused Helene's longings. Helene kissed the lobe of her elder sister's ear, she sucked it hard and the more the hot tears flowed down her sister's cheeks, unrestrained, the more mindlessly did Helene suck, as if this sucking of an earlobe and her sister's salty trickle of tears were the only way of ignoring those tears, of not having to say or think anything. Helene and Martha sat side by side for a while, face to face. It was some time before they were able to think properly again. Martha's weeping, the relief that had set it off and was the sign of it, made Helene guess how much Martha must have been suffering. Martha had been exchanging romantic letters for the last two years with her friend far away in Berlin, hadn't she? And although Leontine was unhappy in her marriage, she enjoyed the nightclubs and theatres of the city. Only a few days ago, when Helene had still been waiting in hope and uncertainty for a letter from Aunt Fanny, she had been unable to resist secretly purloining a letter addressed to Martha. It was from Leontine in Berlin. Helene had taken her chance to open the letter skilfully over the steaming kettle while Martha was on late shift at the hospital. Dear sweet friend, Leontine began. I can't tell you how badly I miss you. It's not so very often that my course means I must go on studying until late into the night, and I'm already giving the younger students lectures on pathology, but the weekends are mine. Yesterday we went dancing. Antonie brought her friend Hedwig with her, I showed them my new outfit – stolen from Lorenz's wardrobe. My friends loved it, but I don't wear his trousers outside the house. I've made myself a new dress for when I go out. Antonie was wearing a lovely dress too, a cream-coloured tea gown. We admired her in it so much. Knee-length and unwaisted! She danced beautifully in that tea gown – she sent us out of our minds, and enjoyed it. What can be more exciting than the hint of a waist and a hip when the whole cut of the dress pretends there's no such thing underneath? She was wearing a silk peony at her neckline. We competed to dance with her. Oh, my beautiful tall friend, I keep thinking of you all the time. Do you remember how we danced half the night away in our attic? You sweet, dear girl, I'm with you so often in my thoughts. It goes to my heart to think I won't be able to come and see you this Christmas! Lorenz won't hear of it. He thinks it would be an unnecessary expense; after all, he says, my father is comfortable with my sister Mimi's family and no one at home misses me. Lorenz always has to be in the right, of course. Nothing he says ever admits the faintest doubt. I tell you, he ought to have been a lawyer. He'd have been really at home in the law courts. Our domestic life together isn't comfortable, not with the righteous glances he gives the world, narrowing his eyes like a lizard's. You can imagine how the things he says annoy me. I could always contradict him, but then I suddenly find I couldn't care less about his remarks, and I usually leave the room and even the house without answering him. He loves to have the last word – well, he's left alone with it more and more often. Does that satisfy him? Luckily we don't see much of each other. He sleeps in the library and every morning I tell him his snoring can be heard all over the house. I wish that were so, but to tell you the truth he snores as little as you and I. However, I'd rather have him sleeping at the other end of the apartment so that we meet as little as possible. I'm going to the theatre with Antonie this evening. The Terra Cinema in Hardenbergstrasse has closed and a theatre's going to be opened there in October instead. The production of *Miss Sara Sampson* is famous all over the city. I'm sure Lucie Höflich must be simply wonderful as Marwood. But why do I tell you these things, my dearest, when you've never seen her on the stage? What wouldn't I give to be going to the theatre with you this evening. Don't be jealous, my sweet honey-tongued love. Antonie's getting married in April, she says she's very much in love. I saw her fiancé at a distance once, he didn't look exactly elegant – a burly, broad-shouldered fellow! Just the opposite of delicate, pretty Antonie. How did Helene's exams go? Give my love to the little one. Love and kisses to you, from Leo.

She signed it just Leo, like a man's name, with a long inky curve hinting at the rest of the name, but it was certainly Leontine's handwriting. Helene did not show that she had read Leontine's letter to Martha, but now, days later, when the girls sat face to face over Aunt Fanny's invitation, with Martha crying over it and laughing for joy the next moment, Helene was sure there was nothing Martha would rather do than pack a suitcase at once and leave for Berlin, to stay there for ever. In fact, Bautzen had a large railway station of its own, but what did that matter? Helene often went to meet her professor's colleagues there on his behalf, other doctors and professors from all over Germany, and Bautzen station couldn't properly be called provincial. Railway carriages built in the carriage factory here were sent halfway round the world, and some of them must certainly go to Berlin. However, Aunt Fanny couldn't be blamed for thinking of Bautzen as a village and she showed extraordinary generosity with those first-class tickets. To think that neither Martha nor Helene had even been on a train at all!

* * *

One afternoon in January, when darkness had already fallen, the professor of surgery asked young Nurse Helene to come to his consulting room. He told her he intended to go to Dresden for a week in March. He was meeting colleagues at the university there, he said, they were planning a jointly written book on the latest developments in medicine. He asked Helene if she would go with him. It would be to her advantage, he said. He didn't want to hold out too many hopes, he added to the fifteen-year-old, but he could imagine her as his assistant some day. Her nimble fingers on the typewriter and her knowledge of shorthand impressed him. She was clever and gifted, he would feel it an honour to take her to his meeting with his academic colleagues. He expected she'd never been in a motor car, had she? His grave gaze made Helene shy; she felt her throat tighten. There was nothing to be afraid of, said the professor, smiling now, she would only have to take the minutes of a meeting now and then, his old secretary couldn't travel any more because of water on her legs and he couldn't ask too much of her. Helene felt herself blushing. Only a little while ago this offer would have seemed a wonderful opportunity. But today she had other plans, not, of course, that the professor could have known anything about them.

We're going to leave Bautzen in March. It burst out of Helene. Both of us, Martha and me. And when the professor looked at her in silence, as if he didn't understand what she had said, she sought for more words. We're going to Berlin; we have an aunt there who's asked us to stay.

Now the professor stood up, and with his monocle in his eye turned to the large Pharus map on the wall. Berlin? He sounded as if he didn't know the city and had to look for it on the map.

Helene nodded. Their aunt had sent tickets for the train from Dresden to Berlin, she said, they just had to find the money for the railway journey to Dresden. If the professor would be so very kind as to, well, to take them to Dresden in his car, she would happily take minutes for him during his meetings with his colleagues and wait until those meetings were over before travelling on by train to Berlin. Could I ask when your meetings there are to take place?

The professor of surgery could not share Helene's pleasure. He did not answer her question about the date, but instead warned her against acting thoughtlessly. And when Helene assured him that they weren't acting thoughtlessly, on the contrary, she and Martha had thought of nothing else for a long time, he became brusque.

Young ladies ought not to overestimate themselves, he warned her. She and her sister were the daughters of a Protestant family of good standing, after all, and their father had been a well-regarded citizen of Bautzen. Their poor mother, so far as he knew, was on her own and in need of care. What could induce them to turn their backs so irresponsibly on the mother who had borne them?

Helene swayed back and forth on her heels. She reminded the professor that Nurse Leontine was living in Berlin too and studying medicine there, largely thanks to his recommendation. That was probably the wrong thing to say, for now the professor lost his temper. Thanks to my recommendation? he cried. You're an ungrateful rabble; you don't know how to behave. Let alone show gratitude. It was more than obvious, he said, that Leontine had not married for love. He had heard every word when she told another nurse that it was a clever idea. Not a good idea, no, a clever idea, she had said! Just imagine that! Was she trying to make him, her professor, look ridiculous, even make him jealous? Perhaps her veneration of him had gone slightly to little Leontine's head! A clever idea? It would have been a cleverer idea for Leontine to stay at his side. What useless trouble we go to when we let women study! Women, he said, have no business to set their sights on a career calling for stamina, strength and concentration, indeed for putting mental and physical pressure on other human beings. Women would always rank second, simply because in his profession only the best could do research and practise medicine. The professor was getting out of breath. A keen mind, it all depends on that, he gasped out rather than stating it. So why would a woman study? Leontine had been an outstanding nurse, really excellent. It was a shame; who could have guessed what she'd do? It seemed as if she had actually betrayed him, he said, putting his recommendation in her pocket, just like that, and going off to get married in Berlin!

Helene buried her face in her hands. She would never have expected the professor to harbour such a grudge against Leontine. Whenever he referred to her in front of the other nurses and the doctors he spoke with great respect, paying tribute to Nurse Leontine's abilities. Helene had thought she heard pride in his voice when he said that his little nurse, as he affectionately called her, was now studying in Berlin.

Take your hands away, Helene, he cried, reaching out his own hands to remove hers from her face so that she must look him in the eye. As he did so, the backs of his hands brushed against her breasts so roughly that Helene found it hard to assume he didn't notice. Now he pulled her up from her chair, his hands either side of her head, pressing so firmly against her ears that it hurt. What are you thinking of, Nurse? Do you suppose you could ever be better off than here at my side, in my ward? You're allowed to hold my instruments when I make incisions in my patients; I even let you stitch up the wound when my own wife had her operation. What more do you want?

Helene would have liked to answer his question, but she felt numb and still inside.

Now the professor let go of her and started pacing rapidly up and down. Helene could feel how her ears hurt, how they were burning. She had admired him ever since she had first been present at an operation and had seen his hands moving calmly, surely, almost gently, as if he were playing a musical instrument rather than handling bones and sinews, growths and arteries, ever since that first sight of his hands when she observed the fine, precise movements of the individual fingers. At first she had been afraid of him, because of her admiration and his abilities; later she learned to value him, because he never misused those abilities to humiliate a colleague, because he was always at the service of his patients and the art of medicine. Helene had never heard an angry word from him, let alone seen him make a rough gesture. Even when they had been working for ten hours without a break – once it was fifteen hours, through half the night, after the accident at the railway carriage factory – even then the professor had seemed to preserve a godlike calm that made her think of his kindness as well as his self-confidence. Now the professor turned the light on his desk so that it shone into Helene's eyes, dazzling her.

Sheer high spirits? asked the professor, as if assessing a case. No, probably not, he answered himself. He moved towards her, cupping her chin in his hand. Thoughtlessness? To be sure. So saying, the professor put his head on one side and his voice softened. Perhaps stupidity? As if he were wondering whether this diagnosis might help Helene.

Helene lowered her eyes. Please forgive me.

Forgive you? Stupidity is the last thing I could ever forgive. Tell me honestly, what do you expect to find in Berlin, child?

Helene looked at the floor, which was polished and shiny. We . . .

we, she stammered, searching for words to say more than she could clearly formulate in her mind, well, the way things are now, rising prices, Professor. People want to protest to the town council, they want work and bread. There've been rumours that people here at the hospital will lose their jobs too. Surely you've heard that, Professor? Well, Martha and I will have opportunities open to us in Berlin, please understand, we'll have opportunities. We want to work there . . . and study – well, perhaps.

Study – perhaps? You have no idea what that means, child. Do you know what commitment study calls for, what self-control, how demanding studies are? You're not up to it. I'm sorry to have to say it so frankly, child, but I really would like to warn you. Indeed, I must warn you. And the expense, you have no notion of the expense. Who is going to keep you while you study? You're not the sort of girl who'd plan to make your way by going on the streets.

No, certainly not, Professor. Helene could think of nothing more to say. She felt ashamed.

Certainly not, murmured the professor. His eyes went to her wide, smooth face, which could surely hide nothing; his look seemed heavy, pressing down on her, she wanted to say something in reply, to ward off his glance, but then she saw a desire in it that made her look away quickly, and she allowed her tears to flow. She took her handkerchief from her sleeve and dabbed her eyes.

Helene. The professor's gentle voice caressed her ear. Don't cry, child. You have no one, I know that. No one to care for you and protect you as only a father could.

These words made Helene cry harder than ever. She didn't want to, but now she was sobbing, and she allowed the professor to place his hand on her shoulder. He immediately put his arm round her.

Stop that, he begged. Helene, forgive me for being so stern with you. Helene. The professor now cautiously pressed her to him. Helene felt his beard touching her hair as he bent slightly and laid his mouth and nose on her head, as if they were man and wife and belonged together. As man and wife. It was the first time a man had been so close to her. He smelled of tobacco and vermouth, and perhaps of masculinity. Helene noticed the trembling sensation in her breast, her heart was racing. She felt hot and cold, then sick. She must have forgotten to breathe. Finally she thought of nothing except that he must let go of her now, because otherwise she would have to push him away with all her might, which was the right and proper thing for a young girl to do.

And he let go. Quite suddenly, just like that. He took a step back and turned away. Without looking at her, he said in a dry tone of voice: I will take you to Dresden, Helene, you and your sister. You say you have the tickets for the rest of your journey?

Helene nodded.

The professor went behind his desk and adjusted the stack of books on it.

Of course I'll take the minutes for you in Dresden, Helene made haste to say. Her voice was low.

What? The professor looked enquiringly at her. Minutes? Oh, that's what you mean. No, Nurse Helene, you will not take any minutes for me, not now.

Over the next few weeks the professor seldom asked to have Nurse Helene with him at the operating table. And he dictated no reports and letters to her. Everything outside the operating theatre was done under the matron's strict supervision. Helene cleaned the instruments, washed and fed the patients in their beds, emptied bedpans. She scraped the furry coating off old people's tongues and dressed their wounds. As she had not yet been asked to return the key to the poison cupboard, she managed to abstract tiny quantities of morphine for Martha. Through the swing door, she heard the screaming and whimpering of women in the delivery room, and on Sundays she watched them showing the snow in the garden to their newborn babies. The midwives were firmly in charge of the maternity ward. If Helene had wanted to stay here, she would probably have gone over there to offer her services. But then if she had wanted to stay here she would still be standing by the operating table, handing the professor his instruments, taking the needles and stitching up stomachs. Helene scrubbed the floors. The advantage was that she was working with Martha more often now, and as they mopped the corridors they could talk about their future and Berlin. Despite the fact that Helene took almost no further part in operations, and the professor had brought in a new nurse to help him, he did not leave them in any doubt that he would keep his promise. They just had to wait for March to come, and then it would soon be the end of the month.

With the help of his junior doctor, the professor managed to get the trunk containing the two sisters' things strapped to the back of his car. The young ladies were invited to climb in at once. During the drive he imparted useful information to the girls at the top of his voice; he was obliged to shout because of the roar of the engine and the other noises on the road. At times like these it was important to invest in durable assets, he said, and a car like his was just the thing. Would they like to drive it too?

Yes, definitely. Martha was the first to take the wheel. After a few metres she steered the vehicle straight towards a ploughed field. The furrows, still black, gave way as it drove into the soil. It stuck fast and stood there steaming. All three had to get out. The water that had collected in the furrows formed a thin skin of ice, which cracked when you trod on it. While Martha rubbed her arm, the professor and Helene pushed the car, bracing themselves against it with all their might until they had it back on the road. After that the professor wouldn't let either of the sisters drive.

They reached the bridge known as Das Blaue Wunder, the Blue Miracle, before midday. The professor waxed eloquent on the brilliance and magnificence of this structure, but Martha and Helene could see only metal struts rising high in the air outside the car window and its legendary blue was nothing compared to the colour of the river. The Elbe, flooding its banks, seemed to them far more magnificent. The drive through the residential area of villas took longer than expected; once they had to stop and add water to the radiator. But after that it all went very fast. They overtook horse-drawn cabs; there was a lot of traffic. Helene would have liked to see the harbour, but they were short of time. As promised, the professor took the sisters to the Central Railway Station. The clocks on the two towers showed different times; the professor was sure that it would be best to believe the one that was ten minutes in advance of the other. Martha and Helene marvelled at the size of the great steel hall with its three aisles. It was the first time they had seen steel arches used to hold up a vaulted glass roof. The sun gleamed out through grey clouds; it was going to rain. Crowds of people were looking into the magnificent display windows of the shops or making for one of the many station platforms. A basket of lemons fell over and people stooped to snatch up the tumbling yellow fruits as if there were no tomorrow. Helene couldn't resist stooping too and slipping a lemon into her pocket. Two little boys pestered Martha and Helene to buy a bunch of pussy willow. An old woman with a baby in her arms held out one hand. It couldn't possibly be her own child; Helene thought the mother might have died in childbirth. But what made her think of mothers dying? Before the sisters knew it, a young porter was loading their trunk on to his cart and walking ahead of them, shouting to the crowd to make way. The professor warned Martha and Helene never to lose sight of their luggage and the porter in the crowd. Although they protested, he insisted on seeing the sisters to their train. He accompanied them to the platform, to the luggage van, to their carriage and finally to their seats in the first-class compartment. With a composed smile, he handed Martha a small package of food that his wife had put together that morning. Sausage and hard-boiled eggs, he said quietly. All through the journey the professor had avoided looking at Helene, and he still did. But he was in friendly mood, he shook hands with them both and climbed out of the train. Perhaps he would appear at the window on the platform and wave a white handkerchief? But no, they did not see him again.

The train hissed and moved ponderously out of Dresden station. The rumble of the engine was so deafening that Helene and Martha didn't talk to each other. Travellers were still pushing and shoving in the corridor, looking for their compartments and their seats. Helene and Martha had been settled in their own velvet-upholstered seats for some time. In all the excitement they had omitted to take off their coats and gloves, but they leaned forward and looked sideways so as not to miss anything that could be seen through the window. They felt sure that a new life was beginning with these elegant seats, this window, this train, a life that would have nothing to do with Bautzen any more, a life that was to make them forget these last weeks with their mother now scolding, now drowsing. On the left, cranes towered to the sky. They must belong to the harbour and the docks, which could not be seen from the train. Mariechen would certainly take good care of Mother; when they said goodbye Martha and Helene had promised to send her enough money on the first of every month. What else was the rent money from Breslau for? Together, they had decided that Mariechen would stay in Tuchmacherstrasse with Mother for the time being. Mariechen was grateful to them for this suggestion. She probably wouldn't have known where else to go in her old age, after spending twenty-seven years in the service of the Würsich family.

The last buildings in the Old Town were passing by. The train was crossing the Marienbrücke so slowly that you could have walked along beside it. The Elbe meadows were still more black than green; the Elbe itself was in spate, but hardly rose above its banks here in the city. A barge with a load of coal made its way slowly against the current. Helene wondered if it would go as far as Pirna. More houses, streets, squares, the train went through a small station. It was some time before the buildings of the city had all passed by, and the low-built houses and gardens of the suburbs were also behind them. Helene thought she saw the first of the Lusatian Hills rising in the distance. She felt happy excitement and relief when they too disappeared from view, and the train was finally puffing through meadows, woods and fields. Mist hung over the arable fields that they were passing, hardly any green yet showed that spring was on its way, but now and then the sun broke through the hovering mist.

It seemed to Helene as if they had been on their way for weeks. She opened the picnic prepared for them by the professor's wife and offered Martha something to eat. They ate the sandwiches with boiled sausage, which tasted like blood sausage and had the same fine consistency, devouring the bread and its dark-red filling as if they hadn't had anything to eat for years, as if blood sausage tasted wonderful. With the sandwiches they drank the tea that they had brought in a flask with a wickerwork cover. Later they felt tired, and their eyes closed even before the train stopped at the next station.

When they woke up again, other travellers were already standing at the windows and out in the corridor. The train's entry into the city, and soon afterwards into Anhalt Station, brought soft cries of amazement from the girls. Who could have imagined Berlin, its size, all the passers-by, the bicycles, hackney carriages and motor cars? After Dresden station, Martha and Helene had thought they were well prepared for the metropolis, but they held each other's chilly, sweating hands tight. The deafening noise of the station concourse came in through the open windows. The travellers crowded out of their compartments into the corridor and made for the doors. Outside, Helene could hear the whistling and shouting of the porters, already calling and offering their services out on the platform. Panic seized the girls; they were afraid they wouldn't get out of the train in time. Martha stumbled as she climbed down and caught her foot in the skirts of her coat, so that she half slipped and half fell off the last step to the platform. She landed on all fours. Helene couldn't help laughing and was ashamed of herself. She clenched her fist and bit her glove. Next moment she took the handhold by the door herself, accepted an elderly gentleman's helping hand, and quickly climbed out of the train. She and the elderly gentleman helped Martha up. The station was full of people, some of whom had come to meet their nearest and dearest from the train, but there were also many traders and young women going up and down offering everything from newspapers to flowers to shoe-cleaning for sale, all of them items which Martha and Helene realized only now that they lacked. At the same time they looked at each other, and down at their dirty shoes, where the Saxon soil of the ploughed field out of which they had pushed the professor's car still clung. And their hands were empty – they ought to have thought before now of taking their aunt a present. Hadn't the physicist Röntgen died only the other day? Trying to think of small talk, Helene was searching her memory for world news that she had heard recently. She seldom took her chance of reading any of the newspapers left lying around the hospital. What did she and Martha know of the way of the world in general and Berlin in particular? Perhaps a little bunch of daffodils? Were those real tulips? Helene had never seen tulips so tall and slender.

As Helene tried and failed to pin down any of her fleeting thoughts – they ought to have started printing banknotes in good time, it occurred to her, and then: what nonsense! Then again: who was Cuno? President of the Reich or Chancellor? Then she thought of those fine-sounding names again: Thyssen and France and cash, cash, cash; printing money would have been just the thing, whether it was legal or not. Come on, she told Martha, who was still disentangling her coat and tucking her hair under her hat. She hoped their trunk was still there.

Together, the sisters hurried along the platform to the luggage van. A queue had formed outside it. The girls kept looking over their shoulders. Their aunt had suggested in her last letter that they should take a charabanc or the tram to reach her apartment in Achenbachstrasse. But wasn't it possible that in spite of this advice she would come to the station to meet them herself?

Do you think Aunt Fanny will recognize us?

She'll have to. Martha was holding the luggage voucher ready, already counting out the right money, although there was still a dense line of people waiting in front of them.

It won't be difficult with you. Helene scrutinized Martha. You look like Mother.

The question is whether Aunt Fanny can see that – or wants to. Perhaps she doesn't remember what her cousin looked like?

She won't have a photograph of Mother. Mother has only one from before we were born, that photo of her wedding.

Has? Martha smiled. She had it, rather. At least I brought the photo with me. We want a souvenir, don't we?

A souvenir? Helene looked at Martha blankly. She thought of saying: Not me, I don't, but then decided not to.

Need a place to stay? Nice hostel, young ladies? Someone was plucking at Helene's coat from behind. Or a private room with a landlady? Helene turned. A young man in shabby clothes stood behind her.

163

Running water and electric light? a second man asked, pushing the first aside.

I can tell you a good place. Those hostels for strangers are full of lice, and who can afford a hotel? You just come with me! An elderly woman took Helene's arm.

Let go! Helene's voice cracked with alarm. No thank you, no thank you, we don't need anywhere, Martha was saying to all the people crowding around them.

We have an aunt in Berlin, Helene added, and now she did up the top button of her coat.

I'm sure they didn't get on because Aunt Fanny thought she'd risen higher in the world than Mother, Martha whispered in Helene's ear. She had, too!

You think so? I don't. Helene often felt uncomfortable when Martha said something spiteful about their mother. Much as she too feared her and often as she had quarrelled with her, she hated it, couldn't bear it when Martha expressed her poor opinion of Selma for no reason at all. Martha enjoyed saying such things, taking a kind of delight in exposing their mother that Helene shared only occasionally and to a lesser extent.

Aunt Fanny stole from Mother, Helene claimed now. She remembered their mother saying so on the evening when they had first told her about their correspondence with Aunt Fanny.

And you believe that? mocked Martha. What would she have stolen? A dried toadstool, maybe? If you ask me she just made it up. Maybe it was the other way round. Aunt Fanny would never have needed to do such a thing.

She'll be a fine lady, I feel sure she will. Helene looked ahead of her. The queue was not so long now and, deep in conversation, the sisters had missed hearing the man ahead of them by the big door of the luggage van calling their number for the fourth time. Now he called their names too.

Petitions from the Democratic parties rejected! a man was shouting at the top of his voice, brandishing a newspaper; a whole stack of them threatened to slip from under his arm. The National Socialist Party's Sturmabteilung forges ahead!

That's all old hat, shouted another newspaper boy derisively, and he too began bellowing at the top of his voice. Earthquake! He was waving a paper himself and Helene wondered if he had just thought up this news item to sell more papers. In any case, people were snatching newspapers from his hand. Huge earthquake in China!

Calling for the last time! Number four hundred and thirty-seven, first class, Würsich!

That's us, that's us! Helene shouted back as loudly as she could, and hurried the short way forward to the man who, in the absence of anyone to take their trunk, was just about to put it on the big truck for unclaimed items.

Rote Fahne! shouted a thin girl with a small handcart of newspapers. *Rote Fahne!*

Die Vossische!

Der Völkische Beobachter! Helene recognized the young paper boy who had been shouting just now. How old would he be? Ten? Twelve? Occupation of the Ruhr goes on! No coal for France! Earthquake in China! He too was now shouting the headline about the earthquake, although it was doubtful that the paper he was selling had any news of it.

Buy the *Weltbühne*, ladies and gents, fresh off the press, the *Weltbühne*! A strikingly tall man in a hat, suit and glasses was striding along the platform. Although he spoke in a strange accent, which Helene immediately assumed to be Russian, his small red magazines were selling well. Soon after he had passed Martha and Helene, an elegantly dressed lady bought his last copy.

Only when someone called: *Vorwärts! Vorwärts! Vorwärts!* did Helene come to the bold decision to take a wad of banknotes out of her coat pocket. The lemon was still in the pocket too and the notes were now lemon-scented. After all, she knew *Vorwärts*, the Socialist weekly paper, and she hoped it would give an impression of elegance and culture if they arrived at their aunt's carrying a newspaper.

They took a cab with several seats in it; perhaps this was what Aunt Fanny meant by a charabanc. The buildings and advertising columns were already casting long shadows. On Schöneberger Ufer the cab stopped; it looked as if the horse were leaning forward; it went down on its knees, its forelegs gave way, there was a loud cracking of wood and the horse slumped sideways in its harness. The driver jumped up. He shouted something, climbed down and patted the recumbent horse on the neck. Walking round the cab, he took the bucket off its hook and went away without a word of explanation. Helene realized that he was going to a pump, where he had to wait until someone else had filled a bucket and it was his turn. The lanterns along the street were lit. There was shining and sparkling everywhere. So many lights. Helene stood up and turned round. A motor car with a funny chequered pattern like a border all round it stopped beside them. Did they need help? asked the driver, leaning out of his window. Maybe they could do with a taxi? But Martha and Helene shook their heads, and looked in the direction their cab driver had gone. The taxi driver didn't ask again. A young man was hailing him at the crossing ahead.

Perhaps we ought to have changed into that motor cab. Helene looked around. Their driver was coming back with a bucket of water. He sprayed the horse, then tipped the whole bucketful over it, but the horse didn't move. The sun had set, the birds were still twittering, it felt chilly.

Got much further to go? It was the first remark the driver had addressed to them.

Martha and Helene shrugged their shoulders, not sure.

Hm, yes, Achenbach, that's a good stretch, can't make it, there's your baggage too. The driver looked worried.

A policeman strolled up. The trunk was unloaded, and Martha and Helene had to get out. Another cab was hailed for them. The sky was dark blue by the time they finally arrived outside the building in Achenbachstrasse. The porch of the four-storey apartment house was lit, a broad flight of five stone steps led up to the elegant front door of wood and glass. A servant was waiting at the doorway to welcome them; he went over to the cab to take their trunk. Martha and Helene climbed the broad steps to the first floor. Was that marble, genuine Italian marble?

So here you are at last! cried a tall woman. She reached out to Martha and Helene with hands in long gloves that covered her elbows. Bare shoulders gleamed above them. Martha didn't hesitate for long; she took one of the lady's hands, bent her head and kissed it.

Goodness me, no, are we at a royal court? My nieces. Aunt Fanny turned on her heel and her long scarf floated into Helene's face. Some of the ladies and gentlemen standing around nodded in greeting, raised their glasses to welcome the sisters and drank to each other. The ladies wore flimsy dresses without any visible waistline, and with cords and scarves round their hips; the skirts only just covered their knees, and their shoes had little straps and small heels. Many of them had cut their hair as short as Leontine had once cut hers, to just above their earlobes, and even shorter at the nape of the neck. One woman seemed to have her hair crimped close to her head in waves. Helene looked curiously at these hairstyles and wondered how you achieved them. Just the sight all those necks confused her, some rising from straight, prominent shoulders, others from shoulders that sloped delicately, always leading the eye to the heads of the girls, young women and ladies as if heads and no longer hips were the crown of creation, the hips had been on show quite long enough. The gentlemen wore elegant suits and were smoking pipes; they looked at the sisters who had just arrived with expressions of avid benevolence. One stout gentlemen gazed into Helene's face in a friendly manner, then let his glance move over her and her coat, which was now opening to show what to him must certainly look like a dress in an old-fashioned country fashion. With a kind, avuncular nod he turned, took a glass from a tray being carried round by a young lady and immersed himself in conversation with a small woman whose feather boa came right down to the backs of her knees.

What pretty children! A friend of Aunt Fanny's took her arm, swaying tipsily, her head thrust forward like the head of a bull with red curls to look at Helene. Her large, sequin-covered bosom glittered as she straightened up to her full height right in front of Helene's eyes. Why have you been hiding these bewitching creatures from us so long, my dear?

Lucinde, meet my nieces.

A gentleman leaned curiously over Aunt Fanny's bare shoulders to look from Helene to Martha and back again. Obviously the guests filled every nook and cranny of the first floor of this building. The front door was still open behind them. Helene looked around, feeling she would like to escape. When she felt something touch her calf and looked down, she saw a coal-black poodle, newly clipped. The sight of the poodle helped her to breathe more easily.

A housemaid and a manservant took the sisters' bags and

helped them out of their coats. Helene's newspaper was taken away – no one had noticed it – and two more menservants came up the steps with their trunk. Helene hurried a few steps after the girl carrying her coat and took the lemon out of its pocket.

A lemon, how delightful! screeched Lucinde the red-headed bull, but in as quiet a screech as possible.

Quick, go and freshen yourselves up and change for dinner, we dine in an hour's time. Aunt Fanny was beaming at them. Her face, thin and regular, was like a painting with her cheeks so dark with rouge, while her eyelids shimmered green and gold. Long lashes rose and fell like black veils over her big black eyes. A young man passed Aunt Fanny and stopped beside her with his back to Martha and Helene. He kissed her bare shoulder, then laid his hand briefly against her cheek and went on to another lady who was obviously waiting for him. Fanny mimed clapping her hands. She looked so distinguished, elegant, graceful – words to describe her tumbled over themselves in Helene's head – she looked so charming as her long hands touched but never actually made any clapping sound. Fantastic, she said. My treasure here will show you everything. Otta?

The housemaid Otta, white-haired and smooth-skinned, made her way through the throng of guests and led the sisters to a small room at the far end of the apartment. It smelled of violets. Two narrow beds had been made up, and in a niche in the wall stood a washstand with a big mirror. There was a lily pattern engraved on the rim of the glass. Candles in a five-branched silver candleholder gave a soft light, like the candlelight on an altar. The housemaid showed them towels, chamber pots, a wardrobe. And there was a bathroom and lavatory, a water closet, at the front of the apartment near the entrance door, the housemaid whispered. Then she excused herself, saying she had to open the door to other guests.

Is this a party? Martha looked in astonishment at the door that had closed behind the housemaid.

Change for dinner? Helene threw the lemon on the bed and put her hands on her hips. I'm already wearing my best dress.

She can't know that, little angel. She won't have looked closely.

Did you see her lips? Did you see all that make-up she's wearing?

Vermilion. And her hair, cut to just above the earlobes – it's the style in town, little angel. I'll cut your blonde locks for you tomorrow, said Martha, laughing nervously as she opened the trunk. She rummaged around in it with both hands and sighed with relief when she found her little bag. Turning her back to Helene, she shook out its contents on the washstand. Helene sat down cautiously on one of the two beds. She stroked the throw arranged over it; it was so soft. The word cashmere came into her mind, although she had no idea what cashmere felt like. Ducking to look under Martha's arms, Helene saw her open a small bottle and fill the syringe with liquid. Her hands were shaking. She rolled up the sleeve of her dress, tied her large handkerchief round her arm with an expert gesture and plunged the needle into the skin.

Helene was surprised to see how openly Martha let her watch all this. She had never used the syringe in front of her sister before. Helene rose and went over to the window. It looked out on a shady courtyard with maple trees, a carpet-beating frame and a small fountain. At this blue twilight hour, daffodils were in bloom.

Why are you doing that now?

Martha did not answer this question asked behind her back. Slowly, she pressed the contents of the syringe into her vein and sank back on to the bed.

Little angel, there could be no finer moment than this! We've arrived. We're here. Martha stretched out on the bed and reached one arm towards Helene. Berlin, she said softly, as if her voice were dying of happiness, drowning in it. We're in Berlin now.

Don't say such things. Helene took a step towards the trunk, found her brushes in its side pocket and let down her hair.

The poison is sweet, little angel. Don't look at me as if I were a damned soul. So I'm going to die some day – what about it? I suppose one's allowed to live a little first? Martha chuckled in a way that, just for a moment, reminded Helene of their mother, left behind at home in her deranged state of mind.

Lying on her back, Martha kicked off her shoes – she had obviously undone their long laces already – undid the buttons of her dress and, as if it were perfectly natural, placed one hand on her bare breast. Her skin was white, thin and delicate, so delicate that Helene could see the veins shimmering underneath it.

Helene combed her hair. She sat down at the washstand and poured some water into the basin from the silver jug, she picked up the fragrant soap, smelling of southern lavender, and washed. Now and then Martha sighed.

Will you sing me a song, little angel?

What shall I sing? Helene's voice had dried up. In spite of her long afternoon nap in the train, she felt tired, and could not find in herself the joy and happiness that she had expected to feel on arriving in Berlin, that she had in fact felt on the station.

Do you love me, dear heart, my golden girl?

Helene turned to Martha. Martha had difficulty concentrating her eyes on Helene; they kept sliding away from her and they looked as if the pupils filled them entirely.

Martha, do you need help? Helene looked at her sister, wondering if she was always like this just afterwards.

Martha hummed a tune that sounded very odd to Helene's ears, winding its way between F sharp major and B flat minor. I wonder if Aunt Fanny has a piano?

You haven't played for ages.

It's not too late. Martha giggled in that strange way again and smacked her lips slightly, as if she were having difficulty in suppressing her giggles. She retched. Next moment Martha sat up, reached for one of the little red glasses standing on the glass-fronted cupboard and spat into it.

Very elegant, a little spittoon like this. Our fine aunt thinks of everything.

Martha, what is all this? Helene gathered up her hair, twisted it to the sides of her head and pinned it up. We have to be out there in half an hour's time. Will you be able to manage that? Can you pull yourself together?

Why so worried, little angel? Haven't I managed everything so far? Everything.

Perhaps I'd better open the window.

Everything, little angel, what choice did I have but to manage everything? But now we're here, my golden girl.

Why do you call me your golden girl? That's what Father used to call me. Helene wanted to wrinkle her brow in a frown, but the dip between her forehead and her strikingly small nose was so shallow that only a few fine lines formed above her nose.

I know, I know. And did the pet name die with him, little angel?

Helene handed Martha a glass of water. Drink this. I hope that'll disperse the mists.

Tut, tut, tut, mists, dear heart. Martha shook her head. This is spring's awakening, little angel.

Please get dressed. I'll help you. And before Martha could turn down Helene's offer she was buttoning up her sister's dress.

And I thought you wanted to kiss me, dear heart. You didn't answer my question. Do you remember what I asked?

Helene was kneeling in front of Martha now to help her get

her shoes on. Martha dropped back on the bed and whispered: Dear heart, dear heart, you *will* answer me.

When Helene had tied her sister's laces, she tugged at her arm to make her sit up. Martha's long torso was heavy and swayed. She sank back once more.

Oh, my poor foot, it's too light to stay on this floor, please hold it. Martha saw Helene stretch both legs out stiffly in front of her so that they reached over the edge of the bed. At the same time she breathed deeply and raised her shoulders.

Can you stand up?

Easy, couldn't be easier. Martha stood up, leaning on Helene's arm, and raised her head. She was only a little taller than Helene now. Her words came out sharply and distinctly, with a hiss on every 's', although the intervals between the words were noticeably long. Perhaps Martha thought she had to speak like that to sound clear and sober.

Someone knocked at the door.

Yes? Helene opened it, and the housemaid Otta took a small step aside and bobbed a curtsy. Her cap was perched on her hair, looking as white and starched as if she had made no effort at all this evening.

Can I help the young ladies?

Thank you very much, we'll be all right. Helene plucked a hair off Martha's dress. How did you speak to housemaids in Berlin, she wondered?

You'll hear the gong for dinner in a minute. If you would like to come and sit down?

By all means, said Martha with dignity, and she walked past the housemaid with her head held high and into the long corridor. You could hardly see her swaying.

There were place cards at the dinner table. As soon as the party was seated a gentleman at the head of the table rose to his feet. He wore a ring on every finger, each more magnificent than the last. *Bonsoir, mes amis, copains et copines, cousin et cousine.* He raised his glass courteously to the company. His oily, combed-back hair rested on the collar of his shirt, his white face looked as if he were wearing make-up. He laughed out loud and now began speaking German with a French accent. It is an honour for me to wish my dear *cousine* . . . ah, why don't we throw the lies overboard today and devote ourselves to other vices? Let me say it's a joy to me to wish my young lover here good health and a long life. To Fanny, to our dear friend!

Astonished, Helene looked around. Could he have meant their Fanny, Aunt Fanny? How could the speaker call her his young lover when she might be in her mid-forties and he wasn't yet thirty? Fanny thanked him; her black eyes smiled under heavy lashes. Stars sparkled in her hair. She placed her hand on her long neck, and it looked as if she were caressing herself here at the dinner table in front of her guests. There was a net over her short dark hair that must be sprinkled with diamonds. Or perhaps they were just imitation gemstones, but she wore them like diamonds. The ladies and gentlemen raised their glasses and cried *enchanté*, and *à votre santé, ma chère*, and *à mon amie* to Aunt Fanny.

Martha was sitting very upright on the opposite side of the table, her eyes shining as she talked to her neighbours, laughing her clear laughter again and again, and letting them pour more champagne into her glass. Helene kept an eye on her; she intended to take care of her sister. Martha hardly touched the delicious food, now and then she put her fork into her vol-au-vent and later she kept blowing on her soufflé as if it were too hot. There was a grating, crackling noise from a large brass-coloured funnel, a voice croaked in song: *In fifty years we'll all be gone.* When the party moved from the table to sit on chaises longues, Martha gratefully took the arm of the man who had been sitting beside her at dinner listening to her chatter. Once Helene thought that Martha was crying. But as soon as she had made her way across the salon to her sister Martha was laughing, dabbing tears of delight from her face with the handkerchief that she had tied round her arm earlier. In the course of the evening Martha accepted cigarettes and smoked them through a holder that Helene had never seen in her sister's hands before. Later Fanny's lover, whose name was Bernard pronounced in the French way, had a pipe lit. Nothing less than opium could be offered in tribute to her, he opined. Her friends clapped.

Martha once called out, raising her voice: Oh, aunt, what a wonderful party – and Helene could hardly believe her ears, because she had never before heard Martha raise her voice like that, laughing, in such company. Aunt Fanny replied, also with laughter, from the other end of the big room: Aunt? Darling, is that what you're going to call me? I feel a hundred years older right away. An old lady – aren't aunts all old ladies? Fanny, darling, just Fanny!

No one offered Helene a pipe or cigarettes; she supposed word had gone round quickly that she was still under sixteen and came from Lusatia. Two gentlemen looked after the flapper, as they called her, pouring champagne for Helene and later on water, and obviously enjoying reminding each other that Helene was still a child. What a pretty flapper! It was charming to see her drink water from her glass. Was she always so thirsty? The two gentlemen were amusing themselves, while Helene took care never to lose sight of Martha. Martha was laughing with everyone, pouting prettily as if to kiss a young gentleman who hadn't taken his cap off. But next moment she put her arm round a half-naked woman who wore a sleeveless dress like Aunt Fanny's, and whose cries of ooh-la-la reached Helene's ears over all those heads, so shrill a sound that it hurt. Ooh-la-la, the woman kept crying, putting her own arm round Martha, and Helene clearly saw her hand fall on Martha's shoulder and later move to her waist, until it seemed as if the woman would never let go of her again. Was that a pipe Martha was smoking? Perhaps Helene was mistaken.

A little more water? One of the two gentlemen leaned forward to pour Helene water from the crystal carafe.

Late in the evening the party broke up. But not to go home, as Helene thought at first; they were all going on to a club together.

Help my niece into her coat, Fanny told one of her admirers, a tall blond man, her glance indicating Martha. She told Helene in kindly tones that she must make herself entirely at home and wished her sweet dreams.

But the sweet dreams were elusive and Helene couldn't sleep. Left alone with the servants, she had gone straight back to her room, but she couldn't help waiting up until the first light of dawn. Only when morning light came falling through the stone-grey curtains did she hear sounds in the apartment. A door closed. There were voices, laughter, steps approaching down the long corridor. Their bedroom door opened and Martha, half stumbling, half staggering, was helped into the room, where she immediately dropped on to Helene's bed. The door closed again. Out in the corridor, Helene heard Fanny laughing with her French lover and a woman friend, perhaps Lucinde. Helene got up, pushed the second bed up to hers and undressed Martha, who couldn't move anything but her lips now.

Little angel, we're here. The forfeit is a kiss. You only have to open the gates of heaven and you can go through. But Martha couldn't giggle any more; she snuffled and fell asleep, her head sinking to one side.

Helene got Martha into her nightdress, unpinned her hair

and laid her big sister down beside her. Martha smelled of wine and smoke, and a heavy scent that Helene couldn't place, both flowery and resinous. Helene put her arms firmly round Martha, and she was still staring into the dim light by the time Martha was snoring softly.

The approaching winter brought heavy snow. Martha and Helene had pushed the trunk far under one of their beds, and even at Christmas it didn't occur to them to pack it and go back to Bautzen to visit their mother. A letter from Mariechen came at the beginning of every month. It described their mother's state of health, mentioned the weather and the domestic finances. While Fanny enjoyed Martha's company, took her to every club and every revue, Helene relished the quiet of the ground-floor apartment. What a large library Fanny had, full of books that she herself had obviously never read, but she must feel flattered by the sight of them. Helene often spent the night reading on the chaise longue. If Fanny and Martha came staggering home in the small hours, with a man in tow but keeping in the background, and their eyes fell on Helene they burst out laughing. But was Fanny frowning? Perhaps she didn't like Helene to read her books. Oh, child, laughed Fanny, raising an admonitory forefinger, you need your sleep if you want to be beautiful. And when Helene was lying in bed later, smelling the smoke and perfume of Martha's evening, she would hesitantly reach out, stroke Martha's back and rest her hand on Martha's hip. Helene fell asleep to the sound of her sister's regular breathing.

I love you girls, Fanny assured them one morning as they sat on her veranda round the low table, which had a tiled top painted with pale roses, drinking tea and nibbling little sticks of ginger. The veranda was full of the scent of bergamot. Fanny drank her tea with a great deal of sugar and no milk. Every morning a plate of poppyseed cake stood on the table, but Helene had never tasted it; she felt shy of reaching over the table uninvited and helping herself to a piece. Fanny's lover must still be in bed – in the boudoir, Fanny liked to say. Or at least one of her lovers. Recently a new one had frequently visited the apartment, tall, fair-haired Erich. Like Bernard, he was a few immaterial years younger than Fanny. She didn't seem to have chosen between the two of them, but they were seldom both her guests at the same time. Also like Bernard, Erich usually slept until midday, but while Bernard spent the rest of the day betting on horses and watching the trotting races, tall blond Erich frequented the Grünewald tennis courts, and now in winter the indoor courts. Once he had asked Helene if she would like to go with him. He had waited to invite her until a moment came when Fanny wasn't around, and he had put his hand on the back of her neck so suddenly and with such passion that she had been afraid of coming across Erich ever since. It was true that in front of Fanny he took not the slightest notice of her, but his glances fell on her all the more avidly when Fanny's back was turned. Today the veranda windows were clouded with condensation; the heating was still full on in the apartment, and February snow lay on the trees and rooftops.

The door opened and the housemaid Otta brought in a tray with a pot of freshly brewed tea. From Ceylon, said Otta, placing the tray on the table. She put a silver cover over the pot to keep it hot, and left.

I do love you girls, whispered Fanny again. Her black poodle, who answered to the name of Cleo – Fanny pronounced it in the English way and said it was short for Cleopatra – wagged her short tail, a soft ball of hair. Cleo's coat shone as she looked attentively from one young woman to another. When Fanny threw the dog a little piece of poppyseed cake, Cleo snapped it up without looking at her, as if she weren't waiting for something sweet at all, but was giving all her attention to the girls' conversation. Fanny dabbed at her nose with her handkerchief; she blew her nose a lot, and not just in winter.

Oh, my poor nose is all inflamed again, she whispered, lost in thought as she stared at her knees, like my mind in general. But children, I do love you.

Leontine was perched on the wooden arm of Martha's chair, jiggling her toes impatiently. Martha had met Leontine again in summer, and since then they had seen each other daily. These days Leontine was spending the night at the ground-floor apartment in Achenbachstrasse more and more often.

My friend says they have only one vacancy. They're looking for an experienced nurse. That's Martha. Fanny made a sympathetic little moue in Helene's direction and batted her eyelashes, to show Helene that she was genuinely sorry. Helene, dear, something else will very soon turn up for you too, sweetheart.

Martha was to start work next week at the Jewish Hospital in Exerzierstrasse, in the north of the city. Fanny had an admirer who was medical director of the ward for the terminally ill. Fanny said he was old and randy, and had described the post as might have been expected of him. The nurse was to be between twenty and thirty. Just like Martha. Yes, the applicant must be the right age, he only liked women of that age, which was why his admiration for Fanny had faded slightly over the last few years. It was difficult to find staff for the terminal ward because of all the incurable illnesses and dying patients, so the management would prefer an older nurse. Well, of course twenty-six was far from old, but all the same Martha had more experience than Helene, didn't she?

Helene tried to look content with that. Martha couldn't suppress a yawn. She was still wearing the silk dressing gown that her aunt had recently passed on to her.

Leontine nodded on Martha's behalf. Absolutely right, no one's Martha's equal in emptying and filling things, cleaning up the patients and soothing them, feeding them and applying dressings.

And you'll learn the right prayers, won't you? Fanny meant it seriously. She took Martha to synagogue with her on high days and holidays, but even at home Martha had not been very diligent over saying her prayers in St Peter's Cathedral.

Martha picked a stick of ginger out of the flower-shaped glass dish, crooked her little finger and nibbled the ginger stick. Over the last few months, Helene and Martha had often discussed their reluctance to be a burden on their aunt, living at her expense. They were enjoying life in the big apartment, but they would have liked to give Fanny some money for their board and also to have money of their own to spend. Accepting financial presents made them feel uncomfortable. There had turned out to be problems with the Breslau legacy. The rents didn't come in regularly, and the agent who was supposed to be managing them hadn't sent any news for months. Martha and Helene couldn't bring themselves to ask their aunt for money to send home to Bautzen. When a letter arrived from Mariechen, appealing for help and saying she didn't know where to turn for money to buy food for their mother, Helene had stolen into the larder and taken some provisions, which they sent by parcel post to Bautzen. At the same time Martha had abstracted one of Fanny's gramophone records and taken it to the pawnbroker's to exchange for some money. A loan was the way Martha and Helene had described it to each other, until one day Aunt Fanny asked casually if they knew what had become of her Richard Tauber record, which seemed to have disappeared. Helene had been overcome by a coughing fit so that they could avoid telling all to Fanny. Martha said at once that she had dropped it and it broke. She just hadn't dared to tell her aunt, she said. False remorse? Martha's look of wide-eyed innocence was astonishing, as always. Fanny proved magnanimous.

Martha and Helene had applied for posts at several hospitals over the last few months, but so far unsuccessfully. The whole city seemed to be looking for work, and those who did have a job wanted a better one with higher pay. If you had no job you did deals, but the sisters didn't understand enough about that. People dropped hints about the black market, and bets, and how only pretty girls could sell their services for some things, at least at the revues. Fanny's friend Lucinde worked in a revue, naked, as she said with relish, wearing nothing but her hair. Helene's nursing certificates from Bautzen won her some admiration, but her age put the hospitals off, she was considered too young for a permanent nursing post in a hospital.

I'll take the job. Martha put the nibbled ginger stick down on the rim of her saucer. She rested her head against Leontine and held her hand in front of her mouth. Fanny looked at Leontine and Martha, smiled, and ran her tongue first over her teeth and then over her lips.

I'm glad. But you know you are my guests – for ever, if you like. So far as I'm concerned you don't have to work. You do know that, don't you? Fanny looked round at them. She might have no husband and no parents any more, but obviously Fanny was still so rich, without anyone to share her fortune, that she had no financial worries. I wasn't including Leontine, of course, said Fanny, but then who wouldn't like to have a beautiful woman as a hospital doctor? When do you take your exams, Leontine?

In the autumn. I'm not hoping for too much – I'll start with Professor Friedrich at the Charité Hospital. He may help me to get my further degree and my lecturer's qualification.

Oh, you disappoint me, darling. I see you in a little doctor's car, stopping outside my house with your medical bag. Why not aim for a big private practice – you could get young assistants to help you, men like Erich or Bernard?

Flattered, Leontine smiled. She had developed a curious flexibility in Berlin, she smiled more often, sometimes just with her eyes, and even her movements had become as graceful as a cat's. Leontine rose and went round the table. She took Helene's blonde braid in both hands, as if weighing it, then placed one hand on Helene's head. Helene felt warm; there was nothing nicer than the sensation of Leontine's hand on her head.

Private patients still don't trust a woman doctor, said Leontine, raising her eyebrows with a rueful look. And I don't have the necessary funds either.

Well, of course your assistants don't need to be men; you could have woman assistants, Leontine. Like Martha and Helene. Fanny chuckled. I hear you're married to some feeble-minded palaeontologist. One might think he had funds.

Lorenz, feeble-minded? Leontine's eyes sparkled. Who says so? My dear husband wouldn't feel at all confident about it if I set up in private practice. Now Leontine was laughing, the wry laughter they knew from the old days.

Surely he must be feeble-minded if he doesn't notice that his wife fails to spend the night at home! Fanny's tongue slid along her top row of teeth again, then licked her lips.

Lorenz is liberal on principle – and he's lost interest in me anyway.

Fanny threw her poodle Cleo a morsel of poppyseed cake and poured herself a glass of brandy. Now her eye fell on Helene. Leontine says you can use a typewriter and do shorthand? Fanny's nose was running, but she noticed too late. She only just managed to catch the trickle on her chin with her handkerchief. Didn't you keep the accounts in your father's printing works?

Helene diffidently shrugged her shoulders. It seemed so long ago that she'd done these things. Her old life had retreated into the distance; she didn't like to think about it. She practised not remembering – that, she had recently whispered to a young man making up to her at a party, was the only way to hold on to youth. And she had looked at him so innocently that the young man had to take her seriously and wanted to agree with her.

Helene had spent most of the last few months in Berlin reading in Fanny's library, going for walks and facing up to her private worries about Martha. She seldom let Martha out of her sight, although she admired the fearlessness with which Martha and Leontine smuggled themselves into every louche club in Bülowstrasse. Helene hated the nights when she was woken by the moans of her sister and her sister's friend. She never felt lonelier than there in her narrow bed, although it was less than a metre away from the equally narrow bed where Martha and Leontine were panting for breath. Sometimes they giggled, sometimes they stopped, whispered and wondered out loud, so that Helene was bound to hear it, whether they had woken her up with their whispers. Then again there were the sounds of kissing, the sighs, particularly Martha's, and the rustling of the bedclothes. Sometimes Helene thought she could almost feel the warmth radiating from their bodies.

You know my friend Clemens the pharmacist – he's looking for a girl to help him, someone who can use a typewriter, a pretty girl who'd be nice to the customers. I could ask him.

184

That's her all over, said Leontine, stroking Helene's hair.

You're discreet, aren't you? Martha wrinkled her brow doubtfully.

That's her all over too, repeated Leontine, still stroking Helene's hair.

Pharmacists keep secrets. Fanny was not exactly whispering, but murmuring in her velvety voice. Mine, Bernard's, Lucinde's, half the city's secrets.

Helene didn't know what to say in reply. Unlike Martha, she had not managed to win Fanny's affection and confidence. They had been living with their aunt for almost a year now, Fanny passed on her clothes to them and introduced them to her circle of friends, but it seemed as if she thought Helene a naïve child and would do all she could to ensure that didn't change. Sometimes Helene thought she detected a kind of reserve towards her in Fanny. She discussed certain things only with Martha, whether they were to do with clothes or society gossip. Helene had seldom felt as much aware of the nine years' age difference between herself and Martha as she did in their aunt's presence. Usually all the doors on the ground floor stood open, but when Fanny called Martha into a room with her she often closed the door, and Helene guessed that behind it her little round box with the tiny spoon and the white powder was coming out, something she shared only with Martha and no one else. Then Helene would stand on tiptoe, listening, and hear her sniffing and sighing, and at those moments, when she stood on tiptoe with her cold feet in a dark corridor, with only the pendulum of the white English grandfather clock and its golden dial to keep her company, she was sorry she had come to Berlin with Martha. Fanny had never once asked if Helene would like to go out with them in the evening.

Only when Leontine and Martha visited the now rather faded

Luna Park was Helene allowed to go too. The girls went in the old artificial wave pool there – the waves were generated only by the wind now – and splashed about, taking no notice of the gentlemen, both young and older, who strolled around the rim of the basin to watch them. The artificial wave pool was nick-named the Nymphs' Basin and the Tarts' Aquarium in the city, which seemed to the girls poor ways of expressing the lively interest shown by the young and old gentlemen. The girls liked the waves and the slide into the lake, and paid for their own entrance. Didn't that mean the male spectators had no right to regard themselves as pimps and potential customers?

I'll tell you girls something: this is a small city. The world thinks it's large because it's such a beautiful soap bubble in our imagination. Fanny lit one of her English cigars and tilted her head back. Each fantastic bubble stretches, grows bigger, brighter, more fragile. Is it falling? Fanny drew on the thin cigar. Is it rising? Fanny puffed little smoke rings. Is it coming down? Fanny was enjoying her flight of fancy, but then her smile disappeared. Well, Helene, if you can keep secrets the pharmacist would appre-ciate that. So would I. I'll ask him about the job. Fanny nodded as if to confirm her words and encourage herself. She drained the final drop of brandy from her small glass and dabbed her nose carefully with her handkerchief. A tear ran from the corner of her eye. Oh, dear children, how I love you. You do know that you don't need to work, don't you? Why should you be any worse off than Erich and Bernard? Stay with me, fill my home and my heart, she said, visibly moved. By her own loneliness, Helene wondered, or by the idea of her generous heart? Fanny blew her nose and caressed Cleo's muzzle.

The doorbell rang. A little later Otta appeared to announce a visitor. Your friend the Baron, mademoiselle. He's arrived with several suitcases. Shall I get a room ready for him?

Oh dear, did I forget that? Dear Otta, yes, please get a room ready, the gold room will be best. He'll be staying some time, he wants to look around Berlin. Turning to Martha, Fanny said, He's a painter, a real artist. Fanny opened her reddened eyes. The ash on her cigar was getting long. She looked around for something. She had lost track of the ashtray and knocked the ash off the cigar on to the plate of poppyseed cake. The Baron tried his luck in Paris, now he's come here. It's only here he thinks he can paint to his heart's content. If only! These days everyone wants to found a club and be head of it. Fanny gave herself a little shake. Only recently, she said, she had met a lively little man who talked a lot about himself and had made a name for himself too, an artist who rejected any notion of meaningful content in his work. It was just the outer form he valued, the artist's way of life, recognition and of course followers. Yes, he founded a club and made himself head of it. He was in earnest, that was what surprised Fanny. There must have been something about the encounter, she said, that displeased her in retrospect. Perhaps it was his claim to have a large following who loved, indeed idolized him.

The girls looked up, curious to see the visitor. Martha and Helene had never met an aristocrat in person before. But it soon turned out in conversation that he wasn't a baron, that was only his surname: Baron, Heinrich Baron.

He didn't have much of anything and in particular he didn't have much money. What little he did have, he would like to share with a pretty young girl who would model for him and get him drawing and drawing until he dropped. The Baron was a small man; any man the same height as Helene wasn't tall. His forehead was high, his hair sparse, with a parting from his hairline to the back of his head. She liked his eyes. Their sad, lost expression easily inspired confidence and yes, they could make a young girl like Helene seem larger, more important.

Even if Helene didn't quite like the way the Baron's eyes lingered on her, to be the object of his attention promised her some protection from tall Erich, who could hardly find a moment now when they wouldn't be disturbed if he manoeuvred Helene into a dark corner, and while Fanny had popped into the kitchen to look for Otta and Martha was working at the hospital, and there was no one around to see it but Cleo with her watchful eyes and the trustful wagging of her tail, he put a hand on her breast and stuck his fat, wet tongue into her ear, breathing heavily as he moved it around inside. As soon as Helene, holding her breath in alarm – for it never occurred to her to cry out – heard first from the light padding of Cleo's paws that Fanny was on her way back from the kitchen, and then Fanny's own footsteps were audible, Erich would let go of her as suddenly as he had seized her and stroll easily away to meet Fanny. Why didn't she get her tennis racket, he asked, and go to Grünewald with him? He had borrowed a car and he knew she liked driving.

One day the Baron took off his glasses, cleaned them and ran his hand lightly over his high forehead. He asked Helene if she would like to earn a little something. Helene felt flattered; no artist had ever wanted to draw her before. She also felt shy and ashamed. Who, aside from Martha, had ever seen her naked?

Shame was for other girls, not for beauties like her, said the Baron out loud from the other end of the room where they had agreed to meet, on a Sunday morning when no one was going to church or even thinking of God. He hoped that this remark would bring Helene out from behind the screen. She wasn't being asked to show herself for nothing, she'd be paid for it. The Baron waved a banknote. He didn't mind that her breasts were tiny, he took it as a sign of her youth. He liked her blonde hair. He laughed: why, she was still just a child. He liked that, and he drew and drew, though he never did drop from exhaustion. Helene felt tired. After several weeks he told her she was an enchantress who looked different every day, she helped him to see in a new way. The Baron said she presented him with new eyes daily. He gave her newly minted coins and banknotes fresh from the printer in the Reichsmark currency, superseding the Rentenmark notes first issued in 1923, and to Helene they seemed like tickets to a new life of her own choosing.

She went to the pharmacist's during the day now, she showed how discreet she could be there, and in the evening she undressed for the Baron who regarded her as both an enchantress and a child, but in whose presence she felt like a woman for the first time. She didn't let him know that. After all, she felt that way because of the sense of shame and the excitement, not because of the assessing look with which he walked around her, asked her to sit down, to lie down, to hold her arm at a certain angle, to move her left leg a little further, yes, to spread her legs like that; and then, quite soon, he contracted tendonitis. Helene couldn't help being reminded of those dragons who lived among rocks and ate virgins. Not that she felt guilty in any way; she was sorry for him. He couldn't hold his charcoal any more, Helene wasn't asked to undress again. So she no longer earned her share of what little money he did have, but worked longer hours at the pharmacy instead.

In the evening, when she came home from the pharmacy, Helene brought back a small box of white powder and placed it on Fanny's bedside table without a word, as evidence that she was trustworthy. Leontine provided for Martha's needs, if reluctantly, and it was only on rare occasions, when a good opportunity offered, that Helene brought some morphine back from the pharmacy for her sister. The Baron sat on the chaise longue in his room in the Berlin apartment, waiting for Helene with his sad, lost eyes. Helene was glad he just looked at her and didn't touch. All the women around her were involved in relationships. Helene didn't feel too young for that any more, it was just that she couldn't make up her mind. She bandaged the Baron's arm and put cold and warm compresses on his tendon. He gave her a bunch of bright yellow daisies, which she happily accepted. As she put the flowers in a vase she imagined that they were late roses and wondered how she would have felt if Clemens the pharmacist had given them to her. Helene wanted to be in love, to know all the boundless ardour and the fears that she supposed went with that condition. Was this all there was to it, a tingling sensation in the pit of her stomach, a trembling below her breasts? She had to smile. She couldn't agree with Fanny's belief that Clemens was one of her suitors. The gaunt pharmacist – Helene thought of him all the time when she had a day off – wouldn't look Fanny or any other woman in the eye a moment longer than necessary. He didn't watch any of them walking away either, he never said a word more than he had to. Only when his wife came into the pharmacy with two or three of their five children clinging to her skirts, to fetch something or ask him a question, her round face red with cold and her big blue eyes shining, did the pharmacist's face open up and then he came to life. He would kiss his wife and hug his children as if he hardly ever saw them.

The apothecary did not come from a prosperous family; he worked hard for his money and still had debts against the pharmacy. If Fanny thought of him as a friend it might be because she didn't realize how important money was to him. Helene typed his orders, letters and accounts for him. He showed her the consistencies to which fats and acids could be mixed, taught her what she needed to know about the reactions of bases with acids, and finally lent her a big book to read at home. Helene knew that this information might come in useful for any future medical studies of hers, and she mastered all the knowledge that came her way. She made it her habit to pack up five of the woodruff-flavoured sweets called May leaves for the pharmacist every evening, and if the big jar holding them was empty to take raspberry and violet-flavoured sweets out of the little jar instead. His children liked them. Helene did his accounts, she mixed ointments, and she stayed in the pharmacy after closing time when he hurried home to his wife and children. Abstracting drugs was easy. After a while Helene recognized the signatures and stamps of the various doctors; she knew who prescribed what for whom and where she could add a nought to the orders. Two grams of cocaine became twenty, but only very occasionally did she make one gram of morphine into ten or a hundred. She took the orders herself and she knew when the supplier came. She arranged the jars and boxes herself too, signed receipts for the substances, weighed them out. The pharmacist knew he could trust Helene. She relieved him of responsibility and of part of his work as well. When she ground crystals to powder and put them into capsules, or poured liquids into small bottles, all she needed was brief instructions and a fleeting smile. In the course of time Helene also learned to mix alcohol with expensive active agents and to calculate the mixture of bases and acids for tinctures, so that she didn't have to pester the pharmacist with questions any more.

But the pharmacist's smile was too fleeting. A gentle tingling in the pit of her stomach, a quivering sensation beneath her breasts, did not yet kindle any fire, did not provide Helene with the relationship that she thought was her due by now.

The Baron flattered her and his attentive eyes watched her, but he missed every opportunity, however good it was, to reach out to Helene.

Early one evening they were all sitting together. Martha had laid her head on Leontine's lap and gone to sleep, Fanny was arguing with Erich over how to spend the rest of the evening and Helene was reading the new translation of *Le Rouge et le Noir*. The Baron was sitting in an armchair beside Helene, sipping a glass of absinthe and listening.

Leontine excused Martha and herself, and made an elaborate business of getting to her feet, while Martha complained that her bones, her nerves, even the roots of her hair all hurt. Leontine had to half carry Martha, half support her to the bed they shared. As soon as the two of them had left the room Erich jumped up, suddenly in vigorous mood. The night was young yet, he said, but not for long, and he wanted to start out at once. Fanny held him back by his shirt. Erich shook her off. Oh, take me with you, she begged. Doors slammed.

Suddenly Helene was alone with the Baron; she went on reading about Julien Sorel and how he offered to leave Madame Rénal's house, apparently to save the honour of the lady of his heart but to save their love too, and how the lady then rose, prepared for anything. Was this not like the moment when the distance between the Baron and Helene would disappear entirely, would melt away? He had only to put out his hand, aroused by the strange passion that seemed even greater here than on the pages of the book. But when he did raise his hand, it was only to place it on the arm of his chair between himself and Helene. He was holding his glass in his other hand, took the last sip and topped it up. Helene felt her impatience turning to annoyance. She stopped reading.

Would you like a drink too, Helene?

She nodded, although she didn't want one. Julien would never have asked anything so mundane. Helene's eyes fell on the first page: *The truth! The bitter truth!* Helene guessed why Stendhal quoted that cry of Danton's. Undeterred, the Baron poured a small glass for Helene, drank to her and asked if she didn't want to go on with her book. Perhaps he had noticed her hesitation, for he started telling her his own story, talking with a certain pleasure. He had lived in France, he said, he spoke French fluently, but he had never found time to read this particular novel. How grateful he was that Helene had opened his eyes to that world too. Helene felt rising weariness and only half-heartedly suppressed a yawn. A virgin should be a virgin should be a virgin. She did go on reading, but with no enjoyment and she soon felt it was a strain. Her cheeks, only recently flushed with expectation, turned pale. A headache was rising from the nape of her neck. When the grandfather clock in the corridor struck ten, Helene closed the book.

Didn't she want to read any more? The Baron seemed surprised.

No. Helene stood up, her throat dry. The taste of the absinthe made her feel slightly sick. She just wanted to be in her bed, and she hoped that Martha and Leontine would be fast asleep in the room they all shared.

S pring flew past and nothing woke or came to life. Helene's nineteenth birthday was in June, on the longest day. Still not twenty-one, but old enough, as Fanny and Martha thought, to go to the White Mouse club with them for the first time. Fanny gave Helene a narrow envelope containing a voucher, made out in her wonderfully sloping handwriting, for a girls' course in grammar-school education, at classes held in Marburger Strasse. The course was to begin in September and would fit in perfectly with Helene's work at the pharmacy, since all the classes were in the evening. For some inexplicable reason Fanny had headed the voucher *On Probation*, underlining this all-embracing title, and it seemed to Helene as if, by that, she meant to point to those invisible pitfalls that her kind gesture must not gloss over.

Helene thanked her, but Fanny just looked at her sternly and began talking to Martha about the first beauty contest on German soil, to take place next year. Fanny thought that Martha definitely ought to enter.

I'm just bones and a bundle of nerves, said Martha, exhausted.

Oh, come on, replied Fanny, people see you better from outside. Look at yourself. Fanny put her long hand on the nape of Martha's neck. Helene had to look away.

On a whim, and to annoy the Baron, Leontine cut Helene's hair short that afternoon, level with her earlobes, and shaved away the rim of hair left in the nape of her neck with a knife. How light her head felt now!

In honour of the day, said Leontine, and got Helene to kiss her by way of thanks. To think that Helene would ever be so close to her own earlobes! Could she, Leontine, kiss those earlobes? Helene merely touched Leontine's cheeks briefly with hers, her kisses flew into the air above Leontine's shoulders, two, three, four, only Helene's nose touched her friend's ears. How did Leontine manage to smell as she once had in Lusatia, even today?

During the hair-cutting operation, the Baron kept passing the open doorway of the bathroom, putting his head round the door on a variety of threadbare pretexts and uttering wails of dismay. He couldn't bear to watch, he cried, one hand going to his flies, barely in time to cover himself. It was a sin and a shame!

Martha gave Helene a knee-length dress of satin and chiffon that she had worn herself last season. It had originally been Fanny's. Helene would be tall enough to wear it now, that was true. But Helene wasn't as thin as Fanny and Martha. Without hesitating, Leontine said she would let out the dress at the seams and asked for a needle. In less than half an hour the dress fitted Helene perfectly. Out of the corner of her eye, Helene saw the Baron bending down to pick up her hair from the floor. He laid the long golden tresses over his arm and left the bathroom almost unnoticed, taking them with him. Fanny announced that she felt both too old and too young for satin. But the dress was just the thing for Helene, Fanny added, and she didn't look again once Helene had the dress on. Presumably the grammar-school course and the dress must seem to her a good way of getting rid of Helene.

A summer night, the air was warm, a breeze was rising. Was Helene a little uneasy about her new hairstyle? She put on the hat that had come to Bautzen from Breslau along with their great-uncle's legacy, the cloche hat like those all the women wore now, except that hers was made of velvet and set with small paste gemstones.

Fanny went ahead with Lucinde and the Baron; Leontine and Martha took Helene between them and linked arms with her. The scent of lime blossom wafted in their faces. Helene was wearing a transparent organza scarf instead of a jacket. The wind was pleasantly cool on her throat.

Two white-faced people stood at the entrance of the White Mouse; their make-up didn't tell you for sure whether they were men or women. These doorkeepers unsmilingly negotiated the admission of guests. Those they knew were welcomed, strangers were turned away. Fanny was recognized and had a confidential word with one of the two doorkeepers, no doubt saying that the Baron, Lucinde and the young ladies were in her party. The door-keeper was happy with that and opened the door for them with a gesture of invitation. The bar was not particularly large; guests stood crowded close together. Further forward, near a stage, there were tables with guests sitting at them. The days were gone when the famous Anita Berber performed her Dance of Vice and Horror here, a spectacle that was also called a Dance of Death; it was said that she now danced in a real theatre but didn't appear often. However, all the guests could still imagine her on this stage. Their eyes kept going to the red curtains as if they thought she might appear at any moment and perform. Everyone had read how her lover stole from her in Vienna and abandoned her, thereafter travelling to America, where he was reported to have married four women within a single year. The latest rumour was that he had died soon after returning to Hamburg.

So there was no Anita Berber, but instead three musicians soon gathered on the stage, a trombonist, a clarinettist and a trumpeter. And while Helene still thought that the long-drawn-out notes were just tuning up, some of the guests began dancing. Helene was pushed on through the crowd, Fanny handed in her cape at the cloakroom and, without asking, removed Helene's hat. Lucinde ordered champagne and glasses. They whispered, wasn't that Margo Lion, standing over there among a cluster of people? The Baron's eyes were turned only on Helene; they clung to her, to her face, her shoulders, her hands. His glances made her feel both safe and uncomfortable. The bare nape of her neck was probably a challenge to him, and not unwelcome, as Helene said to herself, but very exciting. Suddenly she felt breath on her shoulder and the Baron said, in his soft voice that almost squeaked when he tried to make it sound firm: Helene, you're losing your scarf. Helene looked down at herself, at a loss, and then at the Baron, who seemed to her even smaller than usual tonight. Once again his lips approached; he was almost kissing her throat. I can see the little dimples in your shoulders, they're sending me crazy.

Helene couldn't help laughing. Someone pushed her gently in the back.

You'd better put that scarf round your shoulders again or other men will discover you.

She supposed the Baron was trying to claim rights to her bare shoulders. Helene turned. Fanny and Lucinde stood behind her; they had met Bernard and a friend of his. Fanny told her friends and her nieces to take a glass each from the tray. It was lucky that this club was so noisy. Helene didn't want to answer the Baron; she draped the scarf casually over her elbows. Batting her false eyelashes was exciting too, and she had no objection at all if other men saw her little dimples.

Leontine greeted a young man and introduced him to her: his name was Carl Wertheimer. The music was so loud now that

Leontine had to shout, and the young man put his hands over his ears. He was one of her pathology students, Leontine shouted, he'd smuggled himself into her course, he was really studying philosophy and languages – Latin, Greek – and modern literature too, he was obviously going to be a poet. Carl Wertheimer shook his head vigorously. Never. Oh yes, said Leontine, laughing, she'd once seen him standing in a group of students reciting a poem, she was sure he'd written it himself. Carl Wertheimer seemed bewildered by all this. He was a perfectly ordinary student, he said, and if he did quote Ovid or Aristotle, that wasn't to be compared with the efforts of the rising generation of writers to emulate them. Anyway, he added, he wouldn't have the courage to confess to such attempts of his own in the presence of these clever ladies. Leontine ran her hand over his hair in a sisterly way, she made him seem like a small child. Helene looked searchingly at him; his eyes were level with hers, his slender physique was that of a boy. He was probably about Helene's own age. She looked at him for a moment like someone who might be hers, but all his attention was given to Leontine. It was obvious that Carl Wertheimer looked up to her and not just because she appeared to be several centimetres taller than he was. Leontine was an unusual woman and no doubt he valued her as a teacher; perhaps he was a little in love with her.

Other musicians joined the three on stage, also playing trombones, clarinets and trumpets. The notes dragged along, the beat lurched and swayed. To Helene's surprise, more and more people around her began to dance, and soon she could hardly see the dance floor as the parquet under her feet vibrated in time to the music. Fanny and Bernard were ahead of everyone else, Lucinde took Bernard's friend's hand, even Martha and Leontine mingled with the dancers and only the Baron held back. He stood guard over the tray of glasses, his back to the wall, and he never took his eyes off Helene, who still stood there undecided. A hand was laid gently on her arm. Would she like to dance, asked a clean-shaven man; he took the glass from her hand and led her away with him. He held tight to Helene with one hand, as if he had to be careful, as if the music might lure her away; it was slow at first, then fast, and his other hand, as if by chance, touched her bare arm while they danced. The music spared nothing, no living creature, it went through her, took every particle of her and transformed the room into fragments of time. A moment ago the place had been quiet, motionless, but now it was in uproar, or so it seemed to Helene, an uproar that not only set every molecule and every organ swaying but strained the frames of the dancers' bodies and the bounds of the room itself to the utmost without breaking them apart. The music stretched, filled the place with a dull glow, glittering softly, a spray of delicate melodies no longer observing ordinary musical rules; it bent the bodies of the dancers, doubled them up, raised them again, reeds blowing in the wind. Once the clean-shaven man put his hand on Helene's hips and she jumped, but he only wanted to keep her from colliding with another dancing couple. Helene looked around, she saw Leontine's throat, her short dark hair; Helene moved sideways, making her way past the bodies that bent towards her and then turned away, tracing a winding path through the dancers, and the clean-shaven man followed every step she took, past other dancers, ducking below their arms, until Helene caught Martha's hand and saw Leontine's smile. The clean-shaven man gestured frantically, looked indignant, did a handstand and landed on his feet again. Helene couldn't help laughing. She tried to follow the beat, her shoulders and arms moved, the people around her writhed and swirled in the music, became entangled with each other, trod on one another's feet. The music reminded Helene of being on a swing: if someone gave you a push the impetus of the swing carried everything away with it, made straight for its target, but in the next bar it began to falter. It made you swing and stretch your legs first this way, then that, and a reeling, rolling, spinning movement began, an elliptical circling, ever-decreasing with its own logic. Martha's head was nodding alarmingly, her hair was coming loose, she flung out her arms in Leontine's direction as if she were drowning. Helene saw her glazed eyes, their gaze veiled by night, unable to focus on anyone now, unable to recognize anyone. She waved to Martha, but now Martha was leaning on Leontine with a drunken, rather foolish smile on her face. The trumpet cut in strongly, provided impetus, the dancers began sweating, the women's bare arms and shoulders gleamed in the narrow beams of light cast by the small lamps. Next moment Helene couldn't see the violet blue of Leontine's dress any more and Martha's maudlin smile had disappeared; a new rhythm began. Helene looked around, but she could see neither Leontine nor Martha. Meanwhile, she caught sight of the back of her clean-shaven dancing partner, now dancing with another young woman.

Helene found herself alone in the midst of the excited crowd. The music surrounded her, possessed her, trying to permeate her and leave her at the same time. Helene flung out her arms and her legs. Anxiety took over her body; she knew none of the dance movements, but she did still know where the floor was. Even if the floor gave way, her feet were landing on it and rising up again, so feet and floor depended on each other. Helene tried to reach the edge of the crowd, where she thought the Baron might be, although she couldn't see his hat, nor could she see any of the rest of her party, but the dancers pushed her further and further into the crowd, and her legs never stopped following the rhythm. There was nowhere you could more easily disappear than in the midst of all these dancers. Helene gave herself up to the dance;

the sound of the clarinets chased her feet on, the musical beat was catching up with her, she was punching holes in the air with her arms.

A hand reached for her; she didn't know the man. His face was covered with white make-up, his lips were almost black, and Helene danced. With every dance her partner's face and figure changed. Soon Leontine and Martha reappeared. Martha smiled at her as she danced; perhaps, just perhaps, that smile was really aimed in her direction, meant for the music, for her brief disappearance, but Helene wasn't trying to get near Martha any more. Someone else's glance had been following Helene for some time in the darkness near the platform, from one of the little tables with the small green lamps. Helene recognized Carl Wertheimer and was glad that he had finally noticed her. Perhaps he was just curious to find out what Leontine's friends were like. His glance was attentive, but it didn't bother her. Carl Wertheimer still wore his coat; its smooth fur collar shone, perhaps he was about to leave. He was smoking a short, slender pipe. His eyes kept going to the other dancers, to Leontine, then back to Helene. In spite of his youth, Helene couldn't help thinking, his features were grave and dignified.

The clarinet called, Helene leaped after it; the trombone pushed at her and Helene leaned back; the trumpet beckoned her on, but Helene hesitated.

Soon after that she twisted her ankle, stumbled and lost her balance. She grabbed Martha's shoulder to keep herself from falling and leaned on it. Martha must have mistaken her for someone else; she roughly shook off Helene's hand. The little strap of Helene's shoe was broken; there was nothing she could do but hold the shoe in her hand and make her way through the sweet-sour odour of the dancing crowd. When she reached the stage she turned left. As soon as she was away from the stuffy warmth of the dancers and their hot clutches she felt a cool draught coming from the darkness. Were there windows somewhere? She couldn't see any. Perhaps someone had opened the door to let in some air. Helene looked over the dancers' heads; a long way off, at the back of the room, she saw Fanny's white face. Fortunately there was no sign of the Baron's hat. Would she like a drink? Someone jostled her. Helene said a quick no, thank you, and hurried on. She passed figures exhausted by the night's revels and pale early-morning faces. A shiver ran down her back, and unexpectedly she was looking into the eyes of Carl Wertheimer, the thin-faced young man.

Excuse me, he said, I think you're a friend of Leontine's. His voice was remarkably deep for one so young. Her gaze fell on his fur collar. It shimmered so beautifully that she would have liked to stroke the fur.

Helene nodded; of course he didn't know her name. So she said: Helene, I'm Helene Würsich.

Wertheimer, Carl Wertheimer. Fräulein Leontine was kind enough to introduce me to her friends at the beginning of the evening.

You're her student.

He nodded and offered her his arm. Do you need help?

I do indeed, my shoe's broken. Helene held the shoe out to him. She thought of Martha, looked round in alarm, and saw her sister among the dancers with her arms round Leontine. It almost looked as if Martha were going to kiss Leontine in front of everyone. A slight uneasiness, a momentary revulsion overcame Helene; it was not so much the faint sense of being shut out as fear of this stranger's discovering everything, of revelation of the network in which she too belonged, as Martha's sister and ally. Helene wanted to divert Wertheimer's attention.

Have you known Dr Leontine long?

Our aunt invited us to stay. She has lots of friends. Helene made a vague gesture. I'm afraid I have to leave now.

Of course. May I accompany you? I don't think you ought to be limping home alone through the empty streets.

Yes, please. I'd like that. I'm afraid, she said, thinking of the pigeons picking seeds out of the ashes in the Cinderella story, that I don't have either ashes or pigeons to lend me charms. Then she realized that her ears were burning; she had meant to suggest not so much charms as virginal patience.

Helene said goodbye to her aunt. Fanny didn't even deign to look at the young student Wertheimer, but assured Helene that Otta would open the door to her when she got home.

It was light now outside. The birds were twittering softly to greet the summer day, although it had dawned long ago and the street lights were out. A cab was waiting for custom. Clearly people must be beginning to go to work. A newspaper boy stood on the corner offering the *Morgenpost* and the *Querschnitt*.

The *Querschnitt* on the street so early in the morning, said Carl, smiling and shaking his head.

Helene was enjoying her encounter with Wertheimer, and as they asked each other the first tentative questions about their lives she did not tell him how close they were to where she was staying. One foot shod, the other bare and touching the paving stones, Helene felt the sticky surface of the street. The lime trees had been dropping their nectar overnight.

Come, let's conceal ourselves more closely . . . Wertheimer looked enquiringly at Helene to see if she recognized his quotation from the poet Else Laske-Schüler.

Life lies in all our hearts. Quickly, casually, Helene tossed the next line back to him.

As if in coffins. Wertheimer happily completed the second verse of the poem. But Helene said no more; she just smiled.

What is it? he asked. Won't you go on?

I've forgotten how the rest of it goes.

I don't believe that. He looked surprised and a little sorry, but she mollified him.

You say it so cheerfully, but 'The End of the World' is a sad poem, don't you think?

You call it sad? It's optimistic, Helene! What can be fuller of promise than devotion, a kiss, a longing that embraces us and brings us to the point of death?

You believe she was thinking of God when she wrote it?

Not at all, the divine is closer to her. How does the poem begin? Why, with many doubts! She speaks of *weeping as if the good Lord God were dead*. But if she believed in God she'd assume he was immortal, so it's a double rejection of faith; she doesn't believe in the good Lord any more than an evil Lord or any other kind of god. Is the death of God supposed to make the world weep for him or because it's rid of him?

Helene looked at Wertheimer. She mustn't forget to close her lips. Didn't Martha keep telling her to shut her mouth or insects would fly into it? She had never heard anyone discuss a poem like this.

But wasn't the poem hers, all hers? Waxing enthusiastic, Helene was talking away now, for her poem rather than her life, although with a man like Wertheimer you couldn't draw sharp distinctions between the two.

Laske-Schüler doesn't regale herself on God, she doesn't regale herself on mankind and their sufferings either, she grants them only a kiss before dying. Believe me, her own mortality, looking her in the face – whether she's to die of longing and in tears or not – human mortality, her understanding that it's inevitable, all that's clearly opposed to God's immortality.

Do you always read poems backwards?

Only if I meet someone who insists on linearity.

The young man was going to take the tram or a bus and turned the corner.

So you, with your Latinate terms – regaling yourself on them, in fact! – you accuse me of insisting on linearity? I like to take a winding path myself, but I won't insist on anything, certainly not to you. There was severity in Wertheimer's words, but the next moment mischief was sparkling in his eyes. How about all that cultural and scientific stuff? Tell me, don't you think all our efforts are shocking presumption? Doesn't a club where anyone can be chairman have the biggest membership? Is Dada a wastepaper basket for art?

Helene thought about it. What's wrong with differences, can you tell me that? It was an honest question, after all, Helene thought. Who was bothered by all the clubs, so long as everyone could found one and go there as often as he wanted?

At the Kurfürstendamm they let the first tram pass; it was crowded, only brave souls would clamber aboard and their conversation would admit no pause, wouldn't be interrupted even for the courage to try a kiss.

You know Büchner's *Lenz*, what is Lenz suffering from, Helene?

Helene saw the curiosity with which Carl awaited her answer. She hesitated. From being different. Is that what you mean? But difference doesn't always cause suffering.

It doesn't? Suddenly Carl Wertheimer seemed to know what he was getting at; he wasn't waiting for her answer any more. You're a woman, I'm a man – do you think that means happiness?

Helene had to laugh. She shrugged her shoulders. What else, Herr Wertheimer?

Yes, of course, you'll say that, Helene. At least, I hope so.

That's permitted. But only because happiness and suffering aren't mutually exclusive. Far from it. Suffering embraces the idea of happiness, keeps it safe inside itself, so to speak. The idea of happiness can never be lost in suffering.

Except that the idea of happiness and happiness itself are different things. Helene felt that she was walking slowly, hobbling along. Briefly, she noticed how her feet hurt. But Lenz has everything, his clouds are rosy, the heavens shine down – everything that others only dream of.

Helene and Carl boarded a bus going east and sat down. The wind was blowing in their faces and Carl put his coat round Helene's shoulders to keep her warm.

But that makes Büchner's Lenz suffer, objected Carl. What are the clouds or the mountains to him if he doesn't win Pastor Oberlin over?

Win him over? Helene thought she had spotted something vague in Carl's chain of thought; she was paying close attention and couldn't help noticing. Perhaps he had misunderstood her.

What brings you and your sister to Berlin? Just a visit to your aunt?

Helene nodded firmly. A long visit; we've been here three years now. Helene snuggled her chin into the fur collar of his coat. How soft it was, how nice it smelled; a fur collar in summer. Martha works at the Jewish Hospital. I used to be a nurse too, I passed my exams while we were still living in Bautzen, but it isn't easy for a nurse to get a job here in Berlin if she's very young and doesn't have any references. Helene's feet were sore. She wondered whether to tell him that today was her birthday and she was going to begin an evening course in grammar-school education for girls, adding that she would like to study at college after that, but she decided not to. After all, her birthday was eight hours in the past and the morning sun now shining in her face, the first summer sunlight since the solstice, was more important while she felt that fur collar against her cheek.

So young? Carl looked at her, estimating her age. Helene's cheeks were glowing. Her feet were cold now, one shoe lay on her lap, her dress, drenched from all that dancing, stuck to her back and made her shiver, but her cheeks were burning and she smiled as she returned Carl's glance.

He leaned over to her. Helene thought he was going to kiss her, but he only whispered softly in her ear: If I dared, I'd give you a kiss.

Helene drew her thin scarf more closely round her shoulders. She glanced through the leaves of the plane trees and saw the shops they were passing. Oh, she cried, jumping up, we have to get out here.

But we've only gone one stop. Wertheimer was following her down the steps of the bus and out into the street.

Helene was limping, her unshod right leg much shorter than her left leg now.

I'd carry you, Helene, but perhaps you wouldn't like it.

What makes you think that, she asked, rolling her eyes. The night had left her in high spirits and the bright morning made her feel braver. Contentedly, she put her arms round Carl Wertheimer. Surprised, he hesitated for a moment. But he had hardly put his own arms round her to pick her up when she gave him a quick kiss – his cheek was rough – and then, in friendly fashion, pushed him away.

The sun's already shining. Helene stopped, leaned on Carl Wertheimer's shoulder and took off her other shoe. Don't worry, these paving stones are warm.

She was several steps ahead of him now and, as he tried to catch up, she began to run. She told herself he would kiss her goodbye. Suddenly it seemed to Helene as if she could see right through people and knew exactly what action would lead to what result. She could handle people, all of them, pull the strings as if they were marionettes, in particular she could handle Carl Wertheimer, who she knew was behind her, whose steps were coming closer and closer, whose hand she felt on her shoulder next moment. She stopped outside the apartment and turned to Carl Wertheimer. He took her hand, drew her into the entrance of the building and laid his hand against her cheek.

So soft, he said. Helene liked the touch of his hand, she thought she could encourage her new friend, put her own hand on his, pressing it to her face, and kissed its roughened back. Cautiously, she raised her eyes to his. One of Carl's eyelids was fluttering, only one, like a frightened young bird. Perhaps he'd never kissed a girl before. He drew her towards him. She liked the sensation of his mouth on her hair. Helene didn't know what to do with her hands; his coat seemed to get in the way, it was too bulky. She put one hand to his temples, his cheekbones, his eye sockets, seeking out the fluttering eyelid with one finger. Then, protectively, she laid her fingers on the lid as if to calm it down. Helene felt a stitch in her side and took a deep breath. She took care to breathe regularly, as regularly as possible. In Carl Wertheimer's embrace she was neither short nor tall, his hands on her bare neck warmed her and brought gooseflesh out on her bare arms. Helene had to give herself a little shake. This man's touch was still unknown to her, but her desire was all the more familiar for that. A blackbird sang its loud song, a second drowned it out, first trilling, then whistling – its notes were a triad in a lower register than the first bird, then the two black-birds began singing in competition. Helene spluttered with excitement, which he might take as laughter. Then she felt his grave gaze resting on her and her laughter died down. She felt ashamed of herself, she was afraid he might have noticed the sense of omnipotence that she had just been feeling, but now there was nothing left of it, it was an empty husk once the kernel had dropped to the ground, leaving nothing but the appearance of arrogance or even vanity, and he wouldn't think much of that. She wondered what he wanted. What he wanted in general and what he wanted of her. Her heart was in her mouth. They had to part now.

Proudly, she told him that they had recently acquired a telephone.

Carl Wertheimer didn't ask what the number was. It was as if he hadn't heard her. He watched her go and waved. She waved back. Her hands were warm.

As she raised the heavy brass ring on Fanny's fine front door to knock – for she had firmly determined not to look round at Carl again – and as Otta opened the door in her cap and apron, fully dressed already, Helene doubted whether Carl would telephone. Perhaps he wanted an affair, perhaps just a kiss and he'd already had that. Very likely that was all and he didn't want any more.

There was an aroma of coffee in the air, the grandfather clock struck, it was six-thirty. Helene heard the familiar clatter of cutlery and china from the kitchen; the cook would be brewing the coffee there, already preparing breakfast in spite of the absence of her mistress and the rest of them, cutting up poppyseed cake, stirring the porridge that Fanny liked as soon as she felt able to eat something in the morning. Helene did not feel at all tired. Stepping lightly as if her feet were still dancing to the music of trumpet and clarinet, she went out on the veranda and dropped into one of the low upholstered chairs. Her hair, which hardly came down as far as her nose now, smelled of smoke. She felt the back of her neck; she could move her head so easily without her long hair. She felt tempted to make rapid movements, and if she shook her head suddenly her hair fell over her face. Helene pulled off her false eyelashes. Her eyes were burning from last night's cigarette smoke. As she put the false eyelashes on the table, she thought it would be nice if she could put her eyes down beside them. Cleo jumped out of her basket under the table, wagging her stumpy little tail and licking Helene's hand. The dog's tongue tickled. Helene thought of the goats in their garden at home in Tuchmacherstrasse, the goats that she had sometimes milked when she was a child. As she ran her fingers from top to bottom of the udder, its skin had felt rough against the palms of her hands and she had to wash her hands thoroughly, in hot water and with plenty of soap because the slightly rancid smell clung tenaciously. Rancid goat. She had escaped all that, thought Helene in relief, and as she settled comfortably into the soft upholstery of the chair she was only slightly and sweetly ashamed of feeling glad. What was the real point of escaping, Helene wondered, chasing through your life so fast? Be consistent, be consistent, Helene whispered to herself, and as she heard herself whispering she said out loud, in a firm voice, the concluding words of Büchner's *Lenz*: Inconsistent, inconsistent. Helene patted the dog's firm and curly coat. What a sweet little creature you are. Cleo's floppy ears were soft and silky. Helene kissed the dog on her long muzzle; she had never kissed Cleo before, but this morning she just couldn't help it.

The unexpected advent of Carl Wertheimer on the scene passed largely unnoticed in Fanny's apartment. He did not call Helene on the telephone, but a messenger brought her flowers. Helene was surprised, alarmed, happy. She placed her hand protectively round the flowers, round the air encircling them, which seemed too dense to carry their faint fragrance. Like a treasure, she carried the anemones to her room. She was alone there and felt glad that Martha would not be back until late. She wondered where he had found anemones still in bloom now. She looked at the flowers; their blue changed during the day and the delicate petals grew heavy.

The anemones faded that evening, but she wouldn't let Otta take the flowers out of their vase. Helene couldn't sleep. When she closed her eyes she saw only blue. Her excitement was caused by something she had never known before, an encounter with someone with whom she shared mutual ideas, a mutual curiosity and, indeed, as she confided to Martha, a mutual passion for literature.

Martha yawned on receiving this confidence. You mean in common, little angel, not mutual.

Helene knew clearly now that something unique had happened to her. She wouldn't mind what Martha thought any more; her meeting with Carl was an incomparable experience, something she didn't seem able to communicate to anyone like her sister.

When the bell finally rang on Sunday, and Helene heard Otta's voice clearly and politely repeating his name as if it were a question – Carl Wertheimer? – Helene leaped to her feet, picked up the silk jacket that Fanny had only recently stopped wearing and given her, and followed Carl out into the summer morning.

They took the train to Wannsee and then walked to the smaller Stölpchensee nearby. Carl dared not hold her hand. A hare leaped along the woodland track ahead of them. The water of the lake below them glittered through the leaves, white sails swelled in the distance. Helene's throat felt tight; she was suddenly afraid that she might start stammering, that her memory of the interests they shared and her delight in them would turn out to be a single occurrence, never to be repeated.

Then Carl started talking: Isn't the enjoyment of nature for its own sake, the autocracy of the moment, as Lenz shows it to us, a true hymn of praise to life?

That sounds like sacrilege.

You mean doubt, Helene. Doubt is allowed, doubt isn't sacrilege.

Perhaps you see it differently. It's not like this for us Christians.

You're Protestant, am I right? There was no mockery in Carl Wertheimer's tone, so Helene nodded slightly. Suddenly what she said about her adherence to the Lutheran faith and its nature seemed invalidated, not because she remembered her mother's atheism and her different origins, but because her God seemed so far away here. Büchner had routed him. Who wanted to recognize God as the Universal?

May I tell you something in confidence, Carl? Helene and Carl stopped where the path forked; to the right it went to the bridge, to the left deeper into the wood. They were still wondering which way to go when she told him what was weighing on her mind. You know, these last few years, since we've been in Berlin, I've felt ashamed whenever I thought about God, and I knew I'd forgotten him for days and weeks on end. We haven't set foot in a church here.

And did you find a substitute?

What do you mean, Carl?

Has something given you pleasure? And can you believe in that?

Well, to be honest, I've never asked myself that question.

Carl clenched one hand into a fist and shook it at the sky: and he felt, he said, quoting Büchner again, as if he could *crush the world between his teeth and spit it out into the Creator's face: so Lenz swore, so he blasphemed.*

Don't laugh. You're making fun of me.

Helene, I'm not making fun of you. I'd never dare do that. Carl controlled his merriment as well as he could.

Go on, laugh. It was through laughter that atheism got its grip on Lenz.

You think I'm an atheist? It isn't as simple as that, Helene. It's a fact that God doesn't know anything about laughter. Isn't that a pity? Carl put his hands in his trouser pockets.

I'd never have thought of confusing you with Lenz. Helene winked at him. At last she knew why she had been standing in front of the mirror with the lily-patterned rim for hours on end, practising winking one eye: it was for this moment. Then she turned serious again and looked sternly at Carl. I was going to tell you something in confidence.

I know, I'll keep quiet. And Carl did stop talking.

It seemed an eternity before Helene could bring herself to break the silence.

I'm not ashamed any more, that's what horrifies me. Do you understand? I haven't been to church here, I've forgotten about

God; for a long time I've felt ashamed when I remembered him. And now what? Nothing.

Let's walk on. Carl chose the path leading to the bridge. Clouds were towering up, big white clouds sailing singly in the unchanging blue sky beyond them. On the other side of the bridge stood an inn with a garden. There was hardly an empty table in the garden, parties with sunshades and children were talking in loud voices, they too seemed to have forgotten about God. Carl found them a place. He said this was his table, well, once it had been his parents' regular table, and when he came here by himself now and then it was his. Helene imagined that a life in which you and your parents went to an inn with a garden would be wonderful. Pointing to another table, Carl whispered to her that the painters often sat at that one. The magic of this world seemed to Helene so strange that she felt like standing up and leaving, but now Carl took her hand and told her she had a lovely smile, he'd like to see it often.

Carl Wertheimer was from a good family, prosperous and well educated. His father was a professor of astronomy, so in spite of the financial difficulties of the last few years, his son had been able to study. The waiter brought them raspberry sherbet to drink. Carl pointed to the north-east: his parents' house was over there, he said, on the other bank. His two brothers had been reported missing in the war; the eldest had been killed and his belongings sent home, but his parents still refused to believe he was dead. Helene thought of her father, but she didn't want to talk about him.

He himself hadn't had to join the army, to his mother's relief. His sister was finishing her university studies this year; she was the only woman studying physics. And she was getting married next year. Carl was obviously proud of his sister. He was the youngest, there was plenty of time for him, so his mother said. Carl clicked his tongue as if deploring this, although his eyes were twinkling and his regret seemed anything but serious. A sparrow came down to perch on their table, hopping back and forth, and pecking up crumbs left by the last occupants.

This glimpse of Carl's peaceful world by the Wannsee aroused a vague sense of uneasiness in Helene. What could she set against that, what could she add to it? A wasp had fallen into her raspberry sherbet and was struggling for its life there.

Carl must have noticed that Helene, on the other side of the table, had fallen silent. He told her: your eyes are bluer than the sky. And when he had struggled to coax a difficult smile from her, perhaps he thought, she's ashamed after all, she hasn't forgotten her God. No wonder when I seize her hand. Probably to get her out of her difficulty, he said, quoting Büchner yet again: *My love, is there some terrible crack in your world?*

Helene saw the mischief in his eyes and recognized that aspect of his character. It was as if she knew him a little now, and that in itself comforted her. Now he couldn't stop rummaging around in his memories: To drop the subject of Lenz for a moment, may I advise you to let abstract words crumble to nothing in your mouth like mouldy mushrooms? Even Hofmannsthal recovered from his ennui. And what is it but ennui if a void stretching out before us fills us with discomfort?

There it was again, the idea of discomfort. Helene felt that his words were too importunate, something threatened to go wrong, the wasp in her raspberry sherbet tumbled down inside the glass, Helene felt a headache coming on. There was loud laughter at the next table. Helene had forgotten to answer Carl's question.

I'd like to take you out in a boat. You can lie in the boat with the water rocking you, and you must look up at the sky. Will you promise me that? Carl waved to the waiter, asking for the bill.

There was a Mercedes cabriolet standing outside the inn, with people crowding round it, gaping, stroking, patting the carriage-work as if it were a horse. Helene was glad when she and Carl finally got to their feet, leaving the wasp to its own devices.

Carl took her hand now. His own was unexpectedly slender and firm. No *leaden shadow*, she thought, returning to that poem of Laske-Schüler's, no leaden shadow heavy as the grave weighed her down now, the world was a long way from coming to an end. A clattering noise in the sky made them stop. Helene put her head back.

Can I tell you something in confidence too, Helene?

Go ahead. Helene shielded her eyes with her hand; the sunlight was dazzling. You have a weakness for aeroplanes, isn't that so?

Carl took a step towards her. Junkers F 13 planes. She felt his breath against her throat as he spoke.

Without taking her hand from her brow, Helene lowered her head and her hand almost touched Carl's eyebrows.

Carl stepped back again. I can't talk when I'm so close to you. No, it wasn't my weakness for planes I was going to tell you about. Carl stopped. Your mouth is beautiful. And I can't think of a quotation. Why use someone else's words anyway? I'm the one who would like to kiss you.

Some time, perhaps.

You mean next year? Did you know that Junkers are planning a flight across the Atlantic?

That's failed often enough, said Helene, sounding knowledgeable.

All the way from Europe to America. But I can't wait as long as that for your kiss.

Helene went ahead, pleased that Carl couldn't see her smile. They walked in silence for a long time, deep in their own thoughts, each knowing the other was there. Helene was surprised now at the momentary sense of strangeness that she had felt at the inn, and hoped Carl hadn't noticed. She felt far from strange with him at the moment. The man hiring out boats was sitting on a folding chair, reading the evening paper; passed on to him, perhaps, by one of his customers. He was sorry, he said, all the boats were out on the water, and when one came back he didn't want to hire it out again. After eight no one goes rowing on the lake, he said. As they walked along the bank, taking off their shoes and surprised by the warmth that the sand had stored up during the day, Carl talked about the theatre. In a few brief words they had agreed on a shared preference for classical tragedies onstage and Romantic literature at home, but their understanding nods and agreements were mainly due to their impatience; they didn't want to keep their distance from each other any more, they wanted to come close, they were in search of a way to bring what they were both thinking to its natural conclusion. Helene liked the reddish trunks of the pine trees here in the Mark Brandenburg; you didn't see them at home, only in Berlin. The long needles felt pleasant between her fingers. Why did they always come in pairs? A fine little filament connected the two pine needles under their hard exterior. It seemed to her as if the evening sun were setting the woods on fire. The day was coming to a close, the pines gave off a heavy scent, Helene felt dazed; she wanted to sit down on the woodland floor and stay there. Carl crouched down beside her and said he wasn't going to let her stay in the woods, there were wild animals here and she was too delicate for him to allow it.

Martha was very happy to know that Helene had a boyfriend, so that she herself could live even more openly with Leontine. But it was as if Carl Wertheimer's appearance had robbed the sisters of their conversations. They no longer had anything to say to each other. Aunt Fanny's apartment, which she had liked so much until now, seemed to Helene more and more unwelcoming every day. That was not so much because Fanny was taking one object after another to the pawnbroker's, first the little samovar which, she said, she didn't like as much as the big one, then the picture by Lovis Corinth, which she claimed she'd never liked – she had always felt the young woman with the hat repellent, she said, she'd rather have had his self-portrait with a skeleton – and finally the gramophone went; there was no denying the value of the gramophone, or the fact that she really did like it.

On many days Fanny sat with Erich on her little veranda at noon, arguing over plans for the day. When he rose to his feet because he'd had enough of her and would rather spend the rest of the day without her, she called after him in a loud voice that carried all over the ground-floor apartment: I wish I could feel an infatuation! Take me by storm, somebody!

It sounded both pleading and derisive, and Helene took care not to cross either Erich's or Fanny's path. She closed the door to her room. How sweet the hours she used to spend alone in the apartment had once been. But it seemed they were gone for ever, because whenever Helene came home someone was bustling about in the kitchen, someone else was shouting down the telephone, or sitting on the chaise longue and reading.

You don't love me! The words rang through the rooms. Helene couldn't help overhearing; the silence knew no mercy, it followed the long, slow, apparently never-ending definition of Fanny's conjecture. Helene hurried along the corridor on tiptoe when she had to go to the bathroom. Only when Fanny was lying on the floor, claiming that she couldn't live without love, did Erich reach his hand down to her. He pulled her up from the floor and pushed her into her bedroom ahead of him. Helene counted up her savings; they wouldn't even rent an attic room for a month. The books for her classes were expensive, and Fanny made it clear that she couldn't afford the money any more. Helene should be glad to have had the first two years of her course paid for her, she said; Fanny's money was running out and, sad to say, she didn't know what to do about it. Helene had stopped bringing drugs home from the pharmacy; it had proved impossible to forge a bond of confidence between her and her aunt, and Fanny's kindness to Helene was wearing a little thin too. Sometimes Helene came into the apartment, Otta took her coat and Helene went into the living room to say hello to Fanny, but Fanny either did not look up from her book or pretended to be fast asleep, although a glass of steaming tea stood beside the chaise longue.

Nights in her narrow bed beside Leontine and Martha were a torment, since the pair never seemed to tire of their love and their lust. The Baron had begun writing Helene anxious letters. He saw her so seldom now, he said, his heart was both bleeding and freezing. His life was a poor thing without her. But the object of his affections did not reply. After her original bafflement in the face of his expectations, and his announcement of a love she did not share, Helene took to putting the letters she found pushed under the door of her room inside the lid of the big trunk that stood under her bed, still unopened. A first attempt by two Junkers to fly from Europe to America over the Atlantic had failed in August; the autumn storms and winter clouds were regarded as insuperable obstacles, so the next attempt to fly the Atlantic was postponed until spring. Carl and Helene were alone in waiting no longer.

Carl took Helene to the State Opera House, Unter den Linden. They heard Schreker's *The Singing Devil* and stood applauding for twenty minutes, although shrill whistling from elsewhere in the audience rang in their ears, and while Helene's hands hurt with clapping, she hoped Carl wouldn't follow the crowd to the exits. But the inevitable happened. Outside the cloakroom, Helene asked Carl not to take her home yet. She wanted to walk a little way through the night first. Thick snowflakes were falling, but they hardly settled on the surface of the road, which was black as night. Carl and Helene walked past the Hotel Adlon. The snow melted on Helene's tongue. Outside the entrance to the great hotel, handsome cars and a crowd of people suggested that some distinguished guest was expected to arrive.

You're cold and tired. Let me take you home.

Please don't. Helene stayed put. Carl put his hands inside her fur muff in search of warmth.

But we can't just stand around here, said Carl.

I'll come back to your lodgings with you. There, she had said it, just like that.

Carl drew his hands away from her. He couldn't believe his ears. He had so often begged Helene to go back to his room, he had so often reassured her that he had all the keys and his landlady was hard of hearing. I'm glad, he said quietly and kissed her forehead.

On the way to Viktoria-Luise-Platz she insisted that they mustn't phone her aunt. No one at Fanny's apartment minded where she was; they probably wouldn't even notice her absence. Helene knew Carl's attic room. She had visited him before, but in the daytime. Now she hardly knew it again. The electric light made the colours look faded, his books were stacked on the floor, his bed was unmade. There was a smell of urine as if he hadn't emptied his chamber pot. Carl had not been expecting her visit. Now he apologized and quickly put the bedspread on the bed. She could borrow one of his nightshirts, he said, and could he read something aloud to her? His voice was dry, his abrupt movements showed how important her presence here and perhaps her mere existence were to him.

Are you still reading Hofmannsthal? She took the nightshirt and sat down on his chair at the desk, with her coat still buttoned up.

He pointed to the books on the floor. I was reading Spinoza yesterday evening; in our class we're comparing his ethics with Descartes and his dualist view of the world.

You haven't told me anything about that yet. Helene looked suspiciously at Carl. She couldn't wrinkle her smooth brow; the little lines that formed above her short nose if she did just looked funny.

Are you jealous? Carl teased her, although he must know that she meant it seriously and she really was jealous of his studies – not because she wanted to have him all for herself and didn't want him to be studying, but because she would have liked to be studying too.

Your shoes are all wet, wait, I'll take them off for you. Carl knelt down on the floor in front of her and removed her shoes. And your feet are cold, like ice. Don't you have any winter boots?

Helene shook her head. Wait a minute, I'll get you some hot water, you need a footbath.

Carl disappeared and Helene heard him on the stairs. She looked at the nightshirt on her lap and took his absence as a request for her to undress. She draped her clothes over the back of the chair and rolled up her stockings in a ball, keeping nothing on but her new pair of knickers. In the corner under the window, Helene saw a terrarium with an orchid flowering in it. An orchid in bloom in an attic room, surrounded by the drab colours on which the electric light fell. She heard sounds on the stairs and quickly pulled the nightshirt over her head. It smelled of Carl. The second button from the top was missing, she did up the top button and held the nightshirt closed over the gap. Helene was trembling all over now. Carl brought in hot water, placing the basin on the floor and telling her to sit on the bed. Then he put his blanket round her and rubbed her feet until her toes weren't blue any more. Helene gritted her teeth.

While Carl busily moved his books from stack to stack, he added more hot water to the basin twice. Only then did her feet warm up, and he went out to take away the basin and put on a pair of pyjamas that his mother had brought him for Christmas from a trip to Paris. Helene was already lying under the covers on her back, perfectly straight; it looked as if she were asleep. He drew back the covers and lay down beside her.

Don't be surprised if you hear my heart beating, he said in a voice that wasn't so dry any more, and he put out the light.

Didn't you want to read to me?

He propped himself on his elbow, turned the light on again and saw that she had opened her eyes.

Right, I'll read to you. He picked up Spinoza's *Ethics*, lying on the bedside table, and leafed through it. In the days of Greek antiquity, he explained, licence and freedom meant complete indulgence in pleasure and the demand for happiness. But then the Stoics came along and lent God a hand; duty and virtue, all that is spiritual should be elevated above the lower pleasures, the flesh was anathema. The Middle Ages were a vale of woe. For that old moralist Kant there was still nothing but duty – bleakness wherever you look.

Why do you speak so disparagingly? You act as if happiness meant only physical union. Helene propped her own head up; she suspected that while Carl might be condemning Kant's bleak outlook, he himself gave no more thought, however briefly, to the kiss she had owed him for months.

Carl dismissed her reproach. Not to speak of Schopenhauer, he went on, who saw the notion that we are here to be happy as an innate error in the education of mankind, a malformation, so to speak. But it doesn't all depend on happiness, Helene, you know that, don't you? Go on, then, yawn! Carl tapped her gently on the forehead with his bookmark.

Helene took the bookmark away from him. If I could read every book with you I'd be happy, do you believe that? Helene smiled. Most of all I'd like to read books with your eyes, with your voice, with your flexibility of tone.

Flexibility – what are you talking about? Carl laughed.

I like listening to you. Sometimes it's as if you hurry over to the window while you're reading, sometimes you crawl under the table.

And I'll tell you how it seems to me – as if you climb trees and jump *on* the table when I've crawled under it, on principle.

Do I? Helene wondered what he meant. Did he think her annoying, didn't he enjoy it when they measured up to each other, feeling the tension that sometimes existed between them?

223

Well, anyway, here we are lying under the same blanket, there's an angel here with me – how did that happen? Now Carl looked at her so challengingly, with his mouth a whole millimetre closer, that Helene's courage deserted her and her fear of the kiss was suddenly greater than her desire for it. So it doesn't depend on happiness? Helene tapped Carl's book. No lust and boundless licence?

Carl cleared his throat. What do you want, Helene? Do you want to learn to think?

Elbows in front of the book, chin propped on his hands, Carl was laughing into the cup they formed in front of his mouth. Schopenhauer consoles us: intellectual wealth will overcome even pain and tedium – our old friend Lenz obviously wasn't clever enough there.

Helene put her head back on the pillow, exposing her throat to him; she deliberately turned on her side and watched his mouth as he spoke. His slightly pursed lips moved too much and too fast for her to follow. He noticed her glance and his eyelid began fluttering again, as if expecting her touch, as if it wanted nothing more. Suddenly he lowered his eyes, Helene saw his fingers trembling on the pages of the book, but he bravely read a couple of sentences that he had noted down on the first page: *Happiness is not the reward of virtue, virtue is its own reward. We are not glad of it because we rein in our lusts, but because we are glad of it we can rein them in.*

That sounds like good advice for future priests.

You're wrong, Helene. It's precious advice for all young men. Precious because we study for years to learn it and only when we've studied for years do we know a spark of happiness. Carl suddenly held back. He had been on the point of mentioning the importance of knowing there was a girl in bed beside you too, a woman, not just any woman but this one, his Helene.

But he was afraid that might scare her. He didn't want her putting her wet, cold shoes and stockings on again and going back to Achenbachstrasse through the night, to lie down there in bed beside her sister. So he turned back to where his forefinger had been holding the pages apart and read.

The desire arising from the knowledge of good and evil can be stifled or curbed by many other desires, which themselves arise from the emotions that assail us. Carl's fingers made the whole page tremble.

Are you cold yourself now? Helene put her hand beside his, their little fingers almost touching.

Reason can overcome the passions by becoming a passion itself.

Helene, listening, said: You have lovely eyes.

In evidence we may cite the fact that emotion felt for a thing imagined in the future is weaker than emotion felt for something in the present.

Are you talking about us, are you talking about love? Now Helene did touch his finger with hers and noticed him start. He was so captivated that he didn't even turn his eyes to look at her.

You wanted me to read aloud and I am reading aloud. Love, to Spinoza, is nothing but cheerfulness, cheerfulness contingent on the idea of its ultimate cause.

Your eyes are shining. I could lie beside you all evening just looking at your chin, your profile, your nose, the way the lids come down over your eyes. Helene drew up her knees; there was still the blanket between her and Carl.

Carl was going to explain something about desire in relation to love and the relation of both to reason, but he had forgotten the logic of it all; something else had taken him over, something that could not rest any more, could not be a subject for reflection, he wanted to be outside himself, beyond himself, with her. Words flew past. Her mouth was so sweet. He didn't want to think any more, he had cast his will aside, there was no restraining him now. He felt naked. The touch of the blanket separating him from her excited him enormously. With pure desire, he looked at Helene and kissed her, kissed her mouth, her cheeks, her eyes, his lips felt the smooth skin of her curving forehead, his hand stroked her silky hair, the golden brightness of her hair shone through the narrow opening of his eyelids. His hand felt her collarbone, the curve of her shoulders, his fingertip felt the dimples that he knew so well by sight. Her arms seemed so long, her armpit was moist, he buried his hand in it, he lay close. He heard his breath gasping as he lay against her. Helene's fragrance lured him so much it hurt. Her arms were folded over her breasts, he had to breathe deeply, he saw time unfurling before him, he could find peace with her if only he wanted to, if only he wanted to, but where was his will now? Reason, he called silently to himself, he saw the word before his eyes, plain and sober, he didn't know its meaning any more. Nothing but letters with no sound. Sound and meaning were all gone. But his gasping breath was caught between his lips and her curves and hollows, and her breathing was carried to his ear.

The candle hissed, the wick collapsed and sank. The darkness was pleasantly cool. Carl stared into the dark. Helene's breath came regularly, her eyes were probably closed. He could hardly sleep, her fragrance kept him awake, rousing him even if he did fall into a dream for a few seconds. She was not breathing as deeply as he was, perhaps she wasn't asleep. He put his hand out to her.

She liked his gentle mouth, his lips, demanding in a different way from Martha's, with a taste that was new to her.

It will be nice to see your hair grow longer, whispered Carl in the silence. Why was it so short?

So that I could meet you. Don't you know that? It was long

down to here a few hours before I first saw you. Leontine cut it for me.

Carl buried his face in her throat. He caressed her ear with the wingbeat of his lashes. Your hair shines like gold. If we're ever left starving, I'll cut it off in secret at night and sell it.

Helene liked the way he said *we* as she lay there in his arms.

Spring came, the storms died down and the first flight across the Atlantic from east to west had been achieved. Since that winter day, Helene had been spending her nights in Carl's room. She sometimes did go to Achenbachstrasse, and was relieved to see that Martha seemed better now. Leontine had spent days on end shut away with her. It seemed that Martha had been ill, delirious and in pain, the mirror with the lily-patterned rim above the washstand was cracked, bedclothes had been torn and drenched with sweat in the morning, and had to be changed in the evening or sometimes in the middle of the day, but then she was calm again, weak but at peace. There was still a void full of questions: where did it come from, why, from whom? It was a marvel that Martha managed to get to work in the hospital every day. Leontine said Martha was tough. Her body had got used to it. The two of them had pushed the beds together, and only the trunk under one bed still reminded anyone of Helene and the time she used to spend here, because it had her possessions in it. One day Helene came to visit, opened the trunk, pushed the Baron's letters aside, and took out the fish carved from horn and the chain.

You can take that with you, said Martha, who didn't care about the trunk and wanted to be rid of it. Her cloche hat was moth-eaten now; Helene wondered where her own was. She must have left it in the cloakroom of the White Mouse club that evening two years ago.

There's going to be a vacancy on my ward, said Martha. You could apply. Helene said no, she didn't want to be travelling north to work in the Jewish Hospital. The pharmacist was paying her better now, and she no longer thought about him when she stood in the pharmacy alone in the evening, mixing tinctures. Carl wouldn't take any rent from her; his parents gave him an allowance at the beginning of every month. When he went to visit them he took Helene with him on the train to Wannsee, left her in the garden of the inn on Stölpchensee, ordered a raspberry sherbet for her and came back an hour later. Sometimes he asked her if she wouldn't go with him, saying he would like to introduce her to his parents, but she shrank from the meeting. They might not like me, Helene pointed out, and wouldn't give way to either his encouragement or his protests. In fact, she enjoyed those Sunday afternoons when she could sit reading in the garden of the inn, undisturbed.

At the end of the summer, through Bernard's good connections, they got tickets for the new play at the Schiffbauerdamm theatre. Carl sat next to Helene and forgot to hold her hand. His fists clenched, he struck his forehead, he wept, and next moment was shouting approval. Only when the audience demanded the Army Song again as an encore, and people in the back rows stood up, linked arms and rocked in time to the music, did Carl lean back, mildly exhausted, and look at Helene.

Don't you like it?

Helene hesitated and tilted her head to one side. I don't know yet.

It's brilliant, said Carl. His eyes were on the stage again by now, and did not turn back to Helene throughout the perform-ance. He listened, spellbound, to Lotte Lenya, looking almost dazed. When the first verse of the jealousy duet was over and a second followed, Carl was spluttering, doubled up with laughter.

His cheeks were red as he stood up, applauding, even before the final curtain fell. The audience was bubbling over. They simply wouldn't go until the closing verses of 'Mack the Knife' had been sung again. They roared along with it – even Harald Paulsen, playing Macheath, moved his lips, although in all the noise no one could hear if he was singing that song or another one. There was stormy applause. Spectators in the circle and stalls threw flowers on stage. The actors bowed. They looked like dolls, Helene thought, tiny pop-up toys with claqueurs making them bow low, demanding their reappearance again and again. The spotlights wouldn't allow any of the actors to leave the stage or any of the audience to leave the theatre. They were clapping too, thought Helene, cautiously looking around her. Roma Bahn, who had been cast only recently as Polly, tore off her long bead necklace and scattered the glass beads in the auditorium; she looked as if she was about to walk offstage, but men whistled, either in anger or delight, and she stayed. People shouted, trampled their feet and one man in the stalls threw coins all around.

Helene put her hands over her ears. She had stayed in her seat, the only person to do so; she leaned forward, her chin on her chest, looking down at her lap, and wished she could just disappear. It was more than an hour before they could leave the theatre. People were jamming the exits, they kept stopping, clapping, turning to go back, pushing and shoving. The air was stuffy. Helene was sweating. The uproar frightened her. Someone punched her shoulder, she assumed it was a young man who quickly turned away. Helene did not let go of Carl's hand. People pushed between them, and again and again it seemed as if they would be forced apart. Helene felt sick. Out of here, she thought, I must get out of here.

Carl wanted to walk along Friedrichstrasse and Unter den Linden. The water in the canal was black, an S-Bahn train ran by overhead. On the bridge, Helene leaned over the stone balustrade and threw up.

You didn't like it. He was making a statement, not asking a question.

You're mad about it.

I'm full of enthusiasm, yes.

Helene looked for her handkerchief and couldn't find it. The sour taste in her mouth wouldn't let her nausea go away. She felt a little dizzy, so she held on to the stone of the balustrade.

Isn't this a new departure, true modernity? We're all a part of the whole, the barriers between being and representation are breaking down. Being and appearance are coming closer. People are hungry, hungry and thirsty for a world that they'll determine themselves, haven't you noticed?

What are you talking about? What world will they determine? You talk about enthusiasm and the mob screams. It scares me, oh, that pitiless, overbearing attitude at all social levels scares me. Helene had to straighten up; she felt sick and dizzy, everything seemed to be going up and down. She turned her back to Carl and leaned over the balustrade again. How nice the sandstone felt, rough and firm.

Now Carl put his hand on her back. Darling, are you ill? Do you think the meatballs were off?

Helene's face hung over the water. She imagined jumping into it. Strings of mucus streamed from her mouth, her nose was running too, she had no handkerchief.

He wasn't to know that she didn't have a handkerchief, all she needed was a handkerchief to be able to stand upright again. She had to ask him: Do you have a handkerchief?

Of course I do. Here you are. Come on, let me help you. Carl was solicitous, but Helene was losing her temper.

How can you be so simple, calling that enthusiasm? You read Schopenhauer and Spinoza, then on an evening like this you fling yourself into the crowd as if there were no tomorrow, no yesterday, nothing at all but wallowing in a bath along with the common man.

What do you have against the common man?

Nothing. Helene realized that she was pressing her lips together. I respect him. She wondered whether to tell him that she herself was a common woman. But what good would that do? So she said: The little man isn't the little man, the great man isn't the great man. Perhaps people have to be born in comfortable circumstances, like you, to glorify the little man as you do. Open your eyes, Carl.

Carl hugged her. Let's not quarrel, he said.

Why not? Helene asked softly. She would have preferred to quarrel rather than admit that the play's effect on Carl, so obvious to her, was genuine enthusiasm. Goodness, she thought, it was nothing but a lot of popular songs strung together.

Carl put his hand on Helene's mouth to soothe her. Hush, hush, he said, as if she were crying and he wanted to comfort her. I couldn't bear it if we fell out with each other.

We won't. Helene smoothed the collar of his coat.

I love you. Carl tried to kiss Helene, but she was ashamed of her sour-tasting mouth and moved her head aside.

Don't turn away, darling. You're all I have.

Suddenly Helene had to laugh. I'm not turning away, she laughed. How can you think that? I've been sick, I don't feel good and I'm tired. Let's go home.

We'll take a taxi. You're not feeling well.

No, let's walk. I need some air.

They walked deep into the night in silence. The narrow wooden bridge in the Tiergarten creaked and gave off its usual musty smell. There was rustling in the undergrowth; rats scuttled across the path in front of them. They stopped under the lime tree near the lock and heard the monkeys calling out from their enclosure.

It seemed strange to Carl that he was the first to speak. But what he wanted to say wouldn't have fitted into a conversation anyway. He bent down and picked up a lime leaf. Is anyone invulnerable? He held the leaf in front of his chest, roughly where most people think the heart lies. Helene placed her hand on his and carefully guided it to mid-chest instead. She said nothing. Carl dropped the leaf, took both her hands in his, and thought she must feel his heart beating in his own. I could ask you whether you'd marry me, he heard himself saying. You're twenty-one now. Your mother is Jewish, so my parents won't object to my choice.

You could ask me, yes. Her eyes didn't reveal what she was thinking. He looked searchingly at her.

Your shoe's undone, she said, without looking at his feet. She had obviously noticed some time ago. Carl bent down and tied his shoelace.

You don't know my mother, my father, any of us.

I know Martha. Your parents are nothing to do with me, just as mine are nothing to do with you. This is between the two of us, no one else. Will you promise to be my wife?

A monkey's screech met their ears. Helene had to laugh, but Carl looked at her gravely, waiting for an answer.

She said yes. She said it quickly and quietly, and for a moment she was afraid he couldn't have heard her. Next moment she hoped he hadn't, because it had sounded so feeble and she would have liked to say a clear Yes from her heart. But a second Yes would have made the first sound even more hesitant and cowardly.

233

Carl drew Helene to him and kissed her.

Don't I smell as if I were fermenting?

Carl agreed. A little, yes. Perhaps I've waited too long?

He took her hand. The ice was broken. Maybe you'll give me children, he said, imagining how pleasant it would be if they had two or three small children.

Helene had fallen silent again as they walked on side by side.

Could you have been sick because you're expecting a baby? Carl liked this idea.

Helene stopped at once. No.

What makes you so sure?

I just know, that's all. She laughed. Believe me, a nurse knows perfectly well how to prevent that.

Helene was still cheerful, but Carl was shocked.

You shouldn't say such things. I don't like it. Don't you want children too?

Yes, of course, but not now. I want to finish my evening classes. I still haven't given up my hopes of studying at college. I'm working hard and still I'm barely earning enough for me to rent a place of my own.

Of our own. You can rely on me. You give me children, I'll pay for your studies. Carl meant it seriously.

Are you trying to do a deal with me?

My parents will support us.

Well, perhaps. Your parents whom I don't know at all yet. Carl, I must tell you something. I'm not *giving* a man children. Children can't be given. Christians give their Lord something, they give love. There was a lot of talk about giving in the theatre just now. I think that's nonsense. I don't want you *giving* me the chance to study.

Why not? My father has promised me money if I pass my exams with distinction.

That will be far too late for me. Helene could sense her own impatience. When I've finished the course of evening classes I shall work to pay for my own studies.

Don't you trust me?

Carl, please, don't make it a question of trust.

If our children have your hair, your golden hair, I'll be happy. Carl took her face in his hands.

Helene smiled. Carl kissed her again. He didn't seem to mind the sour taste, he pressed her back against the trunk of the lime tree and tasted her cheeks, licking round her mouth with the tip of his tongue.

Some people out walking passed them, and Carl claimed they couldn't be seen in the dim light from the street lamp and in the shadow of the tree. A leaf fell off and landed on his shoulder.

Perhaps all our children will have is my small nose and your thin bones. Helene blew at the leaf, trying to dislodge it from Carl's shoulder.

I wouldn't mind. Carl stroked her face with both hands, then covered it. Let's go home. He put his hand under her summer coat and felt her lowest rib bone. That's the most beautiful part of you. Helene was afraid he might have mistaken the curving rib for her breast; you could make a mistake under a summer coat, however light it was. She blew at his shoulder again, but the leaf still clung. Now she raised one hand; she didn't want him to notice the lime leaf, so she stroked his collar and, out of the corner of her eyes, saw the leaf drifting to the ground.

At the Zoo station they took the tram to Nollendorfplatz. Hand in hand, they ran up the stairs to his attic room. He opened the door, hung his hat on the hook and helped her to take off her summer coat, her shoes, her dress. Let's have a look at you. She revealed herself. He could never have hoped that a woman would ever show herself to him as she did, he had simply had no idea. She laughed as if ashamed, but he knew that she felt no shame. He loved her for the game she was playing. She placed her hand on her belly, as a woman might do to cover herself, but then she moved her hand down to her mount of Venus, her groin, between her thighs. As she did so her gaze grew more concentrated, her nostrils flared and her mouth sketched a smile. Her fingers seemed to know their way. Then she brought her hand to her mouth; it looked as if she were embarrassed and had to bite her nails. Suddenly she turned, looked over her shoulder, where those dimples were tempting him, and asked: What are you waiting for?

He laid her down on the bed and kissed her.

Day was dawning when they finally left each other alone.

Carl got up and opened the window. It was cool; autumn was in the air.

Come here. Helene patted the pillow beside her. Carl lay down with her. He didn't want a blanket. She liked the sight of him naked. He was exhausted; he had last slept long ago. She had been working all the previous day, he had been studying, they had gone into a little café for a meal, Königsberg meatballs, her favourite, they had gone to the theatre and then stood on the bridge. Later there had been her faint Yes under the lime tree. She was ashamed to think of it. She caressed his chest, circling his navel, from which a long scar ran down. Acute appendicitis, an obstruction of the bowel, which had almost been the end of him. Her clever hand touched every part of his body around his sex, sought his loins, avoided the penis. He knew she was playing with him, he knew how she could grasp him just there on other days. There was no part of his body that she feared. That sometimes seemed strange to him; after all, she said he was the first man she'd made love with. Who cared about being the first? He wanted to be the last, so he had told her: You're my last woman, do you hear, my sweet, my very last. He laid his hand on her hip.

What I liked best was Lotte Lenya announcing her revenge. That really gets under the skin, you have to admit.

Helene couldn't believe he was returning to the subject. Poor girl, she said. She let her tone of voice tell Carl that she was keeping her sympathy well within bounds. You let yourself get carried away. Helene shook her head kindly, like a mother humouring her child.

I let that opera-play fire me up, yes. Like a thunderclap.

Crash, bang. Helene blew into his ear.

His hands stroked her belly, his mouth sought her little nipples. They were his, all his. Before Helene gave in to him, she whispered into his shock of hair: I just don't want you to be blind.

Later, when the sun was falling on their bed, Helene watched over him as he slept. His eyes moved under their lids like small living creatures, a sound came from his throat and made him start in his sleep, then he breathed regularly. Helene whispered something into his ear, hoping that words stealing into his dreams in his sleep, words spoken in her voice, would sink deep into him, into every cell of his being. She herself was too tired to sleep.

Y ou have to separate body and mind, said Leontine, if she didn't then she couldn't work.

Separating the affect from the thing it relates to would probably favour the thing. Because an affect without a cause and the thing to which it relates, well, said Carl, filling his small pipe and lighting it, he couldn't imagine them as separate. His new horn-rimmed glasses disappeared in the smoke; he didn't yet have an older man's practised elegance in smoking his pipe. When he spoke in an animated conversation like this, his words came so fast that he swallowed them now and then, and you had to concentrate to work out just what he had said. How could a thing still exist in its own right without anyone looking at it? Even an inanimate object has its appearance, consistency and temperature, and not least a function.

Leontine glanced at Helene, who was lying on the chaise longue and had closed her eyes.

That, I suppose, is the challenge of my own craft: separation. Dissecting the body itself separates single parts from a whole. We can look at the liver, we can look at a tumour on it. We can separate the tumour from the liver and the liver from the body.

But not from a human being, and it will always be that human being's liver. Removing it from its place, the functional interruption of its symbiosis, robs neither the liver of the human being nor the human being of his liver.

Let's take the example of a leg. Carl still wasn't sure whether his ideas agreed with Leontine's or contradicted them. How many of our fathers' generation have one of their limbs missing these days? They can live without an arm, without a finger.

Martha groaned ostentatiously. She was getting tired of this conversation between Leontine and Carl; it was some while since she and Leontine had managed to get a day off at the same time like this. It was in the middle of the week, and they were planning to go and visit a couple of friends in Friedenau. Martha put her arm round Leontine's neck as if to throttle her.

If you two can't leave each other alone our hosts will have eaten all the cakes before we get there.

Leontine removed Martha's arm from her neck. The word cognition in itself can undergo a certain change of nature. The husk remains, but what was the cognition of God and his omnipotence yesterday is an incision into the tumour today.

Carl was smoking; he held his head upright – he was careful about the way he carried himself, careful not to shake his head yet, not until he had a clear idea of his train of thought and had found the right words to argue against her.

Meanwhile Leontine used the opportunity to develop her objections. Carl, it's not just medicine that has added so many new attributes to cognition that we can no longer speak of its having the same character. A glance at the sky, the technology of aviation, the lethal use of poison gas at the end of the war, all those are arguments against God.

No. Carl lowered his head. No, that's the wrong way to look at it; technology and science are the immediate offspring of divine cognition. It's only logical for human beings not to separate themselves from the light, the light of cognition. They're indissoluble.

Human beings learn lessons. I don't know myself whether praying to God does any good. I wouldn't give God human features, he doesn't speak in the way the Scriptures suggest, he doesn't judge. I would deny God's part in every moral capacity, everything that's human. God can be better described as a principle, the world principle. Only humans, with their emotional approach, can be accused of believing in God as the metamorphosis of a person. Carl drew on his pipe.

Human beings cause catastrophes today, just look at the war and its heroes. Could we recover from it? And what would be worse, material losses, the loss of human life, or injury to the feelings? Leontine rose and went over to the large samovar, the only object still standing on the long coffee table, and turned the tap. The heroes of the war were different. The water was too hot; she just touched the little glass to her lips without being able to drink. She went on talking over the rim of the hot glass: It's not ten years ago and see how people have been waiting by the news-stands for days ready to snatch the *Vossische Zeitung* hot off the press from the vendors. When they devour Remarque's accounts of the war, they're looking at their own botched work. We are sufficient unto ourselves.

No, no, if they were sufficient unto themselves they wouldn't feel either intellectual or physical hunger. Carl's voice lost its light note and his words, usually just uttered fast, were only half voiced now. I'd like to correct myself, I didn't mean to claim that we ought to accuse human beings and their passions of anything at all. Instead we ought to look askance at the divine principle which in my view, as I said, is not a moral one. Let's stop waiting to detect good and evil in man, let's feel some sympathy for his existence.

You're crazy, said Helene in a kindly but uncertain way; she wasn't at all sure of his assumption. She sat up, stretched on the chaise longue and arched her back like a cat. Then she spread out her arms and gave a groan of relief.

To me as a doctor, the extent of sympathy is the deciding factor. I want to help people to live in as healthy a condition as possible. Pain is bad, so I watch my patients, I investigate the cause of the pain, I want to relieve it. Leontine took a small sip of black tea and sat down again. She ran her hand through her short black hair. Then, moving forward, she sat on the edge of the cushions and planted her legs on the floor just as she had done when she was a young girl. It was a mystery where she had found that divided skirt in a coarse-weave fabric; it suggested the culottes that Helene knew only from old fashion magazines. Leontine leaned one outstretched arm on her knee and held her tea glass in the hand of the other arm, elbow crooked. There was a challenge in the way she sat there, in an attitude that Helene found as provocative today as ever, but for the first time it looked to her unfeminine.

Helene swung her feet to the floor and bent down in search of her shoes. Carl, she said, particularly if you think morality is a distinguishing feature of humanity, we ought not to despise what were originally human standards.

I don't despise them, I'm only suggesting we ignore them.

Head down on the floor to get a better view, Helene reached her arm far under the chaise longue. Face twisted with effort, she looked up at Carl: Oh, let's go to the cinema instead of this. I'm working until six tomorrow and the evening classes go on till ten. Helene had found her boots, put them on and tied the laces. November made the city grey; you had to wear warm clothing and if possible you went to the theatre or cinema several times a week to make those colourless days tolerable. Carl stayed in his chair and went on smoking. It was hard to tell whether he had even heard Helene's suggestion.

I admire you, Leontine, so let me tell you something else. In my opinion pain is the only condition that we can't equate with ordinary passions. It's pain that makes people imagine a future, whether Utopia or Paradise. If you, as a doctor, relieve the pain of human beings, that's good for the individual but bad for God. The God principle is built on pain. Only if pain were obliterated from the world could we speak of the death of God.

What about it, do we or don't we want to get to Friedenau before night falls? Martha was already standing in the doorway, hoping that Leontine would break off her conversation with Carl at long last.

Leontine looked at Carl, who was over ten years her junior, and a touch of sadness and resignation crept into her expression. Her voice was both firm and clear as she said: That's cruel. She paused and seemed to have to think. Your view is a cruel one, Carl. Yes, this is the right moment to leave. There was a certain harsh, almost bitter note in Leontine's voice. Listening to you, anyone might think that our priests – I don't know enough about your rabbis – that our priests were the first heretics, with their promise of relief from pain. Christians as an organized gang? Leontine shook her head. An expression of contempt came to her face. She looked away, looked at Martha, who was still standing by the open double door. Leontine stood up, put her hand on Martha's arm. Come along, Martha, let's be off.

The two women left the room. They could be heard in the corridor, speaking a few soft words, short sentences. Then the front door of the apartment closed behind them. Helene dared not look at Carl. The silence between them lengthened. Carl was smoking as he sat there, and in the light from behind it his thin face looked like a little old man's. He wasn't used to being left high and dry in mid-conversation. Helene crossed her arms. She wondered what she could say to cheer him up, and felt at the same time that she wouldn't be able to. He had simply ignored her protest just now; very likely he hadn't even been ignoring her on purpose.

We could see Pat and Patachon at six, we'd make it to the cinema in time. Helene spoke almost casually. She too had now gone to the door, and hoped that he would finally stand up and follow her.

Leontine mentioned injury to the feelings, said Carl, now speaking slowly, pausing in mid-sentence. His eyes went to the chair where Leontine had been sitting. She spoke of the wish for heroes or at least heroism. I don't like the ideas of Germanic heroism propounded by people like Arthur Trebitsch. There's no such thing as either redemption of a Nordic race or a Jewish conspiracy. What's tragic is that with the end of personal suffering, let's say at the moment of death, certain ideas are never lost, perhaps we can say not one of them is lost. They go on developing independently of the individual who thought about them during the tiny span of his lifetime. It's impossible to say who first thought of such an idea because something thought up by the human mind, moulded and impregnated by suffering, doubting itself, has no beginning and no end. Such an absence of boundaries makes me feel quite weak. There's no limit to mankind. Man drives God off his earth, *that belongs in the glowing brazier*, as Kurt Schwitters says.

Carl had been talking to himself, still answering Leontine, who had gone a long time ago. Exhausted, he dropped his hands to his thighs.

How about Charlie Chaplin in *The Circus*? Helene crossed her arms and learned against the door frame.

Carl looked at her in surprise. It was a moment before he could answer. The cinema, he said abruptly, sobered up, yes, let's go to the cinema. Isn't that boxing film on? Everyone's making movies about boxing, we ought to see one. *Combat de Boxe*, it's that young avant-garde Belgian director with the unpronounce-able name. Dekeukeleire. Even the name is enough for a film, don't you think? Or that Englishman, his film is called *The Ring* – the local movie buffs have said it's the world champion. Isn't that comical? Carl was trying to convince himself of the humorous nature of his remark.

A film about boxing? Helene wasn't sure, but she was ready to do anything to get Carl out of that chair and through the door with her at long last.

The street shimmered dark grey; cold moisture hung in the air between the buildings. The street lights were already on, and the evening paper was on sale at street corners.

Were you in love with Leontine?

Leontine? Carl dug his hands into his coat pockets. All right, I admit it. He didn't look at Helene and she didn't want to ask exactly what he meant by that.

H elene had run the last part of the way to the Charité Hospital. She had skipped her class that evening; the only subject discussed on the course for the last few weeks had been the questions they might face in the Higher Certificate exam. It was Easter, the pharmacist had given her the rest of the week off. Her small case was dark red and light to carry; she had bought it only a few days ago and hadn't packed much in it. Helene was still breathing hard as she knocked at the door of the doctor's office. Leontine opened it and they air-kissed over each other's shoulders.

Are you sure?

Yes. Helene took her coat off. Fairly sure. I don't feel sick at all, I just get pressure on my bladder at night.

How long ago was your last period?

Helene flushed. Although she had often changed the sanitary towels of bedridden women during her training and could remember washing Martha's little cloths in detail, she had never talked to anyone about her own periods before. And now this first question went straight to the subject of her last one.

January the twenty-ninth.

It could simply have been late. Leontine looked enquiringly at Helene, no blame, no judgement.

That's what I hoped too.

I suppose I won't have to fetch one of Aschheim's mice?

Leontine worked side by side with the gynaecologist Aschheim in his laboratory, but she would have needed a sample of Helene's urine taken first thing in the morning to test for pregnancy in a mouse by his method. She could have taken one of those tiny female mice, still immature and without any fur yet, to inject the urine subcutaneously. Then she would have had to wait two days and perform an autopsy on the mouse. If the tiny female had reacted by ovulating, it was certain that the woman was pregnant. Leontine was helping Aschheim to write a paper on the subject. It was to be ready around the end of the year, if all went well, and would be published the year after that.

I'm going to give you something to send you to sleep.

And I won't feel anything?

No. Leontine turned; she had stirred some liquid in a glass container and poured it into a glass from which Helene could drink. I know how anaesthetists go about their work.

Yes, of course. Now Helene was frightened. She wasn't afraid of the minor operation itself, she was afraid of unconsciousness. She sat down on the chair and drank the liquid in the glass at a single draught. She herself knew, from working at the pharmacy, what substances could be carefully administered in what amounts to induce unconsciousness for a limited period.

There was a knock, and Martha came in. She turned the key in the door and went to the window to pull down the shutters.

We don't want anyone seeing this, she said, and came over to Helene. Now, breathe in. Just a little ether. Helene saw Martha's steps moving in slow motion as she took her hand. She couldn't feel Martha's hand. Martha stood beside her and put an arm round her shoulders. I'm here with you.

There was no dream, no light at the end of the tunnel, no idea of what might have been, nor was there any image of a patriarchal God rising menacingly above Helene.

When she woke up she realized that she still felt numb all over. Only gradually did she feel the burning sensation. She was lying on her back with a strap firmly fastened over her breast. How had the other two women got her on to the stretcher? Helene dared not move. A light on the desk was switched on. Leontine was sitting at the desk, reading.

Is it gone? Helene's voice shook.

Leontine turned to Helene, stayed where she was on her chair and said: Go to sleep, Helene. We'll stay here tonight.

Is it gone?

Leontine buried herself in her book again. She didn't seem to have heard Helene's question.

A boy or a girl?

Now Leontine did turn to her abruptly. There was nothing there, she said, sounding annoyed. You ought to get some sleep. No embryo, no fertilized egg, you weren't pregnant.

Footsteps could be heard in the corridor, then moved away again. Helene was coming round properly now. I don't believe you, she whispered, feeling tears run down her temples and into her ears, lukewarm tears.

Leontine did not reply; she was bending over her book and turned a page. Seen lit from behind, with the light breaking like a prism in Helene's tears, it looked as if there were a thousand Leontines. Was that a pair of glasses she was wearing? Helene wriggled her toes and the dragging sensation inside her became so sharp and violent that she felt slightly sick.

Is Martha on night duty? Helene tried to suppress the pain. She didn't want to let it show in her voice.

All this week. She'll be along later and we'll take you home. You have seven hours until then, so you should get some sleep.

If Helene hadn't been in such pain, she would have managed to tell Leontine that she didn't want to sleep. But the pain would allow her only a few words and no defiance. Could I have a hot-water bottle?

No, warmth would only make it worse. Leontine gave the ghost of a smile. She stood up and came over to Helene, placing a hand on her forehead. You're crying. I could give you some morphine, a little at least.

Helene shook her head vigorously. Certainly not; she never wanted to take morphine, she'd sooner bear the pain, any pain, although she didn't say so aloud. She bit her lips, clenching her jaws.

Don't forget to breathe. Leontine really was smiling now. She stroked Helene's hair, which was damp from the perspiration on her forehead. Her tears kept on flowing; she couldn't stop them.

When you need to pass water let me know. It hurts the first time, but the urine will help, it has a healing effect. You just ought to lie down a lot if possible. Does Carl know anything yet?

Helene shook her head again, despite the fact that she was crying. I told Carl we were going on holiday to the seaside. We're on a trip to Ahlbeck, all right?

Leontine raised her eyebrows. Suppose he happens to meet me or Martha by chance?

He won't, he's studying for his exams. He's stayed in his room for the last three weeks. Helene gasped, because she couldn't laugh very well in such pain. He said it would still be chilly at the seaside and we mustn't catch cold.

Leontine took her hand away from Helene's forehead, went to her desk, pulled the lamp further down to her so that the rest of the room was more dimly lit and went on reading. In the lamplight it looked as if Leontine had a downy covering on her upper lip.

I didn't know you wore glasses.

Well, don't give me away to anyone, or I'll give *you* away.

In the morning Martha and Leontine walked on either side of Helene. Martha carried the small red case with Helene's underclothes in it. Helene had to keep stopping when her stomach cramped; she didn't want to bend double in the middle of the street. Blood was flowing out of her, and it seemed thicker than usual. The wind was whistling, the girls held on to their hats. Helene felt wet all through, moisture crawling up to her kidneys, running down her legs, and she felt as if it had reached the backs of her knees.

You wait here with her, Leontine told Martha. And Martha waited with Helene, putting an arm round her sister's waist. Martha's arm seemed uncomfortably heavy to Helene, as if her touch were irritating the pain and bringing it back. Martha's arm was a nuisance, but she couldn't speak and she didn't want to push Martha away. Suddenly she thought of her mother and felt bad. The sisters hadn't heard from Bautzen for a long time. The last letter from Mariechen had come at Christmas, saying that everything was all right, their mother was better, she could sometimes take a walk with Mariechen now. A spasm seemed to tear Helene's stomach apart and her knees almost gave way. Now Martha lifted her arm and put her hand on Helene's shoulder; unasked, she assured her that they'd soon be there. There was a strange expression in Martha's face, one that Helene had never seen before. Was it fear?

Little angel. Martha drew Helene to her and stood close. She stroked Helene's face. Helene wanted to tell her she didn't have to do that, it was only pain, that was all. She just had to overcome it, stand up to it, wait. Ahead of them in the street, Leontine waved; at last a taxi had stopped. It was beginning to rain, and passers-by put up their umbrellas. Leontine was now vigorously beckoning to them to join her. The blood between Helene's legs had cooled. Martha and Leontine took her to the little room in Achenbachstrasse. They had pushed the beds back into their old position, one against each wall, and assured Helene that the two of them wouldn't mind sharing the same bed for this week. They brought her water and told her it was important for her to rest as much as possible. There was a fragrance of bergamot and lavender. Helene wanted to wash herself, but she was not supposed to stand up. Doors closed out in the corridor. The Baron, perhaps?

No, Heinrich Baron had gone to Davos for the sake of his tuberculosis. He had been so ill recently that Leontine had examined him and prescribed something. The Karfunkels, husband and wife, had rented his room instead, said Martha. Fanny was glad to get a good rent, and had been able to redeem the gramophone and get it out of pawn.

Helene lay down on the narrow bed and closed her eyes. It was too bright.

It would be better if you lay on your front, little angel, then the uterus can drop more easily. Helene turned over. The pillows, the mattress, everything here smelled of Leontine. Helene closed her eyes again. The cramps weren't too bad. And she wasn't pregnant; that was good.

She lay on her front all that week, breathing in the smell of Leontine and being patient.

Martha had found out that the bus from Ahlbeck went to Heringsdorf and the express train from Heringsdorf station would reach Stettin Station in Berlin at two-thirty in the afternoon. So Leontine telephoned a friend in Ahlbeck and asked her to send a telegram to Carl Wertheimer. Arriving Sunday two-thirty, Stettin Station. Kisses, Helene.

Leontine was on duty at the hospital on Sunday. Martha and Helene went out to Bernau by tram. They waited a good half-hour at the railway station. Several newspaper boys ran towards the train as it came in, shouting, offering their Special Editions to the passengers at the windows. The train steamed and hissed even when it stopped. Berlin, all aboard. It was so crowded that Martha and Helene had difficulty in climbing on. The whistle blew and they were off. The train was full of Berliners who had been spending the Easter break by the sea and at other holiday resorts in the north-east, and were now on their way home to the city. They devoured their newspapers, exchanging views on the latest incidents in Schleswig-Holstein. They had no business in Wöhrden, said one old man, what did they think they were doing there anyway? Vigorous argument broke out around the old man. Cowards, that's what they are, he said.

Cowards? Not on your life! Justice is at stake.

It's dangerous to play with fire.

Helene held tight to the pole inside the carriage. They hadn't managed to find a seat. The pain was quite slight now, it had moved from her lower body to her back at the base of her spine, where it throbbed only to an extent that Helene could endure quite well. The people around her couldn't stop talking, everyone arguing with everyone else. Obviously these strong opinions were catching; every man, even every woman, wanted to speak at length about his or her views and arguments.

Underhand, that's what I call it. The woman who said that sounded offended.

We're not having an assembly banned, cried a man, and his neighbour agreed, we're not letting them slaughter us. Martha and Helene had to stand by the door all the way to Stettin Station.

Carl was waiting at the station, waving his arms about as if he had wings. The train groaned and finally drew to a halt. They got out, Carl hurried towards them, shook hands with Martha and took Helene in his arms.

I've missed you.

Helene pressed her face close to him, to his smooth fur collar. She didn't want him to look at her. People streamed past them.

A whole week by the seaside, and there am I sitting in my room and wondering whether Hegel absolutely had to alienate the German language from its original usage in order to express his ideas adequately. I mean, was it really necessary? Carl laughed. Where have you left Leontine?

She had to come back ahead of us. Professor Friedrich phoned her; he needed her urgently.

Let's have a look at you. Yes, you do seem better. Carl inspected Helene like an apricot he was thinking of buying, and tenderly pinched her cheek. A hint of rings round the eyes, maybe. You two didn't go dancing without me, did you?

We certainly did! And Martha handed Carl the little suitcase to carry.

That spring and summer flew by. Helene worked at the pharmacy, took the exams at the end of her course and waited for the results. Carl sat at his desk among his towers of books from morning to night; if he went out it was only for one of his written or oral examinations. At the end of the summer they both believed the world was at their feet. Two professors here were vying for Carl's attention; he just had to decide whether he would rather go on reading Hegel, or follow the general trend of the time and look more deeply into Kant and Nietzsche. He wrote letters to Hamburg and Freiburg, where he knew of other scholars whose work filled him with enthusiasm. After his results were announced – he had passed *summa cum laude* – an invitation from Dresden arrived asking if he would like to study the question of universal validity in Kant's aesthetics. But Carl was still waiting for answers from Hamburg and Freiburg.

You do know that we must get married before I leave Berlin, don't you?

Carl squeezed Helene's hand. They were crossing Passauer Strasse. There was a smell of foliage in the air; the autumn sunlight showed the light yellow of linden leaves against the dark branches of the trees. In Nürnburger Strasse the fallen leaves were being swept into heaps. Helene walked right through the middle of one heap, kicking it up with the toes of her shoes so that the dry leaves rustled. The maple leaves glowed green and red, their veins shining yellow and green, and edged with brown. The brown gold of chestnut leaves. Helene bent down and picked up a chestnut that had slipped out of its husk. Look, see how smooth it is, and such a lovely colour. She ran her thumb over the curve of the chestnut and held it out to Carl.

Carl took the chestnut from her hand, waiting for her answer. Her eyes were bright and looked almost green in the yellow light of the setting sun. There was a smile in them. Must we?

He nodded, he couldn't wait any longer. Be my wife, he said.

Helene hardly had to reach up at all to kiss him on the mouth. I'm yours, she whispered.

Marry me in the spring? He wanted to make sure of it. He took her hand and walked on.

In the spring, she agreed. She wasn't going to follow behind him, she caught up, and they both walked faster and faster. They had been invited to a party. The lights were already on in Achenbachstrasse. Fanny was still busy with her preparations; she needed the help of her domestic staff at home, and asked Carl and Helene to take Cleo for a walk. When they came back later the apartment was full of guests. A hoarse voice issued from the horn of the gramophone, complaining in song of the times they lived in. Their cousin from Vienna, whom Helene knew only slightly, hurried over to her as soon as they came through the door. He was so glad to see Helene, he said, he had never forgotten their delightful conversation two years ago. Helene wondered what conversation he meant. She had only a vague recollection of it; something to do with bringing up children. Such a pity, said her cousin in his rather moist-sounding voice, that she didn't speak French. Now he put his large, soft hand on Helene's arm. He had thought of offering her the post of governess to his daughters. Helene looked at him in astonishment. You could have our maid's room; after all, we're family.

Could she take their coats, asked Otta, obviously not for the first time. Relieved, Helene turned aside, took off her coat and exchanged glances with Carl, who was waiting patiently beside her. Helene took his hand.

I hear from Fanny, the cousin went on, that you've passed your exams with excellent marks. Well, no one would have expected anything else. I'm sure you would teach my daughters very well indeed. There are two of them.

This is my fiancé, Carl Wertheimer, said Helene, interrupting what her cousin was saying. The cousin swallowed in surprise as his glance fell on Carl for the first time.

Delighted. The cousin offered Carl his hand. So you're the man who's going to be lucky enough to . . . Here the cousin obviously had to stop and wonder why he assumed Carl was so lucky. He tried again. Who's going to be lucky enough to lead this lovely young lady to the altar.

Carl did not conceal his pride or his pleasure. It was the first time Helene had introduced him as her fiancé. We'll invite you to the wedding, he said in friendly tones. Will you excuse us now? Gently pushing Helene ahead of him, Carl made his way through the guests waiting in the entrance hall and into the drawing room, where people were sitting and standing crowded close together. Martha was talking to Fanny's new tenants, who looked large, pale and sober beside the other guests. The wife was holding a glass and Leontine had it topped up with more water. To Helene's surprise, she saw the familiar receding hairline of the Baron standing next to Leontine. His back was turned to the door and he didn't see Helene coming.

How lovely to see you, said Helene, tapping him on the shoulder.

Helene! The Baron spread out his arms, palms upwards, fingers slightly curving, a gesture that also suggested he was distancing himself. But he took Helene's hand and kissed it.

Are you better now? she asked. Have you been able to convalesce?

No, no better. When I arrived the doctor diagnosed a chill of the heart, what do you think of that, Helene? For a moment it looked as if the Baron were going to reveal everything about himself in front of everyone. He looked keenly around, but then began laughing heartily next moment. Ah, Davos isn't what it used to be. A few genuine invalids whom one doesn't want to know, and a great many hysterics who love to exchange medical anecdotes all day and stroll around the grounds of the spa. They go on group pilgrimages to the Forest Sanatorium.

Is that so? said a small, slim person whom Helene didn't know. Obviously this delicate-looking creature admired the Baron and was listening with a finger to her ear.

But no normal mortal so much as gains entry. The Baron was pleased to have an audience at last. I simply said, assuming an air of importance, that I was to see a certain Monsieur Richter. That seemed to me a good sort of name. The doorman nodded, satisfied, and let me sink into a big armchair for a while. I acted as if I were waiting. Unbearable, the company there, terrible.

How very true, said the frail creature, pushing a strand of copper-coloured hair back from her face.

Helene was glad to find the Baron in such high spirits. He was obviously better.

Carl Wertheimer, said the Baron now, trying to look pleased. How nice that you could come too.

We're engaged. Helene looked challengingly at the Baron.

Yes, er, yes, I've heard about that already. The Baron scratched his ear. Leontine told me about it. I must congratulate you. As if he found this difficult, the Baron put the flat of his hand to his receding hairline, and absent-mindedly tugged at his thin hair with his forefinger and middle finger. The delicate creature beside him shifted restlessly from foot to foot, looking around in a friendly manner.

My God, yes, what was I about to say? Oh, I wanted to tell you about the philosophical symposium, the argument that we weren't spared at Davos. But perhaps first I should introduce Fräulein Pina Giotto; we met in Arosa.

Staying at the same boarding house, the delicate creature confirmed.

It was like this: the prices in Davos, ah, here in Berlin you've no idea. And Arosa, well, it's almost part of Davos. The Baron fiddled with his hair, his eyes on Helene, and forgot to blink.

Situated even higher up, claimed the delicate creature.

The Baron tore his eyes away and looked uncertainly at his companion. Cautiously, he ventured a gentle but defensive gesture in her direction and spoke again.

As I'm sure you know, Carl, the argument between Cassirer and Heidegger had the whole place in uproar.

Terrible, yes, said Fräulein Giotto. One of them simply left the resort.

Heidegger announced that he was going to annihilate Cassirer's philosophy.

Yes, and then one of them simply went away. Did you ever

hear of such a thing? As I said to Heini, what a coward. Ducking out simply isn't done.

Now the Baron went red and sweat broke out on his forehead. He seemed unhappy with Fräulein Giotto's remark. Well, it wasn't quite like that. Apologetically, the Baron looked from Carl to Helene and back to Carl again. I'll explain. The Baron passed his handkerchief over his forehead and the gleaming bald patch on his head. It was about Kant. Heidegger's altered theory of Being is fundamental, radical, he hardly let Cassirer get a word in, perhaps Cassirer felt he wasn't being taken seriously. He was concerned with symbolic forms. He kept talking about the idea of the symbol. Perhaps that's why his hasty departure seemed to most of us a sign and symbol of his defeat.

Helene avoided exchanging glances with Carl. She didn't want to give him away. Weren't those the two gentlemen in Hamburg and Freiburg to whom Carl had written, and for whose answers he had been waiting several weeks?

When the party was sitting round the big table later, and after many courses the last to be served was a soufflé on a bed of apples, Carl was talking to Erich about the latest developments in the economy.

Buy, I tell you, buy, buy, buy. Erich was sitting opposite Carl and Helene. He had draped one arm round the back of Fanny's chair and was waving a glass of cognac in the air. Erich's neck, a sportsman's neck, seemed to Helene even more massive than usual today. We can only profit by it, believe me. The bursting of the speculation bubble is an advantage to us in Europe.

Don't you see any danger?

Oh, New York. You're still young, Carl. Presumably you don't have money. But if you did I'd give you good advice. The collapse in America will be useful to us. Erich leaned over the table and said, holding his hand in front of his mouth so that Fanny, sitting beside him and talking to the gentleman on her other side, wouldn't hear him: She'll soon be a rich woman again. I persuaded her to take out a mortgage on this apartment. She'll be buying the whole building, I assure you.

At this point Fanny stood up and raised her tall crystal glass. She asked her guests for their attention. She praised her friends, enumerating the anniversaries and honours enjoyed by some of them over the last few months, and every time the company clapped. Helene and Carl were glad she didn't mention the results of their examinations, so they did not have to stand up, nod at the diners around the table in a dignified way and show themselves proud of their achievements.

Carl leaned over to Helene and said quietly: Pride is for Philistines. Helene lowered her eyes; she agreed. To both of them the pride and self-satisfaction of the gentlemen whom Fanny mentioned were not justified by their distinctions, although it was to celebrate those distinctions that the show was staged.

As the evening wore on, Helene found herself standing with the Baron and Pina Giotto. Although she felt she couldn't bear any more of their chatter, she didn't want to leave their side, because Erich's greedy eyes had been following her all evening. Through the open doorway of the veranda, Helene saw that Carl was sitting there talking to Leontine, Martha and a couple whom she didn't know. Pina Giotto was trying to persuade the Baron to go to one of the big department stores with her next day; she wanted a feather boa. The Baron was looking for excuses; he probably guessed how expensive such a boa was. Boa, boa . . . Pina Giotto gave him no peace. Feather, boa, boa, feather. Long feathers, light feathers, shiny or matt? Peacock feathers, foreign feathers, a dress made of feathers. All this talk of feathers reminded Helene of her mother. In her last letter Mariechen had said she was a little better. Not confused any more, a walk was sometimes possible. It was nearly eleven when the first guests went into the front hall to call for their coats. Some were going on to a midnight revue, others wanted to go dancing at the ballroom. Come with us, said Fanny, with an all-embracing gesture over the heads of the Baron, his Fräulein Giotto and Helene. When, later, Fanny saw Helene among her late guests she babbled: You too, you little rascal.

Helene was looking for Carl, but at present the veranda was occupied by two men practising arm-wrestling at the low table. Fräulein Giotto was explaining to the Baron that the diamond she had seen at the jeweller's this morning was a beautiful size, just the thing to hang on a simple chain. Helene began to feel uneasy. Wherever she looked, she couldn't see Carl or Martha and Leontine. In spite of the danger that Erich might follow her, she excused herself almost inaudibly and strolled as casually as possible through the other rooms. She couldn't spot them anywhere. Just as she had crossed the Berlin Room and, looking around again, glanced back, she saw that Erich had her in his sights. He had followed her and was now making haste towards her. Helene opened the door to the back of the apartment. The light in the corridor wouldn't come on; she hurried past the first two doors when she heard footsteps behind her. For a moment the cone of light falling on her in the corridor from the Berlin Room disappeared. Erich had closed the door. In sudden panic, Helene groped along the wallpaper until she found the frame and then the handle of the door. It must be her old one, the room now occupied by Leontine and Martha. Voices and laughter came through the door. At the far end of the corridor Erich had obviously lost his sense of direction. She heard him breathing heavily. But she couldn't open the door. Helene shook the handle.

Just a moment, said a voice inside the room. It was a few seconds before the door was opened and Martha let Helene in.

Oh, it's you. Martha was obviously relieved and asked Helene to come in quickly. She shut the door again behind her sister. Taking no more notice of Helene, she sat down on the narrow bed. Leontine was perched on the edge of it with the unknown woman who had been sitting with the others on the veranda just now. The unknown woman was wearing a feather boa, the object of Pina Giotto's dreams. Dark violet feathers set off her striking cheekbones and shadowed eyes very well, and a fine permanent wave lay close to her shapely skull. Carl was sitting with his back to Helene at the washstand; now he stood up, surprised to see her. Helene noticed that he pushed the little silver box lying under his hand over to the unknown man who, Helene had thought before when she saw them on the veranda, must be the husband of the woman in the feather boa. But the woman with the boa was now sitting on the bed kissing Leontine. Violet feathers covered Leontine's face. Helene took fright when she realized how wide her eyes were opening in her surprise, and tried to look casually in some other direction. Only where? She knew what the box was, and its secret transfer from Carl to the other man could mean only that Carl didn't want to let Helene know what he was doing.

The others are leaving. Fanny wants us to go dancing with them.

She always wants to go to that Royal Club, said Martha, rather disappointed. Let's go to the Silhouette, it's nicer there. Martha opened the door.

Right, let's go, said Carl in a formal tone. Barely audibly, he sniffed. Now he went over to Helene and took her arm. Let's go dancing, my love.

Helene agreed; she didn't want to let anything show in her face. Only later, when they were dancing in a dimly lit ballroom and Carl wouldn't keep his hands off her hips, stroking her everywhere, in places that he never usually touched in company – he was laying siege to her as if they hadn't seen each other for days, as if they hadn't made love only that morning – only then did she find that she couldn't set her mind at rest or hold back any more. So in defiance of the loud music she called in his ear: Do you sniff that stuff often?

Carl had understood; he must have guessed that she had seen the box. Now he held Helene away from him, stretching out his arms, lowered his forehead slightly and looked at her. He shook his head. It mattered to him; she had to believe him. She did, not only because there was nothing else she could do. Their bodies belonged together: when he held her as they danced, when they let go of one another and came together again, his eyes looking into hers, searching and uncertain, looking inside to what he knew there with his kiss on her lips, when she felt that the two of them belonged together, it was a sense of closeness that did not merely admit or allow little secrets and differences; it unconditionally celebrated those secrets.

Helene danced with him until morning. Once she called to him: Hamburg or Freiburg?

Helene, cried Carl back. He drew her to him and whispered into her ear: I want to be wherever you are. His tongue touched her earlobe. If my wife will come with me, let's go to Paris.

On a February day, when the sun shone down out of a blue sky and the snow still lying in the streets was reddish-brown with the ashes scattered on it, Helene was standing in the pharmacy weighing out sage leaves on her scales for a customer. The customer wanted a whole pound. Helene dug the little shovel into the jar and tipped measure after measure into the scales. Perhaps the customer was going to put sage leaves in her bath. The bell rang as the door opened. Helene looked up. The small boy who had been standing in front of the jars of sweets for a long time left the pharmacy, hands in his pockets. The smell of burning coal and petrol drifted in from outside. It was midday, and apart from her present customer there was only another elderly lady waiting to be served. The telephone rang. The pharmacist appeared in the doorway of the back room. For you, Helene, he called and looked at her as if he were pleased. It was the first phone call that had come for her in all these years. I'll take over; you go and answer it. The pharmacist took Helene's place and she went to the telephone.

Yes? She had probably said it too quietly; now she called in a louder voice, against the rushing sound on the line: Yes?

This is Carl, Helene, I have to speak to you.

Has something happened?

I want to see you.

What?

Can you leave work early today?

It's Wednesday. I leave at noon anyway. I'll be coming out in quarter of an hour's time.

Helene had to hold the phone close to her left ear to make out what he was saying.

Excellent, shouted Carl. We'll meet at the Romanesque Café.

When?

Loud crackling interrupted them.

Darling, one o'clock at the Romanesque Café.

One o'clock at the Romanesque Café. Helene hung up. She had been pressing the receiver to her ear so hard that her temple hurt. When she came back into the front of the shop, the pharmacist was wrapping up a packet of Veronal and taking the elderly lady's money.

You can put your coat on now, Helene, he said in kindly tones, smiling at her mischievously, as if it were in his power to fix a rendezvous for her with the man she loved.

Helene crossed the Steinplatz. A thaw had come, changeable weather. She wondered why Carl wanted to see her so urgently. Maybe the philosopher in Hamburg had sent an answer. The man from Freiburg had written just before Christmas rejecting Carl's application. He was impressed, he wrote, by Carl's *summa cum laude*, but not so impressed by Hegel, and the posts for assistant lecturers were all filled. Helene stopped in Fasanenstrasse. A bicycle rang its bell behind her. It suddenly occurred to her that the cyclist might be Carl, who rode his bicycle in all weathers. She turned, but it was only a baker's boy who must have thought the road itself too slushy for him to ride on it. Helene stepped to one side, standing on a small mound of ice that was melting at the edges, and let the baker's boy ride past on the pavement. The wheels of his bicycle splashed slush on her coat. They were just waiting for Cassirer's answer now. In January, all doors were still open to Carl in Berlin. He could choose between those two professors who were vying for him here. But what he really wanted even more was to build up a reputation for research of his own, and for the last few weeks it hadn't looked as if he still seriously expected a reply from the philosopher Cassirer in Hamburg. What else could seem to Carl so urgent; why didn't he want to wait until this evening? Perhaps he wanted to see her to discuss the forthcoming visit to his parents that weekend? She was afraid to meet them. She and Carl had almost quarrelled the evening before. Helene had said she couldn't go to see his parents empty-handed, she wanted to buy them a present. Carl didn't think that was right. They needed the money badly for other things: food, books, and not least for their future life together when they moved to a proper apartment. Helene wanted to give his parents a little green vase that she had seen at Kronenberg's, in a corner at the front of the display window. A green vase? Carl had said incredulously, and it had seemed to Helene that he was mocking her. Even this morning, when they said goodbye to each other, Carl had told her his parents really wouldn't be expecting any present. They had wanted to meet Helene for years and, after all, his parents knew that they weren't exactly rich. Carl had been putting together the books he would need this morning, standing with his back to her, and murmured something else. What did you say? Helene had to ask, and he had turned round and said, in a casual tone of voice: The fact is, they don't know you're living with me. Helene had to sit down. It was a good three years since she had begun sharing his room. Every month she tried to buy as much of the food for their housekeeping as possible with her own money, since Carl refused to take any of it for the rent because his parents paid that. So did he want her to pretend to his parents on Sunday that she was still living with her aunt?

Carl had tried to calm her down, assuring her that he was going to tell them the truth himself on Sunday.

But in Helene's eyes that was worst of all. How could he take his long-standing fiancée to his home for the first time and say, during lunch: Oh, we've known each other for four years now, we got engaged to be married two years ago, but anyway we've been living together for over three years? Helene rubbed her eyes.

Look, you would never come with me to see them, how was I to explain that yes, you were living with me, but you didn't want to meet them?

Oh, so now I'm to blame, am I?

No, Helene, it's nothing to do with blame. It would have struck them as uncivil. How could I say that you simply didn't feel confident enough?

Helene had wanted to answer back but didn't dare, and she felt uncomfortable about that. She had scrubbed at her eyes until Carl came over and held her hands. Who did his parents think, she wondered, was washing and mending Carl's clothes, making sure he had a hot meal in the evening and keeping the room bright and cheerful, feeding the sparrows on the windowsill, watering the orchid in its herbarium when Carl crossed the Monti della Trinità every summer to go on holiday with his parents near Lake Zürich? When they went away his father did research work at the Swiss National Observatory, working out cycloids and mapping sunspots, while mother and son went to concerts together. His sister hadn't accompanied them on those holidays since her marriage. Carl had kissed Helene's hands and assured her that they would clear it all up on Sunday, the two of them. It was only a small thing they had to explain between them then; this was about their life together, after all, and everything that still lay ahead in their future.

Helene had to take care not to slip as she walked along. Ice still lay under the melting snow in many places. She had to wait outside the Memorial Church for a long time; the cars were driving slowly and skidding on the road. Carl was a good cyclist, he'd be careful, or he might have left his bicycle at the library. The big Kurfürstendamm clock said ten to one. Helene felt restless and stationed herself under the awning above the huge window of the Romanesque Café.

She was sure Carl had some good news to tell her. Perhaps he'd been offered another post somewhere? Perhaps he hadn't made up his mind between the two offers here and wanted to ask her which she thought the best choice? But if he had spent the morning in the library, as he had said earlier that he would, then nothing world-shaking could have happened there. Helene smiled nervously. She remembered how Carl would sometimes stop reading in the evening because he wanted to tell her some great idea that had occurred to him. Helene's eyes searched to both right and left of the Memorial Church on the other side of the crossing. Wasn't that a cyclist wearing a cap like Carl's over there? But perhaps he had left the library some time ago and had telephoned from Viktoria-Luise-Platz? And perhaps that was because he'd met the postman and the postman had brought him a letter from Hamburg. Hamburg was said to be a beautiful city. Sometimes Helene dreamed of living in a city with a harbour. She liked to see big ships. It seemed to her one of the disadvantages of her birthplace that it was neither by the sea nor in the high mountains. She knew mountains only from a distance, and anyway the Lusatian Hills were small and not real mountains at all. The sea was clear and distinct in her mind's eye; she had painted it in glowing colours for Carl, but she had never actually seen it.

Helene came out from under the awning and took a few steps to the left towards Tauentzienstrasse, in case he was coming that way. She looked around searchingly, wishing he would arrive. The four points of the compass just weren't enough here, and she didn't know which way he'd be coming. The sea, no . . . but she did know the big ships on the Elbe at Dresden. The clock said five past one. Suddenly Helene thought she knew why he had to see her in such a hurry, and laughed with relief. He had bought their wedding rings. Helene straightened her hat. Why hadn't that occurred to her before? He wanted to give her a surprise, that must be it. Perhaps he'd meant them to meet inside the café here and she had misunderstood. He was inviting her out in honour of the day. Helene looked around her. She couldn't very well go in; she might miss his arrival. A car hooted. Couldn't that woman with her two children move a little faster? But the traffic was getting worse and worse, and suppose there was another storm? Helene looked up at the clock. Quarter past one. Perhaps something had kept him. It wasn't like Carl to be late. When they had arranged to meet somewhere, he was usually waiting for her at the appointed place when she arrived. Helene looked in all directions once again, turned a few steps to the right. He might be coming along Budapester Strasse. The square, the tall church, the pavements, the roadways, they were all clearly visible despite the bright sunshine. Advertising pillars, people standing in line outside kiosks. Both cars and passers-by skidded in the slush; a coachman had to keep cracking his whip to get his horse moving. Helene shifted from foot to foot; her feet were wet and cold. She remembered the horse falling over on the day they arrived in Berlin. Had that horse died? A heart attack, trouble with its brain or lungs. An embolism. She had decided to take her boots to the cobbler this week. This would have been a good day; she'd have had time today. Since she didn't have a second pair she'd have to wait in the shop until the cobbler had stitched them up and resoled them.

A few minutes before one-thirty Helene decided that if Carl hadn't arrived by the time it was half past she would go and look inside the café. Perhaps he was finally planning to grant her long-cherished wish to go roller-skating, and had gone to the roller-skating rink to find out how to hire skates and buy tickets. They said it was expensive. The Russian girls at Helene's evening classes had often talked about the roller-skating rink and the latest acquaintances they'd made there. They met regularly at the rink to pirouette and twirl around. These girls were all younger than Helene and came from good Jewish families. Roller-skating must be fun. Helene waited until the big hand of the clock rested on the numbers six, then seven and finally eight. Then she went in.

The café was full. Customers sat at the little tables, and the mirrors all the way up to the ceiling made it look as if there were even more of them. It was lunchtime, many of the guests were eating meat roulades and potatoes, and the aroma of Savoy cabbage hung in the air. A distinguished-looking gentleman in black waved to a second man in strikingly informal garb; he wore pale, wide-legged trousers, braces over a crumpled shirt and a white beret. All he needed was an artist's palette in his hand. This was a place where people liked to withdraw into one of the attractive *chambres séparées*. Wine was drunk from tall glasses. Helene's throat tightened. She looked around and, sure enough, there were customers both young and old eating alone at many of the tables, but no Carl. The clock above the panelled bar said quarter to two. Why was her heart beating so hard? There was nothing for her to worry about. Helene went out of the café again into the Kurfürstendamm. A small crowd of people had gathered, an elderly lady kept calling Thief! Thief! Others were holding a boy who couldn't be more than ten or twelve. He wasn't struggling, he was crying. You little rascal, said one of the men holding him. But that wasn't enough for the old lady. Rogues like you ought to be locked up, she scolded him, you just wait until the police get here!

Helene decided not to wait any longer. She knew that Carl wasn't going to come now.

Perhaps they had misunderstood each other and he had meant a different time? But she knew perfectly well that he had said one o'clock. Wasn't it possible that he had meant something else? Maybe another place? They had often met on this corner; maybe he had wanted to meet somewhere else today and mentioned the café by mistake, but with another one in mind? Helene didn't know where to turn, where to go; she felt afraid, although she told herself there was nothing to fear. She went to a kiosk and bought cigarettes. It was the first time she had ever bought any for herself. She really needed the money for the cobbler, but she couldn't think about going to the cobbler now, she wanted to smoke a cigarette. She didn't have a cigarette holder; she'd have to smoke without one. She broke two matches before she managed to light the cigarette. A little piece of tobacco came adrift, tasting bitter on her tongue. It wasn't easy to hold the cigarette in gloved fingers. Helene didn't know which way to look now. She was standing in the middle of a busy crowd of people whose lunch break was over and who were hurrying back to work. Some of them might have appointments to keep, and had to run to the station and take a train going west.

The wind blew in her face, a west wind from the direction of the Memorial Church. Helene tried breathing deeply to inhale the smoke. South, east, north. But before she could draw the smoke into her lungs her bronchial tubes closed against it and she had a coughing fit. So she puffed the cigarette instead. Little clouds of smoke came out of her mouth. The rather sour, bitter taste of it made her feel pleasantly light-headed. She took short, quick puffs, blowing out her cheeks as far as she could, and finally letting the cigarette end fall in the slush at her feet, where it went out at once.

Helene didn't know where to go in search of Carl now. She walked down Tauentzienstrasse to Nürnberger Strasse, round several blocks, past the school where she had taken her evening classes – they had finished months ago now – and she did not turn into Geisbergstrasse until dusk was falling. She could see the black roof of their building from the other side of the square; no light, however faint, showed in their attic room.

All the same, she went up to make sure that no one had come in. The door was locked, the room itself exactly as they had left it in the morning. Helene didn't take off her coat. She went downstairs again, past the young man who lived on the third floor and kept forgetting his keys, so that he often had to sit outside the landlady's apartment with a stack of papers, perhaps revising a stage play or the scenario of a film, until someone came to let him in. He generally had a pen in his hand and was scribbling something in the margin of the typewritten pages. Helene went down Bayreuther Strasse to Wittenbergplatz, over Ansbacher Strasse and back to Geisbergstrasse, to Viktoria-Luise-Platz, up to the attic room and back down to the street again. The third-floor tenant must have been let into his room by now.

Helene had stopped wondering why Carl had wanted to speak to her so urgently in the middle of the day; she was just hoping he would appear and they could fall into each other's arms. Something must have detained him. Helene smoked a second cigarette, then a third as she walked around the streets for the third time, and in the end she had smoked eight. She felt very sick. She wasn't hungry at all.

She told herself she wanted to be home when he returned.

They could eat together when he arrived, he would put his hand against her cheek – oh, if only he would come home.

She took off her boots. She didn't want to disturb the land-lady by asking for hot water. So she sat on the bed, wrapped the blanket round her cold feet and tried to read the new book that Carl had brought her two days ago, but she couldn't get beyond the first poem in the volume. She read it again and again, read each line several times, and said the last three lines out loud to herself: *And then I thought I saw/you, far off, drain the glass/from which I drank before.* Then she began again at the beginning: *After that hour has passed/What next, what news is heard? /Those friends who went there last/Will send no word.* Helene understood only a fraction of what the poem said, her mind was somewhere else, half still in her thoughts, half closed off entirely while her heart beat fast and her eyes narrowed. It was as if, as she repeatedly read the lines of verse, some certainty were forcing itself upon her, taking her over. At one point Helene stood up. She was freezing. There was a basket under the washstand and Carl's vest, ready for washing, hung over the edge of it. She put it on next to her skin and his pyjamas over it. Overnight she counted the time by the distant chiming of clocks. When the first sounds could be heard stirring in the house in the morning twilight she stayed sitting on the bed by the wall, thinking: something has to happen now to make you get up, get washed and dressed. See you tomorrow, the pharmacist had said yesterday. She couldn't keep him waiting. Helene heard steps on the stairs, their stairs, the last flight that led only to the attic. There was a soft knock on the door. Helene knew that Carl wasn't forgetful, he always had his key on him; she didn't want to open the door. The knocking grew louder. Helene looked at the door. Her heart was thudding, exhausted with beating all night long. Helene knew that she had no choice: she must stand up, she stood up; she must go to the door, she went to the door; she must open the door, she opened it.

The landlady stood outside, still in her dressing gown. Fräulein Helene, she said, looking not at Helene but at the floor. Helene held on to the doorknob; she was so weak that the floor seemed to move and rise, turn round, sway back and forth. The landlady was in some difficulty. Well, many people found it hard to talk early in the morning. My telephone rang, she said, Professor Wertheimer told me his son wouldn't be coming back, he said he'd had an accident.

Which son? thought Helene.

She knew it was Carl who had had the accident, she had guessed it even before she heard the steps on the stairs and had to open the door. But which son, which son was the landlady talking about now? Helene said: Yes. She didn't want to move her head unnecessarily, no nodding it, no tilting it, after all, if it turned it might fall off her shoulders.

I asked Professor Wertheimer if you'd been told yet. He said he didn't think you could have been. I told him I would do it, I could go up to you. Professor Wertheimer said he didn't know where you lived, but if I could make sure you were told that would be good. He asked me if I had your address. I said I'd have to go and look. I suppose he still doesn't know you've been living here?

Helene clung to the doorknob with both hands.

He's dead. The landlady must be saying that just in case the message had been misunderstood. That's what I had to tell you.

Helene took a deep breath; some time she'd have to breathe out again. Yes. Still holding the knob tight in both hands, she closed the door until the latch snapped into place.

If there's anything I can do for you, Helene, she heard the landlady saying on the other side of the door, will you let me know?

Helene did not answer. She sat down on the bed and took the book on to her lap; she kept blinking: *I knew your glance, your eyes, /And deep there, it still seems, /Our fate, our joys arise, /Our love, our dreams.* She was reading out loud now, as if she were reading to someone and this was the only way the poem could get out of her. She could not raise or lower her voice even slightly. Helene read the poem through to the end again one last time. The night was over. Then she closed the book and put it on the desk. Helene opened the window. Cold air streamed in. The first streaks of light as day dawned were showing in the sky. There was a pale and delicate tinge of pink among them. She mustn't take off his vest. Helene washed and put her dress on again. Her shoes were still wet; she had forgotten to stuff them with newspaper. Her coat smelled of yesterday's smoke.

Helene never managed to get to work that morning. At the last corner, when she could already see the pharmacy's familiar shop sign, she turned away. She went down the street leading away from the pharmacy. She had not made up her mind where she wanted to go, she had no idea where she *could* go. She simply put one foot in front of the other. Cars drove past, people walked by, the tram moved on its rails, perhaps squealing, although the city seemed to Helene to be perfectly silent. She was not out of breath, only silent.

Finding it so easy to put one foot in front of the other aroused a memory in Helene, although it went away again at once. Helene crossed streets; she didn't have to look right and left any more. The pink light had lit up the sky, the world was bathed in pink now, a sallow tone of pink that didn't suit it. Dark-blue buildings turned violet, and next moment morning had come, there was not a trace of pink left. The pharmacist would wonder where she was. But she was here. She could telephone him and say she couldn't come to work today. Let him wonder why; she never took time off for sickness, but today she couldn't, couldn't go to work. Helene put one foot in front of the other. Tomorrow? What sort of a day would tomorrow be? What could tomorrow be like? Helene didn't know. She found herself standing at the foot of the broad stone steps in Achenbachstrasse. Otta opened the door and told her that Martha was still asleep and Leontine had gone out an hour ago – she had gone to work.

Helene sat down by the washstand in Martha's room. It would be only a few hours until Martha woke up. She had been on night duty. Helene was not really waiting, just sitting there and letting time pass. She wasn't waiting for Martha, she wasn't waiting for Leontine. Helene wasn't waiting for anything any more. It was reassuring to find that time passed all the same.

Later, Martha brought her a glass of tea, found her something to eat and telephoned the pharmacist for her. When Martha sat down she held on to the edge of the table, when she walked along she kept touching the wall. Helene knew that there had been some-thing the matter with Martha's sense of balance for some time. Helene watched the steam rising from the tea in the glass. Martha said something. Helene lowered her head until her chin was on her breast; she could smell him better that way: Carl, the smell of him rose to her from the neck of her dress. Very slightly, so that Martha wouldn't notice, she raised one arm. Yes, his smell was there in her armpit too, clinging to her along with his vest. Martha said something in a louder voice now, loud enough to make Helene listen at last; she must drink her tea, said Martha, she ought to eat something too. Helene couldn't imagine ever eating.

She could sit, she didn't know if she could swallow. She tried it, she swallowed, she put the glass down. That might do for this morning.

At midday she drank the cold tea at a draught and then drank water from the jug on the washstand. The jug was empty, her throat hurt from stretching and closing as she drank. Then Helene sat down again and went on not waiting for anything. Days passed.

If Martha was at work, Helene lay down on her back on Martha's bed and moaned. Sometimes she wept quietly.

When Martha and Leontine said Helene ought to put on her coat, she put on her coat and followed them. Martha went to number 11 Viktoria-Luise-Platz and brought Helene's things down from upstairs. She gave Helene's key back to the landlady and asked her not to tell Carl's parents that Helene had been living there with him. His parents had paid the rent until the end of the month.

Meanwhile Helene had been sitting on the bench in the square outside the house, watching the basin of the empty fountain and the sparrows hopping about on the edge of the little puddles, dipping their beaks into the water. They were bathing. The water must be cold as ice.

Martha and Leontine wanted Helene to go out as much as possible, to keep moving. Helene kept moving. Martha said Helene had to eat. Leontine said no, Helene didn't *have* to do anything. Hunger came back of its own accord. It was good that Helene wasn't waiting for anything now, not waiting to feel hungry, not waiting for food. Sunday arrived. The plan had been for Carl and Helene to visit his parents that day, Helene remembered. Were his parents praying? God wasn't there, she heard no voice, no sign appeared to her. Helene didn't know when Carl's funeral would be. She didn't feel brave enough to go to the telephone; she was a stranger to them, after all, and she didn't want to bother his family, especially now. Time contracted, rolled itself up, folded itself.

Sunday had gone, other Sundays would come and go too.

The sun shone with more warmth now, crocuses were in flower in the beds beside the broad streets. Leontine and Martha said goodbye to her; Leontine was sending Martha to a sanatorium for a month. Dysfunctional equilibrium. What a pompous way of saying she had a poor sense of balance. She had to convalesce and detoxify her body. Martha cried when she said goodbye; she was so sorry that now, of all times, she couldn't be there for her little angel. Martha clung to Helene, threw her long, thin arms round her so tightly that Helene could hardly breathe. What did anyone need air for anyway? Helene didn't try to free herself, it was Leontine who had to pull Martha away. Martha was angry, she accused Leontine of hurting her, using expressions Helene had never heard from her before.

Don't you dare separate me from my sister, you bitch, I won't be parted from her.

But Leontine was sure of herself, and there was no way around it: she didn't want to lose Martha, so she must get her out of the city, perhaps for a month, perhaps for two. Leontine took Martha away with her first by physical force, then by dint of severity. Helene heard Leontine still talking to Martha as they left the apartment, much as you talk to an animal, not expecting any answer. Without Martha there, Leontine seemed to feel she had no right to stay in Fanny's apartment. Helene didn't ask Leontine if she had gone back to her husband.

She hardly saw Leontine. Once Leontine brought some medicine for Fanny, another time she came to fetch a pair of winter shoes that she had forgotten. Helene went with Leontine to the door, where she turned and placed one hand on Helene's shoulder. Martha needs me. You do know I have to take care of her now, don't you? Helene nodded; her eyes were burning. She wanted to put her arms round Leontine and hold her close, but she just blushed. And Leontine let the hand slip off her shoulder again, opened the door and left.

Helene was sleeping alone in the room overlooking the court-yard now; she had pushed the beds apart again. She went to work at the pharmacy and was glad that the pharmacist was reserved in his expressions of sympathy. He didn't pester her with questions. Yet he could hardly know how numb Helene felt. In spring the pharmacist told her she was getting thinner and thinner. Helene knew she was; her clothes were hanging off her, she forgot to eat, and when food was placed in front of her she ate without any real appetite.

One day a letter for her came from Carl's mother. She wrote to say she was in deep mourning; life without her youngest child was hard. Was she deliberately saying nothing about her other two sons, whose death, Carl had said, she so persistently refused to accept? Carl was buried in Weissensee cemetery, she wrote. Recent events were bringing some changes to their life. Her husband had been offered a post in New York, and this time they were thinking of accepting it. None of their children lived in Berlin now and their daughter was emigrating to Palestine with her husband. Finally, Frau Wertheimer wrote, she knew that Helene might not welcome this request, but in spite of Carl's death she herself would dearly like to meet her. Carl had spoken of Helene to his parents with such affection, such enthusiasm, he was so much in love that they were sure he had been plan-ning to tell them about a forthcoming engagement in due form when they were all to have met that day in February. Or perhaps she, Frau Wertheimer, was wrong and the young couple had just been friends? She was writing this letter to invite Helene most warmly to visit them, and asked her to telephone. If for what-ever reason Helene didn't want to, she would understand.

She wished her every happiness in her young life and was confident that she would find it.

Helene didn't want to go. No part of her wanted to accept the invitation. But like her free will, her fears had left her too. If Carl's mother wished for a meeting so much, she would grant that wish. Using Fanny's telephone, she called her at their house by the Wannsee and they agreed on a date for her to visit in early May.

She bought white lilac and took it to the Wannsee. A gardener opened the gate to her. A housemaid met her at the front door. Would she like to leave anything in the hall? Because of the warm weather Helene was not wearing a jacket, only her thin organza scarf, and she didn't want to take that off and give it to the maid. The housemaid took the lilac from her, so Helene stood there empty-handed as she heard a voice behind her saying: Welcome.

Good day. I'm Helene. Helene went to meet the lady.

Carl's mother offered her hand. I'm Frau Wertheimer and my husband will be here any moment. I'm glad you came. A light floral perfume rose from her. Thank you so very much.

Don't mention it, said Helene.

What did you say?

Helene wondered whether she had said something wrong. I was very happy to come. The professor's wife's eyelids fluttered slightly; for a moment her candid glance reminded Helene of Carl. She looked around.

Would you like some tea? Carl's mother led Helene through the high-ceilinged entrance hall. Paintings hung on the walls. In passing, Helene saw the Rodin watercolour Carl had mentioned to her. She wanted to turn and look at it, but was afraid his mother might not think that the right thing to do. The dark picture could have come from Spain. In her long, elegant tea gown, which suggested an oriental princess's evening wear, Carl's mother walked through the next room. Its tall windows looked out on a garden where the rhododendrons were in bloom, their pale violet and purple shining against the dark green of the smooth leaves. The grass was tall and sprinkled with wild flowers. Insects danced in the air above. Helene knew from Carl that this garden went down to the lake, and they had a landing stage where their sailing boat and a rowing boat were tied up. Over fifteen years ago, Carl's brothers, lost in the war, had sailed and rowed those boats.

Carl's mother went into the next room. Chinese vases a metre high and furniture in the Biedermeier style stood there. The wide double doors leading to the terrace were open and the lake lay below. The smell of newly mown grass rose in the air with the warm moisture of spring; the gardener must be cutting it, although he was nowhere to be seen. This was more of a park running slightly wild than a garden, for wherever Helene looked she couldn't see a fence. Only some white-painted arches showed where a circular rose garden stood a little way downhill.

Shall we sit down? Carl's mother pulled back one of the chairs and adjusted the flat cushions for Helene to sit in it. The table was laid for three. In the middle was a dish full of strawberries, which must have been imported from the south, since native strawberries weren't ripe yet. The strawberries lay on a bed of young beech leaves. A parasol provided shade. Birds were twittering in the rhododendrons and the tops of old broad-leaved trees. Was this the place that Carl used to visit on those Sundays when they went out to the Wannsee together and Helene sat reading in the garden of the inn? She had formed no idea of the appearance of Carl's home when he visited his parents. Vines climbed up the ochre wall of the house, their leaves still young and soft. So was it from all this splendid colour that Carl came when he fetched her at the inn? Perhaps he had sat at this table, on this chair, and looked at the fading blossom of the apple tree as Helene was looking at it now. Did his mother always wear that fine, sweet, unusually light perfume? The fuchsias in large pots and containers on the terrace were putting out their first flowers and large, almost improbably bright green ferns grew beside the flight of steps that broadened as it went down to the garden leading to the water. The colours dazzled Helene's eyes. She sat down carefully; the chair creaked and wobbled slightly. The tablecloth was delicately embroidered with flowers. Even Mariechen couldn't have done it better. Helene carefully ran her hand over the embroidery.

Would you like to wash your hands and freshen up a bit?

Rather apprehensive, Helene made haste to say yes. Only on the way back to the house did she take a surreptitious look at her hands, but she couldn't see any rim of dirt under her nails, or anything else suspect.

The bathroom was made of marble, even the stove was covered with marble tiles, and the soap was perfumed with sandalwood. Helene took her time. They'd wait for her out there. A pair of horn-rimmed glasses lay on the shelf above the stove. Helene recognized them. It looked as if Carl had only just put them down to go and lie on the lounger in the garden and rub his eyes. When Helene had found her way back to the terrace, she heard a male voice that reminded her of Carl.

Carl's father's likeness to his son took Helene's breath away. She just nodded when he greeted her, her lips forming a smile, while Carl's mother introduced her husband to Helene by name.

The three of them sat down. I don't have much time, said Carl's father when his wife poured him some tea. He didn't say it to Helene, he said it to his teacup, glancing at the large wristwatch he wore.

You're very pretty, said Carl's mother and rather shyly, but admiringly, added: And so blonde.

She's very blonde, yes. Carl's father drank from his cup quite noisily. It sounded as if he were washing out his mouth with the tea.

So pretty, too, Carl's mother repeated.

Leave the poor child alone, Lilly, you'll embarrass her.

Are you studying, may I ask? The professor put this question too without looking at Helene. He took one of the strawberries and put it in his mouth. His wife pushed a small fruit dish with an even smaller fruit knife over to him, no doubt so that he would find some use for it this time, and before Helene could answer she told Professor Wertheimer: No, Carl told us, remember? She's a trained nurse.

A nurse? It was a moment before the professor could think what to say next. Well, nursing is a very useful profession. A friend of our Ilse . . .

Ilse is our daughter, Carl's mother explained.

But Carl's father was not going to be interrupted. A friend of our Ilse trained as a nurse too and now she's a doctor.

In London, added Carl's mother, and asked if she could pour Helene some more tea.

Helene drank her tea. She didn't want to tell them she was working in a pharmacy now, she didn't want to explain, unasked, how she and Carl had imagined their future. They had intended to go together to Freiburg or Hamburg, where Helene would study. Probably chemistry, pharmacy or medicine. Carl was in favour of chemistry, she preferred the idea of medicine, but perhaps pharmacy would have been the obvious choice after her work in the pharmacy in Berlin. The snag was that Helene had no money to pay for her studies. But independently of that, her wonderful idea of studying had now moved into the remote distance; it seemed to Helene as if that wish belonged to another, earlier life and was not her own any more. Helene no longer wished for anything. The visions that they had developed, discussed and conjured up together were all gone, had vanished with Carl. The man who shared her memories no longer existed. Helene looked up. How long were they going to sit there saying nothing? Carl's father had eaten half the dish of strawberries without using the fruit knife. A last trickle of black liquid came from the teapot, and the joy and excitement of Carl's mother, so palpable at first, seemed to have died down as they sat at the table.

Well, then. Carl's father took the napkin that he had tucked into his shirt and put it down beside the unused fruit bowl and the little knife.

My husband works a great deal.

That's not quite right, I don't work a great deal. I just like working. The professor affectionately put his hand on his wife's arm.

He has a small observatory up there. Carl's mother pointed to a terrace higher up the slope, with several telescopes showing above its balustrade.

Only a little one, said the professor, standing up. He nodded to them both and was about to take his leave, but Helene stood up too.

You were so lucky to have Carl as a son. He was a wonderful person. Helene was surprised by her firm and cheerful tone. It sounded like birthday congratulations.

Carl's mother was crying.

He was her darling, Carl's father told Helene. Neither of them had said a word about their other two sons.

Carl's father went over to his wife's chair, took her head in his hands and pressed it against him. She was hiding her face behind her long, slender fingers. Something about the gesture reminded Helene of Carl, the way he came over to her when she was sad and exhausted, the way he had warmed her cold, tired feet.

The professor let go of his wife. I'll tell Gisèle to bring you some more tea. Helene was going to refuse it; she didn't want to stay, she couldn't bear the silence and the beautiful colours here any longer. She opened her mouth, but no sound would come out, and no one noticed that she had risen to her feet to leave when he did. The professor shook hands with her; his hand was warm and firm. He wished her every happiness, and disappeared through the double doors into the house. Helene had to sit down again.

He was my little darling, said Carl's mother, with a tenderness in her voice that sent a shiver down Helene's back. Carl's mother was kneading her handkerchief on the table in front of her, watching its folds as it fell apart again. Her long fingers ended in oval nails with white half-moons which were so regular that Helene couldn't help gazing at her hands.

He wanted to marry you, didn't he? Carl's mother looked straight at Helene. It was a glance that wished to know everything and was prepared for anything.

Helene swallowed. Yes.

Carl's mother had tears running down her delicate, beautiful face. Carl couldn't help it, you know. He was born to love.

Aren't we all? That was the question that went through Helene's head. But no, probably we weren't. Very likely it was a fact that some people loved more warmly than others and Carl really couldn't help it. She was wondering how the accident had happened and whether she could ask, if such a question would seem to his mother inappropriate, indiscreet. How exactly did he die? On the other hand, Carl's mother still couldn't know that they had been going to meet that day, that he had died on his way to her. That she had waited for him in vain.

She would also have liked to know whether Carl had wedding rings on him at the time of the accident, but she didn't dare ask his mother that. It wasn't her place. His last intentions were his alone, or perhaps for his heirs too, and his heirs were his parents.

There was still snow on the ground, said Carl's mother, drying her eyes with her handkerchief. Fresh tears were trickling out and rolling down her cheeks, hanging on her chin, collecting until they were so heavy that they dripped on her oriental dress, where they made dark patches that kept growing larger.

Helene raised her head. We were going to meet that day.

No glance, nothing to show whether Carl's mother had heard Helene's distinctly spoken words.

The sun was shining, said Carl's mother, but snow was still lying on the ground. He slipped and hit his head on the radiator of a car as he fell. The car couldn't stop in time. They brought us the bicycle. It was mangled. I rubbed it clean. There was a little blood sticking to the spokes. Only a little. Most of it must have been left on the road.

The housemaid brought another pot of tea and asked if there was anything else they would like. But when Carl's mother didn't seem to hear her she went away again.

The snowdrops he had been holding were still fresh. The police officer brought us everything. The snowdrops, his glasses, the bicycle. He had a bag of books with him. There were nine marks in his wallet, nine marks exactly, no groschen, no pfennigs. Carl's mother smiled suddenly. Nine marks, I wondered if someone had stolen money from his wallet. Her smile faded. There was a lock of fair hair in it. Yours? He died instantly.

Carl's mother dabbed at her eyes, but in vain. It looked as if dabbing them just made the tears flow more freely. She blew her nose, she wiped the corners of her eyes with a part of the handkerchief that was still fairly dry.

Helene sat up straight. She couldn't sit here any longer, and one of her legs had gone to sleep. My heartfelt sympathy, Frau Wertheimer. Hearing her own words, Helene was horrified by the false sound of her voice. She meant it, she wanted to say it, but the way she had said it sounded all wrong, indifferent and cold.

Carl's mother raised her eyes now and looked at Helene from under her heavy, wet eyelashes. You are young, your life is ahead of you. Frau Wertheimer nodded as if to emphasize what she was saying, and there was warmth in her eyes such as Helene had never seen in a woman before. You will find a man who will love you and marry you. Beautiful as you are, and so clever.

Helene knew that what Carl's mother was foretelling, to comfort them both, was wrong. She was saying it, yes, but her words hinted at a subtle distinction: Helene could look for another man, she would find one, nothing easier. But no one can look for another son. The likening of one man to another, the competing functions of a human being, the reduction of that human being to his place in the life of those who loved him seemed to Helene fundamentally wrong. But she knew that to shake her head and deny what Carl's mother had said would hurt her feelings. It was impossible to compare their grief, and there would have been something cruel in it; each of them was mourning a different Carl.

I must go now, said Helene. Although her cup was still full, she rose to her feet. The chair grated harshly as she pushed it back. Carl's mother stood up; she had to hold the folds of her tea gown. Perhaps she had shrunk inside it. She pointed to the door with one hand, so that there could be no doubt, so that Helene would start on her way through the interior of the house.

Helene wanted to wait for her to go first, but she herself was to go ahead. Do go first, said Carl's mother; she didn't want Helene looking at her. Helene heard her walking through the drawing room behind her, past the place where Carl's glasses lay, past the tall vases and some framed silk embroidery that Helene noticed for the first time, past pastel pictures of herons and moths, bamboos and lotus flowers. They were back in the entrance hall. The Rodin picture was of two women, girls dancing naked.

Thank you for asking me. Helene turned to Carl's mother and offered her hand.

It's for us to thank you for coming, she said, and had to move her handkerchief to her left hand to give Helene her long right hand, which was curiously warm and dry, yet damp at the same time. A light hand. A hand that would not be held any more and would itself hold no one's.

The housemaid opened the front door for Helene and went to the wrought-iron gate with her.

As soon as the gate had latched behind Helene and she could go down the road, past the wood and into the light of the sun shining pitilessly down, she began to cry. She couldn't find a handkerchief in her little handbag, so she dried her tears on her bare forearm from time to time, and when her nose ran she picked a maple leaf and blew her nose into that. Young oak shoots in the undergrowth. She walked through the wood, past the red-flecked trunks of the pine trees, over protruding roots. Dust rose from the sandy forest floor.

NIGHT FALLING

hy did you think I was dead? Carl put his arm round Helene and drew her gently to him. How warm he was. There was a greenish shimmer about his fur collar. Helene buried her nose in smooth hair, a pelt smelling of Carl, fine, spicy tobacco.

Everyone thought so. You'd disappeared.

I had to go underground. Carl wouldn't say any more. Helene thought there could be reasons she wasn't to know. She was glad he was there with her.

Only the twittering bird disturbed her. Cheep, cheep. Green as stone. The curtains were green as stone, green as lichen, the light made the green stream in, made the colour of the curtains look paler. Helene's heart was hammering. A slight wind was blowing in, the curtains billowed. Those couldn't be the curtains of the first-floor room overlooking the courtyard. Not possibly. Helene turned over, her heart racing, lay flat on her front, her heart beat against the mattress, throbbing as if it wanted to go from one place to another, and if she turned on her back again it would leap out of her. It turned a somersault, stumbled, Helene breathed in, she must breathe deeply, breathe calmly, tame her heart, lighten it, nothing easier, her heart was too light anyway, it was already up and away, it was making off. Helene counted heartbeat after heartbeat, she counted to over a hundred. Her throat felt tight, her heart was running away from her counting, she put her fingers on her wrist, her pulse was racing too, pulse at rest, pulse beat one hundred and four, five, six, seven. Ought she to know this blanket, was it hers? What had happened to pulse beat number eight? She must have reached number twelve by now. One hundred and twelve. She closed her eyes firmly, harsh eyes, perhaps she could get back to Carl again. But it didn't work. The more she wanted to be with him the further away he retreated, going back into the dream, into a world where her will counted for nothing. Helene dried her face with the sheet. Dappled sunlight on the mattress, marking a memory of something, of what? Blankets. Helene held her hand in the light, sun on her skin, that was entirely pleasant. Pleasant as if a day like this might hold something in store for her. Dark patches on the sheet, damp, the sweat had run from her armpits, had been weeping from the pores under her arms, tears, thin sweat. Helene would get up now, she'd be expected, although after her night shift she didn't come back on duty until two this afternoon. Helene got up. She wasn't sweating too much. She dressed herself. She had washed her clothes yesterday evening and hung them over the chair in front of the window so that they would be dry in the morning. Her clothes smelled of Fanny's soap, everything did, except Carl's vest that she still wore, his inner garment her outer one by night, when she was where he was now. She didn't want other people to smell Carl, or the mixture that she and Carl had become with time.

Outside the air was full of sunlight. The postman went his way whistling, swinging his bag back and forth, it dangled, a light weight, perhaps he'd delivered all the letters. He glanced at Helene and gave a friendly whistle through his teeth, making it the beginning of a well-known tune. Two children hopped along the paving stones with their school satchels on their backs, one of them fell, the other child had pushed him and now ran away with a mischievous laugh. There was whistling everywhere, and stones and hopping and children and roads, none of it intentional, it had nothing to do with Helene in particular, presumably it would be just the same if she weren't here. No one meant Helene any harm.

Summer heat made the air above the paving stones quiver, liquid air, blurred images, puddles showing where there hadn't been any for weeks.

There was a smell of tar; a wooden fence was being painted black on the other side of the street, and the ground under Helene's feet felt slightly yielding. The tram squealed as it went round the bend, driving slowly, so that the squealing was long-drawn-out, you heard the dragging sound on the curve and saw the sparks flying, and it didn't stop for a long time. Helene liked everything vague and indistinct these days; she lay in wait for it, but as soon as she thought she saw it, it went away. The heat slowed the city down, enfeebling its inhabitants, thought Helene, making them soft and flexible, crippling them. The less Helene herself weighed, the more oppressively did the heat weigh down on her. It wasn't unpleasant. Helene's body had grown thin but not weak. On Leontine's recommendation she had found a post at the Bethany Hospital and was working as a nurse again for the first time in years. The pharmacist was relieved, and indeed it lifted a burden from his shoulders, for he had hardly known how to pay her recently. She was paid no money at the Bethany either to start with; for the first three months she was on probation, but there would be pay as soon as she had her remaining qualifications. For the time being, Helene borrowed some money from Leontine.

She was friendly to everyone, yet she never really talked to anyone. Good day, she said to the bloated, dying man in Ward 27. Are you feeling better today?

Yes, of course; thanks to your pills I finally managed to stop worrying about my will yesterday evening and get some sleep.

The patients liked talking to her, not just about their illnesses but about their families, whose behaviour could be particularly odd around a deathbed. The bloated man's wife, for instance, no longer ventured to visit his bedside alone, but always came with his younger brother, whose hand she sometimes sought and sometimes pushed away. There was something about the hands of those two, and the dying man confided to Helene that he had known about their secret relationship for several years, but hadn't shown that he knew, because he wanted them to inherit his property with a clear conscience. That way it would all stay in the family, wouldn't it? None of the patients had ever ventured to reply to Helene's question by asking how she was herself. Her uniform protected her. The white apron was a stronger signal than any of the traffic lights going up at more and more road junctions in the city these days, shining brightly to show who could go and who must stop. If you wore white you could keep your mouth shut; if you wore white you weren't asked how you were. Courtesy was all on the outside for Helene and hardly tamed her despair, but it controlled it; pity for the suffering of others was her inner prop and stay. She wondered whether her bloated patient could really die more easily for knowing that his wife was having an affair with his brother. Perhaps he was just imagining the affair so that he could bear to say goodbye. It was easy for Helene to remember the names of patients, where they came from, their family histories. She knew who liked to be addressed in what tone and respected the wishes of patients who preferred silence. If Helene did manage to drop off to sleep at night, she was woken by the grinding of her own teeth and her weeping. Only when she dreamed of Carl coming back, kissing her, surprised to find that he had plunged Helene and his family

into distress and mourning, but explaining that it was all a misunderstanding, he hadn't died at all, only then did she sleep well.
However, waking up after such nights and returning to her life
was difficult, coming back to a new day like this one, an ordinary, unasked-for, unwanted, unimaginable new day of her life.
What was her life really like? What was it going to be like, was
it ever to be anything, was *she* ever to be anything? Helene tried
to breathe, to breathe easily, lightly. But her ribcage wouldn't
expand and she could hardly take in air. She kept thinking what
it was like when you fell down flat in childhood and the impact
winded you, making breathing impossible for ages, your mouth
was open, there was air around it, but the rest of your body was
self-contained, closed. Yet living in the usual way, with nothing
showing on the surface, was surprisingly easy. She was healthy,
she could stretch and bend each of her fingers separately until
her hand looked as if it were foreshortened; she could put her
head on one side and her body obeyed. Her internal irregulari-
ties gave her no trouble; Helene could work even if her heart
sometimes skipped a beat and breathing was difficult.

The other nurses went to dances and on moonlit outings
together, and they always asked Helene if she'd like to come too.
In the changing room they tried on the shorts they were going
to wear on the beach of the Wannsee.

Look at this, said the young nurse who was generally known
to be bubbly, swaying her hips and cheerfully sticking out her
behind. Helene liked the gesture and thought of Leontine; yes,
something about the bubbly nurse reminded her of Leontine.
She was like a boy with her cropped hair, standing there in the
new shorts and showing the other nurses her behind, although
she could be both stern and mischievous on her rounds of the
wards. Then another girl would try on the shorts. Wouldn't
Helene like a go, they asked, she really must go to the bathing

beach with them some time. Helene refused the invitation, saying she had a prior engagement. She invented an aunt who needed to be cared for; she wanted to be left in peace. The nurses' giggling and soft laughter were pleasant so long as they left her alone, with silence in the background, but as soon as they tried to draw her into their group, turned to her, demanding answers and wanting her to join them, it felt like too much of a strain. She couldn't swim anyway, she told the bubbly nurse, who perhaps suspected as much and thought that Helene wouldn't go swimming with the rest of them out of embarrassment or awkwardness.

Never mind, most of us girls have only just learned to swim this summer, haven't we? Yes, cried the nurses happily in chorus. Helene liked her colleagues, their cheerfulness appealed to her. She didn't want pity, she didn't want embarrassed silence, she didn't tell any of the others about Carl and his death.

In autumn a rather older nurse told Helene she looked gaunt. Thin. She'd had her eye on her for some time, said the woman, was she ill? Behind the question mark, Helene detected the word *consumption* and a faint hope rose in her. Helene said no, but she was told to go to the doctor, they couldn't run any risks in the ward for infectious diseases.

Helene was not ill; her pulse was rather fast, that was all, and her heartbeat was sometimes irregular. The doctor asked her whether she had any pain, whether she'd noticed anything unusual about herself. Helene said she sometimes suddenly felt afraid, just like that, but she didn't know what she was afraid of. Her heart beat fast, so fast that it caught up with itself and there didn't seem to be enough room for it in her chest. The doctor listened to her chest a second time, placing the cold metal of the stethoscope almost tenderly on the breast that no longer swelled in a gentle curve. Her ribs could be felt under it. He listened to her heart and shook his head. A little heart murmur, that's quite common. Nothing to worry about. Her fear, well, perhaps there were reasons for it? Helene shook her head. She didn't want to talk about Carl, or say that she hadn't had a period since his death. Perhaps she just didn't drink enough fluids, but what business was that of anyone else? She had been to see Leontine at the Charité in spring and asked her to examine her. But Leontine had reassured her; she wasn't pregnant. Helene felt only a moment's disappointment, for how could she have earned enough to support a child? It was only her heart that sometimes played tricks, her ribcage that seemed too narrow. Her greatest fear was of fear itself.

Well, if that's all, said the doctor, with a twinkle in his eye. Helene guessed that he was thinking of the famous Viennese case histories of hysteria. When she had dressed again the doctor asked, with a nice smile, whether he could invite her out for coffee with him some time.

Helene said no, thank you very much but no. That was all she said. She went to the door.

No, just like that? The doctor hesitated; he didn't want to shake hands and let her go until she had said yes. Helene stepped through the doorway, wishing him a pleasant day.

Martha was to stay at the sanatorium until the beginning of winter, and Leontine was looking for an apartment so that they wouldn't have to move into Achenbachstrasse again when Martha came back. That made it difficult for Helene to prevent unobserved encounters with Erich when she was on her own in the apartment. She lacked the strength and willpower to be constantly on the watch for him in order to avoid such meetings. He pressed his lips on hers, he kissed her where and how he liked. She tried to resist, but unsuccessfully. He would draw her into a room, put his tongue down her throat, and recently he had taken to kneading a nipple with one of his rough hands as he did so. He didn't mind Cleo watching, whimpering in alarm and wagging her tail pleadingly rather than, as usual, cheerfully.

At such moments Helene was glad when she heard Otta coming, because then Erich would generally let her go. It was even better if Fanny came home from a brief shopping trip or some other outing and Erich moved away from Helene without another word. There were days when some instinct warned Helene not to move from Otta's side; she accompanied her into the kitchen, she went shopping with her. But there were other days, like today, when Helene thought she was alone in the apartment, picked up a newspaper and sat in the former veranda, which Fanny had converted into a conservatory by adding glazed windows. Then, in the silence, brisk footsteps approached. Erich came in, sat down at the low table opposite her and put one foot on his knee, his leg bent at a sharp angle. Mhm. He made these vague noises from time to time, mhm, as if she had said something, mhm, mhm, he agreed with her, or perhaps it was more of an mhm of disagreement, or an expectant mhm, mhmhm, mhm, just as if he were suffering from some reflex, it was like the snuffling of a guinea pig, mhm, he watched her reading the paper. Ten minutes passed without a word. Erich stood up, took the newspaper away from her and said: I know what you need.

Helene raised her eyebrows. She didn't want to look at him.

Standing over her, Erich stuck his hand inside her blouse. Helene resisted. The buttons of her blouse came off, the fine fabric tore.

Careful now, he gasped, laughing, and what had been suppressed sighs before turned to loud, fully voiced gasping. Erich laughed, and now he had Helene's wrists in a firm grip. He forced her down on her knees and flung himself on her, his wet, slavering mouth on her naked upper body. Torso was the word that shot through Helene's mind, and she thought of the anatomical models used for teaching student nurses about the human body, a torso where the heart beat without any head, without the capacity to think. Limbs had lost their meaning with their function. Everything outside the windows was purple and violet.

Helene tried to push away from him with her shoulders, her whole body, she wanted to free herself, but Erich was heavy as a rock, mindlessly sucking at her skin. He wanted to suck her out of it, moistening every part of her body with his saliva, which smelled of fish oil. As he held her wrists in his grip and pressed her into the armchair, Helene tried to rear up again and push him off her. But it was as if every move she made just spurred him on to greater ferocity. Now his tongue was roughly licking her face, her throat, moving down to her breasts. Helene froze. Got you now, got you now, Erich kept gasping.

I was just about to water the cyclamens, a voice above them said suddenly. If Fanny's voice was not exactly steady, it was shrill and clear. She was holding aloft a brass watering can, a small one with a long spout. Next moment she brought it down on Erich's head. Erich did not collapse, but in jumping up he did keep Helene from being struck by the next blow from the can, which now dropped to the floor. Erich had let go of her wrists.

Fanny shouted. What exactly she was shouting Helene couldn't make out. It was something to do with the hoi polloi, we're not among the hoi polloi here, that was probably what she'd been shouting. Outlines formed in the purple colour, none of the cyclamen flowers was drooping. Helene clutched at her blouse with both hands, stood up and got back to her room. Once there, she pressed her cold hands to her burning cheeks. Something was thrusting at her skull from the inside, but the something was too soft and her forehead too firm for it to get out.

She heard Fanny and Erich quarrelling until late into the night, but that was nothing new. Helene went to work, she came home and she avoided Fanny.

Helene cursed her existence. She was ashamed of herself for living a life that allowed her to breathe, to work and after a while to take fluids and sleep again, without much effort on her own part. She was ashamed because she could have prevented it; she knew how to kill herself quickly and tidily. What did pain matter, what did little attacks of nausea matter, when they would be finite? But Helene knew that she didn't want it to come as a surprise when she was found, she didn't want anyone making much fuss about her or her death, she didn't want Martha and Leontine and anyone she didn't know, not that she could call such a person to mind, well, she didn't want people in general thinking about responsibility or actually blaming themselves for her death. Dying unnoticed, slipping away for the last time was a little more difficult. Ultimately the life and thoughts of other people ought not to be of any interest, you had to say goodbye to that too, we were all solely responsible for ourselves. Helene had so often handled poisonous substances, administering some in small, painkilling doses, others to bring sleep. The box of Veronal that she had taken from the pharmacy with her, just in case, had disappeared from her little dark-red suitcase. Helene didn't really suspect Otta; she assumed that while she was out Fanny had been snooping among her things and couldn't resist the sight of the box. But there was plenty of it at the hospital. It wasn't just morphine and barbiturates, even injecting a little air could kill you if you did it the right way. Life appeared to Helene a pointless affair of living on, of unwished-for survival of Carl. If she wanted to keep her sense of shame within bounds, because it did seem arrogant and light-minded to be ashamed of living when you were still alive, she told herself that if she lived and remembered Carl that would delay his complete extinction for a while. She liked that idea – as long as she lived, thinking lovingly of Carl, and it would be the same for his family, something of him was still left. It was left in her, and with her, and through her. Helene decided that she was living in order to honour him. She would like to be happy and laugh again some day, simply for love of him. Even though he had no more part in it. Helene did not believe people would meet again in another world; yes, that other world might exist, but without the link between body and soul that we know in this one, always demanding union with others, release from our condemnation to isolation and solitude. Hence our thoughts, hence our language, hence our embraces. Helene found herself in a dilemma, torn both ways. She didn't want to think, she didn't want to talk, she didn't want to embrace another human being ever again. But she wanted to live on for Carl, not in order to survive him but to live for him. What else was left of him but her memories? How was it possible to live on without thought or language or human embraces? The crucial point was not to disturb the mechanism of life, which meant sleeping only as long as was absolutely necessary, eating only as much as was absolutely necessary, and it was a relief to Helene that her work in the hospital divided every day into visible, regular units. Much as time is made visible by the ticking pendulum of a clock, work at the hospital showed Helene her life going on. She didn't have to think about when it would come to an end. She could cling confidently to the beginning and end of her duty shift, and in between them she took temperatures, felt pulses, cleaned the operating instruments. Helene held the hands of the dying, of mothers in childbirth, of the lonely; she changed dressings, sanitary towels and nappies, her work was useful.

Her life lay before her, from one duty shift to the next.

When she was looking for an apartment Helene passed the Church of the Apostle Paul. The door was open and it crossed her mind that she hadn't been to church for years. She went in. The smell of incense hung in the air. Helene went forward and sat down in the second pew from the front, folded her hands and tried to begin a prayer, but however hard she racked her brains she couldn't think of one.

Dear God, she whispered, if you're there – Helene hesitated; why would God want to speak to you? she asked herself – if you're there could you send me a sign, just a little sign? Tears were flowing from her eyes. Take away my self-pity and the pain, she said, please, she added. The tears dried up but the pain in her breast was still there, constricting her bronchial tubes and making it hard for her to breathe. How much longer? Helene listened, but there was nothing to be heard except the clattering of a bus outside. At least tell me this: how much longer must I live? There was no answer. Helene strained her ears in the great expanses of the nave.

If you're there, she began again, but then she thought of Carl and didn't know what to say next. Where was Carl now? She heard footsteps behind her and turned. A mother with her small child had come in. Helene bowed her head and laid her forehead on her folded hands. Let me not be here, she whispered. There was no self-pity left; Helene felt only a great desire for release.

Where? she heard the clear voice of the child behind her.

There, said the mother, up there.

Where? I can't see him. The child was getting impatient, wailing. Where is he? I can't see him.

No one can see him, said the mother, you can't see him with your eyes. You have to see with your heart, child.

There was no reply – was the child's heart seeing something

now? Helene stared at the notches in the wooden pew and felt a sense of dread; how could she ask God for something when she had forgotten him so long? Forgive me, she whispered. Carl hadn't died for her to eat her heart out longing for him. He had died for no reason at all. She would manage to live like this, hoping for an answer that didn't come. Helene stood up and left the church. On the way out she caught herself still looking for signs, signs of God's existence and her release. Outside the sun was shining. Was that a sign? Helene thought of her mother. Perhaps all the things she found, the tree roots, the feather dusters, were signs to her? It's not rubbish, Helene heard her mother's voice say. God needs nothing but human memory and human doubts, her mother had once said.

The rent of the apartment that Helene looked at, an attic apartment with a bedroom and living room, was too expensive. She didn't have enough money, and whenever she went to see a landlady she was asked about her husband and her parents. To avoid being a burden on Fanny, the better to avoid Erich, Helene applied for a room in the nurses' hostel.

She didn't have all her qualifications yet, said the matron kindly. Helene claimed to have heard from Bautzen that there had been a fire in which the records of her training were destroyed. The matron was sympathetic and let Helene move into a room, but said she must get new papers as soon as possible.

Martha came back from the sanatorium and moved into an apartment with Leontine. They were working so hard that Helene saw Martha and Leontine only every few weeks and sometimes not for months.

The economic crisis was getting worse all the time. No one escaped its effects. People were buying and selling, speculating, grabbing what they could; they all said they were anxious not to make a loss now, but so far no one had found the knack of avoiding it. Fanny gave a party for Erich's birthday, a big party, celebrating on a large scale. It was to be bigger than her own, a party in his honour grander than any she had ever given before. In the last few months Erich had left Fanny several times, but he had always come back and now he turned up for his own birthday party. Fanny had issued many invitations, to friends of her own and to friends of Erich, and to some people who didn't even know that she was more than just his tennis partner.

Helene hadn't wanted to go, but Leontine and Martha made her. Perhaps the two of them had Helene on their conscience because it was so long since they'd been able to do anything for her.

Fanny's invitation seemed to Helene an attempt at resuscitation, a measure taken to inject and extend life, a pitiful repetition of earlier invitations. The guests were still splendidly dressed, imitation jewellery sparkled, they talked about betting on horses and the stock exchange rates – more than seventy thousand bankruptcies this year and the number of unemployed had just risen above six million. Someone lit an opium pipe. No wonder wages had to fall by up to twenty-five per cent. Views and opinions on the collapse of the Piscator Theatre were exchanged, but Helene didn't want to listen. Should she feel uneasy because she herself had a job? Life was unthinkable without the metronome of her work at the hospital. Helene didn't look at the Baron and his Pina either. They had married the year before last and had been at odds ever since, this time not about diamonds and feather boas but about a dress that Pina had bought, without the Baron's permission and with money they didn't have. The Baron accused her of borrowing from his friends and deceiving him over their joint property. She denied it all. Soon she was flinging her arms in the air and cried: I confess, I stole the dress! You insisted on knowing, so here's the truth: I stole it. I'm a thief. From the

Kaufhaus des Westens. Now what? Helene looked at the other guests, she looked at her shoes and examined her hands. One fingernail had a black rim. Helene rose from the chaise longue where she had been sitting until now, alone and without being pestered, she crooked her fingers as best she could, curled them up so no one could see the dirty nail, and went out into the corridor, where she had to wait a little while to use the bathroom. As soon as the door was open and the bathroom free, Helene hurried in. She bolted the door. The stove for the water was heated, and Helene turned on the tap. Steaming hot water came out, frothing and white. Helene scrubbed her nails with the nail-brush under running water. The soap lathered, Helene scrubbed, soaped, scrubbed and soaped. Her hands were reddened, her nails became whiter and whiter. She washed her face too, and feeling an itch down her backbone she had to wash her neck as well, as far as she could without undressing. Someone knocked at the door. Helene knew she ought to turn off the tap. Her hands were turning red and hot and clean, then redder and hotter and cleaner, it wasn't easy for her to turn the tap. Underneath it, the bluish-green tinge of the residue left by the water showed on the sides of the tub. What salts had the water brought in and left there along with the lime in it?

Back among the guests, Helene had just decided to leave – after all, nurses were supposed to be back in the hostel by ten, and the night shift didn't end until six in the morning – when she found a young man standing beside her, smiling. He kept smiling down at her so persistently that it looked as if he thought he knew her.

Our friend Wilhelm, said Erich, appearing behind the young man.

Now let me guess, said Wilhelm, let me guess her name.

He's guessing everyone's names tonight, explained Erich,

slapping his friend on the shoulder. Erich laughed. He's another Hanussen, oh yes, he's a real clairvoyant.

Wilhelm removed Erich's hand from his shoulder. Nonsense, I'm no Hanussen.

He's only once really had it off with anyone, and not even with a lady. Erich's eyes pierced Helene.

Wilhelm wasn't letting Erich embarrass him. He looked searchingly at Helene. Don't worry, it's only a game. Wilhelm leaned sideways, as if Helene's name were written on a note attached to her temple. Then he nodded. Alice. Her name is Alice.

Erich laughed. Fanny, who had joined them, mopped her inflamed eyes and asked Erich to get her an absinthe. Erich did not comply with Fanny's request; his eyes were on Helene's face, boring into her own eyes, her cheeks, her mouth.

Well, isn't she a woman after your own heart? Willy here adores blondes. Erich clapped his friend hard on the shoulder as if he had to tenderize him, like a schnitzel. There may not be much else to say for her, but she's blonde. Erich laughed, in the belief that he had cracked a joke. His glance showed how readily he would grab Helene if they were alone. Suspecting nothing of that, Wilhelm stood with his back to his friend and there was surprise, almost amazement in his eyes.

At least you're captivatingly beautiful, dear young lady, stammered Wilhelm. Alice. I'm sure you're going to tell me your real name.'

Helene tried to summon up a friendly smile. Over Wilhelm's shoulder she saw the clock in the corridor. The white grandfather clock said nine-thirty. Helene said she was about to leave.

What, already? Wilhelm couldn't believe it. The party's only just begun. Surely you're not going to leave now, on your own?

I must, said Helene with her friendly smile.

Because of the hostel. Erich ran his tongue over his teeth and clicked it suggestively. The effect was obscene. She lives in the sisters' hostel.

A nun, the Virgin Mary. Wilhelm believed it at once.

Nonsense. Erich set him right. Not that kind of sister, you idiot. She's a nursing sister.

A nursing sister. Wilhelm spoke respectfully as if there were no difference to speak of between a nun, the Virgin Mary and a nurse. I'll walk you back.

Thank you, but please don't bother. Helene stepped to one side and tried to get past this tall young man called Wilhelm. He went to the door with her, helped her into her coat and said goodnight.

Next day Wilhelm suddenly turned up at the hospital. Nurse, he said, you must help me.

Helene was in no mood for companionable laughter and meaningful glances; she wanted to get on with her work. The beds in Ward 20 still had to be made, and the patient in Ward 31 who couldn't get to the lavatory without help had rung for her ten minutes ago.

Nurse Alice, I'm going to sit on this bench. You can call the watchman or the medical director if you like, but I'm going to wait here until you come off duty. I don't suppose that will be so very long, will it?

Helene let him sit there and went about her work. She had to keep passing him for over two hours, and the girls in the nurses' room kept on whispering. That charming gentleman in the corridor, he must be courting her. What a handsome man, how good-looking with his fair hair and blue eyes! One of the nurses stopped beside Wilhelm and struck up a conversation with him. Later, passing Helene, she said: Let me know if you don't fancy him and I'll take him.

Helene would have liked to say she could take whatever she liked, but she found it difficult to answer the nurses' whispers. Her tongue was too heavy in her mouth. As she was washing an old man's genitals and buttocks, going carefully with his bedsores and burst boils, all the little wounds oozing pus that she tended with ointment and powder, she couldn't help thinking of Carl, and how he would never come and fetch her now. Never again. Helene's throat hurt, it felt tight and she couldn't swallow. With her fingers covered in powder and ointment, Helene couldn't wipe her eyes.

Your hands are so soft, nurse, they do me good. I always ask after you and whether you're on duty. You were born for this profession, did you know, Nurse Helene? The old man lying on his bed with his back to Helene – she would have thought he must cry out with pain when she touched his sore flesh – twisted round so that he could at least look her way. He put out his hand and pulled her sleeve. There, he said, pointing to the bedside table. Look in the drawer, Nurse Helene, there's some money there, do take it.

Helene shook her head and thanked him, but said she didn't want his money. Whenever anyone gave her a present she returned it. Just sometimes she found coins in her apron pocket that someone had dropped into it unnoticed. This old man had been in the ward for two weeks and his condition was deteriorating. He was disappointed that Helene didn't want his money. Take it, he insisted, if you don't take it someone else will steal it.

Let them. Helene put the lid on the powder box, spread the covers over him, and took the basin to throw away the water and clean both it and her hands. Another patient, behind her, was groaning, saying he couldn't wait any longer. She went over to the man's bed; he needed the bedpan and asked Helene to stay with him, because he couldn't manage on his own. A man in the next bed was wailing with pain in a strained, hoarse voice, to attract Helene's attention. Then he pulled himself together as well as he could.

Two hours later, when Helene had hung up her overall in the locker and put on her skirt, pullover and jacket, Wilhelm was still waiting patiently on the bench in the corridor.

Would she like to come and have coffee? Helene agreed, not that she wanted to, but it seemed the course of least resistance. Outside the door she tried to put up her umbrella, but it stuck. Laughing and ignoring the rain, not to mention her struggle with the umbrella, Wilhelm was telling her something about feedback on the People's Wireless, a radio device to be unveiled and demonstrated to the public in a few months' time at the Great German Wireless Exhibition. From amplifier to amplifier, said Wilhelm, spreading his arms wide to show her how many of these new technological developments there were, more than would fit between them. Helene liked his enthusiasm. They walked to the bank of the Spree Canal. You could create the necessary sensitivity by feedback to the high frequency stage, he said. Helene didn't understand, but she stood there with him out of civility as he stopped in mid-sentence to show her, by gestures, how she must imagine the construction of the device.

Helene now knew that he was an engineer, but it wasn't clear whether he was talking about inventions of his own or other people's. She still didn't understand what he was talking about, but she liked hearing him and watching as he mopped the rain from his brow with his handkerchief. After all, he said, he was sure she couldn't imagine the extent of possible communication and the amount of information that could be transmitted. In the end everyone would be able to receive the same information at the same time, learning about events that otherwise they would have heard of only by going to some trouble or from reading the newspaper days later – and which newspaper anyway? There were far too many newspapers now. Wilhelm's dismissive gesture was friendly but determined. There was something infectious about his pleasure and Helene had to smile. She had managed to open the umbrella. Would he like to come under it?

Of course, said Wilhelm, taking the umbrella from Helene's hand so that she wouldn't have to reach too high. Sweet girls, he knew, need sweet cakes, said Wilhelm, making straight for a little café. They had apple cake and coffee. Helene didn't like either, but she didn't want to be difficult or attract any unnecessary attention. Wilhelm said, and there was no missing the pride in his voice, that within weeks they'd be able to go into full production of wireless sets, so that enough of this new invention could be sold at the Wireless Exhibition. What did she think of naming it Salvation Wireless, asked Wilhelm, laughing. Just my little joke, he added, there are better names. Helene didn't understand his joke, but she liked to hear him sound so pleased with himself.

She hid her weariness behind her smile. After her long day's work at the hospital, exhaustion was now spreading through her as she sat eating cake and drinking coffee. She felt she was behaving properly to Wilhelm if she looked attentive, sometimes raising her eyebrows as if in surprise, and nodding now and then. The words transmitter and receiver took on a significance of their own as she listened to him. A newspaper boy came into the café. There were not many people here, but he took off his cap and cried his wares. The headlines of the evening papers were speculating on the identity of those behind the fire in the Reichstag building.

Over these last few weeks a mood of gloomy indignation had been abroad in the trams and underground trains. Wherever people met, their faces reddened by the cold, their coats sometimes not long enough because fabric taken from them had been needed to make a child a jacket, there was complaint, discontent and argument. They weren't going to put up with this much longer, they said. No one could be expected to take this kind of thing lying down, not any more, they weren't going to let the authorities do as they fancied with them. Men and women alike were upset.

Wilhelm fetched Helene from the hospital as often as he could. Communist after communist was arrested. Wilhelm went walking with his blonde Alice and took her to the café. He said he liked to watch her eating cake, she always looked as if she hadn't eaten properly for days. Helene stopped eating in alarm. She wasn't sure that she wanted to know what Wilhelm thought when he saw her eating. Eating had become a mere nuisance to her, and she often forgot about it until evening. She didn't like the apple cake, she just swallowed it as quickly as possible to get it over with. Wilhelm asked if he could order her another slice. Helene shook her head and said no, thank you. Her dimples were so pretty, said Wilhelm, beaming as he looked her in the face. To her own annoyance, Helene was embarrassed. Did she like the theatre, the cinema? She nodded. It was a long time since she'd been to the cinema; she didn't have the money, and she had only once agreed to go with Leontine and Martha when they asked her. During the picture she'd found herself crying, which she didn't like. She never used to cry in the cinema. So she shook her head.

Yes or no, asked Wilhelm.

No, said Helene.

Wilhelm asked Helene to go dancing with him. One day it seemed like too much trouble to turn him down, so she agreed. They went to a dance, and he took her face in his hands, kissed her forehead and told her he was in love with her.

Helene was not pleased to hear it. She closed her eyes so as to keep him from looking at her. Wilhelm thought that was charming and took it as agreement, an announcement that she would soon be ready to be his. It was a good thing Wilhelm didn't know about the passion with which Helene had invited and responded to Carl's kisses. SA troops stormed the 'Red Block' of the artists' colony in Wilmersdorf, where writers and artists were arrested and some of their books were burned. Spring came, and there were more book-burnings. Helene heard from Martha that the Baron was among those who had been arrested. Pina was trying to find out the reasons for his arrest; she was desperate to know; she visited all his acquaintances asking them to help her. One day rumour said that he was in contact with the Communist Party, the next that he had been distributing Social Democrat leaflets. Wilhelm wasn't waiting to find out whether Helene returned his feelings; his own desire filled him and that was enough. He called her Alice, although he knew now that she was Helene. But Alice was his name for her.

In spring the newly elected National Socialist Party organized a boycott. The idea was to leave certain parasites, useless mouths, to starve to death. No one was to buy from Jewish tradesmen, or get shoes mended by a Jewish cobbler, no one was to visit a Jewish doctor or consult a Jewish lawyer. It was wrong for Germans to be out of work while others lived on the fat of the land, the medical director of the hospital explained to the nurses. They nodded; some of them came up with special instances of this unjust state of affairs. The bubbly nurse, who as everyone knew was Jewish, had been fired suddenly last week. No one wondered where she was, no one missed her. Her family might not be prosperous, but why should she have a job when others didn't? Once she had gone no one mentioned her any more. Another nurse replaced her. There was much talk about the living space that the German people needed.

Wilhelm fetched Helene from work. As usual, she had been on duty for ten hours, and with the two brief breaks in her shift had been at the hospital for eleven hours in all. He took her arm and led her to the café, and although it was already six in the evening Wilhelm ordered cake and coffee. He drew Helene close to him over the table and told her she must keep a secret. He wasn't just responsible for building the 4A Berlin to Stettin road, he said, and what was more, some day, as she'd see, it would go all the way to Königsberg! Wilhelm's eyes were shining. His voice dropped even lower. But the secret was this: he had been chosen as the engineer to take the wireless apparatus developed under his supervision to Stettin airfield and get it installed on the tall mast there, because the airfield was to be converted for use by the Luftwaffe. Wilhelm was beaming, and looked not so much proud as bold and determined. His eyes saw adventure, promised adventure. Wilhelm picked up his cake fork, broke off a piece of cake and put the fork to his mouth. His area of work had shifted so far in the direction of Pomerania, he told her, that it had been suggested he should move there.

Helene nodded. She didn't really envy Wilhelm his ability to enjoy life and his enthusiasm, his belief that he was able to do something important for the German people, for mankind, and in particular for technical progress. But she liked his frank pleasure, the ease with which he laughed and slapped his thigh. It was pleasantly uncomplicated, like the giggling of the nurses.

Are you glad? Wilhelm asked Helene. He lowered his arm and his fork when he noticed that she was not reacting, and didn't open her mouth to eat more of her own cake.

Please don't ask me. Helene looked up from her cup of coffee and out of the window.

But I must ask you, said Wilhelm. I don't want to be without you in my future life, he said, and bit his lip ruefully, because he had meant to keep such a confession for the moment when he asked a certain question. However, Helene didn't seem to have heard him.

When Wilhelm came back from Pomerania in spring, after a good month away drawing up plans, he bought two rings from the jeweller's at the railway station and went to fetch Helene from the hospital. He held one of the rings under her nose and asked if she would be his wife.

Helene couldn't meet his eyes.

She wondered what to tell him. She knew how to beam and smile, that was easy, you just had to lift the corners of your mouth and widen your eyes at the same time. Perhaps, imitating happiness like that, you could even feel a moment of the real thing?

Surprised, aren't you?

Something like me isn't supposed to exist at all. It burst out of her.

What on earth do you mean? Wilhelm was at a loss.

I mean I don't have any papers, any certificate of my descent, and if I did, said Helene, laughing herself now, well, the word Mosaic would come under the definition of my mother's faith.

Wilhelm looked keenly at her. Why do you say such things, Alice? Your mother lives somewhere in Lusatia. Didn't your sister say she was a difficult case? It sounded as if she was ill. Are you fond of her, do the festivals she celebrates mean anything to you? Incredulously, Wilhelm shook his head, and there was confident determination in his face. Come away with me, be my wife and let's begin a life together.

Helene was silent. A man like Wilhelm knew nothing of danger and obstacles that must be overcome. Helene didn't look

312

at him; she felt a strange stiffness at the back of her neck. If she shook her head he might call her cowardly, spineless. She would stay here. But where?

Are you telling me you distrust me because I'm German, with a German mother and a German father, and they had German mothers and fathers too? he asked.

I don't distrust you. Helene shook her head. How could Wilhelm see her hesitation simply as distrust? She didn't want to annoy him. She rather doubted what other options she had open to her. Her own mother was German, but obviously Wilhelm now understood being German in a different way. In modern opinion, German identity was expressed in racial characteristics and required the right sort of blood.

Your name is Alice, do you hear? If I say so it *is* so. If you don't have a certificate of ancestry I'll get you one, and believe me, it will be unobjectionable, it will leave no doubt as to your healthy descent.

You're out of your mind. Helene was shocked. Could Wilhelm possibly be referring to the new laws whereby every deformity seen in the hospital had to be recorded and reported, because the birth of offspring with hereditary disease must be prevented? And weren't certain mental illnesses, like the psychological disturbance that many of their neighbours detected in her own mother, also considered hereditary, to be avoided at all costs? The first commandment was to be bursting with good health, and anyone who couldn't boast such health had better die as quickly as possible before the German people ran the risk of infection, of being besmirched and made unclean by the birth of sick children.

Don't you believe me? I'll do anything for you, Alice, anything.

What do you mean about healthy descent? Helene knew she wasn't going to get a logical answer from Wilhelm.

Pure descent, my wife will be of pure descent, that's all I mean. Wilhelm beamed. Don't look so fierce, my treasure, who could have a purer, more spotless heart than this enchanting blonde woman opposite me?

Helene was amazed by this view of her. Perhaps it was because she had turned down his physical advances?

People are beginning to go away, leave Germany. Fanny's friend Lucinde is going to England with her husband, said Helene.

Well, as for those who don't love their forests and their Mother Earth in Germany, they're welcome to turn their backs on their native land. Let them go, say I. Let them all go. We have work to do here, Helene. We will save the German nation, our father-land and our mother tongue. Wilhelm rolled up his sleeves. We don't deserve to perish. We'll do it with these hands, do you see? No German may fold his hands in his lap these days. Indulging in despair and complaint is not our way. You will be my wife and I'll give you my name.

Helene shook her head.

You hesitate? Don't tell me you'd rather give up, Alice, don't tell me that. He looked at her sternly, incredulously.

Wilhelm, I don't deserve your love, I have nothing to give in return.

That will come, Alice, I'm sure of it. Wilhelm said this in a clear, frank voice, as if only her agreement were at stake, a decision that would unite them. Nothing in what she said seemed to hurt his feelings or shake his confidence in the slightest. His will would conquer, his will alone. Did she have no strong will of her own? Of course it takes a woman a certain time to get over a loss like yours, he said. You were going to get married, you and that boy. But it's years ago; you must end your mourning some time, Alice.

Helene heard Wilhelm's words, which seemed to her

both stupid and bold. He was talking away at her. His air of superiority, the commanding tone of what he said, made her indignant. There were words that cancelled each other out. Helene felt that there was something suspect about his heroic courage, something fundamentally wrong. Next moment Helene was horrified by herself. Was she resentful? Wilhelm was cheerful, she'd be able to learn from him. Helene regretted her annoyance and her rejection of him. Wasn't it just her grief for Carl, a woman's mourning, as Wilhelm so kindly called it, that made her find it so hard to bear Wilhelm's own cheerfulness and enjoyment of life?

What are you thinking of, Alice? The future's at our feet, we won't think just of ourselves, we'll think of the common good, Alice, of the people, of our German land.

She wouldn't be faint-hearted or bitter. It wasn't life that had injured her feelings, there was no God wanting to make her atone. Wilhelm meant well by her and by himself, and she couldn't grudge him that. How could she be so arrogant? After all, what he said was true, she had to come back to life, maybe nursing the sick didn't help much there. But she lacked any real idea of what life should and could be. She would have to turn to someone else for that. And why not someone who meant well by her, who would be happy to hear her say yes, who wanted to rescue her? Wilhelm obviously knew what he wished for, what he preferred, and he was not just close to belief, he did believe. The word Germany was like a clarion call in his mouth. We. Who were *we*? We were someone, but exactly who were we? She was sure she could learn to kiss again, and above all to come to know and like someone else's odour, to open her lips and feel his tongue in her mouth, perhaps that was what it was all about.

Wilhelm paid court to Helene assiduously. It seemed as if every rejection by her simply lent him new force. He felt born to great deeds, most of all he wanted to rescue people and the first thing he wanted was to win this woman, whom he saw as shy and charming, to live with him as his wife.

I have two tickets for the Kroll Opera, we owe them to my good connections. You'd like to see those first television pictures, wouldn't you?

But Helene was not to be won over. She was on night duty almost the whole week and there was no getting around it.

When Martha brought the news that Mariechen had been unable to prevent an incident in which the police had picked up and taken away a woman in the Kornmarkt who was first weeping and then raving wildly, Helene felt anxious. Leontine telephoned Bautzen, first speaking to Mariechen, then to the hospital and finally to the health authority. She learned that Selma Würsich had been taken to Schloss Sonnenstein in Pirna, where they would try to find out just what was wrong with her and use new techniques to decide whether it was hereditary.

Helene packed her things and Wilhelm saw that his moment had come. He wouldn't let her go on her own, he said, she needed him, she must know that.

In the train, Wilhelm sat opposite Helene. She noticed how confidently he looked at her. He had beautiful eyes, really beautiful. How long was it since she had last seen her mother, ten years, eleven? Helene was afraid she might not recognize her, wondered what she would look like and whether her mother in turn would recognize her. Wilhelm took her hand. She bowed her head and laid her face against his hand. How warm it was. She felt it was a gift that he was with her. She kissed his hand.

My brave Alice, he said. She heard the tenderness in his words, yet she didn't feel as if they referred to her.

Brave? I'm not brave. She shook her head. I'm terribly frightened.

Now he put both hands on her shoulders and drew her head close to his chest, so that she almost slipped out of her seat. My sweet girl, I know, he said, and she felt his mouth on her forehead. But you don't have to keep contradicting me. You're going there and that's brave.

Another daughter would have gone years ago, another daughter wouldn't have left her mother in the first place.

There was nothing you could do for her. Wilhelm stroked Helene's hair. He smelled not unpleasant, almost familiar. Helene guessed, knew, that his words were meant to be comforting. She pressed close to him. What was there in Wilhelm that she could like? Maybe the fact that someone would put up with her.

Only a special permit from the public health authority, for which Leontine had applied in Pirna by way of Bautzen, allowed Helene this visit to her mother.

The hospital grounds were extensive and, but for the high fences, you might have thought that centuries ago this was a royal palace where kings lived, enjoying the view. A delightful landscape stretched out before them at the place where the Wesenitz flowed into the Elbe from the north and the Gottleuba joined it from the south. There was something improbable about the bright sunshine and loud birdsong. Was this where her mother was in safe keeping as a mental patient?

A male nurse led Helene and Wilhelm up some stairs and down a long corridor. Barred doors were opened and locked again after them. The visitors' room was at the far end of this wing.

Helene's mother was sitting on the edge of a bench, wearing a nightdress. Her hair was completely silver now, but otherwise she looked as she always had, not a day older. When Helene

317

came in she turned her head to her and said: I told you so, didn't I? I said you'd be looking after me. But first get me out of here, those hands of theirs churn up my guts. Although there's nothing grafted in me, no pears bred from an apple stock. Nothing mixed there. The doctor says I have children. I convinced him that he was wrong. Hatched out and flown the nest. One doesn't have children like that. They should grow from the head, from here to there. Helene's mother struck first her forehead and then the back of her head with the flat of her hand. Shaken out, as simple as that.

Helene went up to her mother and took one of her cool hands. Just skin and bone. The old skin felt soft, brittle on the outside but soft and smooth on the palms.

No physical contact. The male nurse standing at the door and keeping an eye on the visitors looked as if he was going to come closer.

Don't you have any women nurses here? cried Helene, and took fright at the volume of her own voice.

Yes, there are women nurses too, but a little extra strength is needed to handle some patients, know what I mean?

It could be I'd scratch, it could be I'd bite, it could be I'd scratch them and bite them all night, chanted Helene's mother in the voice of a young girl.

I've brought you something. Helene opened her bag. A hairbrush and a mirror.

Give those to me, please. The male nurse held out his hand. I'll be happy to take them and keep them safe. For reasons of protection and security the patients may not have any possessions of their own here.

But Helene's mother had already picked up the brush and was beginning to tidy her hair with it. *Between the mountain and the vale, upon the grass so green, two hares hopped nimbly at their ease, the finest ever seen.* She sang unerringly, warbling like the girl she had once been.

The male nurse stamped his foot angrily. This was too much for him.

God only knows where she gets all those songs from. He reached for the brush and snatched it from Helene's mother's hand. In the struggle, the mirror slipped off her lap and broke as it hit the ground. And that too, cried the nurse, picking up the mirror frame and the pieces of glass from the floor. No sooner had he snatched the brush and retrieved the mirror than Helene's mother let herself slip off the bench to the floor. She was laughing, showing black gaps in her mouth. Helene was horrified to see the missing teeth. Her mother laughed until her laughter gurgled in her throat, and couldn't calm down.

There's no point in it, Fräulein, you can see that for yourself!

What do you mean, no point? Helene asked, without looking round at the male nurse. She bent down and put her hand on her mother's head. The grey hair was dry and tangled. Her mother didn't defend herself, she just laughed. My mother isn't mad, not in the way you mean. She doesn't belong in here. I want to take her away with me.

I'm sorry, we have our orders here and we stick to them. You can't simply take this woman away with you – even if it were your own daughter, you couldn't in a case like hers.

Come along, Mother. Helene took her mother under the arms and tried to pull her to her feet.

With a rapid stride, the nurse moved towards them and separated mother and daughter. Didn't you hear me? Those are my orders.

I want to speak to the professor. What was his name – Nitsche?

The professor is in an important meeting.

Really? Then I'll wait until the meeting is over.

I'm sorry, Fräulein, but he still won't speak to you. You must ask him for an appointment in writing.

In writing? Helene searched her bag, found the black notebook that Wilhelm had given her a few days earlier and tore out a page. The smell of her mother came off her hands, her laughter, her fear, her unkempt hair and the sweat in her armpits. She wrote, in pencil: Dear Professor Nitsche.

Fräulein, please. Do you want us to keep you here too? I think the professor would take a certain interest in such a case – after all, he's doing research into the heredity factor in illnesses like this. What was your name again?

A little respect, if you please, young man. Wilhelm's moment had come; he intervened. You will let that young lady leave at once. She is my fiancée.

The nurse opened the door. Wilhelm offered Helene his arm. Coming, darling?

Helene knew there was no alternative. She took Wilhelm's arm and went out. At the end of the corridor she heard a shrill screech behind her. It wasn't clear whether it came from an animal or a human throat. Nor could she decide, if it was human, whose scream it was. It could have been her mother screaming. Another male nurse opened the door for them. Wilhelm and Helene went along the next corridor in silence. This place was uncannily quiet; there was something very final about it.

In the train to Berlin, Wilhelm and Helene still sat in silence. The train went through a tunnel. Helene felt that Wilhelm was waiting for her to thank him.

Please, she said, don't call me darling any more.

But you *are* my darling. Wilhelm's eyes were on Helene's face. I have to go to Stettin again tomorrow, for a week. I don't want to leave you alone in Berlin any longer than that.

I won't be alone, why would I be alone? My patients are waiting for me, they need me.

Do you think there'd be no patients waiting for you in Stettin? You'll find patients to nurse all over the world. But there's only one of me. Alice, my sweet little girl, your abstinence is noble, but to tell you the truth it's driving me crazy. We must bring it to an end. I need you.

Helene took his hand. You don't have to persuade me of that, she said and kissed his hand. It was good to hear that she was needed. How was she to talk about it?

What documents do I need to marry you? She was whispering. I don't have any, not a single one.

That can be dealt with, stated Wilhelm nonchalantly. Didn't you once tell me you knew how to operate a printing press?

Helene shook her head. The paper, the right print, stamps and seals. Documents like that are very difficult to print.

Leave it all to me. Promise?

Helene nodded. It was good that he wanted to look after her. Wilhelm mentioned a brother in Gelbensande who had been farming since he married, but who knew about drawing up official documents.

For some time the hospital had been urging Helene to produce her papers at long last: her identity card, her birth certificate, her parents' birth certificates, and if possible a book of family records going back beyond her parents; they wanted to see all that. Helene had claimed that she had no identity card, and whenever she was asked she pretended to be taken by surprise and said she had forgotten her papers. They had given her more time. But she must produce her papers by the end of the month, they had said recently, or she would lose her job.

Only when Helene took a slightly wrinkled apple out of the basket, polished it on her white skirt, found a knife, cut it up and cored it so that she could hand Wilhelm an apple quarter, did she see that she had a view over to the valley of the Oder and the hills around it, to the docks and the Dammscher See, then, rather closer, over the flower beds on the Hakenterrasse and down to the River Oder itself, where one of the white steamers was just putting in, inviting people with both sunshades and umbrellas aboard for an excursion. They had all made different decisions about the likely weather on this day early in May. And only then did it strike her that she had never imagined what her wedding might be like. That was herself all over, she supposed. Helene pulled the coat lying loosely over her bare shoulders together over her breast, because it was cool here. You could smell the sea in the air, you knew you were near the coast. When she licked her lips, she thought she could taste salt. This morning the registrar had referred to the wind in his speech of congratulations, saying marriage was a safe haven from storm winds and tempests, and a wife should make a safe and comfortable home for the man who protected her. Then he had laughed and advised them to have a schnapps on this early May day. A cool wind was blowing their way. Wilhelm munched the apple, he chewed it vigorously and Helene heard his teeth crushing it, juice coming through his teeth, his saliva, his lust, he leaned forward, scrutinized Helene, stroked the strands of hair wafting in the wind back from her face and kissed her forehead. He had a right to do that now, and more besides. A gull screeched. A young woman on the road just below was edging a pram forward with her hips, shove by shove; she held her baby close to her with both arms; it was crying; a shawl was fluttering round her; she was trying to wrap it round the baby, but the shawl kept flying out in the wind, and the baby cried as if it were hungry and in pain.

Incredible, don't you think? Wilhelm was looking down too.

I expect the baby has colic.

I meant the traffic here. Apple quarter in hand, Wilhelm pointed to a long ship. Soon there'll be tons of Mecklenburg carrots travelling this way along our autobahn; they'll be loaded up and go off into the world. We're going to break the 1913 record this year, our turnover of goods will reach its highest level ever, eight and a half million tons, that's gigantic. It was only right when we rescinded the internationalization of our waterways. Versailles can't dictate what we do with our own river. Wilhelm stood up and pointed north-east with his outstretched arm. Look at that big building over there. They'll be completing the second part of it in the next few weeks, the biggest granary in Europe. Wilhelm sat down again. Helene contorted her face and pressed her lips together, stifling a yawn only with difficulty. When Wilhelm was in full flight, it was difficult to interrupt his rejoicings over new technological achievements and buildings. See the mast on that ship over to the right? That's its antenna, it can receive radio waves from transmitters and then we can send messages from that mast over there.

What for?

For better communications, Alice. And there's the *Rügen*, two funnels, oh my word, a freighter of the Gribel Line won't make it under that. Wilhelm lowered his arm and propped it on the grass to support himself. Now he was looking at Helene. She felt his eyes roaming over her and resting on her face.

The prospect of the wedding night to come made Helene feel embarrassed. She had been aware of the happy way he looked at her all day and had avoided his eyes. Now she had to narrow hers, because it was bright and windy up here on the heights. She looked back.

Won't you give me a smile? Wilhelm lifted her chin with one finger.

Today he had seemed to her even taller than usual when he was standing up a moment ago, and even sitting down he towered above her. Helene tried hard to smile.

Wilhelm had let nothing deter him. When the law for the protection of Aryan blood was passed in September, he had not mentioned it once. His efforts to get papers for Helene had dragged on; she had had to stop working at the Bethany Hospital and they had asked her to leave the nurses' hostel. Back in Fanny's apartment, Helene had been glad to find that Erich had obviously left her aunt at last. Wilhelm came to see Helene as often as he could. He apologized for the length of time it was taking, and sometimes he gave her some money which, relieved to be more independent of Fanny, she put away in her purse. Once Wilhelm mentioned that a colleague of his had sued for divorce; he didn't want to be accused of racial disgrace. Helene wondered whether he told her that to emphasize the risk he was running for her sake, or whether it was simply meant to show that her origins were beginning to seem immaterial to him. After all, he had mentioned the other man's divorce as if he certainly didn't see himself incurring racial disgrace. A little later they had met at the Lietzensee, near the embankment by the lake over which the road led. Plane leaves lay smooth and yellow on the ground. Well, here we are, said Wilhelm and he gave Helene an envelope. She sat down on a bench near the dappled tree trunk. Wilhelm sat beside her, put one arm round her and kissed her ear. She opened the envelope. It contained a certificate of nursing qualifications and a leaflet with a bronze-coloured cover certifying Aryan descent, a little shabby but almost new. It still had a certain smell. She leafed through it. Her name was Alice Schulze, her father was one Bertram Otto Schulze from Dresden, her mother was Auguste Clementine Hedwig Schulze, née Schröder.

Who are these people? Helene's heartbeat was steady; she had to smile because the names sounded so new to her, unfamiliar and promising. These names were to belong to her, they would be hers.

Don't ask. Wilhelm put a hand over her mouth.

But suppose someone asks me about them?

The Schulzes were our neighbours in Dresden. Simple folk.

Wilhelm was going to leave his explanations at that, but Helene wouldn't leave him in peace. She tickled his chin: Go on, she said and smiled, because she knew that Wilhelm didn't like to refuse her anything.

There were nine of us in our family; they had only one child, a girl. Alice often played on her own in the street until it was dark. What she liked best was coming over to us and joining our family at our big table. She didn't want to eat anything, just sit at our table with us. One day her parents spread the news that Alice had run away. We children helped to search for her, but Alice never turned up. You look a little like her.

I disappeared? Helene laughed out loud. The idea of being a missing person amused her.

She was about your age. Everyone in our street thought Alice's parents had killed her. How else could they be so confident about claiming that she'd run away?

Killed by her own parents?

Wilhelm raised Helene's chin with his forefinger, as he liked to do when he thought she was being too serious. We simply wondered about the way they went on living just as usual, no sign of grief. They didn't even want to tell the police. All of us toyed with the idea of going to the police ourselves. Alice wasn't to start school until the summer, so there was no teacher to notice her absence. My God, didn't several of your own siblings die too? Plenty of children died without death certificates. Soon after that the wife, Alice's mother, fell downstairs and died. Her husband lived on until a year ago; he survived to a great age, but he always seemed old.

And they're supposed to be my parents?

You wanted to know. Wilhelm rubbed his hands; perhaps he felt cold. Nothing to be done about it, and now you do know.

What about their ancestors? Grandparents, great-grandparents – these are just names that no one knows.

They existed, said Wilhelm. He said no more; he had just taken the record of her descent from her hand, rolled it up and put it into the inside pocket of his coat. He had reached for her hand and suggested getting married in Stettin, where he had rented an apartment in Elisabethstrasse several months earlier, and where Dresden stamps and seals might be even less familiar than they were in Berlin.

Helene had nodded. She had always wanted to see a real big harbour. And they had set off for Stettin before Christmas. It hadn't been easy to say goodbye to Martha and Leontine. They had met at Leontine's apartment the evening before they left; the thick velour curtains were drawn, Leontine offered Irish whiskey and dark cigarettes, just the thing for this moment, she said.

So when I write to you, Martha had said, do I write to Alice now? Leontine had objected, laughing, that no one could break off a relationship in that one-sided way. I'll write to you every week, Martha had promised, as Elsa from an address in Bautzen.

In Stettin, Wilhelm had gone to the registry office to give notice of their engagement and fix a date. He let Helene sleep in the room next to the kitchen in the apartment and she was glad of his thoughtfulness. The wedding was to be at the beginning of May. And Helene wasn't to work; Wilhelm gave her house-keeping money, she did the shopping and put the bill on the table for him to see; she cooked, she washed and ironed clothes, she lit the stove. She was grateful. If Wilhelm wanted beef roulades for supper, Helene might have to spend half the morning going from butcher to butcher to find the right meat for them. Wilhelm didn't want her going to Wolff, quite close to them in Bismarckstrasse, however friendly he might be, however good his prices. Such people must not be encouraged, said Wilhelm, and Helene knew what he meant and was afraid he might follow her to see if she was acting according to his instructions. They had once met by chance; Helene had been coming out of the library in the Rosengarten district with two books under her arm when Wilhelm called her over to the other side of the street. He had cast a fleeting glance at her books. Martin Buber, do you have to read that? At such a time, with his ideas . . . I don't like it. What do you think you get out of it? he asked, laughing. He had put his arm round her shoulders and was speaking close to her ear. I see I'll have to keep my eye on you. I don't want you going to that library. The People's Library is just round the corner. You can easily walk the few metres to the park.

If Wilhelm gave her a shirt with a missing button, Helene went from draper to draper until she had found not just one button the right size, but back in the first shop a whole dozen, so that she could change all the other buttons on the shirt to match. Helene felt a gratitude to him that kept her cheerful.

Once Wilhelm said it was only as you came into their apartment that you noticed how dirty the corridor outside it was. He meant it as a compliment because she kept their place so clean. You're a wonderful woman, Alice. There's just one thing I have to mention to you. And he looked at her sternly. Our neighbour on the ground floor told me she saw you last week in Schuhstrasse coming out of that draper's shop, what's his name, Bader? Helene felt herself going red in the face. Baden, Herbert Baden, I've been buying from him since Christmas, he has very high-quality goods; you don't get buttons like that anywhere else. Wilhelm had not looked at Helene; he had taken a long draught from his beer glass and said: My God, then you'll just have to buy different buttons, Alice. Do you realize that you're putting us both in danger? Not just yourself, me too.

Next morning, as soon as Wilhelm had left the apartment, Helene set to work. She scrubbed and scoured the stairs from the top floor to the entrance of the building. Finally she polished them until they gleamed and everything smelled of wax. When Wilhelm failed to notice the clean stairway that evening, she did not mention it. She was glad she had something to do; she did not just obey Wilhelm's orders readily, she did so gladly. What could be better than the definite prospect of things that must be done, tasks where her only worry was that there might not be enough time to do them all? And Helene knew what to think of as well: the brown shoe polish, the streaky bacon for supper. What she liked best was to do jobs waiting to be dealt with before Wilhelm missed anything or had to go without. When he came home from work he said he was happy to know she was here at home and to have her around him. My little housewife, he'd taken to calling her recently. There was just one small thing he didn't have yet, he said, smiling. He was eagerly waiting for the month of May.

The wind on the Hakenterrasse turned, and now it was blowing right in their faces. Wilhelm didn't want her to cut up the second apple, he wanted to eat it properly, round the core. She handed him the whole apple.

And the big ship there, isn't that a fine sight? Wilhelm took out his binoculars. He watched the gigantic freighter and said nothing for an unusually long time. Helene wondered whether she might tell him she was freezing; it would spoil his good temper. But his mouth was twisting anyway. I don't quite like that name, though, *Arthur Kunstmann*. Do you know about Kunstmann?

Helene shook her head. Wilhelm raised his binoculars again. The biggest shipping company in Prussia. Well, that's about to change.

Why?

Fritzen & Son do better business. Suddenly Wilhelm shouted: Get a move on, lads! He slapped his thigh, as if anyone rowing down there could hear him up on the hill. Our boys are going too slowly. Wilhelm lowered the binoculars again. Aren't you interested? He looked at Helene with surprise and a little pity; at this distance she could make out only that he was talking about an eight rowing past the opposite bank down below. Perhaps he would lend her the binoculars so that she could share his pleasure? But Wilhelm had come to the conclusion that Helene wasn't interested in rowing. He jammed the binoculars to his eyes and rejoiced. Gummi Schäfer and Walter Volle, they'll win for us. Get a move on, for God's sake! It's a pity I have to be here to supervise the finishing touches to the work. I'd love to be in Berlin in August.

Our boys? Why would they win, what does it mean to you? Helene tried to pay no more attention to the crying baby and followed the direction of Wilhelm's glance, looking down towards the water.

You don't understand, child. We're the best. The fair sex has no idea about competitive sport, but once Gummi's won gold you'll see what it's all about!

What what's all about?

Alice, darling! Wilhelm lowered the binoculars and looked sternly at Helene. He spoke menacingly, he liked to threaten Helene in fun when she asked too many questions. Helene couldn't summon up a smile. Just thinking of the approaching night, their first night together as man and wife, kept her from even looking at him. Perhaps he took her questions as implying doubts of what he said, or as doubts of his own pleasure in it. Certainly his wife ought not to doubt him, she ought to respect him, and now and then be happy to keep quiet for him. A little jubilation wouldn't be out of place either, just a very little quiet, cheerful, feminine jubilation, she felt sure Wilhelm would like that. Helene thought he seemed content when she nodded approvingly and simply accepted what he said. And could she really not just accept a statement sometimes? Yesterday evening he had complained a little, but maybe he had just been edgy because it was the eve of their wedding. He had said, looking at the paper, that he sometimes suspected Alice had a joyless nature. When Helene could think of nothing to say and went on sweeping the grate in silence, he added that he thought he noticed not just a lack of joy but a certain aloofness in her too.

Now Wilhelm was looking through his binoculars. Secretly, Helene felt ashamed of herself. Was she going to grudge him the sight of something he liked on his wedding day? She held her tongue and wondered to herself what he meant, and what would happen if the German oarsmen did win at the Olympic Games in a few weeks' time. She also wondered why Martha wasn't replying to her letters any more, and decided to write to Leontine. Leontine was a tower of strength; on Shrove Tuesday she had written to Helene to tell her she was glad to say she could probably get her mother discharged from Sonnenstein. Luckily old Mariechen had stayed on in the house, she said, and would be very glad to see her mistress back. Leontine signed her letter Leo, and Helene felt relieved and happy whenever she read the letter and the name at the bottom of it.

The steamer was casting off from the landing stage. Gulls circled around the ship, probably hoping the passengers on their excursion would throw some scraps overboard. Black smoke rose from the funnels. Helene felt a drop of something on her hand. Wilhelm was opening his bottle of beer. Didn't she want to drink her lemonade? Helene shook her head. She knew she had to give herself to him tonight, give herself entirely, so that he possessed her as he never had before. That idea made him glad. Her mind worked slowly, her thoughts were disjointed. It occurred to her that she wouldn't be able to wear her beloved old vest this evening. If they had stayed in Berlin they could have given a wedding party, but whom could they have asked? Martha and Leontine and Fanny weren't suitable company, it would soon have come out that there was something wrong with their papers, and perhaps Martha might have giggled at the registrar's remarks. Erich might have turned up too, to disrupt the ceremony. Better to move right away from Berlin and avoid any party.

Helene took the paper bag out of the basket and put her fingers in it. She felt happy when she was eating raisins.

They were planning to go for a little trip round the harbour on the *Hanni* or the *Hans*, whichever of the two elderly passenger steamers with superstructures like houses they could take today. Every child in Stettin knew the striped funnels of the Maris Line, and Helene had thought for some time that a trip on one of the two vessels would be nice.

Well, here we go. Helene packed up the knife and the apple

core, put the empty beer bottle back in the basket and spread the little cover over it. They set off down to the quay. Wilhelm took her hand and Helene let him guide her. Behind his back she closed her eyes so that he could lead her as if she were blind. What could happen? She felt very tired, overwhelmingly weak, she could have gone to sleep at once, but the wedding day wasn't half over yet. Wilhelm bought two tickets for the *Hanni* of the Gotzkow Line. The vessel rocked on the water. From time to time Helene put her hand over her mouth so that no one would see her yawning.

On the round trip, with the wind getting up and the ship pitching and tossing, there was no conversation between her and Wilhelm. The link between them had not simply slackened but separated, disappeared. Two strangers sat side by side looking in different directions.

Only when Wilhelm ordered a plate of sausage and mustard from the waiter did he speak to her again. Are you hungry? Helene nodded. They were sitting below decks, a shower of rain was beating on the windows and droplets of water were streaming down; the skies seemed to have opened, but Helene felt sick from the rocking of the ship and her feet were cold. Everything on this ship was so dirty, the rail was sticky, even the plate on which Wilhelm's sausage was served looked to Helene as if it had a dirty rim from the previous customer's mustard. With difficulty, she prevented herself from pointing that out to Wilhelm. Why bother? He was enjoying the sausage. Helene excused herself, saying she wanted to wash her hands. The rocking down here would have made her feel sick even if she hadn't been nauseated already. Helene made her way along the rail. How could she have forgotten her gloves? An excursion without gloves was a special sort of adventure. Perhaps Wilhelm might have made fun of her for wearing gloves in May, wearing gloves to her wedding when she had decided not to have a traditional wedding dress, opting for what to him was a simple white jacket and skirt, stubborn as she was. But the door to the little cabin, behind which Helene had hoped to find a container of water for hand-washing beside the WC, bore a notice saying Out of Order, so Helene had to go back without washing. On the ship, preparations for docking were already going on. Men were calling to other men, the steamer was hauled in to the pier by two strong ship's boys. Helene's throat felt rough.

Well, my wife, shall we go for a drive, have something to eat and then go home? Wilhelm took her hand as they climbed off the ship. His words sounded like the prelude to a play in a theatre, and he bowed to her. She knew why. He had waited patiently all day, from the registry office in the morning, through a little excursion in his new car, in which he had driven her to Braunsfelde and shown her a building site in Elsässer Strasse where the foundations of their new house were soon to be laid, on to their midday picnic, and now on the trip round the harbour. Helene sat down in the car, put on her new headscarf, although it was not an open car, and held the door handle tightly. Wilhelm started the engine.

You don't have to clutch the handle all the time.

I'd rather.

The door might fly open, darling. Let go of it.

Helene obeyed. She suspected that further insistence would annoy him unnecessarily.

Wilhelm had booked a table in the café at the foot of the castle, but after only a few mouthfuls of pork knuckle he said that was enough. If she didn't want any more he would ask for the bill. He did ask for the bill, then he drove his bride home.

She had made the bed that morning, the marital bed that he had had delivered a week ago.

Wilhelm said she could go and undress in her old room. She went into it, took off her clothes and changed into a white nightdress. Over the last few weeks she had been embroidering little roses and delicate leafy tendrils on it, in the stitch that Mariechen had once taught her. When she came back he had put out the bedroom light. There was a strong smell of eau de Cologne in the air. It was dark in the room, and Helene groped her way forward.

Here I am, he said, laughing. His hand reached out for her. Don't be afraid, darling, he said, and pulled her down on the bed beside him. It won't hurt. He unbuttoned her nightdress, wanted to feel her breasts, felt about blindly for a while, up, down, sideways, round to her spine and back again as if he couldn't find what he wanted, then he moved his hands away from her breasts and took hold of her buttocks. Ah, what do we have here? he said, laughing at his own joke, and she felt his rough hand between her legs. Then she noticed a kind of regular shaking; her eyes got used to the darkness; he was taking shallow breaths, breathing almost soundlessly and the shaking grew more vigorous, obviously he was working on his penis. Perhaps it wasn't hard enough, or perhaps he would rather find his own relief without Helene. Helene felt his hand push against her thigh again and again. She put her own hand out and touched him.

Nice, he said, nice. He spoke in the dark, still breathing very quietly, and Helene took fright. Did he mean himself or her? Her hand searched for his; she wanted to help him. His prick was hard and hot. Her nose was pressed against his chest, not a place to stay for long, the eau de Cologne irritated the mucous membrane of her nostrils; how could you close your nose, breathe through your mouth, through your mouth, her mouth against his stomach; a few hairs in your mouth ought not to matter. Helene bent her head, it could only be better further down, and her lips sought for him. He smelled of urine, and tasted salty and sour and a little bitter, and she retched slightly, but he kept saying nice, nice, and: You don't have to do that, dear girl, but she was sucking his prick now with smacking sounds, she liked it, she used her tongue, he took her shoulders and pulled her up to him, perhaps her sucking was uncomfortable for him. Alice? There was a little doubt in the way he said her name, as if he wasn't sure who she was. She sought his mouth, she knelt above him. Alice! He sounded indignant. He grabbed her shoulders, threw her underneath him and, with a shaking hand and gasping out loud now, as if he had lost control of himself, he pushed his prick between her legs.

That's how it goes, he said, thrusting into her. Nice, he said once more, and again, nice. Helene tried to raise herself, but he pushed her down on the mattress. He was kneeling, probably so as to watch himself going in and out of her, one hand firmly on her shoulder so that she couldn't twist or turn, and suddenly he sighed heavily and sank down on her, exhausted. His body was heavy.

Helene felt her face glowing. Now she was glad that Wilhelm had put out the light. Wilhelm thought it was silly for people to weep. His breath was calm and regular. Helene found herself counting the breaths; she counted them and then, so as to stop herself doing that, counted his heartbeats as he lay on top of her.

You're surprised. He stroked her hair back from her forehead. What do you say now?

His voice was proud and gentle; he asked as if he expected a definite and very special answer.

I like you, said Helene. She was surprised by the way those words had come to her. But they were true; she meant it in general and in spite of the last hour. She liked his invincible confidence in himself. All the same, she could not help thinking of Carl, of his hands joining with hers to make one body, some-times with two heads, sometimes without a head, his gentle lips and his prick, rather smaller than Wilhelm's and almost pointed. They were inscribed on her mind and into her movements.

And now I'll show you what else we can do. Wilhelm spoke like a teacher. He turned on his back, took Helene by the hips and pulled her on top of him. He made her move. Faster, that's it.

All this talking disturbed Helene. It was difficult to keep listening to him, to hear what he said and then forget it, forget herself, forget herself so that she stopped seeing and hearing.

There. Careful, now. Now, take your hand, here, hold me firmly.

Helene, exhausted, couldn't help smiling. It was lucky he couldn't see her. He thrust at her, talking at the same time, brief words, issuing instructions. She didn't want to contradict or challenge him. He held her hips hard, he was getting a grip so as to make her move on top of him.

There, that's nice.

Helene let him move her about for a while. The less she wanted to do for herself, the better he seemed to like it. A marionette, thought Helene, she didn't like that, and she didn't know how she could take the puppet strings from his hand. Suddenly she reared up and away from him.

Careful, he cried and he sighed: so close, he complained.

Helene took his hands to hold them, but he shook them free, moved her off him, threw her under him and set to work on top of her again. He thrust his prick into her, regular thrust after regular thrust, like a hammer driving a nail into the wall. No more sound, just his hammering, the ceiling and the mattress. A high squeal, then he rolled off her. Helene stared into the darkness.

He was lying on his back, smacking his lips with relish. That's love, Alice, he said.

She didn't know what to say. He suddenly turned to her, kissed her on the nose and turned his back to her. Excuse me, he said, pulling the covers over him, I can't sleep with a woman breathing into my face.

It was a long time before Helene could get to sleep. She was not interested in what women had breathed into his face when, or where; his sperm was running out of her in a little stream, sticky between her legs, and then it was as if she had slept for only a couple of minutes when she felt his hands on her hips again.

That's right, yes, he said, turning her over on her stomach. Kneeling behind her, he pulled her towards him and thrust in.

It burned. He braced his large hand against her back, hurting her, he pushed her ahead of him on the mattress. That's it, keep moving, you won't get away from me.

Helene kicked his knee with all her might. He cried out.

What's the idea of that? He took her by the shoulders and they both lay still. Don't you like it?

Shall I show you how I like it? She asked the question in self-defence; she could think of no answer, she hadn't wanted to hurt his feelings, but he agreed. She approached him, his large body, he knelt on the mattress, sat back on his heels, his prick dangled heavy and limp between his powerful thighs. Shall I lie down? There was a note of derision in his voice, or perhaps he was just unsure of himself.

Helene said yes, yes, lie down. She bent over him, she smelled his sweat through the eau de cologne on his chest, sweat that smelled a little strange. She took the sheet and dried his chest, his forehead, his thighs first outside, then on the inside. He lay on his back with his body rigid, as if afraid.

She licked his skin with her tongue until he laughed.

He asked her to stop, it tickled. That's not the way, he said.

She took his hands, placed them on her flat breasts, where they lay as if at a loss, not knowing what to do. Helene lay on top of him and moved, she pressed her body to his, she felt his skin with her lips, her teeth touched him, her soft finger-tips and nails, she rubbed his prick and, as it began to stiffen in arousal, used it to sit on him. She rode him, she bent over to be closer to him, she leaned back to feel the air, she listened to his breathing, listened to his desire, and felt some desire herself.

What are you doing to me? Wilhelm's question sounded surprised, almost suspicious. He didn't wait for her to answer. You're an animal, a real little animal. He took her face in his hands and kissed her forehead. My wife, he said. He was speaking to himself, confirming the fact, making sure of it. My wife.

Didn't he like her mouth? Helene wondered why he didn't kiss her on the lips, for he avoided them. He got up and went out. Helene heard water rushing; he was obviously washing.

When he came back and lay down on the mattress beside her, heavy and hesitant, he asked hoarsely: May I turn the light on?

Of course. Helene was shivering pleasantly; she had drawn the covers up to her chin. In the light he looked crumpled, the shadows showing lines that Helene had never seen on him before. Presumably he now saw her own little lines and dimples, hollows and dips, previously unknown to him.

I must ask you something. He had pulled the other blanket over himself. He looked seriously at her. Were his eyes exploring her? Was he afraid?

There are ways and means, she said, don't worry.

Ways and means?

Of avoiding a pregnancy, she explained.

That's not what I meant. Wilhelm was obviously confused. Why would I want to avoid a pregnancy? Or you either? No, I must ask you something else.

What?

I've just been out to wash myself.

Yes?

Well, how can I put it? Normally I'd have had . . . there'd have been . . . well, I'd thought there was sure to be . . . As if to encourage himself he raised her chin with one finger. You didn't bleed at all.

Helene looked at his tense and baffled face. Had he expected her to be menstruating, or were there other reasons why she would be bleeding? Now it was her turn to raise a questioning eyebrow. So?

You know what that means yourself. Now he was looking annoyed. You're a nurse, so please don't act so naïve.

I didn't bleed, no. If I'd bled that would have meant I'd been injured.

I thought you were still a virgin. The sharp note in Wilhelm's voice surprised Helene.

Why?

Why? Are you making fun of me? I keep my hands off you for three years, I procure a certificate of Aryan descent for you, I get engaged to you, damn it all, what do you mean, why did I think that? Listen, how was I to know that . . . ? Wilhelm was shouting. He was sitting up and pounding the mattress in front of Helene with his fist. Involuntarily, she flinched back. Now she saw that he had put on a pair of short white underpants. He sat there in his underpants hitting the mattress again. Between the hem of the leg and his thigh she saw his prick, lying on the thigh as if taking no part in this, just jerking slightly when he hit the mattress. You ask why I thought you were a virgin? I'm asking

339

myself the same question. What a hypocritical act all this was! Idiotic! He beat his fist on the mattress again, making the limp prick inside his underpants jump. What is it, why are you shrinking away like that? Not afraid, are you? He shook his head; his voice became quieter and more scornful. Your tears are just a sham, my girl. Bitterly, Wilhelm shook his head, he snorted with derision, a dry snort, expressing nothing but contempt. He was looking at her with contempt. He shook his head again. What a fool I am, he said, striking his forehead, what a stupid idiot. He was hissing through his teeth. What a wonderful show! He shook his head, gave that dry snort, shook his head again.

Helene tried to understand what was making him so angry. She must be brave and ask. Why . . . ?

This is monstrous, don't you know that? Wilhelm interrupted her. He wasn't going to let her begin a sentence, raise her voice however hesitantly. What do you want of me, Helene? He was roaring at her, barking at her.

Was it the first time he had called her Helene? Her name sounded like a foreign word, coming from him. The displeasure with which he looked at her now made Helene feel very lonely. She lay in his marital bed, the blanket up to her chin, her fingers curved into cold claws under the bedclothes, claws that she couldn't open out even if she tried, she had to keep the covers firmly in place, hiding them, hiding her body from him. The burning between her legs wasn't too bad, she was in his marital bed, the bed he had bought for his marriage to a virgin, the bed in which he was planning to teach a virgin about love. What had he thought she was? What misunderstanding had brought them together in this bed?

Wilhelm got up. He took his blanket, draped it round his shoulders and left the room. He shut the door behind him; evidently she was to stay there. Helene tried to think sensibly.

It wasn't easy. Frau Alice Sehmisch, she said to herself in the darkness. Her feet were as cold as her claws, they were claws too, fingers and toes cold and claw-like in May.

When all was still Helene stole into the kitchen, washed her hands, put water on to heat and mixed hot and cold water with a dash of vinegar in the enamel basin. She squatted over the basin and washed herself. A little soap wouldn't hurt, maybe a bit of iodine? With the hollow of her hand she scooped up water and felt for her labia, the opening, the tender, smooth folds, washed it all out thoroughly, washed his sperm out of her. Soft water, hard water. She washed for a long time until the water was cold, then she washed her hands at the sink.

Back in bed, her feet were still cold. She couldn't sleep anyway, she felt like getting up and making breakfast. She had bought eggs – Wilhelm liked eggs so long as they weren't too soft-boiled. Would he speak to her? What would he say?

For that first half-hour, in which Wilhelm had got up, washed, shaved and combed his hair, it looked as if he wasn't going to speak to her, might never speak to her again. Helene thought about the notes she would write him in future, the notes he would write her. She could practise the language of gestures. He would write notes telling her what she was to do for him and what he wanted for supper. She would write to explain why she hadn't bought eels and tell him the fishwife had plaice on special offer today. Helene was good at keeping silent, as he would soon find out.

Wilhelm had sat down at the table to try a sip of coffee. Is this real coffee? he suddenly asked. She knew there were few things he liked as much as coffee made from real coffee beans. Real coffee came directly after cars and before the wireless masts of ships, but she was a little uncertain where oarsmen and ski-jumpers ranked in his esteem.

In celebration of the day, I thought. The first morning of our marriage.

Good idea, he said, nodding with a fair show of appreciation; then he had to smile. He was smiling to himself, he didn't look at her.

And is that toast I smell, or am I imagining it?

You're not imagining it, said Helene, and she took a step aside, opened the toaster and gave him the dark-brown toast.

Perhaps you'll sit down too.

Helene obeyed. She pulled out her chair and sat down opposite him.

Well, this is a fine situation I've got myself into, remarked Wilhelm. Talk about buying a pig in a poke. He shook his head. No idea of honour. And I've sullied my hands for that, forged those damn documents to give you a new identity. Wilhelm shook his head and took a bite of toast.

Helene began to guess at the humiliation he must be suffering.

We will try, all the same. Helene said it hoping that the question of her virginity might soon seem ridiculous to him.

Wilhelm nodded. I am not going to be cuckolded, let's get that clear. He held out his cup for her to add milk.

Wilhelm had got the papers for her, he had committed a punishable offence. They could feel mutual fear, for either would be able to denounce the other. For the first time Helene understood what fundamentally divided the two of them. He was an established member of society, he was someone, he had built up a reputation for himself. Wilhelm had something to lose: his good name, his honour and his wife's respectability were certainly a part of that; so were his beliefs, his support of a people, the German nation, to which he belonged by virtue of his blood and which he wanted to serve with his life's blood.

We could go out to Swinemünde tomorrow. Helene embarked

on the sentence out of sheer fear that otherwise Wilhelm might understand what thoughts were spreading through her mind, how terror and shame were taking hold of her.

Do me a favour, Alice, spare me that today. I know you love the sea and the harbour. Are you telling me the round trip yesterday wasn't enough?

It was not an easy night, said Helene. She wanted to show understanding.

It's forgotten. Last night is forgotten, do you hear? Wilhelm was fighting to speak in a firm voice and Helene saw tears in his eyes. She was sorry. I didn't know that . . .

That what? What didn't you know?

Helene couldn't tell him. She was ashamed of her thoughtlessness. Not for a moment had it occurred to her that his love could depend on her virginity.

I've been with women. But marriage – Wilhelm shook his head, without looking at Helene – marriage is different. He bit his lip; he probably guessed that they would never be able to agree on this point, now or later. There were moments last night when you were like an animal, a wild cat.

A tear fell from his eye. The eye of a man whom Helene had never seen shedding tears before.

She would have liked to embrace him, but what comfort could she offer?

Have you been with many men? Now Wilhelm was looking at her scornfully; it was hard to bear his glance. Then it softened, she saw a plea in his eyes, he obviously wanted her to tell him he was unique, oh, what an amazing lover, not just *an* amazing lover but *the* lover, there was no one like him.

Helene stretched her fingers, curved them, stretched them. Her knuckles inaudibly cracked. She wanted to wash her hands. What difference did lying a little make? She looked at him over the table, she still had time. It was simple. He wouldn't notice. She shook her head and closed her eyes. When she cautiously opened them again, she saw that he wanted to believe her.

Wilhelm stood up. He was wearing the shirt she had ironed so recently. He looked ready to go to work. He touched her shoulder, grateful and angry at the same time. He breathed deeply in and out, then patted her on the back. That's my girl. He looked at the time. I have to go out to the building site, the construction workers all slack off at the weekend. There's going to be a private discussion. If you wait in the car you can come with me.

Helene nodded. Wilhelm took her wrist. But first we're going to bed. There was an expression of triumph on his face. Was what she saw in his eyes the consciousness of arbitrary power springing from his injured feelings? Defiance and lust? And didn't a husband have rights over his wife? He pushed her into the bedroom ahead of him, drew the curtains, opened his trousers with one hand and reached for her skirt with the other. Lift your skirt, he said.

Helene lifted her skirt, which wasn't easy. She'd made it herself from a pattern only a few weeks ago, and it narrowed towards the hem and had only a short open pleat at the back. She had found a lovely fabric, cream cotton printed with blue flowers. It was a daring skirt, tapering where it ended between calf and ankle. Wilhelm became impatient, he was breathing deeply. She'd soon have done it, she'd have pushed the skirt far enough up. She couldn't help thinking that the laundry had been soaking for too long, that she still had to gut the fish for lunch and must soon put the casserole on if they wanted beans for supper, and she didn't have any savoury to flavour the beans with. Wilhelm told her to kneel on the bed.

The great day was 27 September. The day for which others as well as Wilhelm had been eagerly waiting, a day like no other. All Germany was waiting for that day.

In the morning, when Helene had just dressed, Wilhelm's eye fell on her behind. He took hold of her hips and ran his tongue over her mouth. You're the first woman I've liked to kiss, did you know that? Helene smiled diffidently and picked up her handbag. Day by day, Wilhelm's taste for unsettling her, seeing her feel diffident was increasing. Now that she knew he had developed that liking, she made out from time to time that she really was diffident. Nothing could have been easier. Let's see your suspender belt, are you wearing the one with the little anchors on it? Wilhelm felt her suspender belt through the firm woollen fabric.

We must leave, Wilhelm.

Don't worry, I have my eye on the time. He said it quietly, he moved softly. Especially before going out, and especially on a great day like this, Wilhelm didn't want to leave his home before taking her at least briefly. He grabbed her skirt, pushed it up, pulled her knickers down as far as possible – she wasn't complying with his wish for her to wear them over the suspender belt. Helene felt him push himself inside her and as he went on thrusting, with short, quick jabs, she remembered how Carl used to undress her lingeringly to the last. He would caress her breasts, her arms, her fingers. After that first night, it was enough for Wilhelm to lift her skirt.

He hadn't been inside Helene a minute before pushing her up against the table, with her handbag still over her wrist. He stopped, then patted her buttocks. Obviously he had finished. She didn't know whether he had come or whether his desire had left him.

Right, we can go, said Wilhelm. He had pulled up his trousers, which had slipped to the floor, and fastened his belt. He looked at himself in the mirror, unbuttoned his shirt and splashed eau de Cologne lavishly on his chest.

Helene wanted to wash, but Wilhelm said he was afraid there wasn't time for that. All that washing of hers infuriated him, he added. He took his coat and put it on, looked at the mirror again to check his appearance now that he was wearing the coat, took his small comb out of his inside pocket and ran it through his hair.

Do you think that'll do?

Of course, said Helene, you look good. She had put on her own coat and was waiting.

What's that behind me? Wilhelm craned his neck so that he could see his back view better.

What do you mean?

Well, that! See that funny kind of crease? And my coat's all over bits of fuzz. Would you deal with it, please?

Of course, said Helene, and taking the clothes brush out of the console table she brushed Wilhelm's coat.

The arms too. Not so hard, child, this is fine fabric.

At last they were able to set off. Helene's knickers were wet. Wilhelm was flowing out of her even as he walked to the car about three metres ahead of her. Perhaps there was some blood too. Her periods had been back for the last three months and she was due again tomorrow, or maybe even today.

The opening of the Reich autobahn was an endless ceremony full of speeches and commendations, vows made in the name of the future, of Germany and its Führer. Heil. Helene thought everyone near her must be surprised by the reek of sperm clinging to her. Wilhelm's sperm. There were days when she felt the smell of it was like a brand on her. Obviously Wilhelm didn't notice anything. He stretched out his arm and stood motionless beside her for hours with his back very straight. On this day his greatest achievement so far was on show to the public. All the workers were thanked, including those who had risked or lost their lives. No one said exactly how they had lost them. One might have fallen off a bridge, another could have been run over by a steam-roller. Helene imagined the different possible kinds of death. In any case, theirs had been heroic deaths, just as the building of the whole road was heroic. A reference to the drop in the unem-ployment figures was intended to emphasize the claim that, among other achievements, the building of this road and the other autobahns that were to follow was a triumphantly successful way of tackling unemployment in Germany. When Wilhelm stepped forward to be honoured, he did not glance back at Helene; presumably the many pats on the back he received from his colleagues prevented him. Wilhelm shook hands, stretched his arm towards the sky and looked around him with a certain pride. His excitement seemed so great that he forgot to smile. Or perhaps the place and the occasion seemed to him too sacred for anyone to venture a smile. He expressed his thanks in a firm voice, he thanked everyone, from the German Fatherland to the secretary of the first German Ladies' Automobile Club. Heil, Heil, Heil. Everyone had earned a Heil. Unlike the six gentlemen who had been commended and honoured before him, he had not seen and then exploited the tiny loophole left available for him to thank his wife. Perhaps it was because they had no children. After all, the speakers before him could thank their whole families for providing special support in the recent past.

Before the guests invited to the lunch celebrating the occasion set off in a convoy, Helene left, like most of the other wives. After all, she had to prepare supper and do the laundry. As he said goodbye to her, Wilhelm said he hoped to be home by six, but if he didn't get back in time for supper she wasn't to wait for him. He might well be late on a day like this.

Helene waited all the same. She had made pearl barley soup with carrots and bacon, a favourite of Wilhelm's, specially for today. The potatoes grew cold, fresh liver and onions lay beside the stove ready for frying. Helene herself hated pearl barley and liver, she simply could not get any of those dishes down, so there was no point, she thought, in eating any supper herself later in the evening. She wrote two letters to Berlin: one to Martha alias Elsa, one to Leontine asking why there was no word from Martha. Then she wrote a third letter, to Bautzen. It would bear the Stettin postmark, but as sender's name she gave only her first name, Helene, written in a childish scrawl so that the postman might think it was just love and kisses from a little girl and suspect nothing. She had not yet told her mother and Mariechen that she was married and now had a new surname. Martha and Leontine had agreed with her that such news might agitate her mother unnecessarily. So Helene wrote to say she was well and had moved to Stettin for professional reasons, to look for a job here since she couldn't find one in Berlin at the moment. She asked how her mother was and said any reply should be sent to Fanny's address. Helene opened Wilhelm's desk and took out the cash box. She knew he didn't like her to go to his cash box on her own, but once, three months ago, she had asked him for some money for her mother and Wilhelm had just looked at her blankly. After all, he didn't know these people, he said, and he didn't suppose that she still wanted to call them relations of hers. So then she knew that he wasn't going to give her anything. It might be because of maladministration or possible sharp practice, Helene didn't know the precise reasons, but the income from Breslau had dried up. Finally Martha had said she could send their mother money only every three months; there simply wasn't enough to go round. Mariechen had written asking for something in kind; she needed hard soap and foodstuffs, dried food would be useful, peas, fruits, oats and coffee, not to mention material for clothes. Helene took a ten-mark note out of the box; she hesitated; another ten-mark note lay temptingly on top of a third. But Wilhelm counted his money. She would have to think of a credible story to account for the absence of this one banknote. The simplest lie was to say she had lost the housekeeping money that he had counted out and given her the evening before. But Helene had claimed to have lost money once before. She took the banknote, put it in the letter to Bautzen and stuck down the envelope. Whether and exactly where the money would arrive was another question. Helene didn't even know where her last letter had ended up.

She did some sewing and ironing, and starched Wilhelm's collars, before going to bed just before midnight. Wilhelm came home at four in the morning. Without turning on the light he dropped on the bed beside Helene, fully dressed, and snored peacefully. Helene could distinguish between his various snores; there was the hoarse, light snoring of the carefree Wilhelm, there was the defiant snoring of the hard-working Wilhelm who had not yet had his money's worth, every snore was different and told Helene what mood Wilhelm was in. Helene let him snore; she thought of her sister and worried a little. After all, it could be that Martha wasn't well. Perhaps something had happened to her and Leontine, and no one had told Helene about it because it wasn't officially known that Martha had a sister, let alone what her name was.

After an hour Wilhelm's snoring became disturbed. Then it suddenly stopped and he got up and went out on to the landing. When he came back, Helene lay with her back to him and listened for the snoring to begin again. But it didn't. Instead she suddenly felt Wilhelm's hand on her waist. Helene turned to him. A smell of beer and schnapps and sweet perfume wafted into her face. She had smelled it before, but not as strongly as this.

What a great day for you. You must be relieved. Helene placed her hand on the back of Wilhelm's neck. The hair shaved very short there felt strange.

Oh, relieved, well, this is where it all begins, child. Wilhelm couldn't articulate clearly. He pushed his hand between Helene's legs and squeezed her labia with his fingers. Come on, he said as she tried to push his hand away, come on, little animal, you sweet little cunt, come on. He pressed Helene's arms aside and turned her body over. She resisted, which aroused him, perhaps he thought she did it on purpose to entice him and send him crazy. What an arse, he said. Helene flinched.

Every goddam woman, he had once said, thinks she can see into people's hearts, but he could see into her vulva, he could look deep into her vagina, the deepest orifice of her body, the juiciest, the orifice that was all his, one that she herself could never see, or not so directly. It was possible that Wilhelm and his colleagues had been with a tart just now. Helene had smelled that flowery perfume. Even a mirror allowed a woman only a glimpse of it. She could never be mistress of the sight of it. Let her look into hearts as much as she liked.

When he had finished Wilhelm slapped her bottom. That was good, he sighed, very good. He dropped on to the mattress and rolled over. We'll be going to Braunsfelde later, he murmured.

Or we could go to the sea, Helene suggested.

Sea, sea, sea. You're always wanting to go to the sea. There's a cold wind bl-bl-blowing. Wilhelm laughed. A cold wind blowing.

It's still almost summer. I'm sure it was twenty degrees yesterday.

Day, day, day, day. Wilhelm lay in the middle of the bed, turned to Helene's back and smacked his lips. *My good wife Dame Ilsebill always wants to have her will,* like the story of the flounder and the fisherman. I ought to call you Ilsebill. You always know best, don't you? Well, that makes no difference, we're going to Braunsfelde.

Is the house ready?

The house is finished, yes, but we're not going to live in it.

Helene said nothing. Perhaps this was one of those jokes of his that she didn't always understand at first.

Surprised, are you? We're going to Braunsfelde to meet the architect and the buyers. We'll sign everything and then it'll be nothing to do with me any more.

You're joking.

Perhaps jokes are a question of race, child. Wilhelm turned to her now. We just don't understand each other. Why would I buy a house here when the new contracts haven't been negotiated yet?

Helene swallowed. He had never before so explicitly used the word *race* to indicate the difference between them.

There are plans for some important innovations in Pölitz. Getting that job would be quite a coup. Then Wilhelm was snoring, he had begun snoring again directly after this last remark. It was a mystery to Helene how someone could fall asleep in the middle of talking.

*   *   *

After the long winter Wilhelm's skin was giving him trouble. They had finished supper one evening, Helene had cleared the table, Wilhelm had wiped it down with the dishcloth. Helene was wondering how she could begin the conversation – a conversation that was important to her.

These spots are disgusting, don't you think? Wilhelm was standing in front of the mirror looking alternately over his right and left shoulders. It wasn't easy for him to see his back, broad as it was. He ran the palm of his hand over his skin, his shoulders, the nape of his neck. Look, there's a boil there.

Helene shook her head. It doesn't bother me. She was standing at the sink, washing the dishes in a basin.

Not you, no. A wry smile escaped Wilhelm. It makes no difference to you what I look like. Wilhelm couldn't stop examining his back. Will it heal over?

Heal over? You have a good strong back, why wouldn't that place heal over? Helene was scrubbing the bottom of the pan; sauces had been sticking to it and burning for weeks now. People either have spots or they don't, she said, rinsing out the pan under clear running water.

What a charming prospect. Wilhelm pulled on a vest, leaned close to the mirror and felt the skin of his face.

Zinc ointment might help. Helene wasn't sure if he was listening to her advice. She had something else on her mind, the matter she wanted to speak to him about. But if she opened the subject quietly, as a piece of information, as news, as a simple sequence of words, she could feel how the blood would shoot to her face. The spots, on the other hand, really didn't bother her and never had. Disgust was something different. When she had seen the maggots in her father's wound she had been surprised by the way they curled and crawled in the flesh. Or perhaps she was imagining that recollection; she had a good memory, but it wasn't infallible. Disgust, though? Helene thought of the amazement she had felt at the sight of the wound. The wreck of a body. Jews as worms. I am a parasite, thought Helene, but she did not say so. You couldn't compare the human body with the body politic of the German people. Perhaps she could alleviate Wilhelm's trouble.

Would you squeeze the pus out of them? Wilhelm smiled at her, a little diffidently but sure that she would. Whom else could he ask to do him this favour?

Of course, if you like. Helene raised her eyebrows as she scoured the pan. But it won't be much help. The skin will be broken and then there'll be more spots.

Wilhelm took his vest off again, stood close to her and showed her his back.

Helene hung the pan up on its hook, took off her apron, washed her hands and set to work. Wilhelm's skin was thick, the pores large, it was firm and very fair skin.

Wilhelm let out the air through his teeth. He had to ask Helene to go more carefully. That'll do, he said suddenly and turned to face her.

Helene watched as he put on garment after garment and finally fetched his shoes, checked to see that they were well polished and put them on. Obviously he was going out, although it was late already.

We're going to have a baby.

Helene had firmly determined to tell Wilhelm this evening. Something had gone wrong, although she was sure she hadn't miscalculated. Helene could remember how it happened. It must have been on the night when Wilhelm came home late and had woken her up. She had known it was a risky day and had tried to change his mind, but she had not succeeded. Later she had washed for hours and douched herself with vinegar, but obviously it hadn't worked. When her periods stopped, and a weekend came when Wilhelm was away on business in Berlin and didn't want to take her with him, she had bought a bottle of red wine and drunk it all. Then she had taken her knitting needles and poked about. After a while she started bleeding and went to sleep, but it wasn't a period. Her periods had stopped. She had known for weeks; she had been trying to think of some way out. She didn't know anyone in Stettin; there hadn't been a letter from Berlin for months. Once Helene tried telephoning Leontine. No one answered. When she asked the exchange to put her through to Fanny's number, the switchboard operator said the number was no longer available. Presumably Fanny hadn't been able to pay her bills. There was no way out of it now, there was just her certainty. Wilhelm looked down at his shoes.

We are?

She nodded. She had expected, first afraid and then hopeful, that Wilhelm would congratulate himself; she had thought there was nothing he wanted more.

Wilhelm stood up and took Helene by the shoulders. Are you sure? The corners of his mouth twitched, but yes, there was pride in his face, the first suggestion of delight, a smile.

Quite sure.

Wilhelm stroked Helene's hair back from her forehead. As he did so he looked at his watch. Perhaps he had an engagement and someone was waiting for him. I'm glad, he said. I really am. Really very glad.

Really very glad? Helene looked doubtfully up at Wilhelm, trying to meet his eyes. When she stood in front of him she had to put her head right back to do so, and even then it was possible only if he noticed that she was looking at him and looked down at her. He did not look down at her.

Why the question? Is there something wrong?

It doesn't sound as if you're really pleased.

Wilhelm glanced at his watch again. How dreadful your doubts are, Alice. You're always expecting something else. Now, I have an urgent meeting. We'll discuss it later, right?

Later? she asked. Perhaps this was one of the secret professional meetings that took Wilhelm out in the evening more and more frequently.

My God, this isn't the moment. If I'm too late back tonight, then tomorrow.

Helene nodded. Wilhelm took his hat and coat off the hook.

As soon as the door had closed, Helene sat down at the table and buried her face in her hands. For her, the past few months had consisted of waiting. She had waited for letters from Berlin, she had waited for Wilhelm to come back from work so that she could hear words spoken, perhaps she didn't exactly want to talk to anyone, but just to hear a human voice. When she had asked him to let her look for a job in the hospital he had always refused. In his view the words *you are my wife* were explanation enough. His wife did not have to work, his wife was not to work, he didn't want his wife to work. After all, she had plenty of housework to keep her occupied. Not bored, are you? he had sometimes asked, and told her that she could clean the windows again, he was sure they hadn't been cleaned for months. Helene cleaned the windows, although she had done the job only four weeks ago. She rubbed them with crumpled-up newspaper until the panes shone and her hands were dry, cracked and grey with newsprint. The only people with whom she exchanged a word during the day were the woman in the greengrocer's, the butcher and sometimes the fishwife down on the quay. The grocer didn't speak to her, or at least only to say what the price of something was, and her greetings and goodbyes went unanswered. On most days she didn't utter more than three or four sentences. Wilhelm was not particularly talkative in the evenings. If he was at home and didn't go out again, which recently had been the case only one or two evenings a week, his replies to Helene were monosyllabic.

Helene sat at the table rubbing her eyes. She felt dreadfully tired. She still had to wash Wilhelm's shirts and put the sheets through the mangle. There were bones for soup in the cool larder cupboard under the windowsill. A little air bubble inside Helene burst. Wind? She hadn't eaten anything to give her flatulence. Perhaps it was the baby. Was this how it felt when a baby started moving? My child, whispered Helene. She put her hand on her belly. My child, she said, smiling. There was no way out of it now, she was going to have a baby. Perhaps it would be nice to have a child? Helene wondered what the baby would look like. She imagined a little girl with dark hair, hair as dark and eyes as bright as Martha's, and an inscrutable smile like Leontine's. Helene stood up, put Wilhelm's shirts in the big boiler and placed the boiler on the stove. Then she washed carrots, scraped them, and put them in a pan of water with the bones. A bay leaf and a little pepper. Helene peeled the onions, stuck them with a clove and put them in the pan with the bones. She scrubbed the celery, cut it in half and stuffed it in between the carrots and bones. Finally she washed the leek and the parsley root. She mustn't forget the leek later. She didn't like a leek to soften in the soup overnight, and then disintegrate next morning as soon as she tried to fish it out.

Wilhelm didn't come home until Helene was asleep. Next day was Sunday, and when he didn't mention the baby of his own accord, Helene told him, unasked: It will come at the beginning of November.

What will? Wilhelm was cutting up his bread and jam with

a knife and fork, an oddity that Helene had only recently noticed. Did he feel that her hands soiled the bread she cut for him?

Our baby.

Oh, that. Wilhelm chewed noisily; you could hear the sound of his saliva. He munched for a long time, swallowed, and put down the knife and fork.

Another cup of coffee? Helene picked up the coffee pot to pour him more.

Wilhelm did not reply, as he often forgot to do, and she refilled his cup.

Do you know what I think . . . ?

Listen, Alice. You're expecting a child, all right? If I said yesterday I was glad then I am glad, do you hear? I'm glad you'll soon have some company.

But . . .

Don't interrupt me, Alice. That really is a bad habit of yours. We don't belong together, as you know for yourself. Wilhelm sipped some coffee, put down his cup and took another slice of bread from the basket.

He must mean the two of them as a couple, their marriage, he as husband and she as wife. Something about the coming child seemed to upset him. If Helene had assumed he was glad of it, obviously he was glad of it only for her sake, for the prospect of her having company and not bothering him any more. But he wasn't pleased about the child for himself. There was neither pleasure nor pride in his face today. Was it the connection with her impure race that he didn't like? Helene knew he would lose his temper if she suggested that out loud. He didn't want to talk about it, particularly not to her.

Don't look at me like that, Alice. You know what I mean. You think you have me in your power? You're wrong. *I* could inform on *you*. But you're expecting a child, so I won't.

Helene felt her throat tighten. She knew it was unwise to say anything, but she had to. Because *I* am expecting a child? I am expecting your child, our child.

Don't get so worked up, for God's sake, shouted Wilhelm, and he slammed his fist down on the table, making the cups and saucers clink.

You are the child's father, Wilhelm.

So you say. Wilhelm pushed his plate and saucer aside; he didn't look at her. There was more indignation and self-righteousness in his voice than dismay. Suddenly an idea occurred to him. A look of contempt came into his face. Although who's to say you aren't sleeping with other men again, you, you . . . ? Wilhelm was on his feet now and couldn't find a suitable term of abuse to hurl at her. Bitch – could he really not think of that? His lips were firm and you could see his teeth in straight rows. He was angry, just angry. I'll tell you something, Alice. It's my right, do you hear, it's my right to sleep with you. And you enjoyed it too, admit it. But no one told you to go and get pregnant.

No, said Helene quietly, shaking her head. No one told me to do that.

Well, there you are. Wilhelm clasped his hands behind his back and paced up and down. You'd better start thinking how you're going to feed and keep your brat. I'm not prepared to provide for you and your baby on my own.

This was not unwelcome news to Helene. Over these last few months she had so often asked his permission to get a job – she would have loved to work in a hospital again. She missed her patients, the knowledge that what she did helped other human beings, that she was useful. But Helene had no time to go into that now. There was something else she must say, it would make trouble for her but she had to say it. Helene looked up at him.

I know why you don't inform on me. Because you forged those papers, because you can't inform on me without giving yourself away too.

Wilhelm lunged at her. She raised her hands over her head to protect herself, but he seized her arms, held them tightly and forced her up from the chair. It crashed to the ground. Wilhelm pushed her through the kitchen and up against the wall. He held her there, let go with one hand just to press her head against the wall with the flat of that hand so hard that it hurt. Never say that again, never, do you hear? You serpent. I forged nothing, nothing. Your name was Alice when I met you. It's no business of mine how you got those papers. No one will believe you, just get that into your head. I'll say you lied to me, Helene Würsich.

Sehmisch, my name is Sehmisch, I'm your wife. Helene couldn't move her head, writhe as she might in Wilhelm's strong grip.

He put his hand over her mouth; his eyes were blazing. Hold your tongue. He waited, but she couldn't say anything with his hand pressed to her mouth. You'll keep quiet, is that clear? I won't say it a second time.

One September evening, Wilhelm had invited two colleagues with whom he was working on the great construction projects in Pölitz to supper. Helene was not supposed to know about their plans for rebuilding, she had only picked up a few things in passing and was careful not to ask Wilhelm any questions. He was probably planning the new design of the whole site with his colleagues. Workers had to be accommodated, the camp on the building site had to have space for whole columns of them. The hydrogenation works needed a building plan which, over and above the chemical processing plant, called for good logistics in the matter of traffic and supplies. Wilhelm introduced

Helene to his two colleagues as his wife. At his request she had cooked fresh eel and was now serving the three men sitting at the table.

Beer, called Wilhelm, holding up his empty bottle without turning to Helene. The bottle almost hit Helene's belly. She took it from him. And you gentlemen?

One of them still had some in his glass, the other nodded. Go on, can't have too much beer.

My word, Wilhelm, your wife can certainly cook.

Fresh eel, that was my mother's speciality, the other man said appreciatively.

Everyone's good at something. Wilhelm laughed and took a good gulp from his bottle. His eyes passed fleetingly over Helene's apron. Something growing in there, eh? He laughed, and in high spirits reached with one hand for her breast. Helene retreated. Had his colleagues seen and heard? She turned; she didn't want anyone to see her blushing.

When is it due? His young colleague looked down at his plate as if asking the eel for an answer.

Alice, when is it due? Wilhelm was in a good mood. Well pleased with himself, he looked round for Helene, who was putting the last steaming potatoes in a dish and setting it down on the table.

In six weeks' time. Helene wiped her hands on her apron and took the spoon to help the men to potatoes.

Six weeks, as soon as that? It wasn't clear whether Wilhelm was really surprised or putting on an act. How time flies!

And you're applying for posts in Berlin? His older colleague sounded startled. Helene knew nothing about Wilhelm's making any such application.

These days people are needed everywhere, Königsberg, Berlin, Frankfurt. Wilhelm drank to his colleagues. We'll soon be through with Pölitz, then we'll have to see what's to be done next.

Right, said his younger colleague and drank some beer.

Helene served Wilhelm's potatoes last. They were still steaming; perhaps it was too cold in the kitchen. She'd have to add coal to the stove. Since she had been expecting her baby Helene didn't feel the cold as she used to, and was slow to notice when the apartment was getting chilly.

Never mind that, Alice, we can look after ourselves. You can leave us now. Wilhelm rubbed his hands above his steaming plate.

It was true, the men had their food and Wilhelm knew where the beer was. He could get up himself to find fresh supplies. As Helene was leaving the kitchen she heard him say to his friends: Do you two know the one about Renate-Rosalinde with the barbed-wire fence?

His colleagues were roaring with laughter before Wilhelm could go on.

She asks the holidaymaker: What do you think of my new dress? Fabulous, says the lance-corporal, reminds me of a barbed-wire fence.

The men roared again. Helene put up the ironing board in the bedroom next door.

Barbed-wire fence, says our beauty, how do you mean? Why, says the lance-corporal, grinning and rolling his eyes, it protects the front without keeping it out of sight.

More laughter. Helene heard bottles clinking, and knocking on the table. Very neat reply, said one of his colleagues, probably the older one.

Wilhelm's laughter outdid the mirth of the others.

Helene took the shirt that Wilhelm would be wearing next day out of the basket and ironed it. A few weeks earlier Wilhelm

361

had given her an electric iron for her birthday. The electric iron was amazingly light in weight. Helene could glide it over the fabric so quickly that she had to tell herself to iron more slowly. There was still loud laughter next door and Helene kept hearing the clink of bottles. The child inside her was kicking, it struck a rib on the right, her liver hurt, and Helene put a hand to her belly to feel how hard the bump inside it was. It was probably the coccyx there, turning with difficulty from left to right, with the bump pressing against her abdominal wall. The little head inside her sometimes rested on her bladder so painfully that she kept having to go out to the lavatory on the landing. Wilhelm didn't like her to keep using the chamber pot in the night, so she had to go out to relieve herself. He must find the slow trickle into which her flow of urine had turned in the last few weeks intolerable; perhaps she disgusted him now. Since their altercation in the spring, Wilhelm hadn't touched her again, not once. At first Helene thought he was just angry and his desire would revive. She knew him, she knew only too well how often that desire, that unassuageable lust overcame him. But as days and weeks passed by, she realized it was not directed at her any more. Helene seldom asked herself whether it was because she was pregnant and he didn't want to sleep with a pregnant woman, not wishing to disturb the child in her and feeling increasing distaste for her body, or whether it was simply that the outcome of his lust, the awareness that a child had been conceived, filled him with alarm and dismay. Once, towards morning, she had woken to hear his shallow breathing on the other side of the bed in the dark. His blanket was moving rhythmically, until a point came when the hint of a high squeal could be heard as he let out his breath. Helene had pretended to be asleep, and it was not the only time she had heard him doing that during the night. She didn't feel sorry for him, nor was she disappointed. A pleasant

362

indifference towards her husband had taken hold of Helene. On other nights he stayed out very late, and she smelled sweet perfume so strongly when he staggered into the bedroom early in the morning, drunk, and collapsed on the bed, that she knew he had been with another woman. She pretended to be asleep on those nights too. It was as well for them to leave each other in peace. In the daytime, when Helene came back from shopping, had cleaned the apartment and put the washing to soak and then to boil, she liked to read for half an hour. Everyone needs a break now and then, she told herself. She was reading a book by a young man who had been to a training school for servants in Berlin. It was called *Institute Benjamenta*. Think well, mean well. The total eradication of your own will was the idea of the training, what a wonderful idea. Helene often had to laugh out loud to herself. She had hardly ever found a book so entertaining. When she laughed her belly went firm and hard, her uterus contracted, its huge muscle protected the baby from any violent movement. She had borrowed the book from the Rosengarten library, where she wasn't supposed to go, because there were no books from this particular publisher now in the People's Library. Helene thought of Leontine's dark and magical smile, the sweet tenderness of Carl's lips, his eyes, his body. It wasn't so easy to reach past her big belly with her arm, nor could she, as she had once liked to do, put a pillow between her thighs, lie on her stomach, and try to make those movements; her belly was too big for her to lie on it, so now Helene just stroked herself and thought of nothing.

In the middle of the night Helene was woken by a contraction. Wilhelm was spending November in Königsberg, where he had business: plans and discussions about major building projects. The contraction came again, and her belly hardened. Often a hot bath would either halt or accelerate a baby's birth. Helene boiled water and poured it into the big zinc tub; usually only Wilhelm took an occasional bath there. Helene climbed into the tub and waited. The pains were coming more often now. She tried to feel herself, but her arm couldn't reach far enough round her belly and her hand couldn't go deep enough into her vagina, all she could feel was the soft, open flesh. Helene counted the intervals: every eight minutes, every seven minutes, then every eight minutes again. She poured in more hot water. Seven minutes, seven and a half, six minutes. The intervals were getting shorter now. Helene got out of the tub and dried herself. She knew where the hospital was. She had often gone there to try to apply for a job, with a forged letter giving Wilhelm's permission in her pocket; she had worked on imitating his handwriting. Although Wilhelm had told her she had better think about providing for her child, he didn't want her taking a permanent post while she was pregnant. Sooner or later he would have found out, he might have hauled her out of the hospital by her ears. He had once pulled her ear really hard when he was in a fury because she had overlooked a crease in his shirt, had taken her earlobe between his fingers and dragged her out of the kitchen and into the bedroom. Another contraction; they were so painful now that Helene bent over her tense belly. She took Carl's vest out of the cupboard. She had managed to keep it there so long, unnoticed by Wilhelm, only because he left it to her to put out his clothes for him. She put on Carl's vest. It stretched over her belly and rode up. You had to breathe too, in spite of the labour pains, breathe deeply. She put on long johns, a pain, suspender belt that had to go under the bulge, a pain, stockings, a pain, her dress on top. She mustn't forget her certificate of Aryan descent and family records; she took both documents from Wilhelm's desk. She took some money too. It was a freezing night, the pavements were icy, and Helene had to take care not to lose her balance and slip. She had to stop every few metres as she walked along the empty street. Breathe, breathe in deeply. What did this pain matter? Helene laughed, the pain would end, her child was going to be born today, her little one, her little girl. Helene went on, stopped again. It seemed to her that the baby's head was already coming down between her thighs; she could hardly move if she kept her legs closed. Breathe deeply and go on. Legs wide apart, Helene trudged over the ice.

A midwife came to her aid in the hospital. She carefully felt Helene, her belly first, and it immediately became firm and hard as a stone. The contraction went on a long time. Then the midwife felt inside the vagina with her hand.

There's the head.

The head, did you say the head? Helene couldn't help laughing. She laughed nervously and impatiently.

The midwife nodded. Yes, I can feel the baby's hair already.

Hair? Helene breathed deeply, deeply, even more deeply, all the way down to her belly. She knew how she had to breathe, but the midwife told her all the same.

Would you like to lie down, Frau Sehmisch?

Maybe. Breathe, breathe, breathe; breathe freely, breathe deeply, hold the breath and breathe out.

Don't you want to telephone your husband so that he can at least come to collect you later?

I told you, he's in Königsberg. Breathe deeply. Helene wondered what it must be like for a foetus when everything all around it went so hard and stony. Perhaps the baby didn't feel anything yet. How did existence begin? Were you yourself if you couldn't feel anything? Breathe deeply. I don't have a number for him there. He's coming back at the end of the month.

The nurse was filling out her card for the card index.

Excuse me, I feel sick.

It's a good idea if you go to the lavatory again. The midwife showed Helene where it was. Helene knew that the sickness was a sure sign; it couldn't be much longer now. A certain nerve was stimulated, the *nervus vagus*. Seven centimetres open was still three centimetres too few. The stimulation of the *parasympathicus*, what else?

On her return Helene was to lie on the bed and make herself comfortable, but nothing about her felt comfortable. The doctor wanted her to lie on her back. The pains weren't coming so fast, only every four minutes, every five, but then they speeded up again. Helene sweated, breathed, pushed down. She wanted to turn on her side, she wanted to stand up, she wanted to squat. The midwife held her down.

Lie there, that's a good girl.

Her sense of time was lost, it was day now, the night midwife had been replaced by another midwife. A good pain, said Helene to herself, a good pain. She gritted her teeth, whatever she did she wasn't going to scream, certainly not as loudly as the woman

366

in the next bed who had already had her little girl. Helene pushed down; it burned. There were tears in her eyes.

You must breathe, breathe, keep breathing. The midwife's voice sounded curiously distorted. She *was* breathing.

You can do it, come on, come on, you can do it. Now the midwife took on the commanding tone of an officer. Helene wished she hadn't gone to the hospital. She didn't like this nurse and her military tone. Come on, come on, again, and again, stop, stop. Can't you hear me? You must stop. Stop pushing. Now the officer was angry too. Helene ignored her orders, she could have her baby any way she liked, it was no business of the officer's. Breathe, breathe deeply, that was good, and push, of course, push, push, push. The midwife felt her vagina with her hands, and it scratched as if she were digging her nails into the soft flesh, the soft, indeterminate, stretchable flesh. What was the officer doing with her hands? There was pressure on her gut, such pressure that Helene felt sure the midwife would catch nothing but excrement. Blood and faecal matter in the officer's hands. This was no time to feel ashamed, she must breathe.

Now the officer slapped her on the arm, took hold of her. Stop it, you must stop pushing or you'll tear yourself wide open.

Helene heard this, yet didn't hear it; what if she did tear herself wide open, what did she care? Let what had to tear her do it, let what wanted to tear her have its way, there'd be something left, she must get her baby out. Helene breathed deeply, a good pain, only why did it hurt so much? No, she'd meant to ask that question, she felt her tongue ready against her gums, but she wouldn't ask it, she didn't want anyone marvelling at her, ever.

Keep breathing! The military officer was obviously losing her nerve. Scream if you must, go on, now push, yes.

The *yes* was spoken quickly, the officer's hands moved fast, the doctor pulled something out between Helene's thighs, there was a squelching sound. The doctor nodded. Here came the head.

The head? Is the head out? Helene couldn't grasp it. She felt something thick between her legs, something that wasn't part of her any more, she felt it for the first time, not inside her now, her baby's body, hers. The doctor took no notice of her. Helene put her hand down to feel. She wanted to touch the little head. Was that hair, the baby's hair?

Hands off! Helene's arm was yanked away, someone was holding her wrist in a tight grip. You just keep on breathing, do you hear? The officer was intervening. And push when the next pain comes. Take a deep breath, breathe in, now. Helene would have had to take a deep breath even without the officer's commands.

It slipped out all in one movement. The midwife caught it skilfully in her hands.

Her baby was here. What did it look like? Was it grey, was it alive? It was taken away at once. Was it breathing, had it cried? It was crying. Helene heard her baby crying and wanted to hold it tight. Helene turned, trying to catch a glimpse. The nurses' brown and white aprons were in the way, all she saw was their backs. The baby was being washed, weighed and dressed.

My baby, whispered Helene. Tears were running from her eyes; she saw the nurses' overalls and the midwife's. My baby. Helene was happy. The midwife came back and told her to press down again.

What, again?

I thought you were a nurse.

But why again? Is there another one too?

The afterbirth, Frau Sehmisch. Now, give a proper push, Frau Sehmisch. Helene knew that meant her. She did as she was told.

She had to wait for ever before they brought her the baby.

Three and a half kilos, a fine little thing. The maternity nurse handed Helene the little bundle. Helene looked at her child, the folded slits for eyes, a tiny mouth, a furrow above the nose, a deep one, and little dots on the nose itself. The baby was crying. Helene held it close. My little one, my dear little girl, said Helene. What lovely long black hair she had, how silky and smooth her hair was.

You have to hold the head like this. The maternity nurse adjusted Helene's hand. Helene knew how to hold a baby, the nurse telling her made no difference. Let her knead and press her hand. Nothing and no one could touch Helene's happiness.

Are you going to breastfeed him?

Helene looked at the nurse in amazement. Him?

Yes, your son, are you going to breastfeed your son?

It's a boy? Helene looked at the grey little face. Her baby opened his mouth and yelled, going dark red. Helene hadn't expected this. She had never thought of a boy, it was always going to be a girl.

Make up your mind now, or we'll give him a bottle.

I'll breastfeed, of course. Helene opened her nightdress to put the baby to her breast, but once again the military officer intervened.

Here, this is the way to do it. The officer took hold of Helene's breast roughly, with two fingers, and stuffed it into the baby's mouth. There, like that, see? You must take care the baby's lying properly. And whether you'll be able to keep going with those breasts of yours, well, we'll see.

Helene knew at once what the officer meant. Her breasts had become large and plump over the last few months, in a way that Helene had never dreamed they could be, but still only relatively large. Compared to the breasts of other new mothers they were small, even tiny. Helene knew that.

The baby at her breast swallowed and breathed heavily through his tiny nose. He had attached himself firmly to her breast, he was sucking, tickling her, and sucking in a way that put pressure on her, he was sucking for his life. The baby didn't open his mouth, but sucked so hard that Helene wondered if he had teeth already.

Name? Someone had come up to Helene's bed. Why was the military officer so stern? No doubt she had a lot of work to do, there must be reasons. Perhaps Helene had done something wrong. What a humiliation, a nurse lying here in a hospital.

Name?

Sehmisch. Alice Sehmisch.

Not your name, we've got that. What's your son going to be called?

Helene looked at her child breathing through his nose and sucking at her breast as if to suck her up entirely. What delicate, pretty hands he had, tiny little fingers, all those folds, the thin skin, his hand was clutching her forefinger as if it were a branch and he must cling to it at all costs. How could she give him a name? He didn't belong to her, what presumption to give a child a name. When she didn't have a name herself any more, or at least not the one that had been given to her at birth for her lifetime. Well, he could call himself something else later if he liked. That made Helene feel better. And she said: Peter.

Only when the nurse had gone away did she whisper to her baby: This is me, your mother. The child blinked, he had to sneeze. How Helene would have loved to show him to Martha and Leontine. Didn't he look like a girl? My little angel, whispered Helene to his cheek and stroked his long, soft hair.

Wilhelm came home before Christmas. They had sent telegrams in the meantime. He was not surprised that she had had her

370

baby. A boy. Wilhelm nodded; he had expected no less. Peter? Why not? She ought to feed the boy properly, he told her, a few hours after arriving. The baby was hungry, didn't she hear him crying? And why did it smell like this in the apartment, was it the baby's nappies, he asked, and his eye fell on the yellow-stained nappies hanging on a line to dry. What's the matter with you, have you forgotten how to wash clothes? Can't you see those nappies are still dirty?

They won't come any cleaner, said Helene, thinking that if the sun would shine she could have bleached them in the sunlight. But it hardly got light outside all day; it had been snowing for weeks.

When little Peter cried at night and Helene got up to take him into bed with her, Wilhelm said, with his back turned to her: You're coddling yourself, if you ask me. Go and sit in the kitchen if you must feed him. A working man needs his sleep.

Helene obeyed his order. She sat in the cold kitchen with her baby and fed him there until he went to sleep. But as soon as she put him back in his little basket he woke up again and cried. After two hours she slipped into the bedroom, exhausted. Wilhelm's voice came out of the dark. Get that baby to shut up or I'm leaving again tomorrow.

Not all babies sleep through the night.

You know best, I suppose, do you? Wilhelm turned round and shouted at her. You listen to me, Alice, I'm not having you tell me what's what.

In the dark, Helene dabbed the spray of his spit off her face. Had she ever tried to tell him what was what?

It's time you were back at work, he said more calmly as he turned his back to her again. We can't afford any parasites.

Helene looked at the window. There was only a faint glimmer of light behind the curtain. Wilhelm began snoring, in a strange, chopped sort of way. Who was this man in bed with her? Helene told herself he was probably right. Perhaps she was too used to her baby's crying to tell when he was hungry. Her milk wasn't enough for him, yes, he must be hungry, that was it. She must get some milk in the morning. The poor child; if only he'd go to sleep. Peterkin, whispered Helene, who usually disliked pet names, Peterkin. Her lips moved soundlessly. Her lids were heavy.

When Helene woke up her left breast hurt. It was hard as stone, and a red mark was spreading on the skin. She knew what those symptoms meant. So she went over to the basket, took her Peterkin out, carried him into the kitchen and put him to the breast. Peterkin's mouth snapped shut on it, it was like having a knife thrust into her breast, stabbing, boring, red-hot, the pain stopped her thinking. Helene gritted her teeth; her face was glowing. Peterkin wouldn't suck, he kept turning his head away, gasping for air rather than milk, spitting and crying, clenching his little fists and writhing.

What's the matter now? Wilhelm was standing in the doorway looking down at Helene and her baby. Can you tell me what this is all about? His indignant look fixed on her breast. The baby is crying, Alice, and you just sit here, you've probably been sitting here for weeks letting him go hungry, have you?

Should she say it? I'm not making him cry. Little Peterkin was bellowing now, his face was red and a white mark showed round his mouth.

Turned mute on me, eh? You're not going to let the baby starve, are you? Here. Wilhelm gave her a banknote. Get dressed at once, go out and buy milk and feed him, understood?

Helene had understood. Her breast was throbbing, the pain was so terrible that she felt sick and could hardly take in Wilhelm's orders. She would do as he said, of course, she would simply obey him. She put the baby down on the bed and dressed herself.

Without looking at Wilhelm, Helene wrapped a blanket round her baby, picked up the bundle and went downstairs with Peter in her arms.

Your eyes look quite glazed, said the grocer's wife, do you have a fever, Frau Sehmisch?

Helene tried to smile. No, no.

She took the bottle of milk and the little pot of curd cheese and climbed upstairs with the crying baby. Halfway up she had to stop. Her discharge hadn't quite dried up, the pain in her breast made decisions impossible. She put down the milk and curd cheese, and laid the baby in his blanket on the steps. Helene went to the lavatory on the landing. When she came out again she saw the cheerful face of their new neighbour, who had opened her door and was putting her head round it. Can I help you?

Helene shook her head and said no. She picked up the bundle of baby and went on up the stairs. As she passed her neighbour, the name on the door caught her eye. Kozinska. It was easiest to notice unimportant things just now. Kozinska, her new neighbour was called Kozinska.

Once she had climbed the stairs she saw that Wilhelm already had his coat on. He had to go out to Pölitz to see how the work was getting on, he said, and she wasn't to wait up for him. Helene put the baby in his basket and warmed up the milk. She put the milk in a little bottle that had never held anything but tea until this morning, made a compress of curd cheese to cool her breast and fed the baby. By the afternoon her body felt so hot and heavy that she could hardly stand up to get down to the half-landing. She could tell that the baby had wind, the result of the milk and all that crying, swallowing air, but he would soon be full, she was sure, fed and happy. There was no part of her body that Helene could lie on now, her skin itched, she was so thin that she felt the sheet was rubbing her harshly and the air made her itch, she wished she could be out of her skin. Helene was freezing, shaking, there were beads of sweat on her forehead. Once an hour she got up, her legs shaking, and went to make a new compress. She was so weak that she could hardly wring out the cloths and nappies. The fever stayed with her overnight. Helene was glad that Wilhelm didn't come home. She wanted to put the baby to her breast again, but he twisted and turned and screamed, biting her hard, hot breast. He cried indignantly.

Helene bottle-fed her baby. At first he was still indignant and brought up curdled milk, almost choking, the milk was still too hot and then quickly got cold. Helene gritted her teeth. He would drink, she was sure he would, he wasn't going to starve to death. Her inflammation went down, so did the swelling of her breast, and a week later it was not quite all right yet, not entirely, but almost. However, when the inflammation passed off her breast milk had dried up. Wilhelm thought that he had taken care of everything. There was just the question of her work, which he wanted to get cleared up before he had to set off for Frankfurt early in the New Year. Wilhelm went to the Municipal Hospital in the Pommerensdorfer district with Helene.

Yes, we can certainly employ your wife, the personnel manager told Wilhelm. You know, she added, we can't motivate half as many nurses to come and work here as we need. And we've just had to dismiss one. A Polish nurse, mixed race in the second degree, they're supposed to nurse only their own kind. Your wife's family records, her certificate of Aryan descent, excellent, you've brought it all with you. We can make out a certificate of health for her here. The personnel manager looked at Helene's papers.

Only when she showed Wilhelm and Helene to the door did the woman see the pram standing by the cellar stairs outside the building. I suppose the child's grandmother will be looking after him?

Wilhelm and Helene looked at the pram. We'll find someone, said Wilhelm with his confident smile. The personnel manager nodded and closed her door. Helene pushed the pram. Wilhelm strode along beside her. He seemed to take it for granted that he would not go straight back to his car and instead walked to the suburb of Oberwiek with Helene and the baby. The water of the Oder was grey, the wind ruffled it into waves. Wilhelm looked at his watch and announced, glancing back in the direction of his car, that he would have to start straight out now, he was expected in Berlin that afternoon. He was sure the tram would come along soon, she could manage to get back on her own, couldn't she? Helene nodded.

The baby's fine, gleaming dark hair had gradually fallen out in his first months of life, until his little head was bald and a pale gold down began to grow on it. It turned into golden curls, he was golden blond like Helene. According to her conditions of employment, Helene was to work sixty hours a week in shifts, but in fact it was more than that. She had a day off every other week. She collected her child from Frau Kozinska and would have a nursery school place for him when he reached his third birthday. She was glad of that, because quite often, when she had knocked on Frau Kozinska's door, no one had opened it and she could hear her son crying behind the locked door, calling Mother, Mother, and sometimes calling for his auntie, as he called Frau Kozinska. Then Helene had to wait outside the door because Frau Kozinska had just popped out to do some shopping, and sometimes it was an hour before she came back.

When Helene first took him to the nursery school the teacher asked: What is your little boy's name? Helene looked at his golden corkscrew curls lying softly on his shoulders.

Peter. She had never yet cut his hair.

Well, we'll look after your son, said the teacher in friendly tones. Such a pretty little boy.

Helene would have to cut his hair now. The teacher stroked Peter's head and took his hand.

Helene followed them for a couple of steps, crouched down and kissed Peter's cheek. She hugged him. He was crying and holding tight to her with his little arms.

I'll soon be back, Helene promised. I'll come for you after supper.

Peter shook his head. He didn't believe her. He didn't want to stay here, he screamed, he clung to her with tears flowing from his eyes and bit her arm to make her either stay or take him with her. Helene had to conjure up a smile quickly and stand up straight to shake him off, turn her back and hurry out. She mustn't cry in front of Peter. That made it even more difficult.

When Helene collected him, he gave her a strange look. Where were you, Mother? he asked.

Helene was thinking of the injured nurse from Warsaw who had lost both her legs. She had been brought in only a few days ago and was the first of the war wounded that Helene saw. Her lymph nodes had swollen all over her body, and in many places she had the copper-coloured nodules typical of the condition. They had developed into large papules in the folds of her skin. Helene had to wear gloves and a protective mask over her mouth when she was treating the nurse's sores, because the papules were already weeping and could be infectious. It was lucky that the patient's skin was not itching. Thanks to the Prontosil antibiotic, the stumps of her legs were healing well, but her heart muscle wasn't used to her lying down for a long time, with poor circulation of the blood as a result, and she suffered from insomnia. Medical opinion was that antibiotics might perhaps be useful in treating syphilis too.

Where were you, Mother? Helene heard Peter ask. They were sitting side by side in the tram. Should she tell him she'd been to the observatory or the butterfly house, make up a pretty story?

But that would make it even harder for him to understand why she'd left him for twelve hours.

Mother, say something. Why don't you say anything?

I've been at work, said Helene.

Doing what? Peter tugged her sleeve and she wished he would stop it. Doing what?

Couldn't he give her any peace, must he always be asking questions? Don't ask so many questions, Helene told Peter.

An elderly lady rose from the seat in front of Helene, probably to get out at the next stop, and held on to the pole. The woman patted Peter's recently cut hair. What a smart little fellow, she said. Helene looked out of the window. Not many of the wounded came as far as Stettin; most of them stayed in field hospitals and it was only because Helene had a child that she had not been transferred to one of those. Apparently nurses were in short supply; in desperation the authorities were looking for volunteers to work in the field hospitals after a reduced period of training. Unmarried nurses were sent to work in the field hospitals, married women were needed to keep the municipal hospitals going. One day two nurses were sent to Obrawalde and the question of sending Helene as well arose. They could do with an experienced nurse like her there. But Helene was in luck; a doctor made it known that experienced nurses were also urgently needed in the Stettin Women's Hospital, and the management realized that it would be difficult for Helene to take her child to Obrawalde. Rain beat against the window. Dark had fallen long ago and the lights of the cars looked blurred.

I must say, thank God women like you are still having children. The woman nodded appreciatively.

Helene looked at her only briefly. She didn't want to nod, she didn't want to say anything, but there was no stopping the woman.

Briefly, Helene thought of the girl she'd seen at noon today.

What lovely auburn hair she'd had. Eyes as brown as almonds under red-gold lashes. Her breasts were apple-sized. She had a smile like the morning sun, she had only just come in, aged sixteen. In sign language, the girl had made gestures before she was anaesthetized and Helene guessed what they meant. She was asking questions, and frightened questions too. She had been given a general anaesthetic. Helene had held the retractor. No one had hands as steady as hers. The surgeon cut the Fallopian tubes. You had to be very careful of the tubes when stitching them up. The surgeon had asked Helene to hold the needle while he sneezed and blew his nose. She was always to be relied on, the surgeon had told her, and he asked her to finish the stitching.

She should be proud of herself, said the elderly woman, changing hands and holding the pole with her other hand as the tram went round a bend. Really proud, added the woman with a kindly nod. She was clearly referring to Peter. Helene did not feel proud. Why should she feel proud of having a child? Peter didn't belong to her, she had given birth to him but he was not her property, not her own great achievement. Helene was glad when she saw Peter laughing, but she didn't see very much of him and usually he was asleep when they were together. He slept in her bed; he was often frightened at night and didn't want to be alone. After all, human beings were mammals, weren't they? Why should a human child sleep alone while all other mammals kept their young with them for the sake of warmth? Helene did not often see Peter awake, and even less often did she see him laughing.

We'd all die out otherwise, you know.

Helene stared through the glass at the street. What did the woman mean by we? The Nordic race, humanity itself? The girl whose tubes had been cut today was a healthy, cheerful girl. Only she was mute. The idea was to avoid her having deaf mute children. Why was it so bad for someone to speak in sign language instead of sounds? Why should that girl's children be any unhappier than Peter, who didn't get answers to all his questions either? Later, when the girl had come round, Helene had gone to see her and taken her an orange. She was not supposed to have done that; the oranges were meant for other patients. Helene had given it to the girl in secret. She had held the retractor, she had finished the stitching. If the surgeon had told her to make the incision, she would probably have cut the tubes herself. Helene felt the cool glass against her forehead.

Mother, aren't you listening? Peter pinched her hand. He looked desperate, almost angry. Obviously he had been trying to attract her attention for some time.

I'm listening, said Helene. Peter was telling her something, saying the other children had throwed marbles.

Thrown, said Helene, thrown marbles, and she thought of that young girl again.

Thrown. Peter's eyes were shining. He could talk very clearly when she reminded him. The girl would be alone in her bed in the ward now, with the thirty-eight other women patients. Had she been told what the operation on her was for? Helene could tell her next morning, she had to tell her. The girl mustn't be left wondering later, she should at least know. But perhaps she would no longer be there in the morning.

Hungry, Peter was complaining now. It was time to get out of the tram. Helene remembered that she hadn't done any shopping first thing in the morning. What shops were open before the beginning of her shift? Perhaps she could ring the grocer's doorbell. His wife didn't like it when people rang their bell in the evening, but often Helene had no other option if she hadn't been shopping earlier, and today she had nothing to eat in the house.

She bought two eggs, quarter of a litre of milk and a whole pound of potatoes from the grocer's wife. The potatoes were beginning to sprout shoots, but never mind. Helene was pleased to have them.

Don't like tatoes, complained Peter as Helene put a plate of potatoes in front of him. She didn't want to lose her temper, she didn't want to shout at him and tell him he ought to be glad to have them, he'd better eat up. She'd rather say nothing.

Don't like tatoes, said Peter again, letting a piece of potato fall off his little spoon and drop on the floor.

Helene snatched the spoon away from him and felt like banging it down on the table. She thought of her mother, the angry light in her eyes, her unpredictability. Helene laid the spoon gently on the table. If you're not hungry, she said, keeping her voice down, you don't have to eat. She took Peter's wrist and led him over to the washbasin. He was crying as she washed him.

Eat rinje, whimpered Peter. Eat rinje. He pointed to the picture hanging over the chest of drawers. It showed a basket full of fruit in glowing colours. Did he mean the orange it showed? Should she have brought that orange from the hospital home for him? The girl needed the orange, Peter had potatoes.

Rinje! Peter was shouting now, deafening Helene. She bit her lip, she gritted her teeth, she didn't want to lose patience, patience was all that mattered, it gave shape and form to life. Helene picked Peter up, turned the picture to the wall as she passed it and carried him to her bed.

Another day, she whispered. There'll be an orange another day. Peter calmed down. He liked to be caressed. Helene stroked his forehead and pulled the blanket up over him.

Mother sing?

Helene knew she couldn't sing well, she stroked him and shook her head. A woman in the hospital had taken her arm today with a bony old hand and told Helene she wished she would just let her die. Please, I just want to die. Go to sleep, Peterkin.

Sing, please sing! Peter didn't want to close his eyes.

Perhaps she just had to make a bit of an effort. Helene would have liked to sing, she simply couldn't. Could she think of a song? *Mary and Joseph walked in a garden green,* but Christmas was over long ago. Her voice was scratchy, the musical notes wouldn't come. Peter was watching her. Helene closed her mouth.

Sing.

Helene shook her head. Her throat was hard, the opening too small, she had too little strength and her vocal cords were rigid and creaky. Was there some kind of premature ageing of the vocal cords, a medical condition, voice failure?

Auntie sing, Peter demanded now, trying to sit up again. Helene knew that Frau Kozinska had sometimes sung for Peter. She was often singing when Helene met her in the street or on the stairs too. Sometimes you could hear her voice up in their own apartment. Helene shook her head. Frau Kozinska liked to sing, she was always enviably cheerful, but she had left Peter alone too often, and when she was at home in the evening she was fond of the bottle. It was a blessing that he could go to nursery school now. The weeks when she was on night duty were difficult, however. Helene had to leave Peter alone; he slept most of the time. She told him before he went to bed that she would be back, and locked the door. When she came home in the morning the first thing she did was to fetch coal from the cellar, usually bringing a good load upstairs all at once, carrying the coal in a pannier on her back and buckets of briquettes and logs of wood in her left and right hands. Once upstairs she lit the stove. Peter would be asleep in her bed. She stroked his short fair hair until he stretched and wanted her to pick him up. Then she washed and dressed him, gave him something to eat and took him to the nursery school, where he wanted her to give him a hug, but she wouldn't, because if she did they would not be able to part company. Home again, Helene saw to doing the laundry, mended the straps of Peter's lederhosen; now that Baden had had to close his shop she couldn't find a good cheap draper's. Baden had disappeared, he'd been taken away in February with the rest of them, to the East, it was said. So Helene mended the straps of the lederhosen and found a coloured button to replace the artificial edelweiss flower he had lost. Then she slept for a few hours herself, added a couple of briquettes to the stove, fetched Peter from nursery school and took him home, gave him his supper and put him to bed, switched off the light and slipped out of the door. She had to hurry to catch the tram and reach the hospital in time for the night shift.

Every two weeks, when Helene had a day off, she took Peter's hand and they went down to the harbour to look at the ships. Only very occasionally did a warship come in. Peter marvelled at the warships, and she showed him the flocks of birds.

Ducks, she said, pointing to the little formation in the air, five of them flying in a V-shape. Peter liked eating duck, but Helene couldn't afford to buy it for him. Now and then Wilhelm sent money from Frankfurt. She didn't want his money; it was hush money, and she didn't need to be paid to keep her mouth shut. Every few months he sent her an envelope with money and a note from him. Dear Alice, buy the boy gloves and a cap, it might say, but Helene had knitted Peter gloves and a cap long ago. She took the money, put it in an envelope and wrote the address on it: Frau Selma Würsich, Tuchmacherstrasse 13, Bautzen, Lusatia. She sent off the letter without any sender's name on it right to the end, until the day when she received a long, narrow package from Bautzen. The package contained the carved horn fish. The necklace that had once been in it wasn't there. Perhaps money had been needed in Bautzen, so the rubies were sold, or perhaps the package had been opened in the post and someone liked the look of the necklace. There was a letter inside the fish. The letter itself stunned her, it smelled of Leontine and it was in her handwriting. Dear little Alice, it keeps on raining in Berlin but the frost has gone at last. I wonder if you are still living at the same address? Martha has been very ill for the last few years. You know her, she doesn't complain and she didn't want you to hear about it. We didn't want to burden you with our news, and Martha wouldn't let me write to tell you. She had to give up her work in the hospital. They've sent her to work in one of the new labour camps. My hands are tied. She could do with a husband now, or influential parents, some close relation. As soon as I'm able to visit her I must tell her that a letter arrived yesterday from the Charitable Foundation for Institutional Care, saying that your mother died of acute pneumonia a few weeks ago in Grossschweidnitz. I am truly sorry, although I know that many consider it a merciful death.

The sirens of the big ships sounded a deep note, making your insides vibrate. Helene could feel the humming right to the soles of her feet. Peter asked his mother where the ship's guns were. The letter was signed, in Leontine's handwriting: With love from your sister Elsa. As a postscript, she had added the following note: Do you remember our old neighbour Fanny? She has been taken away. An Obergruppenführer lives in her apartment now, with his wife and three nice children. Helene knew what the letter meant. Leontine had to cover up her tracks or both their lives would be in danger, and had chosen the only possible words to describe that monstrous event. She had enclosed some dried rose petals in the letter. They fell out when Helene opened it. Helene wanted to weep, but she couldn't. Something prevented her; she couldn't take in what she had read. The petals gave off a sweet scent, or perhaps it was just a trace of Leontine's perfume. Her real name must not be dangerously connected with Martha, Helene or any other such person. Was Leontine still working at the hospital? Did she have to cut Fallopian tubes and remove ovaries? Did they want to send her too to a field hospital? After all, Leontine was divorced now, she had no children, they could send her anywhere they liked, however many names she adopted: Leo, Elsa, Abelard even. Helene would always have known her firm, swift handwriting again; it had left its mark on her. A great longing came over Helene and made her feel dizzy. She was perspiring.

Guns? Peter tugged impatiently at his mother's sleeve. Where's the guns? Helene didn't know.

Are you sad? Peter looked up at his mother.

Helene shook her head. It's the wind, she said. Come on, let's go to the railway station and look at the trains. Helene couldn't help thinking what it would be like if she simply bought a ticket and went to Berlin with Peter. It ought to be possible to find Leontine. It must be possible. But who knew how dangerous that might be?

The railway station lay on the river Oder just below the city. The trains were coming in and out. Wind blew over the plat-form, bringing tears to many eyes. They had sat down on a bench and were holding hands. There was a new nurse at the hospital, Ida Fiebinger, who came from Bautzen. Helene had felt strange when she first heard Ida Fiebinger speaking, the melody of the local accent, the closed vowels, the slow lilt of the sentences. Helene kept seeking Ida out. One day Nurse Ida said, when the stormy wind had blown down a tree in the hospital yard: *When the wind doesn't know / where it can blow, / over Budissin it will go*, using one of the dialect words for Bautzen. Helene was astonished when she heard it and suppressed a smile with difficulty. It was so long since she had heard that old saying.

Peter said he was cold, he wanted to go home. Helene consoled him and said let them wait for one more train. Once, when the nurses were standing around with their plates in the hospital canteen at lunch, Nurse Ida had turned in mid-sentence to Helene and said: Now I know why I always feel as if I knew you. You're from Bautzen. Helene had calmly put down her fork, feeling the blood come to her face so suddenly that she had to pretend she had a violent coughing fit. Excuse me, she said. I'm sure you know my uncle, Ida added eagerly, he was a well-known judge in Bautzen until he retired.

Helene shook her head. No, she made haste to say, I'm from Dresden. I once passed through Bautzen on a visit. Isn't there a leaning tower there? Nurse Ida looked at Helene with disappointment and a little disbelief, but definitely disappointed. You passed through? On my way to Breslau, claimed Helene, fervently hoping that none of the nurses here came from Breslau and would want to talk to her about a city she didn't know at all. Since then Helene had several times felt Nurse Ida's enquiring gaze resting on her. The wind howled and hummed around the telegraph poles. Helene looked over the tracks to the locomotive. Only a little vapour still rose from its funnel. It looked as if it wouldn't be leaving the station today. No one had arrived, and Helene would not buy a ticket. She stood up, Peter held her hand tightly, and they walked up the steps and back into the city in silence.

Helene had not expected Wilhelm to visit her again, least of all during the summer when Peter was starting real school. She had cleaned the apartment, repainted the wall by the kitchen window where rain had come in; she had stuck down the bedroom wallpaper and put nails into the wobbly chair until it stood steady at the kitchen table, and finally she had washed the curtains, cleaned the windows and bought a bunch of cosmos flowers. Everything must be spick and span when Wilhelm arrived. She didn't want him shaking his head and thinking that she couldn't manage with the child on her own. With Peter's help, she carried the sofa borrowed from their old next-door neighbours into their kitchen. She told Peter he would probably have to sleep on the sofa that week. But then Wilhelm said he would sleep on the sofa himself, so Peter could stay in her bed. Wilhelm said he was on leave. He had come in a civilian suit, so Helene didn't really know whether he was in the army or not. He made a secret of it. He was not the sort to wriggle out of fighting; his proud bearing suggested to Helene that he had an important job in strategy or some such thing. And his short letters every few months, containing money, always came from Frankfurt or Berlin. Recently she had been putting the money in a thick woollen stocking, which she hid at the very bottom of her work basket. Once, when Peter had hurt his knee, was crying and wanted a bandage, and Helene told him that his graze would dry better exposed to the air, Wilhelm interrupted her, tapping the boy on the back of the neck. Don't cry, Peter. And remember this, men are there to kill and women are there to heal their wounds. Peter had tilted his head back and looked up to his father. Perhaps there was a smile? But no, his father's gaze was serious.

Wilhelm was looking well, strong and cheerful, bursting with health. His snores at night were loud and contented; Helene couldn't get a wink of sleep. His collars were clean, his shirts ironed, he carried the photograph of a smiling woman in his wallet. When Helene had taken his trousers to wash them, the wallet fell into her hands. It was none of her business; she asked him no questions, and didn't want to be asked any herself. On the fourth morning of his visit Wilhelm said that on Sunday, before he went back, he was going to take the boy on a little expedition to Velten. His brother might come from Gelbensande too. Helene had never met Wilhelm's brother and to this day she didn't know if he was the person who had got hold of her documents for her. Peter put his arms round his mother's waist; he didn't want to go without her. But his father told him not to be a sissy; a boy must go on a journey without his mother some time or other. Velten? Wilhelm thought he saw distrust in Helene's eyes.

Don't worry, he said, half laughing, half setting her right. I'll bring the boy back to you. Even on leave you sometimes have to meet colleagues. Wilhelm had left his car in Frankfurt, so father and son went by train. It was a great day for Peter; this would be his first train ride. Wilhelm probably wanted to cut short the time he spent with his wife by going on this little expedition with Peter in the second half of his week's leave. Or perhaps the trip was to do with his work.

At the moment Helene was working in the maternity ward,

where it was hard to look after all the women properly. Sanitary towels were constantly being changed, bedpans brought, compresses had to be changed every hour, cold compresses to ward off childbed fever and curd compresses at any hint of mastitis. There were genital tears to be tended, navels to be powdered. Helene brought the women their babies from the nursery and put them to their breasts. Pink healthy babies sucked sweet milk from their mothers' full breasts while their fathers were fighting on the front far away, in east and west, on land, at sea and in the air, waiting for Leningrad to be starved out. Helene preferred not to think, there were directions, procedures to be carried out, calls for her, she had to act, she had to hurry, she put the babies to their mothers' breasts, she changed their nappies, weighed and inoculated them, and wrote one last letter to the old address she had for Leontine. She would not send any more; she had not received a single reply to any of her letters. The long-distance telephone exchange informed her that there was no number for that address any more and no lady doctor of that name was known. Helene went home only to sleep.

On Sunday, after coming back from Velten, Peter said they had been to see a foundry and stayed the night at a boarding house. His uncle hadn't been able to come; he probably couldn't get leave. They ate herring salad with onions, apples and beet-root, it was only capers that Helene hadn't been able to get. Peter licked his plate clean; his mouth was pink from the beetroot. Wilhelm had to go back to Frankfurt.

I have more of this than I can spend, said Wilhelm, giving Peter a ten-mark note at the door when he said goodbye and telling him to buy chocolates with it. Helene was glad that Wilhelm had gone away again.

When she was lying in bed with Peter that evening, he was still awake. He turned to his mother.

Father says we're going to win the war.

Helene said nothing. Presumably Wilhelm had been telling the boy about the bombs. Wilhelm was firmly convinced that only military service made a boy into a man. Helene stroked her son's forehead. What a beautiful child he was.

Father says I'm to grow big and strong.

Helene smiled. Wasn't he big and strong already? She knew he was often afraid, but who could be brave if he didn't know what fear was? While Wilhelm and Peter were away she had bought Peter a clasp knife. She was going to give it to him in November for his sixth birthday. She knew he wanted a clasp knife more than anything. He wanted to use it to make himself a fishing rod and to cut his bread.

Father says you're so silent because you're a cold woman.

Helene looked her Peter in the eye. People said his eyes were like hers, clear as glass and blue; it was difficult to shake her head lying down. She caressed his shoulders now and Peter buried his head in her breast.

But I don't believe it, Peter said to her breast. I love you, Mother. Helene stroked her son's back. It was hard to move her arm. Perhaps she had lifted too many patients today. She felt weak. What could she be to her Peter? And how could he be her Peter if she couldn't do anything for him, if she couldn't speak or tell stories or say anything to him? Another woman, Helene suspected, would weep at this idea. Perhaps what Wilhelm said was right, perhaps her heart was a stone. Cold, icy, hard as iron. She didn't cry because she had nothing to cry about; her feet hurt, her back hurt, she had been running around all day, she knew she had only five hours of sleep before she got up, did the ironing, mopped the kitchen, made breakfast for Peter, woke him and sent him to school, before she herself went to work in the hospital. The arm with which she had caressed

Peter ached, the arm now lying over him, her sleeping child. She could do without an inflammation of the sinews. Nurses did not fall ill. Wilhelm had told her on Sunday, when he left: Alice, you are tough as iron. You don't need me. It was impossible for her to know just what he meant. Was he proud, were his feelings injured, was he pleased because her self-sufficiency to some extent justified his turning away from her? Perhaps he felt hurt because she didn't need him. Men wanted to be needed, no doubt about that. An iron fist would not miss its target, would not fail to strike it, iron on iron, and certainly would not be robbed of its justification for existing. Was it different with a woman? Didn't she strain every nerve to get to the hospital on time every day? Was iron a criterion, a quality, a peculiarity? Iron discipline. She so often worked overtime. No nurse left when she saw the bedpans stacking up on the trolley, when a patient had vomited on her nightdress, or another lay dying. An iron sense of pity. She had made sure that Peter was used to not falling ill too. Iron reason. When he was little, he had caught chickenpox and measles; she'd had to ask Frau Kozinska to look after him so that she herself could get to work on time. Frau Kozinska hadn't even managed to wash her Peter during the day, she had forgotten to make a cold compress for him and he hadn't had enough water to drink that evening. Presumably she'd been too busy singing.

Peter woke Helene in the morning when it was already light. He pressed close to his mother, put his arms round her, whispered: I love you so much, Mother. Suddenly he was lying on top of her, burying his face in her throat. His silky hair tickled her. He ought not to lie on top of her, didn't he know that? And as she pushed him away, he said: Your skin is so soft, Mother, you smell so nice, I want to stay with you for ever and ever. And he tried not to let her push him away, he held on tight, his hand touched her breast and she felt something small and hard against her thigh. It could only be an erection; his erection. Helene pushed him away and got up.

Mother?

Hurry up, Peter, you must get washed and go to school, she said with her back to him. She said no more, she didn't want to turn to him and see his face.

Many people were now sending their children out into the country because of the war, but if she did that they'd send her to Obrawalde, or to Ravensbrück or a field hospital. Helene didn't want to be sent anywhere, so she couldn't send Peter away into the country.

The sun was sinking to its low autumnal angle over the earth. The wind was blowing, it whined, it whistled. One day Helene was hanging out washing in the yard when she heard the children playing and calling. They were chasing each other, getting cross. Helene clearly heard Peter's voice rising above the voices of the other children.

> *Ikey, Ikey Solomon*
> *Has been shitting marzipan.*
> *Marzipan is bad for you,*
> *Ikey is a dirty Jew.*

The sheet was in her way, the wind blew it into her face, it was a cool wind and she couldn't see the children, only a girl from the building next door standing hesitantly in the entrance. Helene got the final clothes peg over the sheet and turned. Where was the wretched boy? She was often glad when he was out and about on his own, so that she could work in peace; he had friends, he was becoming independent, one day he wouldn't need her any more, but now she wanted to know where he was. How on earth had he learned that rhyme? Marzipan is bad for you. Because of the bitter almond flavour? Like cyanide? There had been no Jews in Stettin for almost three years, none at all, they'd all been taken away.

Have you seen my Peter? Helene asked the girl in the doorway. She shook her head: no, she didn't know where he was.

Helene waited for him, with his supper ready. Food was rationed, the grocer's wife had let her have an egg, quarter of a litre of milk and a lettuce; she had bought a mackerel from the old fishwife's daughter down on the quay; she had stuffed it with her last little bit of butter and a dried sage leaf, and baked it in the stove. Peter liked baked fish. When he came in, both his knees were grazed and a scab on his elbow was coming off. His hands were black and he had a streak of coal dust on his nose. His eyes were shining; he'd obviously been having fun.

Go and wash your hands, please, said Helene. It hardly even occurred to Peter not to do as his mother said. He washed his hands, scrubbed his nails with the nailbrush and sat down at the table.

And wash that coal dust off your face, please, said Helene.

I'm Black Peter, said Peter, laughing at the mention of the card game. He liked playing games and if the others laughed at him he laughed with them.

I heard you saying a rude rhyme just now, said Helene. She put the top half of the mackerel on Peter's plate and cut the piece of bread in half.

Me?

Do you know what Jews are?

Peter shrugged uncertainly. He didn't want to annoy his mother; nothing was further from his mind. People?

So why say a rude rhyme about them?

Peter shrugged again.

I don't like it. Helene spoke soberly and sternly. I never want to hear it again, is that clear?

Peter looked out from under his fringe and had to smile. He looked mischievous, smiling like that. He couldn't believe she was so upset just over a silly rhyme.

What sort of people are Jews? Peter was still smiling. He really wanted to know, but he would have to accept the fact that Helene wasn't going to answer him. She felt inadequate, painfully inadequate. Was she being cowardly? How could she explain what kind of people Jews were to her son, who she was herself, why she couldn't talk about it? No one knew where a child of Peter's age might take what he knew; he could come out with it tomorrow at school, telling the teacher or the other children. Helene didn't want that. She didn't want to think of him in danger. He understood her, Helene was sure of that, Peter was a clever child. Jews were just people, surely that was enough by way of explanation? Helene did not respond to his smile; they ate their fish in silence.

Mother, he said when he had cleaned his plate, thank you for the mackerel, that was a fabulous mackerel. Peter could tell most fish apart, he liked the differences, their different names and flavours. Helene didn't like the word fabulous. Everyone was using it, yet it was a very vague word, totally misleading. When she gave him the clasp knife in November it would be too late for fishing near the city, most of the river banks would be frozen, the fish would be swimming too far down, he probably wouldn't be able to catch anything edible. Helene sketched a smile. Where did these sudden polite thanks come from? Had she ever told him he ought to thank her for a meal? The cat down in the yard would get the fish bones. No one knew whose cat it was; it was a beautiful animal that looked like a Siamese, white with brown paws and bright, clear eyes. Peter was going to wash the dishes, and Helene thanked him in advance. He liked doing it, he helped his mother whenever he could. Helene took her ironed overall and said goodnight. She was on night duty.

Dense mist lay over the water, the ships' sirens were sounding in unison. Up in the city, the golden sun shone, casting long shadows as day dawned.

Let's go picking mushrooms, said Helene on her day off. After repeated requests, she had been given a Sunday off because of the child. She packed her basket. Conditions couldn't be better; it had rained yesterday and last night the moon had been full. Half the city might be out and about in the woods on a Sunday, but Helene knew her way around and would find the really remote clearings. A tea towel, two knives, some newspaper, because she didn't want the mushrooms rubbing against each other and bruising when they were lying in her basket.

They took the train to Messenthin and soon left its thatched, half-timbered houses behind. Helene knew her way through the forest. The spruce trees stood close together, then beech and oak trees were foremost. The air was cool, with the scents of early autumn, of mushrooms and earth. Smooth beech leaves, many of them already turning bronze, shrivelled oak saplings. Helene went first, walking fast. She was familiar with these woods and the clearings in them. She felt hungry, which was not ideal when you wanted to find mushrooms. Her eyes searched the thickets, the undergrowth, it was too dark here, too dry there, they'd have to go further into the forest, to places where bees still settled on the tree trunks and basked on the wood, moving sluggishly now as the coming cold weather numbed them.

Mother, wait, you're going so fast. Peter must be twenty or thirty paces behind her. Helene turned to look at him. He was young, he had nimble legs; don't dawdle, she told him. She went on, climbing over fallen branches, twigs cracked underfoot. She didn't like the agarics that grow on trees, let them stay on their mouldering stumps; she kept going, she was looking for ceps and chestnut mushrooms. Light broke through the trees, further on she saw green, the tender dry green of a small clearing, perhaps it was there, yes, it must be there that she'd find one or two, or a whole fairy ring of mushrooms to be plundered. Helene strode on, hardly hearing Peter as he stumbled along after her, calling. Ah, there was one. It had an old, brown cap, not what she might have expected to find on a morning like this. Hadn't it rained last night and hadn't there been a full moon? Late dew still hung on many grasses. There was only one explanation, someone had been here before her, poaching mushrooms in her wood, on the outskirts of her clearing. Helene stopped, out of breath, and looked around her. Had that branch over there only recently broken?

Wait for me, called Peter, who hadn't yet reached the clearing, as she turned to go further on into the thickets. She didn't wait, she just went more slowly. She heard a dog barking in the distance, then a whistle and another. Surely no foresters went hunting on Sunday? Rabbit with chanterelles. Helene thought of the tender rabbit she had once braised for Wilhelm, a long time ago. She wished she had a gun. Chanterelles, or even better ceps. Helene's eyes wandered over the ground, almost straining from their sockets. A fly agaric with a big cap, young and plump, straight out of a picture book. Helene went on, with Peter still behind her. They crossed the railway line. A breathtaking stench blew towards them. A stench of carrion, of urine and excrement. Some way off a cattle train stood on the tracks. The sides of the rusty trucks were closed. Helene went along the tracks with Peter after her. From a distance she saw a policeman. Perhaps the locomotive had broken down and the cattle in the trucks were in distress on a long train journey. A dog barked and Helene just said: Come on.

She went back towards the woods. They had to skirt round the cattle train, giving it a wide berth to escape the stink and avoid the dogs.

Why are you running, Mother?

Couldn't Peter smell the stench? She retched, she had to breathe through her mouth, better not to breathe at all. Helene went on, twigs snapped, whipped into her face, she shielded her eyes with her arms, rotten wood broke beneath her feet, there was something slippery under her feet, she nearly stumbled and fell on it, there was a mushroom, probably just a bitter boletus, she didn't want to stop, she wasn't going to spend time hanging around, she must go on towards the smell for now. Once they were to the north-west of the train it would be better, the stink was drifting south-east with the wind off the sea. Helene heard the whistle again. Perhaps some of the cattle had escaped? Perhaps they were hunting cows in the woods this Sunday, or little piglets. Helene felt hungry and thought of potato dumplings with mushrooms. Beechnuts crunched under her feet. She mustn't bend down, pretty as they were, those bristly husks with their three chambers, the smooth threefold nuts inside, they had a nice nutty flavour if you roasted them; she wanted to show Peter the beechnuts, but she mustn't stop for that now.

They had done it; obviously they had rounded the train and the stink was gone. The silence of the forest, the humming of insects, a woodpecker.

Mother, I can see a squirrel.

Helene wiped the sweat from her brow with the back of her hand.

The thick trunk of a tall beech tree lay in her path, its bark still shimmering silver grey. Flat-shelled beetles with red and black spots were swarming between the knotholes, hooked together in pairs, little Pushmi-Pullyous. She could at least have read *Dr Dolittle* to Peter, if not Hauff's fairy tale *The Cold Heart*, which she thought too scary. So it would have to be *Dr Dolittle*, if she ever got round to reading it to him he'd enjoy it, but there was plenty of time for that, she'd just have to get home from the hospital early for once and go to the library – the book must be there for her to borrow. A big fallen tree trunk was in their way, they'd have to climb over that. Helene put down her basket and braced her hands on the trunk, she didn't want to crush any of the beetles, the trunk seemed quite steady.

Mother, wait for me!

Helene felt for a suitably smooth surface, leaned both hands on the trunk and swung one leg over it. The trunk was so broad, and although it had been uprooted it still stood so high, that she had to sit on it to get over. But how would she get down on the other side? There was a crack. It could hardly be the tree trunk breaking. The cracking sound came from quite close. The stench was back again. Helene's throat tightened, she retched, swallowed and tried not to breathe, not another breath. It was a terrible stench, not carrion, more like liquid manure. How could that be? They'd got away from the cattle trucks, the train was behind them, she was sure of it. Someone sneezed. Helene turned round. Someone was cowering below the trunk, in the hollow pit left by the roots that now pointed to the sky. Helene opened her mouth, but she couldn't scream. Her fear was so deep inside her that not a sound came out of her throat. Whoever it was had ducked, there were branches above his back, his head was out of sight, he was almost forcing it into the earth, probably trying to hide and hoping he wouldn't be noticed. He was shaking so much that the withered leaves on the branches he had piled over him were shaking too. A crack came again. Obviously the man found it difficult to keep so still that nothing touched him and he touched nothing.

398

Mother? Peter was less than ten metres away now. His mischievous smile flashed over his face. Were you trying to hide? He spoke in a normal tone, he didn't have to shout now, he was so close. Helene slipped off the tree, she slid and ran towards him, seized his hand and drew him away.

I can help you, Mother, if you can't get over that tree, I'll help you, I can do it, you just watch! Peter wanted to go back to the tree trunk, he wouldn't go in any other direction, he wanted to balance on it and show his mother how to climb over a fallen tree. But his mother, steadily putting one foot in front of the other, hauled Peter along behind her.

Let go, Mother, you're hurting me.

Helene didn't let go, she ran, she stumbled, cobwebs stuck to her face, she ran holding the basket out in front of her as if to fend off the cobwebs, the wood was thinning out a little here, ferns and grasses on the forest floor, there was almost no wind, they had to get away. The cow being hunted was a man, there were probably several of them there on the rails, decomposing, stinking. Prisoners, who else would huddle under the branches of the fallen tree in such flimsy clothing? An escaped prisoner. Perhaps this was one of the transports taking supplies to Pölitz. Once the war had begun not enough fuel could be provided, not enough workers found, prisoners were taken away and made to work. Even women, so the nurses whispered to each other, were working in the factories, toiling away until they couldn't work any more, or eat and drink any more, and one day they wouldn't have to breathe any more. Had she seen the face of the runaway prisoner, had he raised his head, had she looked into his eyes, frightened eyes, black eyes? Helene saw Martha's eyes before her. Martha's frightened eyes. Helene saw Martha in the cattle truck, she saw Martha's bare feet slipping on the excrement, trying to find somewhere firm to stand, she heard the groaning of the people crammed into the trucks, heard the man's groaning, saw him trembling under the oak leaves, heard him sneeze. A shot rang out.

A huntsman, hooray, cried Peter.

Dogs barked in the distance and a second shot was fired.

Wait a minute, Mother. Peter wanted to stop and look around, work out which way the shots were coming from. But Helene wouldn't wait, his hand slipped out of hers, she hurried on, stumbling, falling, leaning on fallen trees for support, clinging to twigs and branches, she went on and never stopped, putting one foot in front of the other. She could run. Rabbit with mushrooms, a really simple dish. *The cunning hare sits in the dale, / between the hills and the deep, deep vale.* Ah yes, in the vale. Cattle. How could she ever have eaten rabbit?

They went on through the forest for she didn't know how long, until Peter, behind her, called out that he couldn't go any further and stopped for a rest. Helene was not to be deterred. She just went on.

Do you know where we are? Peter called behind her.

Helene didn't, she couldn't answer him, all this time she had kept her eye on the position of the sun, making sure that when sunlight fell through the leaf canopy it cast their shadows to the right. Did the sun or the trees cast shadows? Helene didn't know. A simple question, but insoluble. Perhaps it was her hunger driving her, making her heart race, making her sweat. Yes, she was hungry. There wasn't a single mushroom in her basket, she had just run and run, not even knowing where she was going. She had meant to make sure she was going west, leaving the train behind. Perhaps she had. They had to go on. Helene saw that it was getting lighter over there; they must be coming to a clearing, or a road, or a broad bridle path.

A hand took hers. Peter had caught up with her; his hand

was firm and small and dry. How could a little boy have so much strength in his fingers? Helene tried to free herself, but Peter was clinging firmly to her hand.

Forward, one step, two steps, three steps. Helene caught herself counting her footsteps, she just wanted to get away, well away. Peter clung on, reached for her coat; she shook her arm, shook it hard until he had to let go. She went on ahead, he followed. She walked faster than he did. The thinning of the woods proved to be a mirage, they were not thinning out at all, the trees grew closer and closer together, and so did the undergrowth. Clouds had gathered above the treetops. They were driving over the sky up there, chasing inland. How late was it? Late morning, midday, after midday? Her hunger told her it must be late, two or perhaps three o'clock, judging by the position of the sun in the sky. Mother! Mushrooms fried with thyme, simply tossed in butter with salt and pepper, fresh parsley, a few drops of lemon; mushrooms steamed, baked, simmered. Raw, she'd eat the first one raw, here and now. Helene's mouth was watering, she stumbled on mindlessly. Leaves and twigs, thorns of berry-bearing plants, maybe blackberries, but where were the mushrooms, where were they? Mother! She had left the beech trees behind, she was in an old plantation, all spruce trees now, growing lower and lower, branches hanging down, needles crunching underfoot, the forest floor was going downhill. A little clearing, soft mossy mounds rising from the needles. A fly agaric and another, poisonous, on guard. And there it was before her, a mushroom, its cap curved, dark and gleaming. Snails must have been at it already, one or two little nibbled places showed that someone else had been feasting here. Helene knelt down, her knees pressing into the moss, bent over the mushroom and smelled it. The leaves, the cap of the mushroom, it all smelled of the forest, of autumnal food. Helene laid her head down on the moss and examined the mushroom from below; the gills were still white and firm, an excellent mushroom. Mother! His voice seemed to come from very far away. Helene turned. There they were, standing lined up in the hollow, mushroom after mushroom, last night's offspring. Helene crawled under the branches on all fours, making her way along on her hands, holding back twigs, wriggling forward, and lay flat on the forest floor. What a wonderful fragrance. Mother! Helene reached for a mushroom, broke it off and put it in her mouth whole. The tender, firm flesh almost melted on her tongue, delicious. Where are you? Peter's voice was faltering, he was afraid, he couldn't see her and thought he was alone. Where are you? His voice broke. Helene had left her basket in the clearing. The second mushroom was smaller, firmer, fresher, its pale stalk almost as broad as its brown cap. Mother! Peter was fighting back his tears; she saw his thin boyish legs through the branches as he trudged across the clearing and stopped at the place where she had left her basket, leaned down and straightened up again. He made a trumpet of his hands and put them to his mouth. Mother!

There was no echo. The wind was blowing up in the tops of the trees, lashing the top branches, trying to get down to the ground. Mother! called the boy, turning to all points of the compass as he looked for her.

Was it so difficult to keep still? The simplest exercise of all, no trembling, no snapping of twigs, just silence.

The boy sat down and wept. It was no joke. If she came out of the bushes now, just a few metres away, he would know she had been watching him and had hidden on purpose. What for? Why? Helene felt ashamed of herself and stayed still, and the boy shed tears. She kept her breathing shallow; nothing simpler. No sneezing, nothing to give her away. The ants tickled her, she felt a burning sensation on her hip, the tiny creatures were getting into her clothes and biting. A red spider with delicate legs, no bigger than a pinhead, climbed on her hand. The boy stood up, looked all ways, picked up her basket and set off south-east. He wasn't stupid, that was the way to the village and then the city. Helene stuffed mushroom after mushroom into her mouth. How nice it was to be alone, chewing in peace.

When she couldn't hear his footsteps in the undergrowth any more, she crawled out from her hiding place. Needles and bits of bark stuck to her jacket. She brushed down her skirt. There was a rustling, a bird flew up. Helene walked through the spruce trees and young oaks in the wood, going the way Peter had gone. She called, Peter, and on the second syllable of his name he answered in a high voice, relieved, happy, laughing impatiently as he shouted: Here I am, Mother, here I am.

Fine stitching, the skin above the eye was so delicate, the eye of the wounded man, of a father, of the war. The eye itself could hardly be seen under the swollen flesh. Helene took tweezers and removed splinters of glass from the man's face, his forehead, his temple, very tiny splinters of glass from the cheek that was still recognizable and from the other, which was only raw, bleeding meat. The wounded man didn't move. After several attempts, and in spite of the low dosage, the doctor had managed to anaesthetize him. Medicaments were running low and most of the patients had to be treated without anaesthetic. They lay on camp beds, on bedsteads that had been dragged out of people's houses, some huddled on the ground because there were not enough beds available, lying under tarpaulins and in the outbuildings of the hospital, which had been largely destroyed. Helene dabbed the rust-red tincture on the man's wounds, she asked for gauze, but none of the nurses had any left. The little girl stared at her in silence; she had singed her hair slightly in front, had a boil, no more, and she had lost her mother. She never said a word. She'd have to be removed from the hospital, she must go somewhere, anywhere, but who had time to think about that? She would get soup here when someone managed to make any, when the gas was back on, when water came out of the tap again.

In March, soon after the last air raids, the Women's Hospital had been evacuated to the seaside resort of Lubmin near Greifswald. Helene had promised to follow as soon as they had done what they could for the wounded in the city. She didn't even mention her son any more.

Forceps, Nurse Alice, tweezers. Helene hurried about, handed instruments, opened a peritoneum, made incisions when something had to be done quickly and the doctor was in the other tent with a young pregnant woman who had only injured her foot, but might yet lose it. Helene made incisions and stitched them up, staunched bleeding with cotton wool, a girl held the instruments for her, the scalpel and scissors, the forceps and needles. Helene worked day and night, sometimes she slept for one or two hours in the shed that the nurses had fitted out as a kitchen. She thought only very seldom that she ought to go home and make sure everything was all right there. Peter should be going to school. He said no, there wasn't any more school, well then, to lessons, oh God, he must just get himself something to eat, he had two legs, didn't he, he'd have to find a place to stay. Hadn't he been lucky? No harm had come to him in any of the air raids. Once, in winter, he had brought home a severed hand and wouldn't say anything about it. Perhaps he had found the hand in the street, a child's hand. Helene had had difficulty in prising it away from him. He didn't want to let go of it. The boy had to leave the city, no doubt about it, she couldn't have him around, he ought to be doing his homework, heating the stove for himself, looking for coal or wood, it was lying around everywhere, she'd had to leave him alone for weeks, for months. When she did come home he looked at her wide-eyed, always wanting to know something, asking questions, asking where she'd been, saying he wished she'd stay with him. He put out his hands to her, lay close to her in the bed they shared, wound his arms round her like an octopus. Tentacles, he was sucking her into them. His arms squeezed the last of the breath out of her. But she couldn't stay, she had work to do. She wasn't talking to anyone any more. Mummy! That was an old woman, on her deathbed, calling from where she lay. She didn't mean Helene, Helene had never been a Mama or a Mummy, she didn't have to turn to the dying woman, she could keep quiet while she dabbed, stitched, applied bandages and dressings. As soon as there was water again she washed her injured patients as best she could. She could hardly hold the hands of the dying, there were too many of them, too many hands, too many voices, moaning and groaning and finally falling silent; sheets had to be drawn up over faces, bodies put on trolleys. Back in the operating theatre, where a man was having his fourth operation on his skull, the doctor wanted Helene to help him; whether there was still any way to save the man no one knew, but the operation was performed. The bridge-head had been blown up, the Red Army was waiting outside the city with the fury of the starving, the first rumours said that they had licked up blood as they made their way forward, they were to be feared, the Red Army was already coming in, there were no muslin bandages left, give me a compress, anything to dress a wound. How long was it since she'd been home, one day or two? She couldn't tell. She had last slept for a few hours lying in a shed the night before this, taking turns with other nurses; she had dreamed only once in these months, a dream in which she had been stitching people together to make a great web of human tissue, and she didn't know which part of it was alive and which was dead, she just went on stitching the pieces together. All her other nights or hours of sleep had been dreamless, pleasantly black. Helene hurried home, it was dark already, she didn't look up, didn't look at the damage, didn't take an objective look at what had happened to this or that building, she hurried on. She must tell Peter to get a new lock. Helene hurried, wanted her

406

legs to carry her faster, but she was making no progress, the ground beneath her feet gave way, she slipped, stones, rubble, sand, she tried to get a footing, slipped lower, slowly going down and down, her feet sank into the sand at the bottom of the bomb crater; she used her hands to help her, she had to get out on all fours and kept slipping back. A crater could be a trap, a nocturnal time trap. One step took you in and even a thousand wouldn't take you out, try as you might, much as you wanted to. Helene didn't call for help; there were still a few people out and about, but all going their own way in any case, not hers. Her hands groped, she tried again, groped up and down until she felt something solid and was able to grab hold of it. It was so dark that she couldn't make out what it was. She worked her way along the solid thing, a cable perhaps, a firm cable, a bent water pipe, then something soft, she let go of that, it might be a body or part of one, she was still working her way along her solid handhold, she hauled herself up by it and clambered out. The street was dark, the sky was dark, no light burned in any of the buildings, perhaps there was a power cut. The paving stones were smooth from the drizzling rain. From afar came the voice of an agitated woman complaining about looting. Who was going to join her in her indignation tonight, tomorrow night, the night after that? A young man leaned out of one of the dark windows. Arms outstretched, he shouted into the night: The Redeemer! The Redeemer! You didn't see many young men here these days, those who were still around had to call on the Redeemer. Perhaps he believed in redemption. But what was gone was finished, over. Helene had to be careful not to slip. She heard men behind her. Insinuating remarks, she walked faster, she ran. Mustn't turn round. Disguise would be a good idea; the ground smelled of spring, a dusty spring night.

She had to make a decision, she knew that; no, it was not exactly a decision, it was just something she had to do. All Germans were being ordered to leave the city, there was nothing here any more, no lessons, no fish for Peter. Where could she send him? He wouldn't part from her, ever, not of his own free will. She had no time for long journeys, she couldn't take him away and she didn't know where they could go either. In no circumstances would Peter allow himself to be sent away. He would guess the meaning of any excuse, he would see through any threadbare pretext. Yet she had nothing more for him, her words were all used up long ago, she had neither bread nor an hour's time for him, there was nothing of her left for the child. Helene's time meant relief for her patients, helping them to live a little longer with a little less pain. *There is a longing in the world, and we will die of it.* Why did Else Lasker-Schüler keep haunting her? We don't die of it, Else, we just cease to be. And that was good. Helene gave herself to the injured and sick who asked for nothing except for her to lay her hands on them, she must and could do that.

At home she found Peter in her bed. He was already asleep. She lit a candle and laid the sprat that she had brought home in her overall pocket, wrapped in a piece of newspaper, on the table. He would be glad to have a sprat for breakfast. She took the little dark-red suitcase out of the cupboard and opened it. At the bottom of the case she laid the woollen stocking with Wilhelm's money in it. On top of that two shirts, two pairs of underpants, a pullover that she had knitted for him in the autumn. The pyjamas he was wearing were too short for him. Why did Peter have to start growing so fast just now? She would sit down at the sewing machine this very night; she had salvaged it from the fire in the next-door apartment and brought it into hers. She would make him a new pair of pyjamas, nothing elaborate, perfectly simple. She had material for it. Why else had she kept a pair of Wilhelm's pyjamas all these years? She put two pairs of long socks into the case, and his favourite book. He had been reading and rereading the stories in it for months: the myths of Greece and Rome. Without stopping to think for very long, she wrote a note on a piece of paper: Uncle Sehmisch, Gelbensande. Surely that brother of Wilhelm's existed? At least there'd be a woman waiting for her husband to come home from the war. There was still food to be had in the countryside. Let them look after Peter. Wilhelm's money might help. She put the note with the uncle's address and Peter's birth certificate under the stocking full of money, right at the bottom; she didn't want it found too soon, not until the right time. And Peter could have the fish too, he should take it in the suitcase, the carved horn fish. What would she do with it? She burned Leontine's letter in a pan on the stove, she burned all her letters now. As soon as she had to leave Stettin she would set out in search of Martha, she had to find Martha. She felt certain that Martha was still alive, of course she was alive. Perhaps the labour camp had been a safer place. A safer place to live? Martha was tough too, tough enough. Who knew what would become of them? Helene meant to travel back by way of Greifswald, by way of Lubmin, her patients needed her. She made the pyjamas for Peter; working the treadle with its regular rhythm calmed her. He must want for nothing, that was why he must go, go away from her. Helene shed no tears; she felt relieved. She was cheered by the idea that he would be better off and have someone to talk to him about this, that and the other, that he'd see sunlight in the evening. Helene made a double seam in the waistband of the pyjama trousers and sewed a small bag into it. She put her wedding ring in the bag and a little money; that couldn't hurt. Then she sewed up the little bag. She put the pyjamas on top of the other things in the case. She mustn't tell him that this was goodbye, or he would never let her go.

EPILOGUE

Peter heard what his uncle was telling him. So that woman who calls herself your mother is coming to see you. His uncle snorted into his checked handkerchief and spat scornfully in the direction of the muck heap. Well, let's get on with it, he said, glancing up at the cranes in the sky. The others had all flown south weeks before. Peter was to help his uncle muck out the cowshed. He needn't think he was there to idle about. Just because he seemed so clever at school was no reason for him to consider himself too fine for mucking out. Peter did not consider himself too fine. He helped out in the cowshed, he helped with the milking, and he slept on the bench in the kitchen. They tolerated him.

Not a word from her in all these years, his uncle complained. Makes off just like that. Calls herself a mother. His uncle shook his head scornfully and spat again. He dug the pitchfork into the big heap. Mind this at the bottom doesn't get spread around, Peter, keep piling it well on top.

Peter nodded. He went ahead to the cowshed door, which was kept closed because it was an unusually cold autumn, and opened it. He liked the warm breath of the cattle, their grunting and mooing, their munching and lip-smacking. She had said she was coming on his birthday, his seventeenth birthday. Peter knew that his uncle bore his mother a grudge. He and his wife had no children of their own and obviously never would. Peter had turned into a good farm labourer, helping about the place, but the first years had been difficult; they realized they would have to get used to each other, but none of them knew whether it would be for a few weeks or a few months. By now it was clear to everyone that it was to be for ever, or at least until Peter was old enough to leave. And none of them had really got used to each other, they simply tolerated one another. His uncle and aunt moaned whenever they had to spend good money on something for him to wear. He had had to build his own bicycle, the one he rode to school first in Graal-Müritz and later to the railway station for the train to Rostock; he had made it out of spare parts that were still worth using, finding or if absolutely neces-sary earning the money for those spare parts himself. He had earned cash by turning hay all day long in his first summer holi-days. After that he had been able to convince his uncle and aunt that he could make himself useful. Which was just as well. He wasn't expected to eat too much either; if he did they would say: That boy will eat us out of house and home. Again and again his uncle and aunt had expressed the hope that someone would come to fetch Peter, his mother was the one who ought to come, after all, she had known their address at the time. Uncle Sehmisch, Gelbensande. Just like that, without asking them. But nothing had been heard of her for a long time. Nothing had been seen of Uncle Sehmisch's brother either, the brother now living it up in the West on Braunfels market place near Wetzlar with his new lady friend. Oh yes, he was a big shot there, he had no time for a brat like this. Another mouth to feed, that was how they had referred to Peter on the farm in those first years.

Where is she coming from? The West? Peter knew that his question would merely anger his uncle again, but he wanted to know. He really did want to know where she'd be coming from.

The West, huh! Lives near Berlin. Says she wants to see you.

Huh. His uncle wrinkled his nose and didn't look at Peter. Your aunt wrote straight off asking if she wants you back. That's what we asked her. Not likely! Have you back – her situation wouldn't allow it, huh, living in a very modest way with her sister in a one-room apartment, working all the time. Huh! His uncle bent down. Aren't we all working hard? Here, Peter, take a hold of this. Peter picked up one end of the trough, his uncle picked up the other and together they carried it to the most distant of the sheds, where the eldest sow was due to farrow any day now.

So Peter knew that she came from near Berlin. She had no husband, but all the same she didn't want him back. She just wanted to see him. Peter felt himself tightening his lips, his teeth nibbled at the dry skin on them, softened it, bit strips off. What was she after? All these years later. He wasn't going to show up anyway. Let her come.

His uncle fetched his mother from Gelbensande station in the morning, she was coming by train, changing at Rostock. Would Peter like to go to the station with him, his uncle asked, but his aunt said the sow had farrowed in the night and someone had to see to the piglets. The sow had had too many, she was two teats short, and the two extra piglets risked being bitten to death or starving, because each of the others jealously clung to its own teat. Peter was happy to go to the shed. He knelt down beside the sow where she lay and chose the strongest of the suckling piglets. The sow's light-coloured bristles were curiously soft along her belly, some of the teats were fuller than others, some large and knotty, others small and long. The piglets kept their eyes closed. Peter hauled the strongest piglet off its teat and it squealed as if its throat were being cut. He would carry it around for a while so that one of the two runts of the litter could have a go. With the piglet in his arms, Peter trudged through the straw and climbed the narrow ladder to the hayloft. It was dry and warm up there, warmer than down below. Peter sometimes hid here to read and dream. You could see the whole farmyard through the cracks in the skylight. From up here he had a view of the gate, the entrance, the beginning of the poplar-lined road. He took his clasp knife out of his trouser pocket and cut a little notch in the frame of the skylight, which was already heavily carved, another notch, making a pattern, an ornament. It wasn't long before a clattering sound was heard and the little truck appeared in Peter's line of vision. His uncle got out, opened the gate, got in again, drove into the yard and climbed out once more to close the gate. Hasso started barking and jumped up at his uncle. Hasso was a good-tempered German shepherd, but bright enough to guard the farmyard. The last dog, a large mongrel whom Peter had taken to his heart, had been put to sleep because he didn't bark loudly enough. The other door of the truck opened and a young woman climbed out. At least, from up here she still looked like a girl, slender legs under her skirt, fashionable shepherd's check coat, blue headscarf. Peter recognized her blonde hair, as fair as if it had turned white. Her familiar figure, the way she walked, the way she put one foot in front of the other gave Peter gooseflesh. She was carrying a little handbag and a net shopping bag. She looked around hesitantly. Perhaps she had brought him a present. How old would his mother be now? Peter did a quick calculation, she must be forty-seven. Forty-seven! Still, six years younger than his uncle and aunt. The piglet in Peter's arms squealed. Peter watched his uncle disappear into the farmhouse with his mother. He quickly climbed down the ladder and took the piglet back to the sow.

Peter! That was his uncle's voice. He must have come out of the front door to call for him. Peter kept still and didn't respond. Come on in, time for coffee!

His uncle had never invited him to have coffee. Peter had once helped himself to some out of the pot on the sly, tasting it with plenty of milk and sugar.

Peter waited until he heard nothing but the snorting and breathing of the animals, then climbed back up to his hiding place. He could see the house from the skylight. There was a wooden roof over the porch, with benches to left and right where you sat to take off your wellington boots and put on wooden clogs. If it was as cold as today, Hasso lay there on the planks of the porch among the shoes and the benches. He liked chewing shoes, it was his one vice, but he was forgiven because he barked so well. Peter could see Hasso's tail from the skylight, thumping down on the porch floor at regular intervals. Then he saw Hasso jump up and wag his tail. His uncle appeared on the porch, shouting: Peter!

That call, just his name, showed that they were being thoughtful of the visitor. Usually his uncle was never as patient as that, calling his name instead of cursing that lout, where could he be this time? Peter had to smile. She would soon come out on to the porch too. Would she call his name? Peter felt excited. He wasn't going to show himself, never. Peter! Let her call, let her wait for him, let her hope he'd turn up. Peter felt his trousers with one hand; they were covered with bits of hay and straw.

Wait a minute, he heard his uncle say, turning to the dog, I'll soon ferret him out. Peter needed to pass water, but he didn't want to leave his place here, he wanted to see her come out on to the porch and look for him.

Where's Peter? he heard his uncle asking. Find, Hasso, find. His uncle slapped his thigh impatiently. His aunt must have put the potatoes on indoors. His mother was staying for lunch. His aunt had made cabbage roulades. Peter had suggested pickled herrings; he remembered that his mother had liked those as

417

much as he did. Rollmops and pickled herrings. But his aunt didn't like fish. They lived eight kilometres from the coast and his aunt had never eaten fish in her life, so there was never any at the farmhouse. Peter remembered how his mother often used to cook fish for him. With juniper, he thought, what a nice word. He said it out loud: Juniper. The little black berries that his mother used to flavour the fish. Peter liked to smell her hands; even when she had been gutting and cooking the fish her hands had their own special smell. Perhaps he could forget the smell of his mother some day. It wasn't until four in the afternoon that her train would leave Gelbensande, taking her to Rostock, where she would change for Berlin. Hasso wagged his tail. Obviously he didn't take Peter's uncle's command to find him seriously.

Peter took his handkerchief out of his trouser pocket and wiped his hands with it. He washed his hands often, several times a day. The other boys at school said that made you infertile, which was a good idea. Peter couldn't imagine ever having children. Now his mother did come out on to the porch. She wasn't wearing her headscarf any more, and she must have left her coat indoors too. Her hair was piled up on her head. She must be freezing. Peter saw her fold her arms and stand uncertainly at the top of the few steps under the porch. Her breath was white vapour in front of her face. She had a beautiful face. Wide and regular. Her high forehead, her narrowed eyes – Peter remembered how bright they were, as bright as the Baltic Sea in summer. His uncle had come out into the yard and was telling Hasso to look for Peter. Seek, Hasso, seek. Peter saw his uncle going to the outhouses; after all, Peter had been told to look after the piglets this morning. His uncle disappeared from view, and Peter heard the door of the shed underneath him open. Cautiously and quietly, he squeezed in among the bales of straw. He heard his uncle call his name, then a clattering, a thumping as if his uncle were stamping his foot and kicking over a bucket, the squealing of the piglets as if he had kicked them.

His uncle's footsteps went back through the cowshed; perhaps he thought Peter was there with the cows. Once again he heard his name, its sound muted by the straw. Hasso barked, only briefly this time and far away.

After the back door of the shed had closed and he thought the coast was clear, Peter crawled out of hiding. Now the skylight showed him the porch as well as Hasso and his uncle. His mother must have gone back into the warm again. Was she asking questions, asking about him? Perhaps she was proud that he was going to secondary school. His aunt and uncle didn't like to talk about that, but they hadn't dared to disagree with the teacher and his strong recommendation. Oh, very well, his uncle had said after that interview at the school. So long as Peter went on helping on the farm he could stay at school. Peter knew where he wanted to go later. A few weeks ago a College of Film Studies had opened in Potsdam near Berlin; he had read about it in the newspaper. And one Sunday there had been a long talk about it on the radio, saying how it was going to train talented young people. Who knew, perhaps he was one of those? They'd all be marvelling at him yet, his uncle and aunt, his father, his mother.

Down in the shed the geese were cackling and flapping their wings. Someone must have scared them; geese didn't start cackling for no reason. Only when they were hungry or when someone had alarmed them. Peter would have liked to climb down and take a look, but it was too risky. Smoke was rising from the farmhouse chimney. Peter was hungry. Time for dinner, his aunt called this time, coming out under the little roof of the porch. Come along, dinner time, Peter!

It was a pleasure to resist his hunger and the sight of his

mother, a huge, compelling, sweetly painful pleasure. Peter imagined them sitting there, his uncle cursing, his aunt embarrassed and complaining quietly, his mother in silence. Was she sitting on the bench in the kitchen where he slept at night? He was sure she wouldn't ask: Where does he sleep? She didn't ask such questions, she'd be thankful that he'd been able to live here for the last few years. Peter had once heard his aunt and uncle quarrelling about money, and it had sounded as if his father sometimes sent some money for him. But Peter didn't know about that; what he did know was that he had to earn his keep, and he did, he was earning his keep and earning the time he spent at school instead of on the farm. How would she speak of him? Was she saying *my Peter*, was she just saying *Peter*, or simply *the boy*? Perhaps she wasn't talking about him at all. Perhaps she was sitting there in silence. She might not understand why he didn't show up. It could be embarrassing to her to think her son was so rude that he didn't want to see her. Well, let it embarrass her. Peter rammed his fist against the bulge in his trousers, pressed it, handled it delicately. Let that mother of his down there leave, she could piss off. Didn't she realize she was waiting in vain? She wouldn't ever get to see him, not now, not today, not ever. Let her push her fair hair back from her forehead, wash her white aprons and go back to that sister of hers near Berlin. Go away, he thought, just go away!

Peter stared through the crack in the skylight frame. Large, soft snowflakes were whirling in the air. You couldn't say they were falling, they were hovering, dancing down towards the east and settling on the cobblestones in the yard. How often, as a child, he'd imagined running away from his uncle and aunt, out into the fields in the snow. Lying there in the snow and just waiting to stop breathing. But that was all over now, he wasn't going to do them the favour, he would let them wait and keep them guessing. And then he'd simply go his own way. He didn't need anyone.

Hasso barked and ran to the gate, wagging his tail. Someone with a bicycle and a milk can hanging over the handlebars was opening the gate, wiping snowflakes off her face. She was wearing her red anorak. It was Bärbel. Bärbel was posh, or at least she thought so. Her parents sent her over at the weekend to fetch milk. Bärbel was Peter's age and was learning how to be a sales-girl in Willershagen. In summer you sometimes saw her on the beach at Graal-Müritz. Peter was seldom allowed to cycle over the Rostock Heath to the coast. But it didn't take long and he sometimes went without asking for permission. You could see boys and girls almost naked on the beach. Bärbel too. Bärbel thought the world belonged to her because she had the beach and the summer visitors at her feet. No one saw what she looked like coming to the farm with her milk can over the handlebars of her bike in winter, slipping in the farmyard. She really did slip over and fell flat, the bicycle with her, and Hasso came out barking and wagging his tail. Peter's uncle appeared on the porch. He wasn't to know what Bärbel looked like on the beach in summer because he never went to the beach. All the same, he liked Bärbel and didn't want either Peter or his aunt to fill the can with milk for her. His uncle preferred to do that himself. Bärbel was a silly goose. She had told Peter he was a late devel-oper. She was right, everything she said was always right.

Peter heard the cowshed door down below opening. Just buggered off, he heard his uncle telling Bärbel, today of all days, would you believe it? Bärbel giggled. Bärbel usually giggled when she went into the cowshed with his uncle. She giggled on her bicycle too, and in the shop where she was a trainee, standing behind the cash desk, she giggled there as well, and she groaned when Peter asked her when real honey would be available again.

Peter listened to them down below. His uncle and Bärbel were talking quietly now, whispering. Or perhaps they weren't saying anything. Peter heard the milk flow into Bärbel's can from the big tank. Then he heard the cowshed door close and looked through the crack, to see Bärbel shaking hands with his uncle, opening the gate and pushing her bicycle out. His uncle went back to the house. He turned once, looking at the gate as Bärbel closed it. Hasso stood in front of his uncle with his ears pricked, thumping the ground with his tail and whining. He could probably smell the cabbage roulades and was hoping there might be some left for him. His uncle was looking in several different directions. He wasn't calling for Peter any more, they weren't to know that he'd disappeared only for the time being and hadn't run away for good. The air darkened and turned blue. The twilight of a November afternoon; time for his mother to go. Perhaps it was only the snow clouds bringing evening on early. Perhaps his uncle was feeling glad, was relieved to think that Peter had gone for ever. Wouldn't he just be furious when Peter turned up that evening claiming his place to sleep on the kitchen bench! Making demands too, his uncle would say.

What had his mother imagined? She wanted to see him – so then what? Did she by any chance want to ask him to forgive her? Was he supposed to forgive her? He couldn't forgive her, he'd never be able to do that. It wasn't in his power; even if he had wanted to. What did she hope to find out by seeing him? She was brave, yes. Coming now, after so many years. Just like that. She had picked his seventeenth birthday and now he was spending his birthday hiding in the hayloft. He put his eye to the crack so as not to miss the moment when she left. The falling darkness made it difficult to see. The little light at the entrance had come on. There was light behind the kitchen window. Peter wasn't cold, but he did feel hungry again. He quietly climbed down the ladder and went over to the milk tank. The darkness didn't bother him, he knew his way around the cowshed. He turned on the tap and drank. The sucking noises and quiet squeaks of the piglets added up to a comfortable sound. None of them crying or squealing, perhaps the two extra piglets were already dead. Outside, Hasso barked for a moment. Peter wiped his milky mouth on his sleeve; he must hurry, he didn't want to miss the moment when she left. He quickly climbed the ladder again and took up his post by the crack in the skylight, staring out at the dark-blue farmyard. It was warm in the straw above the animals. He had peed in the corner before when he had to. What else could he do? No one would notice or smell it up here in the cowshed. Peter liked to pee in the straw. What could be nicer? He did it again in a high arc, as far as it would go.

He heard voices coming from the farmyard. Did she still smile sometimes? When she smiled she'd had dimples in her cheeks. Peter remembered those dimples. She hadn't often smiled. Peter knelt by the crack. In this blue light he saw his mother walking over the thin covering of newly fallen snow, putting on her head-scarf and opening the truck door. What was left to him of his mother? Peter thought of the fish, the funny fish carved from horn. No one knew what to make of the fish, not his uncle, not his aunt. Peter had looked at the fish for a long time, every evening he had opened it and looked inside, but there was nothing there, just a hollow space. Down below, his mother had tied her scarf on. From up above it didn't look as if anyone was smiling, and their goodbyes must have been short and sharp. His mother was carrying her handbag and the net shopping bag. Was she taking the present away again? Or perhaps she hadn't thought of bringing any present, and it was just provisions for her journey in the net bag. Peter had felt that the hollow space in the fish's belly was weird. Perhaps it was three years ago, perhaps only two that he had taken the fish to the coast with him and thrown it into the sea. Stupid fish, it wouldn't sink, it floated on the waves. Peter liked the curve of the horizon. You could see it particularly well from the steep coast to the east, from the Fischland peninsula. Perhaps his mother's back was a little bent, curved like the horizon? Only very slightly, as if she were grieving. Let her grieve. Peter wanted her to grieve. But he wasn't going to mind about that, there was just one thing he was quite sure of: he never wanted to see her again in his life. Peter saw his mother take the handle of the truck door and climb in. His uncle closed the door and went round to the other side to get in himself. Peter heard the wind in the poplars. His aunt opened both sides of the gate. The engine was switched on, the little truck turned in the yard and drove out. His aunt was talking to Hasso; she closed the gate. Peter lay down flat. The straw tickled the back of his neck. The darkness soothed him; he was quite calm now.